Moon

in

Grundy Center

Struggles of a Disfigured Boy

Gary Sutton

PublishAmerica
Baltimore

First printing

At the specific preference of the author, PublishAmerica allowed this work to remain exactly as the author intended, verbatim, without editorial input.

ISBN: 1-4241-1491-8
PUBLISHED BY PUBLISHAMERICA, LLLP
www.publishamerica.com
Baltimore

Printed in the United States of America

To those villagers who care for the misbegotten.

Jenny, enjoy!
(I hope.)
Gary Sutton

Mom and Dad couldn't marry.

He was an Irish sharecropper and nothing's wrong with that. But Catholic? Now there's a whole different matter.

Dad worked four miles east of Grundy Center on the Rasmussens' 160 acres. They let him settle near the creek so the guy didn't live half-bad. And he was no dummy. Each spring he'd hitch up his trailer, haul it onto higher ground and stay put until that water got over its notion to flood. So Dad pretty much had it made.

Except there was no getting around one thing. He was Catholic.

This ruined another Sunday supper with Grandpa and Grandma. Mom and I perched at their knotty pine table with our backs straight as cornstalks, yet somehow it felt cozy while gusts rattled the dead leaves outside. Grandpa stood for attention, him being almost six feet, and started right in again.

"You know them Catholics pray to statues," he said, bristling inside his starchy white shirt and still wearing those black suspenders from church.

Grandma nodded.

Mom stared into her plate, twisting a napkin into knots.

"And it makes good sense," Grandpa said, turning toward me, "that those fish-eaters call their priests fathers," his fingers gripped the suspenders until each knucklebone flashed white, "because most of 'em are."

Mom slid her chair back. I didn't move a muscle.

Grandma clanked down bowls of chicken, green beans and spuds; each onto a doily. Her glasses fogged when she lifted the lids.

Mom rose up, lips tight and flung her balled-up napkin onto the table. She marched away.

Whiffs of chicken fried in cornmeal and bacon drippings drifted across their table. Grandma shuffled the pieces around, mumbling something about the lovely weather, hunched over, mashed the spuds, her thistles of white hair wobbling with each arm thrust. She wiped a palm on her apron and scurried back to the cookstove.

"Chow down," Grandpa said, like nothing had happened. The chicken probably still smelled powerful good but I can't remember. I just didn't feel hungry after Mom huffed out.

"Them spuds aren't Catholic," Grandpa said, "so they won't stay hot for eternity."

"Oh, they'll keep overnight," Grandma replied, "the iceman delivered a fresh block yesterday."

"Home is the place where, when you have to go there,
They have to take you in."

Robert Frost

Chapter 1

Mom had been a country schoolteacher until I came along. She concealed her pregnancy by wearing a girdle a couple of sizes too small. That hid everything until the students left for their summer chores. Then Grandpa packed Mom's stuff and sent her off to the Methodist Home for Wayward Girls.

Meanwhile Grandpa and Grandma moved clear across Iowa to Grundy Center, escaping the shame of my bastardly arrival.

This fresh start turned out lucky. In just a few weeks Grandpa found work delivering milk with a horse who remembered the route. That's right smart for a horse. Grandma taught school, smack-dab in the city of Grundy Center itself, not out somewhere in the sticks.

Eventually Grandma talked Grandpa into letting Mom move back in. He even granted permission to bring me along. They didn't make Mom turn me over to the orphanage. That was hardly discussed, Grandma said, and I believed her.

Mom gave piano lessons on an upright we rented for five dollars a month. She didn't put on recitals, or anything showy, so Grundy Center wouldn't get upset by our intrusion.

Our only other music cost was the piano tuner from Des Moines. That ran ten bucks every time. Paid in advance. He was blind as a bat and if you didn't like it, tough, he wouldn't be back until next year. Talk about your monopoly, he could squeeze. Just because you're blind or deaf and dumb or a cripple doesn't mean you can't be a shyster, the way some regular people are. We watched our backsides when trading with those Des Moines hucksters. They're slicker than peeled tomatoes.

A college-educated lady controlled the Grundy Center piano lesson business and captured most of the hard-coal brats. She charged those rich kids twice what Mom dared ask, put on recitals and let them borrow sheet music. But Mom invented a practice song. She wrote it all by herself.

"Grundy Center...finest town...in the state."

And the notes went ABC, CBA, BAC. Kids could play that after their very first lesson and their mothers always beamed. That college lady never wrote any song. She owned one of those silly, flattened-out pianos that take up half a room. Why would anyone with a brain waste space that way?

Speaking of space, after his stroke we laid Grandpa out on a bed in the hall, away from the windows so he wouldn't chill. He hollered sometimes and went funny in the head. Most nights he'd ask me to rub his feet and legs. I would and Grandma kept a quart of Rexall Isopropyl Denatured Alcohol nearby. That liquid felt good to his skin and covered the stink.

One evening I massaged Grandpa's left calf and knee, string and bone they were, studying his eyes and breathing so I might guess when he nodded off. Grandpa's head jerked up.

"We raised you like one of our own," he said.

"I reckon you did, Grandpa."

"And you wasn't even legitimate."

I kept quiet. His eyelids flickered and shut.

When Grandpa got sickly we lost his milk route money, so Mom snagged more kids for piano lessons. Grandma hustled weekend work at the John Wesley Pentecostal Redemption in Jesus Second Methodist Church, known as Wesley Redemption Methodist for short.

"WRM is the best church in town," I said in the basement one evening. The Women's Christian Auxiliary was dishing up cake, potato salad and Kool-Aid but they all sort of froze, the rest of the crowd too, when Reverend Dawson jumped from his steel folding chair and headed straight for me.

"John Wesley Pentecostal Redemption in Jesus Second Methodist

Church to you, Moon," he said. Driplets of sweat flew off him while he shook a finger over me. Grandma had always said that horses sweat, men perspire and women glow, but Reverend Dawson seemed to do all three.

"And members may call it Wesley Redemption Methodist," he went on, "but only members, Moon, and you are nothing more than a guest."

"But Reverend Dawson," I asked, "then why is it okay to call the youth club MYF?"

That did it. His cheeks puffed and that vein on the side of his temple pulsed as if preparing to burst. Everybody hushed and looked in all directions but ours.

"Blemished kids, of all people, should not blaspheme our Lord's House," he said.

I scooted out of there and everybody felt better, including me.

For my part, I delivered the Des Moines Register before sunrise. Besides my paper route, I'd shovel sidewalks in the winter and mow lawns each summer. I got a pile of loot at Christmas from customers. Mr. Grifhorst, the druggist, normally handed me a silver dollar. Mrs. Hank "the Tank" Schmidt, our mayor's wife, gave us a fruitcake which I always passed on to Mom, and Grandma donated it to the church. Mr. Nordstrud, who ran our Coast-to-Coast Hardware store, handed me a set of fishhooks one holiday, a length of chain another season and 500 BBs once. That Christmas paper grew so fat my shoulder nearly wrenched off, so I deserved something.

When North Korea invaded South Korea, which are countries in the Orient, the paper thickened to forty-eight pages. This made it impossible to ride my bike around the route, even in summer. I didn't get any extra tips, but that didn't matter, since several more citizens then subscribed.

Grundy Center took good care of me.

Each August, during Korn Kastle Days, most farmers came to town and I'd order twenty additional copies of the Register. Walking through the VFW in the middle of the afternoon, some of the patrons would give me a dime for a newspaper, even one or two pretenders who couldn't read. Since they got soused I would drift back through, about two hours later, pick up their copies, refold them and sell each paper again, unless they had slopped beer over it. During one Korn Kastle Days I cleared twenty bucks.

A few farmers whooped it up at Korn Kastle Days if the corn and beans were healthy. When crops withered that same handful of farmers got lubricated to forget. That struck me as contrary, since prices went up if the weather hurt the yields, but they were lucky to get fifty cents a bushel when there was a bumper crop. It seemed not to matter near as much as they carried on. Maybe it was pride. They loved to brag on their yields, stretching the numbers sometimes to frustrate neighbors.

The carnies trucked into town for Korn Kastle Days and set up a Ferris wheel, Tilt-a-Whirl and booths where citizens might win kewpie dolls and plaster figurines.

Carnies didn't mind my affliction. They had plenty of their own.

So I'd work a booth, after delivering the papers, usually the one where folks paid twenty-five cents for trying to set a Coke bottle upright. Sometimes I ran the "guess your age and weight" scales, but usually I was the star at the Coke bottle booth.

"Test your luck," I'd shout. "Just one thin quarter, the fourth part of a dollar to win a kewpie doll or sculptured piggy bank, all original works of art."

As soon as one customer stopped, several others always gathered behind him or her. I'd step outside the booth, reach back in with a bamboo pole, loop the rope on its end around the neck of one of the Coke bottles, laying flat, and would set it upright.

"Hey, how easy was that?" I'd ask.

Some guy would shrug and flip me a quarter. I'd drop it into that short apron with pockets that we booth carnies wore.

"Here you go and good luck." I'd hand the pole to the customer. Either the Ferris wheel or Tilt-a-Whirl would whisk past with flashing lights and screaming riders. This didn't help the customer concentrate. The guy would lift the bottle about an inch, maybe two, before it rolled out of the loop and clattered on the gravel.

"Oh, too bad, great try." Most customers would shake their heads while the audience chuckled. Maybe about then a diesel generator would start chugging to power another ride or the barker from the freak show might shout over the loudspeakers.

"See the amazing spider woman...right here, the astounding two-headed calf...you won't believe it when plastic man ties himself in a square knot...inside this tent in two short minutes, ladeees and gentlemen, only one hundred and twenty short seconds to go."

This distracted my players further.

"Try your luck again?" I asked. Usually they would. They'd fail. And I'd show them how, one more time. Some other distraction would take place, maybe an electrical connection on a spotlight arced with a "zap." There was always a new noise and another flash of light.

"Care to try a third time?" If they did, I'd see that they won, unless it was Doctor Throckmorton.

The secret came each year while I dug through the empty Coke cases behind Grifhorst's Drug Emporium, looking for bottles that were cast off-center, showing one thin side while the opposite was thick. Those were cash in the bank. When I laid the bottles for myself, I put the thick side down, which was heavier, with the light side on top. Those stood up easy. Then for the customers I put the lighter side down so they could never make that very same bottle stand.

Some days I'd make five dollars at the booth and Grandma let me keep half. I'd bring home a cotton candy for Mom. She'd groan but she'd take it. If Mom was in good spirits, she'd hand me the paper cone at the end so I could lick the sugar beads, but that was rare.

One year the carnies brought a spectacular ride to Grundy Center called the Flying Saucer. It was like a gigantic pie tin with pennants on top. Everybody flocked into this thing, stood against the outer wall and it would start to whirl. Passengers got pushed back against the side, harder and harder. It tilted up a bit, the riders hollering, finally dropping back down and stopped.

I had to try that thing but some mud had caked on my soles and heels. I scraped it off using the angle iron that supported the entry gate and stepped in. Gloria Throckmorton, the doctor's daughter, pranced through with a gaggle of friends, chattering and giggling.

"Hi Gloria," I said. They floated past wearing their yellow, red and green Capezio shoes, unspotted, without noticing me.

I turned my left side, the good side, toward her.

"This is some crazy ride, huh Gloria?" I asked.

She looked the other way.

The carnie buckled us all in. We spun and twirled. The Flying Saucer rotated faster while the pennants above our heads crackled and fluttered, some of the screamers went quiet and the whole thing started to tilt, thrusting one side into the sky.

Gloria pointed at me.

"Moon's rising," she said.

They laughed. This didn't upset me at all, but it wasn't so funny that they'd make The Ed Sullivan Show with that dumb joke.

The ride kept tilting until we swirled at a sharp angle to Main Street. I glanced at Gloria just when she puked. Centrifugal force pulled her vomit back in a lumpy, brown trail across both cheeks and over both ears, into that flip hairdo, oozing through her Korn Kastle Kween Krown.

She didn't call me "Moon" again that day. Then again, girls hardly ever talked to me anyway.

In spring, summer and fall, Grandma beat the carpets every Saturday at "Wesley Redemption Methodist," as some called it. She set up folding chairs in the basement for the socials and passed out cardboard fans. Each fan had a color photo of Jesus on one side and Farber & Ottoman's Funeral Home, "Friends When You Need Them Most," printed on the back. Those fans helped, but in July and August the sweat still darkened your collar before the benediction, and unless you had your own seat cushion, your pants stuck to your rear when you stood. Most farmers didn't wear deodorizer under their arms at church. Grandpa said that's where the word "pew" came from.

Grandma even took Mom and me to eat at the Copper Kettle once after Sunday services. Our bachelor neighbor stayed with Grandpa, for which I gave him a free Sunday paper. The Copper Kettle had four booths with Formica tops, a linoleum counter with several stools and two tables with red and white checkered cloths that nearly matched. The patrons looked startled when we stepped inside so Grandma hustled us to the back booth, near the stove.

We scooched across to the far side of its bench, where grease popping from the grill couldn't hit us. Pieces of chicken or hamburger patties hissed when slapped onto that stove and quickly settled into a deeper "shhhh" sound, adding to everybody's appetites. We had to raise our voices to talk in that corner, but were careful not to say much, so others wouldn't grumble over us being out of place. There were wieners on the stove too, but they cooked quieter.

Mom sipped her chocolate malt through a straw. She took care to not slurp at the end, since people might have heard that over the sizzling, and that could start them grouching about us.

Grandma ordered a vegetable burger, which they created with a fried patty of ground chuck under two pickles, a tomato slice, lettuce and onion in a bun toasted on the grill.

I ate a hot roast beef sandwich, chewing real slow, and that thing tasted so good I wished it could last forever. It wasn't really a sandwich, but a slice of white Wonder Bread on the plate, a slab of beef with hardly any gristle and a scoopful of mashed potatoes on top, plus brown gravy ladled across the whole thing, and cost us three whole quarters.

The King of England had nothing on me that day.

Since Grandma did so much for The Most Reverend Dawson, pretty soon the parish agreed to let me attend Sunday school, except I could not take catechism, which I didn't care about anyway. Are you kidding? Memorize all that? Stand up to recite in front of the whole congregation? No ma'am and no sir. It was just fine that they included me out of that torture.

Everybody at church started calling me Moon. But Dad never would. He suffered from a nervous condition and acted jumpy during our secret meetings. Dad and I got together often. He gave me a fishing reel once and a Louisville Slugger baseball bat another time. The bat was an official Duke Snider model, signed.

I got good with the reel.

Mr. Nordstrud saw me practicing my casts with that reel. He took my daily and two Sunday papers. Mr. Nordstrud displayed a used fishing pole in his front window. He noticed that I always studied it.

"Why doesn't anybody buy that thing, Moon?" he asked one day.

"It sure is nice, fiberglass and all," I replied.

The next Saturday, after collecting, he said I could hold it. I did, and by swinging it around was able to hide my hand tremors.

"That's a great whip action Mr. Nordstrud, my rod's metal, and won't bend half this much."

"Could I suggest something?" he asked.

"Of course, Mr. Nordstrud."

"You're pretty good at casting, right Moon?"

"Yes sir, fair."

His forehead wrinkled. "Do you understand, Moon, what a big favor you'd do me by just taking that thing? Wouldn't it be good advertising? See all that window space it would free up?"

My heart stopped.

"Are you kidding, Mr. Nordstrud?"

He scratched his head. Maybe he was just joking around. Mr. Nordstrud stepped out from behind his counter.

"You understand, Moon, that this wouldn't exactly be free?" He bit his upper lip and squinted. He was thinking hard.

"I'm trying to save the paper route money, Mr. Nordstrud, for my future education."

"It's not a cash expense, Moon, but can you handle a different kind of cost? You know how happy I would be to get that fishing rod out of my front window? But could you promise me to use it? That'll take some of your time, won't it? If people see how well you cast with it, doesn't that promote my store?"

Wow.

"Think you could, Moon, promise me to get better with that rod? And show it off regularly?"

Mr. Nordstrud stepped away to measure and cut a length of chain for a farmer. I stood there and steadied myself by gripping the counter. They talked on and on for about a century but finally he clipped the chain, the farmer left and Mr. Nordstrud strolled back.

"Oh yes Mr. Nordstrud," I said, "surely, and often, and Mr. Nordstrud I can tell anyone who asks about your store and the other stuff you have here that's so keen, Mr. Nordstrud, and certainly I will and is it really that important to free up your window space?"

Luckily I wore black trousers. I was scared that I might wet myself from this excitement, but it wouldn't show so much with my dark pants.

Mr. Nordstrud nodded. He stared at the rod, not blinking.

"And I'd mention what a swell selection you've got in your store."

He extended his hand.

"Well it's a deal then, okay Moon? I'm only pleased with our agreement if you are, so what do you say?"

I told him how happy and delighted I was with the arrangement and how I'd make sure everybody saw me casting with that rod and shook his hand until finally he suggested we had shaken long enough to confirm our deal in every single state of the union.

"Could you free up my window space now, Moon, and get that blankety-blank rod out of here?"

I did.

"May I say thank you, Moon?"

"Sure, Mr. Nordstrud, but gee, thank you too and I'll…"

"Can you just get that cantankerous thing out of here Moon?"

I did, without dampening my pants, but needed to duck into the bandstand bushes right after leaving his store.

Every eyelet on this rod except one in the middle was still on it, and I even retied that. You could bend this rod double and it would snap back as if nothing happened. I got so I could cast thirty yards and drop the line into a tire behind the gas station every time.

Well, maybe my cast hit center with about half my tries, but that's pretty good for such a distance.

Okay, I guess it was only once that I hit it five times out of ten, and that was the best I ever scored, but several other times I nailed it three or four times. That's respectable. Any fisherman would agree. Dad would be impressed.

But I never did get to try that baseball bat Dad gave me.

"Moon has a dangerous lack of depth perception," Doctor Throckmorton explained to the school PTA. Grandma attended their monthly meetings and told me what went on.

The fluorescent lights flickered, she said. Doctor Throckmorton ran both hands over his mud-colored hair without moving a curl. A crowd of forty parents sat in the school lunchroom, dipping ginger snaps in their coffee and milk. Doctor Throckmorton added that he thought it would be too risky for me to play baseball. He marched to the room's center and all heads turned to follow him.

"There is simply no point in distracting and disturbing the other teams with Moon's condition," the good doctor said, turning to walk toward the door. Everybody twisted to watch him.

"We want Grundy Center remembered for positive things, not tragedies."

He walked out the door backwards, making his usual grand exit. He was wrong about me.

It's not like I was ever asked to join some freak show. My right eye slants a little lower than my left, but not so much. My cheekbone there is pushed in flat but most folks say they don't even notice. Well, some small kids comment. Every once in a while, not often, toddlers cry the first time they see me. Hitting a ball could be tough, but thanks to big shot Doctor Throckmorton, I'll never know.

The first time Gloria Throckmorton had said my face was shaped like a half moon, I made the mistake of talking back. Then everybody made a big deal out of her stupid comment. By the next weekend my name became Moon all over Grundy Center.

"Which of us has looked into his father's heart? Which of us is not forever a stranger and alone?"

Thomas Wolfe

Chapter 2

The worst lie I ever told was when Dad asked about that baseball bat he gave me and I claimed to have hit a home run. Dad and I had snuck out to Grundy's Marsh for a meeting. The mosquitoes were biting fierce. We swatted them non-stop on our face and arms.

Dad couldn't suspect that I fibbed. He didn't dare set foot inside Grundy Center, being my illegitimate father. I never really figured him out, especially when I lied about that home run. He grinned and hissed in a breath, through his teeth, hugging himself, and looked away for a minute. When he gazed back toward me his cheeks were wet. Several mosquitoes landed on his face and hands, but for a spell Dad didn't notice.

Mom escorted me out to Grundy's Marsh for those get-togethers. She and I hiked over to this place where duck hunters beached their flat-bottomed boats in the reeds. I'd sit in one and she'd slip away. In a few minutes, sometimes not even a half-hour, Dad would emerge from the reeds and cat-tails, trudge over and plunk down right next to me. We'd talk about the White Sox and squirrel hunting and how you could make a little camp stove from an empty Folgers can and fry an egg on it. Stuff like that.

"If ye could ever get into Ames, that'd surely be a proud thing," Dad said once.

"What's Ames?" I asked.

"Iowa State, lad. A college town. A triumph of that nature might win over a measure of respect for yer kin." I didn't know what to say back.

"If that seems a bit of a stretch, of course, there's little reason to beat yourself up tryin."

His neck blackened in the summer sun, his chin and cheeks went brown but his forehead didn't appear to belong atop the same head. The skin above his eyebrows shined whiter than a Perch belly, one with freckles, having been shaded by a straw hat.

After awhile he'd pat my shoulder.

"I'm wishin things were different," he'd say, "but you're my pride, boy. Best ye never let the citizens be the wiser about us. Make no mention of me." When he talked that way I knew he was fixing to leave.

He'd stoop low, holding the sides of the boat, step out and walk away. I never answered. That talk confused me. I'd try to focus my eyes on something small to keep from having another fainting spell. I hardly ever passed out, after learning to anticipate this dizziness.

Once I studied the Oshkosh, B'Gosh label stitched to the middle of Dad's bib, concentrating on every thread when he started itching to go. Dad crouched. He stood. I looked away and started examining an oarlock on the side of the boat until I heard his boot squish in the mud. Then I got brave and glanced up. He was pushing the reeds apart and stepped through, but slowly. He was thinking about staying longer, that's for sure.

I never saw Dad again. Probably he croaked. But I took bigger steps and flexed my shoulders back ever after Mom told me the secret about him. I had just finished collecting for the paper, a spring mist cooled me. That drizzle and a breeze kept the bugs away. Mom's last piano student was skipping down the street. She slouched in our doorway.

"Hi Mom," I said from the sidewalk.

She nodded and stepped out to smoke.

"It's wet out here, Mom."

"You think I don't know that?" She stood in front of the door for a few seconds, her hair dampened and drooped over her forehead, black roots peeking out from under the peroxided curls, and finally turned inside and opened a window.

I ducked inside. I figured this was as good a time as any to ask.

"Mom, what do you hear from Dad?"

"He ain't your dad."

"Well, okay, but where'd he go?"

Mom flung her cigarette out the window. The screen bounced it back inside, she said some bad words and stomped the ashes into the rug. I grabbed a broom and dustpan.

"That bum followed us here and you better not tell anybody, I mean nobody, you hear?"

"Sure Mom." I swept up the ashes and tobacco, dumping them into our trash can.

"That's why he could visit you," she said.

"Is he still near by?"

"Who knows? Have you gotten a dollar from him lately? I sure haven't."

"Can I see him again, Mom?"

Her eyes squinted so tight you couldn't see into them.

Mom swore.

She ran straight at me.

Mom jerked the dustpan out of my hand and raised it over my head.

I didn't flinch.

I didn't move.

Mom had blown her stack before, but she hardly ever clobbered me. Give her credit for that.

Mom turned, flung the dustpan into the corner and slumped to the floor. She dropped her face into her hands.

"That tramp dug ditches in the summer," she said.

"What?"

"Can't you hear?"

I kept my mouth shut and Mom spoke louder.

"After the ground froze," she said, "the guy tended the furnace at Saint something-or-other, not so far from here. And I'm not about to tell you where. You're in big trouble if you ever repeat one word of this."

"But Mom, he told me he worked on the Rasmussens' farm."

"Grow up." She stomped out into the mist. I fell asleep before she returned, so she must have taken quite a hike and didn't even wear a raincoat or scarf. Maybe Dad's life wasn't as glamorous as the farming he pretended to do, but he probably wanted to give me some pride in him, just like I exaggerated to become his baseball hero.

That's how I discovered that my dad had followed us. So he must have liked me. Not every kid can say that. Willy can, but Carla's dad hardly talks to her.

If Dad were alive, he and I'd still be messing around together, that's for sure. Before he vanished, he and I had met as much as three or four times a year, but only when there wasn't snow blanketing the ground. There was a season when he didn't show, so I suppose work took him out of county.

He never said.

I was afraid to ask.

But I figure anybody who tried that hard to be near his boy must have passed on, or he'd still visit. Dad departed from his earthly toils and found glorious peace with our Almighty Father. I know this.

A gully-washer downpour had soaked the county the night before that final visit with Dad. After he disappeared in the reeds I sat there, trembling. Mom finally showed up, struggling through the muck around the edge of Grundy's Marsh.

"Get going," she said, "before all those snooty busy-bodies notice we're not in town." We shuffled to the woods and took the path curving toward Grundy Center. I glanced down, since tree roots gnarled over our trail. Mom stepped ahead, arms swinging high.

"Does your face ever hurt?" she asked, talking into the air. I stared at the back of her head, glancing down in time to spot a fallen branch. We stepped through the clearing. I wanted to stay calm, but we had never discussed this.

"Nope," I said. That was mostly true. Everybody gets a headache sometime. She slowed. I picked up a pebble and tossed it towards the trees, trying to act as if we weren't talking about anything that mattered.

"Well, how does that caved-in cheek feel?" I stumbled but didn't fall and kept walking.

"Oh, fine Mom, just like other kids, you know." Of course I couldn't guess how anybody else's head felt but I sure didn't want Mom suffering pitiful thoughts for me.

Mom planted both fists on her hips. She kicked the ground. I shuffled slower so I wouldn't catch up and agitate her. I started thinking that maybe, if I studied harder, I might be accepted by Iowa State. But for sure I wouldn't mention that to Mom. It made no sense to stir up a fuss with uppity talk yet.

We passed the woods, hiking the railroad tracks to town. Cocklebur leaves shaded the ties. Mom walked faster. Most of the spikes had worked loose and the rails were rusted brown. I imagined how much respect our family might enjoy in Grundy Center after I earned a college degree. The grain elevator pierced the tree line along the horizon ahead, which meant we should be home in a half hour.

"If I'd known wearing a tight girdle could bend a kid's face," Mom said, "I'd never have hidden your damn pregnancy that way."

I stumbled but scrambled back to my feet. Mom didn't hear. At least she didn't look back.

"Maybe I'd have just left town earlier. Then you'd have a normal head." She hiked on, crossing her arms.

"But how would I have fed us? Teachers can't marry, let alone be with child." She spit sideways.

"Moon, you were a disaster from the start."

Along with everybody else, Mom had started calling me Moon. That was okay. We slipped back into town without being noticed.

"This village belongs to the Castle..."

Franz Kafka

Chapter 3

My pal Willy Geiselman could roller skate on gravel. I'm not saying this looked pretty. But being able to move across loose stones at any speed, without tripping, counted for something. After a dozen jerky steps over his lawn he stumbled north, flailing like a scarecrow through the rocks, potholes and little gullies of Main Street until he'd reach Grundy Center's only hard road, Highway 24, running east to west.

Then Willy sailed.

One day the Iowa State Highway Commission came to town and set up lawn chairs and an umbrella two blocks from school, right where that cement road intersected the gravel of Main Street. They plunked down with their clipboards and jugs of Kool-Aid. Our Mayor, Hank the Tank, knew what that meant.

To make this short story long, I'll explain first that he called Mr. Ericsen at the grain elevator.

"Ericsen, don't you think our school kids should have a tour of your elevator today?"

Hank the Tank explained why, and called Mr. Scarletti, our principal, next.

"Scarletti, wouldn't this morning be perfect for a school tour of the grain elevator?"

Hank gave his reasons again. And so Mr. Ericsen and Mr. Scarletti scheduled everybody in high school to have a tour of the elevator that afternoon.

When all eighty-three of us hiked across the highway you should've seen those bigwigs' pencils scratching their clipboards, like starved roosters let loose in a granary. The Iowa State Highway Commission Officials had no choice but to count every one of us. For good measure, Mr. Scarletti walked back to school, got all five teachers hiking over to the elevator with him, returned that group to school, as if they all forgot something, then sauntered back to get us and escorted the entire student body across the highway one last time, returning to their classrooms. Those "roosters" marked every single pedestrian crossing of that pavement on their clipboards.

Within one month a state truck arrived and began putting up Grundy Center's own stoplight, right there on the northeast corner of main and the highway.

I never saw two cars or trucks or tractors enter this crossroad at the same time, but that stoplight surely put Grundy Center on the map.

The GRUNDY CENTER MONTHLY BUGLE, which came out seven or eight and sometimes nine to ten issues a year, pictured the new traffic signal on the front page, with interviews of state officials plus prominent citizens inside.

"This shows," Doctor Throckmorton said on page one, "that Grundy Center is moving forward, on the go and our honorable mayor is a proven, smart leader."

Our mayor was never called Hank the Tank publicly, since he got named that from his beer consumption at the VFW.

Only one plumber existed in all of Grundy Center County, and that was none other than Willy's dad. He taught Willy and me how to sweat a copper joint for plumbing and how to flange one for a gas stove. He explained why you put a vent pipe in the plumbing, and that's so the sewer gas can't back up into the house. If you didn't put in that vent, the S-trap might siphon itself so there wouldn't be anything keeping that stench where it belongs, which is not in your home.

Willy's father hauled off cracked bathtubs at no charge, but resold them to Catholic farmers, so the Geiselman family lived well. He had a 52 Ford with tires that matched. It started almost every time you turned the ignition and didn't smoke out the back.

Willy's dad even owned a Piper Cub. Looking close, you could see that airplane was skinned with painted cloth. Any half-hearted hailstorm could perforate it. The Geiselmans sheltered their plane in an empty barn and paid the farmer to not grow corn or beans on a narrow strip of grass that ran a hundred yards for their landings and takeoffs. The Geiselmans basked in that kind of wealth, but it never turned Willy's head.

Willy's dad and Hank the Tank conducted the "TURKEY DROP & COW PLOP" every Fourth of July. The citizens milled around while officials marked squares in the gravel on Main Street with a hoe. They scratched a number in each. Then everybody bought a square for a quarter, except Doctor Throckmorton, who purchased ten squares annually, donating nine to the less fortunate. That could have been anybody in town, of course, but he gave his extras to those who were rock-scrabble poor.

Finally the Rasmussens turned loose a Holstein or Angus cow, they raised both, onto the street to the cheers of the crowd. When that animal pooped whoever bought the square that got decorated won a bag of free groceries at Hardcastle's.

That was the first half of Grundy Center's famous "TURKEY DROP & COW PLOP."

One year Widow Chizek won. She spent so much time putting stuff in her bag and taking it out and putting something else in that Mr. Hardcastle finally just told her to take what she had plus whatever she could hold in one free hand and be done with it.

Widow Chizek did.

Maybe she planned that. Sometimes folks think harder when they're scraping the bottom.

After the animal marked a square each year, Hank the Tank always waltzed out carrying a scoop shovel.

"On behalf of the citizenry of Grundy Center, I proudly remove this cow pie and announce the winner." He'd then scan the list of names and numbers, hesitate, start to shout the winner's name, stopped to double check the list again, looked up and smiled.

The crowd cheered every year when he yelled out the name.

Next Hank the Tank scooped up the cow pie and faked a toss into the crowd. A few people always ducked and screamed while everybody else laughed.

Doctor Throckmorton stepped into the center of the street and the crowd hushed.

"Fellow citizens," he began.

He would look out at the crowd on one side, lift a foot onto one toe, twist to face the other side, say nothing, glance up the street and down the street, run several fingers through his wavy hair and start again.

"It is not a light burden I accept in guiding our fair city; my responsibilities were not sought by me but requested by you, the citizens. And again I agree to watch over our officials in the government, school and bank."

He slipped one hand into a pocket, walked up the street several paces, scratched his chin, nodded, turned, strolled back looking straight ahead and suddenly stopped. He'd rotate towards the other side and glare into the crowd.

"While agreeing to guide our mutual fortunes, I must humbly ask your support, for your unquestioned faith in my decisions, plus your loyalty to my medical practice, if I am to continue."

He would usually hold both arms out, like a crucifix, at this point.

"When those simple requests are too much, just say so, and I'll happily step aside to enjoy my private life again." Then Doctor Throckmorton would talk about our great country and Grundy Center's place in it.

Next Hank the Tank and Willy's dad roared out of town, hopped in the Piper Cub and circled overhead. Everybody yelled when they started, some because of the upcoming spectacle but more because the annual lecture from Doctor Throckmorton was over.

When the plane shrunk down to a speck in the sky, and the engine buzzed instead of roaring, Hank the Tank threw out coupons good for prizes followed by the turkey. The bird fluttered down and about a hundred people calculated the wind direction from the coupons' drift and swarmed through yards, running into clotheslines, tripping over fences, trying to grab the wide-eyed bird.

That was the rest of Grundy Center's famed "COW PLOP & TURKEY DROP."

One year Hank the Tank forgot the historical reasons for these procedures and instead of a live turkey, he got a dressed one, frozen in waxed paper and tossed that from the sky. Nobody saw that artillery coming until it conked a dent right in the roof of Doctor Throckmorton's Midnight Blue, four-door Cadillac. Hank hid out for a few days. Carla's dad pulled the bump out smooth using a toilet plunger. The paint didn't even crack, so Hank the Tank could show his face again.

(Carla sounds like a guy's name, but she's a girl and one who talks to me.)

That Cadillac proved how money piled up in Grundy Center. Lots of folks cut a fat hog. Willy lived in a house with central heating and doors inside, separating the rooms.

Doctor Throckmorton resided in the only three-story house in town, all brick, and drove a brand new car every other year.

"As soon as the ashtray's full, he trades for a new one," folks joked. Those Midnight Blue, four-door Cadillacs seemed to float. More unbelievable yet, the Throckmorton house featured wall-to-wall carpet. That means there were no gaps around their edges. It's true. I saw it once. Their main floor rugs went all the way to the walls and were trimmed to fit. Doctor Throckmorton also had a sun parlor and a basement finished with plaster walls.

Des Moines bragged about having three millionaires, but Grundy Center had a bunch of thousandaires and some folks guessed Doctor Throckmorton might be worth a hundred thousand dollars. That story got repeated so often that half our town started to believe it.

Grandma and Mom and I lived in a duplex. Grandpa departed for the better world on the fifth day of a January. We couldn't afford to pay Farber & Ottoman to chill him inside until the ground thawed, but they gave us their economy plan, where his box sat outside, in a snow drift but fenced to keep away varmints. They did this right on his permanent site, in the Protestant section of the cemetery, until his resting spot could be dug in the spring.

Since our landlord was too poor to paint and too proud to whitewash, the duplex we lived in faded to gray. The boards weathered until the grain stood out bigger than Grandma's hand veins. I wasn't embarrassed for our landlord. At least he had enough cash to paint his own house. A few years later he nailed some asbestos siding over his home. A Des Moines salesman guaranteed he'd never have to paint again. It didn't quite work out that way.

Like many others, we didn't have doors inside but used curtains to separate the three rooms. Our linoleum shined in the summer and fall when a waxing lasted a week.

Grandma bought a used car, a '48 Kaiser. She learned to drive. I'm proud of her for that. I figured out how to tune it. This kept me hopping since we drove on recapped tires and fed it used oil. The gas station charged twenty cents for a new can but we got the drained oil for a nickel.

Willy's home nestled at the edge of town, like ours, and even though they were rich, they also burned soft coal, bituminous instead of anthracite, so each spring they washed the soot from their walls just like us. One year Grandma and I bought a truckload of corncobs to fill the stud spaces in our outer walls. Our coal bill dropped almost $3 per month that first winter, so that investment paid off. I asked our landlord if we could get a break on the rent since we improved his property, but he said we'd benefit more than he would. That was a point.

"Squawk, squawk, squawk."

That was the early Sabbath sound. Willy's mom walked over carrying a chicken by the feet.

"Looks like about three pounds," Grandma said.

The chicken fluttered its wings, sending white feathers into the air. Mrs. Geiselman handed it to Grandma. She walked over to the stump with our axe, chopped its head and let the body run around to spurt out the blood.

That always made me light-headed.

After that chicken minus a head stopped running around, Grandma tied its feet over the clothesline to drip. Both women would then waddle into our chicken coop.

"That one about right?" Grandma would ask while pointing at one of ours.

Willy's mom would nod okay. Next Grandma waded into the chickens, grabbed the victim, feathers flying, handed it to Mrs. Geiselman and she'd twist its head off, by hand. She'd drop the head into her apron pocket and hold the fluttering bird out straight, by the feet and legs, while it bled over the dirt. That encouraged me to always keep a couple steps between Mrs. Geiselman and myself.

"Never can kill one of my own," she'd say.

"Me neither," Grandma replied, "works better this way. I get attached to those birds."

Boiling off their feathers stunk up our house.

"My family will always have meat on Sundays," Grandma liked to say, and we did. Sometimes with a bigger bird there'd be enough pickings left over for a Monday sandwich with pickles, Miracle Whip and lettuce.

Hardcastle's Grocery kept mayonnaise, Jell-O, lettuce, baloney, fancy bar soap wrapped in paper with rounded corners, milk, hand-packed ice cream, sliced bread and a side of beef plus one butchered hog. Mr. Hardcastle carried Velveeta but cream cheese was a special order. That railroader who moved into town from Minneapolis, his whole family talked with accents, asked for garlic, but Mr. Hardcastle told them to shape up and become true Americans.

"No tea either."

Mr. Hardcastle took a newspaper, so I was in his store daily, except Sundays when I tossed the paper on his porch step. One summer he generated some excitement with a bushel-basket full of peanuts. For a nickel any Grundy Center resident could have all they could hold in one hand. He was some promoter.

Mr. Hardcastle made a show out of backing away from the scale while the meat weighed, taking a small step, arms out. That way nobody worried about his thumb on the scale. The State of Iowa calibrated his scale once a year and the certificate on front proved that.

But when Grandma stopped in to buy a half-pound of ground chuck one day, I happened to be delivering his paper. I kind of sharpened my eyes at moments like that. This was November. It was cold enough they didn't need to worry about meat spoiling but Mr. Hardcastle fixed up some for Grandma fresh. He didn't shove an unfair amount of gristle into the grinder, but he did reach up and pulled a string while grinding. That turned on the overhead fan. I slipped behind his counter.

"Mr. Hardcastle, sir?"

"What Moon?"

"Why do you turn on the fan?"

His cheeks flushed.

"Got to keep the flies away, boy."

"I surely appreciate that, Mr. Hardcastle."

The problem with his answer was that this was the cold season, and flies generally disappeared. Maybe they went south.

"Mr. Hardcastle, sir?"

"Now what?"

"Did you notice when that fan goes on, your scale measures two ounces heavier?"

"What? No."

"It sure seems to Mr. Hardcastle, sir, just look."

"Well I'll be. Thank you Moon, I'll watch out for that."

He never pulled his trick again, at least on Grandma. He never tried to with anybody else either, at least not while I stood inside. Mr. Hardcastle was too pretentious to hang flypaper in the summer anyway, so I don't think bugs bothered him as much as he said.

He walked me into his meat locker the next week and cancelled the paper.

"You see, Moon, in business, to treat customers fairly, we have to watch our expenses."

It was cold in that locker, and his words came out in white puffs.

"I just wasn't reading the paper enough, so I need to stop my subscription, out of respect for our grocery's customers."

"I u-understand M-Mr. Hardcastle." I shivered in my short sleeve shirt.

"I don't plan to raise prices a pinch, as a service to Grundy Center, but sometimes that means a personal sacrifice."

"Okay, Mr. H-Hardcastle."

"So Moon, you won't need to hang around my store anymore, right?"

"I guess n-not, Mr. Hardcastle." I noticed Mr. Hardcastle bought a new davenport that year and went fishing in Minnesota, so his sacrifices didn't seem too unbearable.

But nobody starved in Grundy Center. Here was me, a kid with a bent head and parents that didn't get hitched, yet I never suffered a frostbite, except delivering papers once, and I ate in a restaurant and got two new shirts and a pair of Lee rider jeans with a zipper fly from the Sears catalog every Christmas. Carla lived like me. Willy had more. And the Throckmortons even owned a motion picture camera. They could put on private picture shows, I guess.

Willy thought Carla liked him and me because she was supposed to be a gypsy, my face was bent and he couldn't talk right.

Most of the country kids, no matter if they were Catholics or Protestants, didn't have indoor plumbing. They kept thunder jugs under their beds for relief in the winter and used a privy in the summer. Flies tickled everybody's rear when they used the outhouse, which wasn't a kind of sensation anybody enjoyed or could do much about. Despite this tougher rural living, Bohemian Catholic farmers like the Prohaskas, Zrostliks and Kopaceks all maintained Mother Mary shrines between their house and the road. Each stood about a yard tall, with a white backdrop surrounding the statue. A few had lights.

Years later some folks worried about the loss of family farms. Anybody who said that never worked on one. Until you've lifted bales of hay off the machine, one after the other as long as the sun shows, and spent early evenings under a bare bulb in the haymow stacking them, blowing black dirt from your nose and like to choke in the heat, well, do that for just one season and you'll never sob over the loss of some family farm. Or try detasseling corn in the hundred degree temperatures, wearing long-sleeved shirts so the leaves don't cut your arms. Then pull some cockleburs out of beans. Shovel manure from the barn. If there's a full winter layer, the manure ferments down deep and steams when you push your pitchfork into it, so your eyes water from the fumes.

Get up at four to milk cows, and each one will kick if you aren't careful where you place the stool. Slop the hogs, feed the chickens, put down a few bales and break the ice over their water. Then tell me why we need family farms. Do that every day, year round.

If just a few of their animals died, the farmer was halfway to the poorhouse. Yet if he ever fell down in the hog pen, those animals would eat him in minutes. I always wondered who was working for whom.

When a farmer made it through harvest he paid off the loans and prayed that the banker would loan him seed money for the next year. This required squirming on the chair in front of the banker's desk. Everybody walking past could glance in to watch. If the farmer's yields and prices came in okay the banker almost always would loan again, but the farmer never knew that for sure. The banker always mentioned that hailstorm when hardly anybody made their annual mortgage payment on time, but forgot the other years when everybody paid right after harvest.

The only benefit to country life was that farmers never got polio, which put Jimmy Blackman in leg braces and Sally Lomen into an iron lung for her life, which wasn't so long.

In time, America learned that polio had been around forever, but only turned into an epidemic after city folks got plumbing and sewage. This caused them to lose some of their natural immunities.

Doctor Throckmorton served as chairman of our bank. He hoped this reassured Grundy Center. The bank manager stood and hustled to the front whenever Doctor Throckmorton entered. The banker dried both palms on his pant legs before shaking hands with Doctor Throckmorton. Sometimes Doctor Throckmorton paused until the bank manager blotted his fingers on a red kerchief. Then Doctor Throckmorton extended his hand.

When the manager grilled each farmer, he told them that he was merely making sure Doctor Throckmorton didn't become nervous. Making loans to farmers who couldn't deliver a top yield endangered the bank, he'd explain, over and over, and if the bank failed all of Grundy Center would suffer.

Each year one farmer failed to get a new loan. And Doctor Throckmorton, for the community good, stepped in with his personal money and bought that farm, letting the previous owner work it as a sharecropper.

"I respect and love the gritty American farmer," Doctor Throckmorton said in the town hall. Three or four dozen citizens sat there on the wooden folding chairs below him. The overhead fan swished around, stirring up the heat, and every window was open but the air outside sat still. Nobody stirred and nothing moved but drips of sweat running down necks and cheeks. Not a chair squeaked.

Doctor Throckmorton held both arms out in front, palms up, like he was carrying firewood, but his arms were empty and he gazed above the audience.

"It is a barely comprehensible surprise to me that the Lord decided I should also become a man of the soil, for the greater good of Grundy Center."

Everybody nodded. Like they'd better. Doctor Throckmorton dropped his arms and surveyed the room, nodding with a half-smile. I sat in the back, but noticed Doctor Throckmorton's shirt anyway. His sleeves had two buttons on each cuff and there were eight buttons down the front. I could get in and out of any of my shirts quicker than him, since mine had four buttons in total. I don't know why his wife didn't remove those unnecessary ones.

The farmers who lost their land to Doctor Throckmorton knew they could always survive a few more years as his sharecropper. When their tractor would wear out it became time to move to Waterloo or Des Moines for a factory job. Understanding that risk, smarter farmers either sold out to a neighbor when they could or bought out that neighbor, both hoping to avoid the banker's squeeze.

Money's funny. Doctor Throckmorton always sauntered out to his Midnight Blue, four-door Cadillac and turned the key with confidence. He then cruised four blocks to his office. Grandma, Mom and I guessed that our car might start about four times out of five. Grandma would drop me off at the drug store, where they tossed my papers in bulk.

Main Street would be dark. Only the bakery windows glowed, dim, since they fed their ovens in the back, but the front wouldn't be open for another hour.

Grandma chugged on, hunched over the steering wheel, gripping it with both hands. She reached school in another minute. The ground sloped several feet behind the building. Grandma always got there first so she could park on that incline, guaranteeing her next start. If her battery failed, she just rolled the car down and popped its clutch, starting the engine, and her head jerked while that car lurched, engine sputtering to life. Hopefully.

Attitudes scratched lines across Grandma's and Doctor Throckmorton's faces.

Doctor Throckmorton arose every morning expecting his car to run. On maybe one morning a year, when it was twenty below zero, he'd be disappointed. The good doctor would get furious. He'd trudge to his office late, cursing.

Grandma and I bounced up every morning wondering if our car would run. We started earlier in case things didn't go our way. So we were never late. And Grandma sang hymns on those days when our car started. Those were times when the Almighty smiled upon us. And we were never tardy when our car wouldn't go, since we always started out sooner and would just walk when the engine failed.

Who was richer?

Sure, his cars always had power windows, which could hurt your hands and busted about once a year. We stayed with crank windows. They never broke and wouldn't smash a finger.

Was he so rich?

Doctor Throckmorton owned more stuff, but that doesn't always settle the thing. If you looked close at him and Grandma, you could notice the cheek wrinkles proved Doctor Throckmorton spent more time frowning than smiling, while Grandma's face was cracked with happier lines.

But the drivers to pity most were the farmers, some with pickup trucks but most freezing or baking or getting rain-soaked on a tractor. That's not all bad since a tractor could cross washed-out roads, any snowdrift and even make it through some rivers when a bridge let go. But being exposed to the weather made riding those machines less than healthy. If you had chains on the tires and your jacket was loose, a link might jerk a fellow out of his seat and run him over before the engine quit, even if the ignition had a dead man switch.

That's how Max Schultz and Louie Bartik bought it. Or, if your pant leg got too close to the power takeoff that could thrash you to death. Tom Kumsher lost his left leg like that, just before Bob Zrostlik widowed his wife the same fall and that same way, but neighbors finished the harvest for her.

Farmers lose one year to corn borers, another season in hail and imagine one-legged Kumsher trying to squeeze a living from our black dirt. Townies lived the "Life of Riley" compared to farmers.

Maybe if I got into college and came back to Grundy Center as a graduate, I would know how to set up a bank so farmers weren't always on the edge. Doctor Throckmorton, that piano lady, Grandma and I would be the only four citizens with degrees. Doctor Throckmorton's daughter Gloria would go to college, of course, but she'd head for some big city like Des Moines and marry a rich guy. So Grandma and I would be two of the four distinguished people in town. Maybe that's why Doctor Throckmorton resented me. Maybe he was scared I would set up a friendlier bank for the farmers.

I could help Grundy Center someday.

"He had but one eye, and popular prejudice runs in favor of two."

Charles Dickens

Chapter 4

Willy snapped my legs with a rubber band while the teacher turned to the blackboard. It hit the seam of my Lee jeans, so I barely felt it but flipped a spitball back at him anyway, off the end of my ruler. Carla stopped drawing Cinderella coaches and giggled at us.

Sometimes when the sun shone through our classroom window early in the spring or fall, it outlined Carla's chin, nose, cheeks and forehead. Her eyebrows glowed. Whenever Carla spoke to me, I'd be in a trance for awhile afterward.

The teacher turned around fast but saw nothing.

"What have I written on the board, Willy?"

"Coroner?"

"Carla?"

"Coronet?"

"Moon?"

"Coronation?"

"Correct, Moon. And what is a coronation?"

"I don't know, ma'am."

"Willy?"

"It would be a trumpet like?" Willy asked.

"No, Willy, that's a coronet."

"Carla?"

"It's a royal ceremony, like the one to crown Queen Elizabeth this summer."

"Good, Carla, good."

Our teacher explained that Hollywood people planned a flight to London for this event, and they installed film processors in a twin engine plane. (Probably one with metal covering its wings, not cloth.) They would load the exposed film onto that aircraft, take off and develop the motion pictures while over the Atlantic, heading for America. Television could then broadcast this event the very next morning, an amazing thing.

"Our leading citizen and benefactor, Doctor Throckmorton, has graciously offered to open his home for nine of Gloria's schoolmates so they might see and learn from this spectacle."

She paced in front of us. Something creaked with every step, but I couldn't tell if it was the floor or her shoes.

"The good Doctor Throckmorton points out that this is Cultural History. Since Doctor Throckmorton serves our community as President of the School Board, his opinions on such things carry great weight."

Gloria picked four kids and the teacher drew five more names from a hat. None of the country kids put their names in since they would be working at summer chores. Gloria picked her best friends, of course, there's nothing wrong with that, but Willy and me and Carla were luckily among those that the teacher pulled out.

The teacher kept Willy and Carla and me after class to explain how to behave. Willy probably knew, but Carla's dad did the body and fender work plus some farm implement welding, so she might appreciate the tips. Her father pulled that turkey dent out of Doctor Throckmorton's roof with a toilet plunger. Carla's dad also befriended John Barleycorn, so they drank lots of hot dog soup in that household. John Barleycorn's the nickname for whisky. Hot dog soup's the water left after you boil hot dogs, but when you put some ketchup and salt in it, it's tastier than Campbell's.

Carla's ear lobes had holes and she wore hoops through them. This didn't bother me but it unsettled most townsfolk. Carla's eyebrows bushed out, she smiled quick and I sometimes imagined her and I being pals and doing things together. I never admitted that to Willy. There was no denying that Carla's mom and dad divorced, the only other tragedy in Grundy Center, besides me being a bastard, which hardly made Carla or her dad citizens of the year.

Once, when our teacher explained that pierced ears were common to some cultures, Doctor Throckmorton and Mr. Scarletti suggested the next week that she also explain the health risks.

"When you're outside Doctor Throckmorton's home," our teacher said, "notice the 'tennarotor' on their roof. With the twist of a dial, from inside his living room, Doctor Throckmorton can turn the antenna north for KGLO, Channel 3. Or he can aim it southwest for WOI, Channel 5. And on some days, by going just a little further south, the Throckmortons actually see WHO, Channel 13, all the way from Des Moines."

"What if I have to unirate?" Willy asked. He didn't always pronounce words conventionally, but we knew what he meant.

The teacher gave him a look.

"You excuse yourself and go home, young man."

Carla and I didn't peep.

"Scrub up," the teacher said, "and wear your Sunday-go-to-meeting clothes." We all nodded despite the fact that Carla and I didn't have any fancy duds. Willy didn't have much either, but sometimes he wore a red necktie. If that thing ever caught in some machinery he'd be a goner.

My stomach ached the morning of the coronation so Grandma heated a cup of warm milk with cinnamon, and that settled me down. She ironed a shirt for me. I squeezed some Brylcreem out of Grandpa's old tube, rubbed it in my hair and splashed on that Old Spice sample Mr. Grifhorst handed to me once.

Mom even got up. She told me to have a good time and behave.

Willy whizzed over on his three-speed bike, the kind with skinny tires that actually had gears so if you ever traveled to someplace with a hill, you could shift. We guessed that would work pretty neat.

"Peeuuw," he said, "you on got sweet-water."

"No I don't, Willy."

Willy clipped a baseball card onto his fender with a clothespin. The card stuck into his spokes so he sounded like a motorcycle. Carla joined us, riding alongside.

"Carla, do I smell?" I asked.

She steered her bike closer to mine, then dropped behind me, pedaled along and pulled back next to me.

"That's a sophisticated odor," she said.

That sounded like a good way to be. The Old Spice would be okay.

Throckmorton's lawn was so plush you couldn't use the kickstand on your bike. It would just fall over when the stand sunk into his soft lawn. That didn't matter to Willy since his axles were chromed but Carla and I had to figure a way to keep our bikes upright. It would be poor manners to block the sidewalk, so we leaned ours against the maple until Doctor Throckmorton gazed out and raised an eyebrow. Carla and I rode our bikes around the corner, stacked them against the neighbor's tree and scurried back on foot.

"Did you walk her house?" Willy asked.

"What?"

"Did you walk home her?"

"Well, it's right on the way," I said.

"Did you held hands, you sissies?"

"No, Willy. Of course not. We made a Solemn Pact, remember?"

He snorted. Willy was a pal, but acted funny when I mentioned Carla. So I reminded him that Carla couldn't jump a fence like him. Willy chuckled and everything was okay.

This would almost be the first time he or Carla or I saw something real on a television. Willy and I stopped a couple times on our way home from school in front of the Motorola store and looked at the TV going in their window, but all it ever showed was a test pattern. With luck, sometimes it wiggled or got snowy, so we could tell it wasn't just some magic lantern show, but most of the time it stayed still. Once Willy got lucky and saw it when Howdy Doody was on. Another time Carla and I caught it with John Cameron Swayze giving the news, but I didn't dare mention that to Willy.

Our Solemn Pact was a promise between Willy and me to never let any girl come between us. We wrote it on tablet paper, twice, and pricked our thumbs with a pin and spotted both copies with blood. Of course Carla, also being an outcast, was the only girl that paid any attention to us. Willy was my only friend. We had to be careful.

At the Throckmorton palace Gloria swept into the living room.

"Rebecca, you may sit on the right, front row, then Gretchen, I shall be in the middle, and Betsy, you're next to me with Susan to the left."

Betsy and Gretchen smiled wide. Rebecca and Susan scowled.

"Jane, you take the left front chair."

They ruffled their petticoats and sat, dresses overlapping and squeezed down to fit, but still running across the length of the room.

"Our guests," Gloria said, turning slightly in her chair, "may spread out behind us." Carla and I and Willy and the two others stood behind them.

A strange thing is that to this day, I cannot remember who those other two were and generally I recall everything. I stayed against the wall. It wasn't painted like ours, or cracked, and had red flowers papered on it. You could do that with hard coal heating, it burned so clean.

Doctor Throckmorton emerged. He nodded to the row of seated girls, took a deep breath, turned to the television and flipped its switch. During the time it took to warm up he adjusted the antenna dial. When the picture came in he pushed another button and a frame around the screen glowed.

"This is known as a Sylvania 'Halo Light' television," he explained, "the best dealer in Mason City made sure we received the first model in our progressive state of Iowa."

The image wasn't room-sized, like a picture show, but when he flipped those switches and dials the magical thing was that motion pictures with sound came out of his Sylvania 'Halo Light" television, right into Doctor Throckmorton's living room. That must've given Mr. Sheetz, owner of the Chief Picture Show, something to lose sleep over.

Queen Elizabeth floated down the aisle, wrapped in bleached rabbit fur, and these guys in sheep wigs and band uniforms stood at attention for a couple of hours while they said things you could understand once in awhile. It was hot enough in that living room that the Brylcreem dripped off my hair and slid down my neck.

Doctor Throckmorton stood. He looked us up and down.

"I presume you all to be fully baptized Christians," he said, looking only at the front row of girls. Doctor Throckmorton went on to say that this ceremony, conducted in Western Minister Happy seemed distinctly Protestant, if a little high-end. That didn't really matter, he explained, except this was the most important event of our lifetime.

"It does seem that our God, when overseeing this most historic event," Doctor Throckmorton said, "clearly decided that it should occur in a church free from Rome's despicable influence."

Doctor Throckmorton stared at us to make sure we understood, turned and sat.

That church might have joined the Protestant side, but West Minister Happy was a new flavor to me. They swung those same smudge pots around and sprinkled water in a way that didn't feel Protestantly modest.

Gloria and her friends sipped Cokes, Nesbit Orange Soda or Hires Root Beer and passed around Bazooka Bubble Gum. It was fortunate the rest of us didn't drink anything because this moment was exciting enough and it would be bad luck to have to leave and pretend to race home for the bathroom. If Willy or I just ducked into the shrubbery outside we'd have to delay before returning, because if either of us came back too soon they'd all know what we did. So them drinking and laughing without offering us any was just fine.

Gloria's friends used the Throckmortons' bathrooms. It's hard to believe, but there were two. Really. Nobody ever danced cross-legged outside the toilet door in that house. When the lights came back on her group drifted upstairs.

"Did you appreciate your first television experience?" Gloria asked Willy and Carla. Gloria talked like that. Their faces bobbed up and down. I stepped forward to leave. Gloria gasped and pointed at the wall behind my head.

"Moon, what, just what is that stain?" she asked.

There was a dark splotch of Brylcreem on her wallpaper, several inches across, right where I had leaned back.

"Moon, you oily freak," Gloria said.

I stared at that spot on the wall but still noticed the blur of a hand just before she slapped me. I fell to one knee.

"Leave now," she said.

We left fairly quick.

I had embarrassed Willy and Carla but they both spoke up for me when we turned the corner.

"She's spoiled rotten," Carla said.

"Least at," Willy replied. That was one of the rare times I had no idea what he meant and I was too upset to ask. Carla and I picked up our bikes.

But it was me that stained the Throckmorton's expensive wallpaper.

Nobody else. I didn't mean to, darn it, and I didn't need anybody feeling sorry for me either.

We didn't talk so much. We just kept riding. Carla thought we'd never see the inside of that house again, but all three of us felt okay about that.

Willy and Carla pedaled alongside me an extra block.

"Okay you?" he asked.

"I'm fine Willy."

Willy asked Carla if she was going home, she said yes and would turn off at the next street. Willy asked if she was sure and she said yes, kind of irritated at his checking. Willy waved good-bye and turned towards his home.

"Forget about her," Carla said, right away.

"You're worth two Glorias."

By looking away and pretending to stretch or something casual like that, I was able to rub a forearm across my eyes so Carla couldn't see how the misery took me. The grief might pass but I couldn't be sure so I didn't look back and cycled ahead with both hands off the bars, showing it didn't matter to me.

"Wow, coronation, big deal," I said, using a brave voice. Carla heard and she offered to ride all the way to my Grandma's house with me and I wish she would have but told her it wasn't necessary. I didn't care what the town thought of Carla, she was a neat girl. I'd never say that to Willy since that might upset my best pal. And Carla might feel awkward if I said something out of place. If she ever gave me a signal that she liked me and it was okay, then I'd have a dilemma. But if Carla ever felt something for me more than a friend, I didn't want it to be out of pity.

Maybe Willy hankered for Carla too. He never said.

It's not like Willy or I had five million other choices. Carla shouldn't ever go for a moron like me, I figured. What a jerk I was to stain Throckmorton's wallpaper. Maybe Carla would like Willy. I turned into a chump that day.

When I got onto Grandma's grass I started to melt, but stiffened back up when I heard the putt-putt sound.

It was Willy on his bike. The baseball card still made that sound against his spokes.

"Okay you?" he asked, not even stopping.

"Oh just fine, Willy, yup." I waved and he kept right on going. Willy was a true friend. Sometimes closeness creates jealousy. Maybe he also rode past to make sure that Carla and I weren't still hanging out together.

That night I had another bad dream, the same one, but it hadn't tormented me since I laid out the canvas. A few months earlier I had noticed a tarp behind the counter at the hardware store.

"Mr. Nordstrud, is that material waterproof?" I asked.

"Could you use it, Moon?" he asked. His pockets were full of ten-penny nails, so he tinkled with every move.

"That depends, Mr. Nordstrud, on what it costs."

"Would two dollars be okay, Moon?"

"Oh yes, Mr. Nordstrud, if it's eight by four feet and has grommets all around."

"Shall I set it aside, Moon? Could you pay me a quarter each week? Might you pay Saturday afternoons, after you've collected from your paper route?"

Mr. Nordstrud got twenty-five cents from me every Saturday, and fifty cents on one good collection day, so that canvas became mine in no time. I figured I had only paid Mr. Nordstrud one dollar fifty on the day he tried to hand me the tarp. He calculated I had paid it off. That didn't match my notes, so we split the difference.

I never told anybody, but I snuck my canvas out to the "Bone Orchard." That's what they call the Grundy Center Cemetery. I found Grandpa and took out some sharpened dowels I saved, stretched that canvas over his grave and staked it down taut. After that I didn't have any more nightmares about Grandpa lying down there in the rain. That is, not until that evening after I ruined the Throckmorton's wall, and I kept seeing that stained wallpaper and Grandpa getting soaked. That only lasted for a few nights.

Most of my dreams about Grandpa, after installing the canvas, featured him plodding along in the white milk wagon, white cap and white pants and white jacket, hoisting full bottles out of the back, carrying them up to the porches, picking up the empties and whistling while his white horse and white wagon waited.

Grandpa took care of me early and he didn't have to. I kept him dry later. Fair's fair.

Trouble struck. Willy got the mumps. Doctor Throckmorton told Hank the Tank who told our part-time cop, Billy Blue Pants, to quarantine their house. Billy nailed the pink quarantine notice on their front door, they locked it, Willy's mom stayed in the den and kitchen, his dad slept on the couch for a week and Willy couldn't leave his corner bedroom.

I went over and he opened the window further so we could talk through the screen. Willy seemed okay, but his cheeks and neck puffed out.

Carla walked up, too close for safety.

"Willy, how are you feeling?" she asked.

"Better much," he said, but not loud since his throat was sore. He almost smiled but said it hurt.

"I made you a present," she said.

"Me for? What?"

"A tapa."

"Huh?" Willy asked.

"What?" I asked.

Carla smiled and unwrapped a napkin.

"Can you open the screen?" she asked.

Willy shoved at the frame, hit it with the heel of his shoe but it wouldn't budge. Probably the paint stuck it shut. I took out my pocketknife and wedged into the crack but my blade started to bend when I pushed against it and the frame didn't move a hair.

"Damn it," Carla said.

"Okay if I give it to Moon?"

"Sure," Willy said.

Carla handed it to me, I was nervous about eating the thing but bit into it and this tapa tasted swell.

"Wow," I said.

Carla smiled and walked off. Willy disappeared from the window.

"Willy, this is good."

His window slammed shut. It was still hot. He should've kept it open to avoid baking.

I had just got a present from a girl for the first time in my life and my true friend stopped talking to me, all in one minute.

"Invention, in my opinion, arises directly from idleness, possibly also from laziness. To save oneself trouble."

Agatha Christie

Chapter 5

Willy's mumps went away. After several days of doing small things together, just him and me, we became comfortable again. Carla was never mentioned.

Lake Poytawukie rippled some twenty miles east of Grundy Center. Too far to hike. My bike couldn't be trusted to get there without a flat tire or chain jam. Even Willy's fancy rig might bust. So we hitchhiked.

Willy understood the ordeal. Stick your thumb out. Wait 'til some car pulls over. I keep the left side of my face towards the road but when we walk up to the window, they ask where we're going, see the rest of me, claim they're not going far enough and squeal away. Those would be the nicer ones.

Others let Willy and me in, said nothing, twitched and pulled over after a mile, saying they were headed the other direction, and a few would actually turn but others wouldn't even pretend after they dumped us. It normally took a couple of those before we hitched a ride all the way.

"I'm sorry to slow us down," I said the first time.

"Friendship has price," Willy said. I surely appreciated him.

"You could get there faster alone."

"This price," he said, "is bargain for us being pals." When somebody acted disgusted at my appearance, Willy took this as our problem, not mine.

"We're the best friends ever, Willy."

"And we have Solemn Pact," he replied, and that said it all.

Willy's father owned a boat with a five-horse Johnson plus an automatic cord recoil to start it. We will never be passing the hat for Willy. His father hauled out four busted bathtubs that spring, and sold every one of them to Bohemian Catholic farmers. Willy said they were considering using the extra money to install a deck on their boat. On some older maps and signs the lake and village are both spelled Lake Potawuka. Either way, Lake Poytawukie is the Lakota Sioux for "sparkling waters where the deer drink."

The second driver pulling over took us all the way to those sparkling waters where the deer drink.

Willy's dad's boat anchored fifty feet from shore at Lake Poytawukie, where nobody could tamper with it. Willy towed the gas can through the waves, and I took the towel. My job was to swim out and keep that towel dry, so I side-stroked and held up one arm. Willy had to drag the gas can. It floated when a wave hit him, so there was no worry about losing it, but if water got in the gas then we might as well head home. We smelled like fuel by the time we rolled into the boat, so staying distant from the spark plug until we dried made sense.

Willy fired up his engine on the third pull and we chugged across Lake Poytawukie, taking turns steering. When he felt like going left, he just turned left. When it was my turn and I wanted to go right, I did. We even threw in circles once in awhile.

Willy straddled the bow when I steered. The water looked like glass where we hadn't churned it yet. I was watching the branches and shore reflections when Willy jumped up and pointed.

"A water skater," Willy said.

"Huh?" I asked.

"Boat and boy not together."

"What?"

"Guy roped to the boat," Willy said.

"Where?" Then I spotted it. This boat had a steering wheel and windshield, so it must've been from Des Moines. It zipped along with a wave fanning behind. That's not unusual. I had seen several fancy boats before. Willy too. Some were even in the water. But this one had a rope tied to the stern and it stuck straight out horizontally until there was a fellow, standing on the water, gripping the other end. Water sprayed from his feet. When they got closer we saw the guy crouch slightly, with a ski under each foot and they just planed over the surface like a flat rock skipping forever.

I leaned out too far, lost my balance, the boat rocked, Willy spilled over the edge and my body splashed into the drink before he even surfaced.

"He speeds so fast quickly," Willy said, bobbing in the waves, "that he doesn't sink over the water."

Willy never lost his confidence and was still chattering about the first water skiing we'd ever seen. I forgot it for a moment, thinking we could both drown, or, if we lost the boat, might wish we had. The motor turned, so the boat circled back at us, which gave me some other thoughts about how that propeller might process us into bacon strips. Willy just dove down and kicked himself up when the bow came close, hugging the point with his arms and slowed it. He swung a leg over, rolled in, grabbed the controls and killed the motor. He paddled over to pull me in.

Willy invented moves like that. He could not have practiced this one. But he relied on me for help with long division and spelling, so we teamed well.

Willy and I sat. I tossed the towel to him. We kind of looked at each other and without even saying it, knew what had to happen.

Just a week later I ambled down the alley behind Doctor Throckmorton's. There was a green apple tree back there, but I wasn't going to take one. Really. And I wasn't going to pick any of their grapes either. Sometimes an apple might be hanging so wobbly on Doctor Throckmorton's tree that you knew it would drop and spoil if you didn't pick it. And the same held true for grapes, although you had to look harder through the vines to spot those windfalls. But unbelievably, Doctor Throckmorton's trash barrel sat next to the alley and there were two scratched-up skis sticking out of it. No fooling. And I never took Catechism.

I pulled them out, slow so the noise wouldn't disturb anyone, brushed coffee grounds off and scraped away some dried orange peel. I sat them down on the ground and stared at the perfect shape of these skis.

I laid the first ski over my shoulder, but hoisting the second one got complicated and it clattered against the barrel. Throckmorton's cocker spaniel bounded out their back door, yipping and yapping and I could see how my luck was about to change. Most probably this involved that animal's teeth in my ankle. Running with two skis on your shoulders is tough enough, but when a smart aleck dog with saddlebag ears bites the cuff of your jeans, making any kind of speed grows into an insurmountable challenge.

"Moon!" somebody shouted.

I stopped.

"Get back here you wretched brat!"

It was Doctor Throckmorton. He stood on that screened porch, chin out like he owned half the world, which, of course, he nearly did. I trudged back, dragging the skis and stood on the grass around his porch while he shook a fist at me.

"I should be obliged and compelled to turn you in," he said.

"Yes sir."

"Yes who, boy?"

"Yes, Doctor Throckmorton."

He sighed. He crossed his arms and scowled, standing on the porch. I slouched below him, looking at the grass between my shoes. My head lined up with that medical belt buckle of his, the one with the two snakes wrapped around a stick, a symbol that never seemed so awful healthy to me.

"Listen up, Moon, the whole of our school board would love to see me pack you off to Woodward for special training and I happen to be the only person stopping that. Now I catch you stealing my polished hickory skis."

"But they were in your trash Doctor…"

"Says who, might I ask?"

I didn't reply.

"Look here, Moon boy, do you covet those Deluxe Nordic skis?"

"Well, Doctor Throckmorton, yes, if you could spare them Willy and I…"

"You stand right there. Do not move one foot. I am going inside to call up and consult some folks, and decide what to do about you. This is not the first time you have disrupted our fine city, Moon. But it could well be the last."

He slipped through the door and disappeared. I dropped down on his royal lawn, kind of worrying for a few minutes. Then I remembered how much of my life went this way. For example, if Gloria had slapped me twice, it wasn't so much more than if she just hit me once, so go ahead, do what you want to and get it over with, I thought. Grandma had whispered that those waves in Doctor Throckmorton's hair didn't look natural, but he wouldn't dare get a permanent in Grundy Center. Grandma suspected he drove to Hayfield and probably did so at the end of a day, after all the other customers would have left, and paid cash. Paying by check would cause some snickering back at his bank.

Doctor Throckmorton returned, looking disgusted, like he usually did.

"Moon, listen close. Use those fine skis, since you have already scratched them badly. But you shall repay me for the next three months by giving me a free paper. I mean daily and Sunday, without charge and then I just might suggest the Grundy Center Police look the other way."

"Billy Blue Pants?" I asked.

Billy Blue Pants served as Grundy Center's part-time cop and helped out during harvest at the grain elevator. The town council bought him a siren that attached to the roof of his Chevy with suction cups while he was on duty. If anybody planned mischief while Billy Blue Pants was working, it was best to drive a V-8, since Billy's car was six-cylinder and didn't have overdrive. Getting away was no problem.

"Yes Moon, Billy Blue Pants. I argue that you do not belong in that Woodward school for retards and morons and idiots, but am weary of fighting the other opinions on your miserable behalf. When I called the city fathers and reported, regretfully, that I caught you stealing my skis, they suggested you be sent, without delay, to the Eldora Training School for boys, if not Woodward. I managed to salvage your sorry butt from that. Can you explain why I should bother?"

"No sir, Doctor Throckmorton."

"I thought not, and that is because there is no reason to defend you, Moon."

That scared me. The Eldora Training School contained Iowa's toughest kids. When Grundy Center met them on the football field, we had practiced every offensive play running both right and left. The point was to be able to avoid getting tackled anywhere near their bench. Do that and you'd be mobbed, despite those games having more referees than players. Our grass stayed green near the Eldora bench after each game while the Grundy Center side got chewed into mud.

"Your attempted theft, even as a failed effort, is a sin," Doctor Throckmorton said.

"Stop shuffling your feet, Moon."

I stopped.

"Being a Protestant Christian makes it possible for me to forgive, but how the Lord views your act I cannot presume to judge.

"However, Moon, you may give me a paper with no charge for six months and we can look past your depraved behavior."

"But Doctor Throckmorton, I thought you said three months."

He glared. Doctor Throckmorton was building up steam, so I shut up and dropped my head, looking at my shoes. He repeated his demand for the paper, no charge, for six months and I agreed that this would not be a problem.

"Wait just one more minute, boy," he replied, "that also means you wash the windows on my medical office every week, but do so on Thursdays, just after sunrise, so nobody sees you and gets bothered."

I agreed that was fair.

"You better also check the street lights on my block each night and report any burned out bulbs."

I said okay. Those skis looked nifty.

"If I hear of any more disgusting incidents," Doctor Throckmorton said, "like that rebellious scene in the grocery store, you shall be done in Grundy Center. Through. Mr. Hardcastle is an upstanding citizen. You, of all people, have no right to question how he weights the meat in our upstanding grocery. I will protect you no more. Your ugliness and deformed face is a blemish upon our otherwise fair city, so a little humility from you is merely appropriate."

"Yes sir."

"Yes who, kid?"

"Yes, Doctor Throckmorton."

I still could make some money on my paper route, even with his free subscription. And for the street lights, I popped one a week with my slingshot to make sure there was something to report. I usually hit one near his house. Doctor Throckmorton got a free paper, lived on a darker street and enjoyed cleaner windows while I got a great set of skis. Life works out, but sometimes you need to grease things.

Willy and I went to the dump and found a pair of galoshes that fit us both; our feet measured the same. We screwed those galoshes onto the skis. Willy slipped into Father O'Brien's backyard and cut a clothesline. I sawed off a broom handle and we were set to give those folks on Lake Poytawukie a show.

We tied the clothesline to our stern and the other end to the broomstick. It was natural that Willy, being athletic, tried to ski first. He buckled the galoshes on his feet, jumped in the water with the skis attached and grabbed the broomstick. I twisted the throttle and the boat groaned, but Willy just kind of swished in the water, his skis waving back and forth, not even close to getting up and they clattered against each other while he wallowed along. That outboard developed asthma.

Willy jerked the rope and stood upright for a glorious half second and sank. He did it again and stayed up for a moment until one ski tip knifed the water and snapped under. He flipped instantly, both skis rocketing toward the sky whil his head and shoulders sprayed a wake, and in a giant eggbeater move flipped over again. He sat in the water, ski tips fluttering while the motor sounds dropped lower.

What neither Willy nor I could realize was that all the while his ski tips waved from the water, that plastic clothesline stretched. If we started with a twenty-foot length, after five minutes of churning up Lake Poytawukie we probably owned forty feet. This sounds like we're gaining assets, if you avoid thinking too hard. Willy wasn't any higher in the water but looked a lot wetter and shakier and further away by the minute.

About then our line snapped. The broomstick cracked Willy's forehead. He slumped into the water and the boat lurched ahead, me with it. I pulled myself off my back, nearly tumbled over the stern, slowed it and turned. I got back to Willy and he hadn't passed out. He was thrashing the water and looked like a 49 Chevy grille whacked his face where that broom handle struck.

That's how water skiing started in Grundy Center.

When we talked to other folks about this, we observed that ours seemed to be snow skis as compared to water skis, which apparently were distant cousins twice removed. We had tried snow skis on water with an outboard motor at least twenty horses short. The plastic rope had been the smallest of our problems.

Willy and I got back to Grundy Center that night, and I made it home for a turnip, cabbage and potato dinner. Grandma slathered that food with margarine and pepper. Maybe there was too much pepper. Mom's face went pale. Grandma suffered a coughing fit that shook her upper body.

"Is it the pepper?" I asked.

Grandma shook her head yes.

"All I said was that Doctor Throckmorton suggested I might be happier in Woodward."

Grandma fanned herself. She hoisted herself up and wobbled into their bedroom.

"What's Woodward?" I asked.

"Nothing," Mom said, "nowhere, Moon. Forget it." She followed Grandma into the other room and flung the curtain shut. It didn't matter much, I could hear whispering, upset sounds, stomping the floor and hushing each other.

Maybe it wasn't the pepper.

Willy agreed I should make the water skis. I appropriated two ash boards, one-half-inch by six feet by six inches from the Grundy Center Grand Lumber & Coal yard. "Appropriated" was how Willy's dad described it when he came upon copper piping that wouldn't be missed. Sometimes it was wiring and he'd burn the insulation off in a backyard fire, and then sell it for scrap.

Anybody could appropriate wood from the lumber yard if they were quick in the evening and leaned over the higher fence sections where their German shepherd couldn't reach. That animal always gave it a good try. I didn't flinch and drop our material when the dog snapped at me.

I put our boards on the school shop's band saw, slitting their ends the long way, which is a lot harder than the short way, and more difficult yet to explain. I mean I slit them along their 1/2" side for about six inches, so there was a front part with two 1/4" slats sticking out. Of course I rounded them too.

Grandma let me borrow a cook pot and her car. I filled the pot with water, piled up some cobs and coal and fanned a blaze under it. After it bubbled to the top, Willy and I boiled the notches for three hours. They softened, we pulled them out and I squirted glue into the slits. We braced them against sawhorses with the tips down and rolled the car's front wheels over the ends, bending them. That was around lunchtime. It was dark before we pushed the car back. With the headlights on, we saw that the tips stayed curled. Willy and I hustled those boards into the garage and sealed them with paint before the grain could change its mind. We screwed on the same pair of galoshes.

If only Dad could've seen what happened that summer. Or Grandpa. I think maybe they did, maybe chuckling together, without any religious problems between them. Grandma heard all about it, for sure, but Mom wasn't so interested. We took those skis to Lake Poytawukie every week. This time we made our tow rope from a length that seemed unnecessary in the second story of our school. It was knotted and tied next to the window, but with a brick building, a fire seems unlikely and nobody missed it anyway.

June and July were heavenly. We didn't appreciate how much until later, when the leaves fell. Willy found an outfit that loaned us a 25-horse motor at Lake Poytawukie every weekend for a couple hours, if we delivered ten pounds of night crawlers, unless the place was too busy. It never was. At first, we had to hunt for the worms every night with flashlights just to get enough for a Saturday boating, but after a few weeks, we kept some extras in an orange crate with dirt, sawdust, leaves, cigarette butts, fruit rind and eggshells. They started reproducing, kind of like wire hangers in a rich person's closet.

"Carla ski wants to," Willy said one night.

"Willy, that's okay with me if it's okay with you."

"Remember our Pact Solemn," Willy replied.

"I will honor our Solemn Pact until I die, Willy."

So Carla came with us to Lake Poytawukie several times and Willy didn't mind as long as she didn't ski too much. When she did, in her swimsuit, you could tell things were changing for all of us. I used to watch her constantly when she'd ski, for safety purposes, not just because her suit tended to slip and she didn't seem to have on a brassiere underneath. Willy and I got so we could swing behind the boat and jump its wake. Carla hardly ever fell but she didn't leap the wake either.

Folks noticed. Willy and I were champs. And I bet nobody on shore ever said Carla had cooties, the way kids teased her in Grundy Center.

"Carla wink at me," Willy said after one day at the lake.

"That's wonderful, Willy." My stomach churned.

"But we have Solemn Pact."

"Willy, she didn't just get dust in her eye, did she?"

"No, no," Willy replied, "she turned right me at and dropped eyelid, slowly."

"Wow, Willy, wow." I got dizzy but didn't fall.

We returned to Lake Poytawukie the next day, and I was relieved Carla couldn't go. It confused me intolerably to imagine my only two friends becoming a couple. Instead of feeling good for them, it made me lonely.

A white wooden ramp bobbed on the water when Willy and I arrived. We couldn't figure out what it was and wondered, until about an hour later we saw some guy, probably from Des Moines, skiing behind a boat. He swung over to the ramp and by golly, like he meant to, hit that ramp and went up into the sky for about twenty yards before coming down.

Willy looked at me. I looked back. We nodded. There was no need to talk. We had no option.

"You're best at this sort of thing," I said.

"Yeah," Willy said, "but you okay."

I jumped in, buckled the galoshes, Willy fired up the engine and there we were, Willy gunning the boat across the water and me, Moon, throwing up spray from my feet and skiing across Lake Poytawukie like, well, I don't know what like, but it must be what a football champion hears from a crowd or maybe a President in a parade or Moses dispensing tablets, and I mean like "The Commandment" tablets, not aspirin.

Willy roared past the ramp and whipped his arm in a circle. I knew what he meant.

"Hoo-ya!" he shouted.

"Hoo-hoo, ya-ya!"

"Wahoo!" I replied, not as loud as Willy. He was acting for the folks watching from shore but I concentrated on the jump.

The boat turned in an arc, I followed and we headed for the ramp. I swung left, then cut back to the right where that jump floated, pointing into the sky.

My ski tips hit the bottom of the ramp first.

"Wahoo!" was my last shout.

What I could not have perceived at that moment, and this was before plastics, was that ski jumpers back then splashed water over the ramp before using it, to make it slick.

The tips of my skis stopped instantly.

They just stuck.

This fact didn't register with the rest of my body, which had its own plans and just a split-second before had been streaking towards the ramp at thirty miles an hour. And so my torso, which was a significant part of me, continued at one half a mile per minute, give or take, about eighty-eight feet every second, and slammed into the ramp. That same dry wood that stopped the skis screeched across my chest, stomach and thighs, removing many little patches of skin.

If I was doing thirty miles an hour at the low point of the ramp, my guess is that I was down to about three miles an hour by the time my skinned arms draped over the top and I rolled into the water, feeling somewhat less majestic. It sounded like a "Wahoo, thump, thump, splat," except faster than that. I couldn't separate the noises, they came so quick, it just seems that should've been the sequence. Maybe it was "Wahoo, thump, thump, thump, thump splat."

When people talk about seeing stars they don't quite have it right. I would describe it more like sparks and flashes with a dark background and you can hear voices but they tune in and out like a radio during a thunderstorm. Even then, there's still a moment when you can think under water, and give serious consideration to staying down, just to avoid the humiliation. Fortunately my lungs convinced me differently, and the sting of peeled skin helped me to not hear the laughter from the shore while Willy pulled me out.

Carla and Willy and I still tugged night crawlers from the ground most nights, dropping a can full into our orange crate. Sometimes Carla wore a t-shirt and shorts, without any unmentionables underneath, but Willy and I never discussed that. She might catch as many worms as we could, after all. But sometimes she sucked on candy cigarettes, and that, combined with her earrings, made Carla seem older than Willy and me. She had stopped reading Nancy Drew but Willy and I still followed the Hardy Boys.

I wished Carla liked me. She must have fallen for Willy, but didn't show it that I saw, and I couldn't tell if Willy liked her back or not and I stewed over this a goodly amount. Maybe she could like us both. I'd settle for that. Willy and I had sworn out and bled upon our Solemn Pact but I was afraid to mention how exciting I thought Carla was. Maybe Willy was afraid to say anything to me. This was our $64,000 question but I felt too nervous to ask.

We got so good at capturing night crawlers every Saturday that summer we'd have that 25-horse Johnson for a couple hours most weeks, and got famous on Lake Poytawukie. Since we harvested night crawlers easy, especially if it rained a little, the rest of the time we just had fun. Grandma tuckered out earlier those days, went to bed by eight and it didn't get dark until after nine. With weekend water skiing and nights free, Carla and Willy and I became a trio.

"This become could a problem," Willy said after Carla left one night.

"Willy, you and I, we're best friends forever." I punched his shoulder.

"What her about?"

"Man is by nature a political animal."

Aristotle

Chapter 6

We experienced a misfortune with the piano lessons, and that came when the town council decided to license all services. The beauty shop, for example, needed a license, which put another $25 in the council's budget every year. Widow Chizek, who put up and colored some hair out of her farmhouse, couldn't get a license but kept doing permanents anyway.

This caused a ruckus that never settled. Catholics claimed she didn't need a license, being outside the city limits and what was Billy Blue Pants going to do, shoot some women for just wanting to patronize their own faith, simply trying to look decent for a season or two?

Hank the Tank's wife, who ran the beauty shop in town, got busy enough that she had to add a second chair. Widow Chizek's Catholic customers became so antagonized that they started getting perms twice a year, so her illegal business boomed, and she joined the other fish-eaters, installing her own Mother Mary Shrine next to the gravel road passing her house.

The council also decided to license music lessons. Mr. Weed, the school band and driver training instructor, earned an exemption, of course, and that music license was set at only $10. But it also required a college degree to teach.

This cut Mom out of the business.

The city council said Grundy Center needed to raise all standards to improve our children, or we'd revert back to primitives. The city loaned their gravel truck to that college lady across town, so she could haul our piano over. She put it in her hallway and said Mom could help her, but fifty cents an hour was all she could afford.

Some of these leading citizens weren't much brighter than rusty nails. If they wanted to push Mom down, their license plan didn't work. But if they wanted to make life easier for their society friend, that other piano teacher, it worked. I guess that's government.

"It is a professional and civic disgrace," Doctor Throckmorton said, "that there is not a single, trained nurse in Grundy Center County, not a one." This was his speech to the city council. His eyes gazed into the smoke curling across the tin-stamped ceiling while he strolled in front of them.

For these winter meetings, a council member would stoke the furnace at dawn, open the ducts to the main hallway, set out some folding chairs and the chimney would do its best to carry the smoke away, sometimes succeeding, but always leaking enough to make everybody's clothes stink.

Attendees were expected to leave their galoshes in the foyer. Since the galoshes were all black, and the farmers wore buckle versions and the town people wore zippered models, there wasn't much confusion when they left.

If a pair fit your shoes, it didn't matter, as long as you came in buckles you and you left in buckles, or the same for zippers. If they were caked with fresh manure, there usually wasn't any argument.

"No great city can operate with a renowned medical leader only," Doctor Throckmorton said. "There must be a trained and competent staff."

He shook his head. He paced in front of the citizens. Just under fifty came through the cold and dark and blowing snow that night. It was warm enough that everybody unbuttoned their jackets. Doctor Throckmorton kept a scarf around his neck, which was a style nobody else copied.

"How do we get professional medical assistance?" He looked at the council. He glanced through the crowd. The part in his hair lay straight as a bean row.

Nobody said a word. Those were the rules, of course. Doctor Throckmorton preached that the council members, only, should express their consent, but, the citizens were there to learn democracy, and could do so better by listening than by talking. This made sense to most folks.

Several days later, Mom agreed to take nursing instructions from Doctor Throckmorton. He would charge her nothing, and the city would pay for her books.

"The inarguable shame of Moon's birth," he said to Mom in front of me, "is hardly a thing of civic pride. But it is history, recent, but history, the filthy circumstances of his existence fading slightly with time. You may depart now, Moon." I scurried out of his office. It smelled like iodine anyway.

Doctor Throckmorton also mentioned that most of Grundy Center had overcome their embarrassment of my disfigurement, and my lack of a father, so it was okay for Mom to be seen around town, as long as she didn't become flagrant.

"I have stooped to pull you out of the trash," he told Mom, "and you shall repay me and stay fortunate by keeping your head down and Moon out of sight."

Doctor Throckmorton gave Mom evening lessons and books to read and before we knew it, she became a certified nurse's aide. I don't want to brag on Mom too much, but just think about being a country schoolteacher, then a piano instructor and finally a medical professional.

All while in her twenties. I had expected Mom to run off that night she got mad at Grandpa and Grandma's supper table, like she threatened to sometimes, but she didn't. So Mom had her good qualities.

Soon she was authorized to measure blood pressure, give enemies, take urine samples and administer eye tests. In a month, Doctor Throckmorton got the city to buy an X-Ray machine, which Mom learned to use, and pretty soon every patient got X-Rays, just to be safe, but that sure boosted the bills.

We'd all seen the miracle of X-Rays at Gildner's Florsheim store in Mason City. You could put your toes in their machine, flip a switch and view your foot bones inside any pair of shoes. This made the fit better and if done often enough, cured athlete's foot.

Mom's night work gave me even more freedom.

Her lessons with Doctor Throckmorton started to take up most evenings, so I could stay out and play with Carla and Willy more. Carla's dad passed out early most evenings. Willy's dad allowed him to run around at night as long as we didn't get caught at any mischief, and we hardly ever did. Get caught, I mean. Grandma turned in early.

We'd drop the night crawlers in our orange crate every evening, maybe toss in some apple cores and other stuff worms love to eat. Carla, Willy and me usually had a full tin of worms in an hour. Then we'd slip over to the gas station and if nobody was around, I'd straighten out the hose. Almost always there would be a quart of Texaco's best left in the curve of the hose, so we'd put that in a can and sneak over to the hard road and pour a puddle across the cement. We'd dribble a line to the ditch and crouch in the culvert.

Willy or Carla would peek through the grass when cars approached. If it was someone like Mr. Nordstrud, we'd let him pass. But once it was Doctor Throckmorton, and even though we saw the back of his head every Sunday in that front pew, reserved permanently for his family, I lit that thing and fire blazed to the sky just before his Midnight Blue, four-door Cadillac reached our inferno.

His tires screamed like a dozen hawks, and for some reason he honked the horn, as if that could extinguish the flames. He must have figured his car couldn't stop in time. First he slid sideways, then gunned it and roared through the blaze, screeching sideways. That Cadillac lurched around like a bloated cow trying to stamp out an ant hill.

"Oh, oh, now we've done it," Carla said.

The car was still skidding.

"Let's scram," I said.

His royal barge spun around. It came to a stop on the wrong side of the road, a hundred feet past us, headlights pointed our way.

"Idea good, run," Willy said.

We scrambled through the culvert under the road and into the corn. We walked through the whole field before turning right and hiked across Widow Schultz's pasture all the way to the gravel, sneaking back into Grundy Center from the other direction.

The grass was slick and Carla grabbed my arm.

She hung onto my elbow after we got out of the pasture and onto the gravel.

Willy noticed. He walked behind us. When I turned, Willy was nowhere to be found.

Carla let go of my arm.

I told her she could continue but I guess she didn't hear me.

I remembered how that felt for a long time. Even now.

The next evening, Carla and I invented a new activity involving the rotten egg barrel outside the hatchery. And the night after that we discovered power lines with frayed insulation could be made to short-circuit and spark, just by hanging on a support cable and bouncing it from a pole two blocks away. But Carla and I did things like this for a week without Willy.

Finally he came by, sitting on his bike in front of our house.

"Is Carla you girlfriend?"

"No, Willy, how come you won't play with us at night?"

"I don't want to in butt."

"Willy, we're the Three Musketeers, one for all and all for one."

"Except Carla touches you."

"Just that one time, when the pasture was slippery."

Willy crossed his arms. I stood there.

"Is that only the time?"

"Sure," I replied, glad to give Willy the answer that honored our Solemn Pact, but wishing it weren't so true.

"We have Solemn Pact, right?"

"Pals to the end, Willy, you bet."

"See you tonight."

"Carla too, okay Willy?"

"Yeah, but no hand holding." We continued our evening antics, all three of us. This girl stuff was a problem, and Willy was my only friend.

Grandma swayed over her ironing board one evening, sprinkling clothes, just a step from my feet. I crouched under the sink looking for a leak. She'd been saving lard for weeks and just bought a can of lye, so I knew we'd be making soap that weekend.

Mom sauntered in.

"We almost crashed Doctor Throckmorton's car," Mom said.

"Really?" Grandma asked.

"It was dark," Mom said, "and a flame jumped across the road. Doctor Throckmorton hit the brakes, we skidded sideways and slid through it."

I dropped the wrench.

"A single woman shouldn't be out after dark," Grandma said.

"It was scary, but Doctor Throckmorton handled that car perfectly."

"Why is it necessary to work nights?"

"The way our Doctor handled that emergency, it's no wonder he runs Grundy Center so well."

"A mother should tend her child."

I rattled the wrench a couple times so they wouldn't think I was listening.

"Doctor Throckmorton is the only meal ticket I've got."

"The rumor is he gets permanents for his hair, out of town."

"This town's stupid. That's jealousy talking."

"But child..."

"I'm no a child."

"What are you?"

Mom walked to the clinic and slept in an empty bed that night. That's what she said when Grandma interrogated her the next morning.

Me? I stayed under that sink about twenty minutes longer than necessary, knocking the pipe with the wrench once in awhile, just to stay out of it. I was also wishing there was some other pipe I could hit to keep me from wondering about Grandma's questions and Mom's answers.

Classes started. Willy, Carla and I pedaled toward school for opening day. Carla didn't talk. The trees reached up, bare. Piles of leaves dotted the curbs. Willy and I used them as jumps, pretending to be Joey Chitwood's Hell Drivers at the State Fair while Carla dawdled behind. Willy had clipped another baseball card onto his fender. Dogs barked when he putt-putted past their yards. After a few of Willy's and my jumps Carla stood on her pedals, pumped and pulled alongside.

"Moon," Carla finally said, "I heard something."

"What?"

Willy veered at another leaf pile.

"Our teacher said they're sending you to the Woodward School."

Willy braked, his rear tire skidding out from under him. My front wheel twisted and I flew over the handlebars.

Nobody said a word.

Willy got up and stared at me like I was a ghost. I wiped the gravel off my hands and stood. My head felt like it was somewhere else and I looked at my palms, full of gravel scratches, to avoid getting dizzy. I had never heard about Woodward except when Doctor Throckmorton threatened to send me there.

Mr. Scarletti stood, hands in his pockets, at the school's front door. He said I wouldn't need to go to class that day but should follow him. The secretary didn't look up or say a word when we walked past. Her typewriter clacked faster and Mr. Scarletti turned into his office.

I lingered outside the doorway.

Mr. Scarletti pointed at a wooden chair. I stepped in and sat. He eased into his swivel chair, half disappearing behind a shiny walnut desk that stretched so long any decent pilot could land a plane on it.

Sometimes I exaggerate to make a point.

"Why don't we leave that here?" Mr. Scarletti asked. He reached for my empty newspaper bag. It was the yellow one with red lettering I won for getting eleven new subscribers during the Register & Tribune's delivery boy contest. I didn't move. He tugged the strap off my shoulder.

"Moon, there's a special place in Iowa that takes better care of young retards and cripples than our public schools are capable of handling."

"Mr. Scarletti, if a retard won your spelling bee last year, what does that make our school?" I asked. That would be me. I had won that contest.

He leaned back and frowned out his window. We both knew that the summer before our library had received a World Book Encyclopedia set. It came in the economy blue covers. But those books contained all the same information as the red edition or even the deluxe white leather-bound version with its own official pine bookrack. Mr. Scarletti understood that I checked out every book in the set, one at a time. I studied aardvarks during corn planting and finished zygote cells during harvest. I read them cover to cover. Mr. Scarletti knew this and he was a decent enough to not recall things differently. But the school board decided whether he got rehired each year and Doctor Throckmorton ran that group.

"And Ole Ericsen," I continued, "advances each year." Mr. Scarletti turned around but looked at something on the wall behind me. "Ole is a nice enough fellow," I said, "but he does have difficulty adding and spelling or reading. He rolls clay into thin strings all day and traces alongside them, Mr. Scarletti, and he gets passing marks."

Mr. Scarletti let out a long breath. He mumbled something about Ole Ericsen's father running the grain elevator, and attending school board meetings, but he didn't even glance my way.

"I can water ski," I said. "So assuming I'm no moron, then I must be a cripple, but a water-skiing cripple could sure make some town famous, if you follow me, Mr. Scarletti."

He reached under his desk and pulled out a cardboard box. It had my bat, rod and reel, underwear, socks, jeans and shirts in it with a winter parka. Mr. Scarletti slipped an envelope out of his drawer.

"There's a letter of introduction for you in here," he said, "Doctor Throckmorton wrote it and your mother and grandmother signed it last night. Moon, are you wetting your pants?"

I was not. Well, just a little, but I mean it wasn't dripping or anything. Just a small spurt slipped out and Mr. Scarletti took me to the bathroom so I could finish and I stuffed toilet paper in my pants to dry up.

"Ole Ericsen ate everybody's black crayons in first grade," I said from the stall. Mr. Scarletti heard me. His shoes scuffed across the tile.

"His teeth turned black, Mr. Scarletti."

Mr. Scarletti shuffled back and forth. I didn't feel like leaving the stall.

"Ole Ericsen thought they were licorice."

Mr. Scarletti didn't answer but I heard him shuffle, scuff and shuffle back and forth.

"Did the school board ever discuss sending Ole Ericsen to Woodward, Mr. Scarletti?" He didn't answer. I stepped out. We walked back to his office. The secretary hunched over and stared into her typewriter real hard without moving. Doctor Throckmorton stood in the middle of Mr. Scarletti's office, appearing to be quite aware that he was standing in the center.

"Are we all ready?" Doctor Throckmorton asked.

"I'll head home," I said, "to check with Mom and Grandma."

"In these most awkward of situations," Doctor Throckmorton said, "we always find it best to make a clean and quick break."

Mr. Scarletti developed a cough and walked away. A trance swept over me and I don't remember falling. When I woke up the secretary had my head propped against Mr. Scarletti's desk and she shoved a glass of water at me. I choked down some.

"This proves we are doing the right thing," Doctor Throckmorton said. Mr. Scarletti was gone. The secretary and Doctor Throckmorton lifted me. My legs kind of worked, but my mind stopped like I wasn't there, yet I could see, but like through a frosted window.

Doctor Throckmorton tugged me outside.

"Your grandmother shall visit you, Moon boy, once a month should she want to."

Willy and Carla's faces pushed against the school window, looking mournful. The teacher yanked them back by their shoulders in a slow pastel motion and they went limp. I didn't wet my pants any further, for which I remain grateful.

Doctor Throckmorton had borrowed the ambulance from Farber & Ottoman Funeral Home, "Friends When You Need Them Most." He tossed a blanket over the rear seat, shoved me in and started driving.

"Moon, we should be there in fifty short minutes, and you are going to enjoy this professional institute," Doctor Throckmorton said. He turned on the siren and blinking light. Cars ahead pulled over when we shrieked up behind them. Doctor Throckmorton floored it until we clipped along at eighty miles an hour.

"See how we progress?" he asked. We were on a cement road, of course, nobody would roll along that fast on gravel, at least not for long.

The Woodward Institute looked like a bunch of farmhouses, five of them, although I couldn't see too well by then. My head hurt right behind my right eye. Doctor Throckmorton told me to get my box and follow him inside. I did.

This first room stretched big enough to host a basketball game, but had an upright column in the middle with two kids tied to it wearing football helmets. One banged his head against the beam. It was wood, not steel, and his helmet kept him from doing much damage. Then we walked through an area with a half dozen cribs. One kid stretched out in each, with their hands tied to the slats. They had big heads and little bodies, diapered. Several howled non-stop. Each had two or three rows of teeth and you could wave your hand in front of their faces, but they never blinked.

Every crib had one tin cup of milk with a fly or two sharing most of the drink.

In the next room all the childrens' eyes took that almond shape. They drifted towards us the instant we entered. Most reached out to touch me and grinned. This was a happy group, probably gone around the bend a little, but friendlier than cats in heat.

Doctor Throckmorton yelled, they scattered, he left, they came back and shoved their hands into my box of possessions. I stopped to play with them until Doctor Throckmorton jerked me into the main office.

There was no urine stink inside that room. The desks and chairs must have been built at the same factory that turned out Mr. Scarletti's stuff, all walnut so smooth it reflected without a nail or screw showing anywhere. Several Air-Wicks sat on desks and windowsills, which explained why my nose thought we were touring a Christmas tree lot.

Woodward's principal sat behind the desk. He wore a stethoscope. He motioned for Doctor Throckmorton to take the stuffed chair.

"Moon," the principal asked, "why did the President fire General Douglas MacArthur?"

"Insubordination, sir. General MacArthur wanted to attack more aggressively, risking bringing China into the war, sir," I replied. Being a newspaper boy paid off.

"What's the square root of eighty-one?"

"Nine, sir. If you care I can tote up some figures in Roman numerals."

The principal's eyes widened. A Folgers can hissed when he opened it, he spooned out two dabs, poured water into the percolator and pretty soon it gurgled, with coffee smells pushing away the pine. He stepped outside and motioned to Doctor Throckmorton, who followed. That door had a cracked panel and I could hear bits of what they said, but not all.

"...doing here anyway, Throckmorton?"

".... savant, knows some but..."

"...scaring townies doesn't qualify, if we put every ugly person from any county in here, our budget..."

Their voices grew louder for a minute, then drifted away and I fixated on the envelope Doctor Throckmorton left, the one Mom and Grandma supposedly autographed to make my entrance official. They'd miss the letter if I grabbed it. In ten minutes, I might steam it open with the coffee percolator and see the truth, but there probably wasn't time. And sure enough, both guys strutted right back into the room while I was thinking about all that.

"Moon, get your pathetic, scroungy box back into the car," Doctor Throckmorton said. He pushed me along, unlocked the car door, spread the blanket over the back seat again, shoved me in and we headed home.

"It just did not seem to me, Moon, that Woodward was quite right for you, so I urged them to allow your return to our fair city."

I said nothing. He didn't fire up the siren this time. We poked along about forty miles an hour, him not talking. I started whistling the song Mom invented, three notes up, three notes down and then a skip, but Doctor Throckmorton turned up WOI and we listened to the weather report followed by crop prices the rest of the way. He kept the envelope next to him on the front seat. I feared that envelope.

Our trip down had been so bothersome I saw nothing. I didn't miss a thing coming back. A couple times I tried to imagine what Grundy Center would be like if Grandma and I became two of its four college graduates. I couldn't figure how we would change things but knew that somehow life could be better for all.

Doctor Throckmorton's shirt still had too many buttons. His face shined like wax. I remembered Mom saying Doctor Throckmorton rubbed moisturizer into his skin. With deodorizer in his armpits pulling out the dampness and moisturizer pushing water back in his head, no wonder he got cranky. His body was confused.

The road pointed straight. There were no other cars. Just outside of our town, I noticed Mother Mary Shrines dotting some farmyards. While not believing their religion, Willy's dad supported it. Every time he hauled out a broken bathtub he took it straight to the next Bohemian Catholic farmer in line and sold it. The farmer would dig a hole, bury the tub halfway in the ground and leave the white curved end, opposite the faucets, sticking out from the grass. They'd tuck in a plaster statue of Mother Mary and there would be another shrine. The white porcelain tub and statue glowed if lit at night. Most of them used Christmas tree lights for that. Once in awhile you'd even hear a Protestant admit that those made a clever backdrop for the Madonnas, but they'd never say that inside their own church. The Lord works in mysterious ways.

Suddenly Doctor Throckmorton squealed the brakes and pulled over, stopping on the shoulder. He turned around. "You know, Moon, next week they take photos for our school's annual yearbook."

Annual yearbook sounded repetitious, but it wasn't a good time to mention things like that to him.

"Yes, sir."

"Yes who, Moon?"

"Yes, Doctor Throckmorton."

"There seems to be little reason for you to participate," he said, "since your appearance is so very unusual. Why should we disturb people and cause any commotion? Stay out of our good school's photographs, okay Moon?"

"Sure."

"Sure?"

"Sure, Doctor Throckmorton."

He nodded and eased back onto the road.

"It is important that you understand something else, Moon."

"What's that, sir?"

"Who?"

"What's that, Doctor Throckmorton?"

"I have always admired you, Moon. My life has been far easier than yours, being born to a respected family, well educated and physically impressive. You, on the other hand, have an embarrassing birth, look disgusting and cannot possibly hope to get a university education."

It seemed smart not to talk about my college plan just then.

"You've done well, Moon, considering those terrible deficiencies."

"Thank you, sir."

"Who?"

"Thank you, Doctor Throckmorton."

We'd only been gone five hours, but Grundy Center looked greener to me. The breeze made the heat tolerable. Grandma burst out in her apron and carried my box in and just couldn't stop gabbing and fussing over me, but Mom was indisposed.

Willy and Carla came by and Grandma fell asleep in her chair. Mom didn't have a nursing lesson that evening and told me she might reconsider her career options. She kind of stared at the corner where our piano used to sit and didn't say anything, finally deciding to walk down to Doctor Throckmorton's office to check some patient records. Willy and Carla and I skipped out to play.

Carla's dog went after Willy's cat, which applied its claws to the dog's nose in a manner that established a new Grundy Center yelping record, we agreed. Carla and Willy laughed so hard I thought they might choke. My mind floated. Our breeze shifted, coming from the northeast, so you could smell the corn and beans, which is difficult, but couldn't detect any pigs or cows, which would've been easy.

Carla didn't touch my arm. She didn't brush up against Willy either. We all just had fun, but I was wondering if she liked me more than a friend and I wondered if she liked Willy in a special way and I wondered if Willy, my pal, wondered.

Then it happened.

Carla leaned toward me with a smile. She kissed my forehead, stood and walked towards her home. Willy jumped up and sprinted away, leaving his cat behind.

I'm not sure the sun ever set that evening. Oh, sure, it had to. I just can't recall it.

I'd been kissed.

But the envelope that almost put me into Woodward had disappeared in the commotion of my return, and so did Willy.

"To be out of society is simply a tragedy."

Oscar Wilde

Chapter 7

Two or three new homes popped up in Grundy Center every year, a gravel road got blacktopped and several folks talked about moving back to the country where they suffered less noise. And some did just that.

Carla's dad disappeared again.

He ran off with John Barleycorn about once a year and usually came back in a week or two; unshaven, wobbly and smelling worse than when he left.

Carla tended to her younger brother while her dad was gone. That cute little fella stood barely knee-high to a grasshopper. She cooked and cleaned and sent him off to school with his face scrubbed, lunchbox filled and hair butch-waxed. This time her dad was missing for a month so Willy and I hardly saw her.

Willy and I rode our bikes past her house on a Sunday afternoon.

"You break our Solemn Pact," Willy said.

I just pedaled on, not knowing how to answer. Willy looked straight ahead with his jaw tightened.

"We is supposed to be friends."

I kept my mouth shut.

"We mark our Solemn Pact with blood."

"Willy, I did not break our Solemn Pact."

"How can you said that?"

I pedaled.

"How?"

"Jeepers, Willy, I almost got imprisoned at Woodward that day, escaped and Carla kissed me on the forehead. What did I do wrong?"

We pedaled on. When my bike chain came off, Willy stopped and came back to help me reconnect it.

At school, in the locker room for physical education, Stan Bartik and Merle Jacobsen and Roger Schlaefke sprouted hair first, and I mean on places other than their heads. Mr. Scarletti talked to all of us guys about this and explained deodorizer. Mr. Grifhorst set out beginner tubes at his drugstore. He put them on the back shelf so a guy wouldn't be flustered buying them. If somebody else lined up at the cash register, they said it would be okay if we just read a comic book until people cleared out. That's how we avoided embarrassment.

Roger Schlaefke was so proud, however, that he waited an hour to buy his, until there were customers to observe his purchase.

Mr. Scarletti got stuck explaining those tasks to us. A few years before he taught us to cut toenails straight across, instead of curved like you might expect to, in order to avoid ingrown toenails. His other lecture, of how important it was to dry between your toes after a shower, became so famous we knew it before he told us.

His birds and bees talk, of course, was the most eagerly anticipated, with snickering before he started.

"Can we ask more?" Willy asked. Our pollen and sperm and pistils and eggs lecture was due that afternoon. We knew because the science teacher pulled the window blinds shut.

"Why not, Willy?"

"I don't speech so good, and your irregular face might mean we never get girls. This could be only way we ever learn."

I didn't answer. Willy was right, of course, he and I might die lonely bachelors. We went to the birds and bees talk wondering, but didn't have the guts to ask anything.

When my different places grew hair, I bought the deodorizer without mentioning it to Mom or Grandma and tucked it under the davenport where I slept.

About that time Grandma figured I needed more privacy. She partitioned off my davenport with a chenille bedspread. By using a curtain rod, we could pull it back during the day, so we enjoyed a regular living room. I'd tug the curtain across at night for seclusion and have my own sleeping quarters.

Mom and Grandma shared their bed. But Mom's nursing got complicated. Being a professional like that required more study for a small town clinic, where you might be the only nurse and cared for tuberculosis, tractor crushes, polio, broken bones, births, deaths and nervous disorders. City nurses enjoyed the luxury of specializing, Doctor Throckmorton explained. Plus the medical office had a couple of patient rooms. When somebody was there and couldn't bathe themselves or pee then a professional needed to look after them.

Mom spent more and more time at her profession, sometimes being forced to sleep at the medical office if a patient required it. Grandma fussed over that.

Had Grandma kept her chin up things might have relaxed more around our house. There were reasons to be proud. Years earlier Mom had to stay at home and not mix with the citizens, being an outcast. Now Mom worked alongside everyone and kept them healthy. Nobody did more for Grundy Center except, well, maybe King Doctor Throckmorton Fancyhair.

But Grandma wore herself down worrying about Mom's career. She started to fall asleep on my davenport, sometimes before dinner. I'd carry her into bed.

She'd shrunk.

I'd grown.

Carla changed after her dad returned. She didn't care to join Willy and me anymore. Carla started riding around with an older guy, Donny Zrostlik, in his 48 Chevy. That car purred through dual glasspaks, he lowered the rear springs and installed fender skirts.

Some kids said Carla necked with Donny in the back seat, but Willy and I doubted that. His car body was so sleek that it didn't even have running boards, which looked pretty swell, but also meant you couldn't hang onto the door post and ride outside.

"Maybe our Pact Solemn will never necessary be," Willy said.

Willy and I spent summer evenings hot wiring cars and hitching bumpers in the winter.

Hot wiring came easy. If I had a stick of Wrigley's gum, I'd jam the tin foil across the three terminals under the ignition and the engine would crank up. Reach left to unthread the speedometer cable so the mileage wouldn't change and the owners never knew. Then check the gas station hose for free fuel or maybe stop at a farmhouse and appropriate some more, being careful not to get any diesel.

Nights belonged to us.

We always put the vehicles back where we got them. We never took six cylinder vehicles and that thinking paid off one night when Billy Blue Pants did try to verify a vehicle's ownership with us. All he saw were the back of two kid's heads, fading away in his headlights while our v-eight outmuscled his straight six.

Winters were for bumper hooking. After a second storm, the streets would be hard packed ice, dusted with new snow. Willy and I hung out downtown, maybe shot a game of eight ball at the VFW if they weren't having a meeting, and slipped outside to a street corner.

When a car came by, especially if their side and rear windows frosted over, we'd slip in behind them and dive at their bumpers, catching hold. We pulled both feet under ourselves and rode. We'd sway back and forth, go on one foot, finally let go and skidded away. Then hook a ride back.

This was best done with galoshes found in somebody's trash, since even on ice some gravel poked through and moms wondered how your soles wore out so fast.

Grandma would notice in my case. Mom focused on her career.

Another magical part of winter in Grundy Center was the Christmas decorations. Main Street lit up with different colored lights, Grifhorst Drug Emporium added bubble lights and Mr. Nordstrud played White Christmas for a week through outdoor loudspeakers. But Mr. Robert (you can call me "Bob") Ford outdid everybody. His lawn display lit up the whole block, with a manger out front, Santa and his reindeer on the roof and Reddy Kilowatt wishing everybody a Merry Christmas. Mr. Robert (you can call me "Bob") Ford ran the Grundy Center Rural Electric and Gas Company, so he was doing his job, selling power. Anytime his safety inspectors looked at your furnace, smarter customers would readjust the gas to mix in more air afterwards, otherwise their fuel bills jumped.

I mention these things to prove that winters weren't all glum. We traveled to Lake Poytawukie and ice fished too. But for the most part, winter was about surviving until spring.

Each April we took down the storm windows, put up the screens, washed the walls, beat the carpets and none of that seemed like work. It was anticipation.

Beating the carpets especially gave me a chance to imagine I was swinging a bat, like the school never let me do, and we borrowed a rug beater from a neighbor. We hung those rugs on a clothesline and I'd whack the dirt into the next county.

Taking down the screens to put up the storm windows in October, well, the glass was heavier than the screens of course. But something additional weighed on your soul while lifting those things onto each rectangle. We understood we were sealing ourselves inside for six months. When you stepped outside in winter, you were still trapped, wound up in fourteen layers of cloth, and when you needed a bathroom it became a race against nature.

Seasons continued these rhythms, but a few things changed and never came back. Carla dropped Donny Zrostlik for Robert Horstman. She still ignored Willy and me. Zrostlik and Horstman shaved and drove cars. We all could drive, of course, but those guys could cruise Main Street in daylight, in unstolen cars.

Zrostlik said something too loud about "Carla the Harlot" near our school so Willy hit Zrostlik from behind with a stone and ran. Willy had to sneak around town for a few weeks until the lump on Zrostlik's head went down.

Everybody clamped knobs on their steering wheels. That way they could turn with their left hand only, draping the right arm around their girl who'd sit straddling the transmission hump. In summer, girl or not, they'd steer with their right hand on the steering knob and drape the left arm out the window, since having a tan on that arm was status. That proved you were a driver. A tan right arm was embarrassing, marking passengers, so you rarely saw that side sticking out of car windows.

Some guys dropped the cars' rear ends. A few used lowering blocks. Others just torched the leaf springs until they flattened. Horstman installed a continental kit, making his car the longest in Grundy County. A few guys took off the air filter for more horsepower. Most ripped off the mufflers and put on glasspaks, and some installed dual exhausts with chrome tips. Main Street looked like the cover of Hot Rod magazine, almost.

Willy and I met kids at the Chief Theatre for a picture show on our bikes, but the girls our age migrated up and made out in those older guys' cars. This may have been natural, we didn't know what was going on. A couple of times guys our age were invited to feel Dorothy Lassen's blouse, and not just on the outside, but most were too scared. Maybe that went on in those souped-up cars, I don't know and neither did Willy. Dorothy Lassen didn't encourage anybody; her older brother Jerome promoted her. The stories suggest, however, that she remained unoffended.

Carla got jumpy when I tried to talk with her at school.

One day Robert Horstman punched me for standing around Carla's locker. He didn't need to do that.

If there was something wrong, well, if they just explained I'd leave them alone. Carla and I were pals and suddenly I was supposed to disappear or something. When he slugged me in the face I fell. My eye swelled shut. None of the teachers asked. I guess they agreed. I didn't realize things had become so different. Carla walked past my locker the following week, glancing over her shoulder. Nobody else was in the hall.

"Moon," she said, "we all change. You took one path and I chose another."

"What?" I asked.

"We'll both always remember the things we did, won't we?" Carla asked. "But don't talk about them, that's ancient history."

"What paths?" I asked.

"If you can stay away from me, especially when Donny or Robert are around," she said, "our memories can stay happy."

Geez. With 901 people living in Grundy Center, I supposed we could live forever without running into each other again.

"But why avoid each other?" I asked.

"Get with it," Carla said. She walked off in a hurry. Criminy. With only twenty-eight in our class, should we never talk again?

Her dad was a fall-down drunk. My Mom was professional. Grandma graduated from college. Why should I feel put down by Carla? Willy's family owned more stuff than hers and mine put together. And Willy didn't get huffy with Carla or me.

Willy just nodded when I reported what Carla had said.

Maybe he thought I'd get jealous if he let me see how much that bothered him.

Maybe he was right.

Maybe Willy thought I'd be angry if he didn't get upset.

That could be. Girls confused us.

Willy knew everything I thought except one little dream. I imagined myself graduating from Iowa State and cruising back into town, driving an MG. My girlfriend would sit beside me. This would attract attention in Grundy Center, being classier than just a custom car, and because it's British, the steering column's on the right hand side.

Because of that, my girl would sit on the left, and not be bothered by seeing the right side of my face. Everybody in town would know that Moon had a girlfriend and a college degree. Willy would approve and have his own girl, maybe even a wife. Our Solemn Pact might hold forever.

That railroader's family, the ones who ate garlic, left town. This made everybody more comfortable and was probably better for those foreigners.

Doctor Throckmorton fixed the typing class too.

"Communism is insidious and surrounds us," he explained to the school board, "and it disappoints me that nobody, not a one of you, detected this entering wedge." They squirmed on the gym bleachers. Doctor Throckmorton turned, walked onto the Grundy Center Eagle painted on the center and spun around.

"Can you not keep your eyes open wide, can you listen harder, is it possible for you to think?"

It wasn't yet winter, but coughing and throat clearing noises bounced around the bleachers. They nodded, mumbled agreement and walked out with heads hanging. Never again did anybody type "Now is the time for all good men to come to the aid of the party." From that moment forward, all typing practice was "The quick brown fox jumped over the lazy dog." Everybody also became careful not to use the word "comrade."

I was strolling down Main Street, feeling lucky and not thinking of anything in particular when Mr. Nordstrud stepped out of his store after I walked past.

"Moon?" A hammer dangled from his tool belt.

"Yes, Mr. Nordstrud."

We were the only ones on the sidewalk, but he put a finger to his lips, looked around and stepped toward me.

"Could you ride to Ames with me tomorrow? Might you be able to help me that way?" He stood so close I got nervous.

"Sure, Mr. Nordstrud."

"Moon, I've got business with Iowa State, and shouldn't you see that place someday?" He must've cleaned some paintbrushes before asking since the smell of thinner on him started to give me a buzz.

"Okay, Mr. Nordstrud."

"There's no reason, Moon, to tell anybody this, okay?"

"Sure thing, Mr. Nordstrud."

We stopped at Story City on the way and purchased a Pepsi. Mr. Nordstrud drank down to the "P" on the label and let me finish the bottle.

The startling thing about Ames, besides being Utopia, was we could see it from more than five miles away. Two power plants accented the skyline, one for the town and one just for the college. When we got closer the houses went on and on. This metropolis, a sprawling place, is where I might study and work hard and earn respect. And return to Grundy Center to help everyone.

After a few minutes Highway 69 dropped under another road. They called that an underpass. It means that while we cruised south cars passed over us going east and west on a separate road, bridged above us. I'm speaking hypothetically. There weren't actually vehicles overhead when we went under, just one bicyclist pedaling west, but still a car could have passed above us if we'd been a few minutes later or earlier. That biker proved it.

We turned west onto Lincoln Way, heading for the campus and the road widened to four lanes. This was all hard road, no gravel. Strictly concrete. Two lanes went side by side to the west, with the others for traffic to the east. This let cars pass each other without changing lanes. I looked into one automobile next to us and could almost lip-read what they were saying. Mr. Nordstrud didn't have to worry about oncoming traffic or rush to get back into our lane after passing a car.

I didn't talk for several minutes. Looking into a car next to us, both vehicles traveling some thirty miles per hour was scary.

How could people live that way?

Mr. Nordstrud did his business with the maintenance warehouse at Iowa State, which took about ten minutes after our hour and a half drive. Then he asked if I'd like to take a look around the campus.

"Wow. Will they let us, Mr. Nordstrud? Gee."

We went to Beardshear Hall, where it seemed they expected him, walked up the two stories of stairs, seventy-eight steps in all, and into the Registrar's office.

Registrar is a college word for admissions boss.

Mr. Nordstrud, the Registrar and I talked for about fifteen minutes. The Registrar was a skinny, bald guy, bouncing in and out of his chair, talking loud and waving his arms. He asked me a hundred questions which I respectfully answered. We walked to a few places that the Registrar suggested.

We listened to a professor in the chem lab and you'd hardly believe it, every student did experiments and had their own locker, filled with flasks and burners and chemicals and hardware. Mr. Nordstrud showed me a lecture hall where we sat in the back and listened to a professor work some calculus problems. These were about fifty pounds and twenty miles beyond the trigonometry that came easy to me. This appeared to be the brain of our universe.

I got dizzy seeing things like the lake in the middle of campus with two swans. We drove past that on the way to Beardshear. And so much grass between buildings that you'd expect cows to graze, or at least a few sheep, but no. There were only students walking to and from the library. The grass was planted there just for looks, imagine that.

I hoped Mr. Nordstrud wouldn't hear my heart thumping. I relaxed when we headed back to Grundy Center on a road where you could look straight in every direction, without anything blocking the view.

"What'd you think, Moon?" Mr. Nordstrud asked.

"It's Hollywood and New York but better," I replied. "Iowa State is the center of the universe."

Mr. Nordstrud looked at me, the road, me again and the road.

"That college and what I'll learn there will make Grundy Center a better place for everybody."

Mr. Nordstrud pursed his lips.

"Moon, isn't it a great place? Don't you think you'll do well there and make us proud? Just keep our trip quiet, okay?"

"Yes, Mr. Nordstrud."

"Do you understand, Moon, that some of our civic leaders don't realize that you have ambitions? Just like regular people?" Mr. Nordstrud dropped me off.

Grandma had waited up. We mixed navy beans with ground chuck for sandwiches. She stayed up late that night, until eight o'clock, listening to my adventure.

I laid in bed imagining myself at Iowa State. Grandma and I could make things better for Grundy Center. We'd be a proud family with two college degrees. Smart's better than rich any day.

Picking pickles only lasted two weeks, but, as soon as school got out officially you could start weeding the beans and corn. That paid seventy-five cents an hour. This went on until the Mexican and Negro families arrived and we got laid off.

For a while blacks were called Negroes and for a while they were called colored but I forgot which was the proper name for that time. They were better workers, farmers claimed. More important, they put entire families in the field. When a farmer paid a migrant seventy-five cents an hour, that went further since their kids would help, making us local boys obsolete. This was how the season progressed. We took the pay while we could.

After we got fired, the Chief Theatre filled up.

Willy ran the projector. I helped. Talk about an easy job. All we did was load the reels and most motion pictures had seven. When a reel neared the end we stared at the upper right hand corner of the screen, until a little squiggle flashed. Then Willy or I counted to seven, a second squiggle appeared and we threw the switch to the next reel. Folks in the audience never noticed the changeover. It didn't go so smooth when we loaded up a cartoon or the newsreel, since those were separate film cans without any squiggle marks to help us. Like many jobs the better opportunities hid elsewhere, which involved John Barleycorn in this case.

Mr. Sheetz owned the theater and was no bumpkin. He hung pictures of himself in the lobby shaking hands with Roy Rogers, Gene Autry and Johnny MacBrown. They all signed the photos. He took down the Dale Evans photo after The Most Reverend Dawson raised a ruckus about her not changing her last name to Rogers and thundering on about whether Roy and she were married or not.

You wouldn't know Mr. Sheetz was so famous, the way he acted around Grundy Center, although he drove the other Grundy Center Cadillac. His White Cadillac was decked out with gold trim, dual rear-view mirrors mounted on the front fenders, mud flaps and a foxtail tied to the antenna. He had white sidewall tires, just like Doctor Throckmorton, except his were slip-ons which scraped off when he parked against a curb in Mason City.

After Mr. Sheetz bought his first pair of Florsheim shoes he carried the empty box around in his rear window for a month, making sure everybody knew, but other than that, the guy acted pretty modest.

The picture show benefits to Willy and me compensated for the migrants putting us out of field work. They filled every theater seat, and Mr. Sheetz put on double showings Saturdays. Money flowed. If Mr. Sheetz hadn't been a front-row Lutheran he could have opened the theater on Sunday and hauled in even more dough.

We ran the same picture show through the whole harvest. Some films bleached and several frames melted. We'd resplice them and the migrants still filled all sixty seats. They all bought popcorn which Mr. Sheetz salted heavily, keeping up his Coke sales.

Air conditioning made the picture show business.

We all slept with windows wide open in summer and still sweated through the sheets. Nobody moved quite as fast. But one evening in the Chief Theatre with cool air revived folks. Still, there was a threat to Mr. Sheetz, and that was television. There were now five sets in Grundy Center. With three channels, it seemed that trend might kill motion pictures.

"Can you imagine what's around that next corner?" Mr. Nordstrud always asked me.

"Isn't change constant here in Grundy Center?" he'd ask.

Maybe the air conditioning would always keep the picture show business strong in summer.

Pretty soon Kraft Theater broadcast Sunday night programs; neighbors would join the TV owners for a potluck dinner and the Velveeta sales shot up for Mr. Hardcastle. But the citizens still dripped sweat every June, July and August so the motion picture business stayed strong, and got even better during harvest.

Part of that harvest cash spilled into my paper route. Some people added the Sunday paper during the picking of corn and beans. Willy's dad noticed folks paid quicker and yowled less.

Besides the money Mr. Sheetz paid us, two other benefits made the entertainment business special in summer.

First, Willy and I took turns pretending to escort someone to a seat. We did this with a flashlight pointed to the aisle so the imaginary customer could follow us without tripping. So we'd just glide to the front alone, with a flashlight pointed down, step to the side, click off the flashlight and look back.

There were always several women nursing babies right there in the picture show and Willy watched them from the front of the theater. Reflections off the screen lit up the audience. If a daylight scene played those women sat naked from the waist up, right in front of Willy.

Well, sometimes I snuck up and peeked too.

Okay, we took regular turns.

If the motion picture showed a night scene at that moment, we could still make out the shape of their, uh, we might see plenty of, well, it was some kind of show. Even when somebody lit a cigarette, the glow from his or her match revealed so much that Willy and I needed to go to the bathroom, separately, and lock the door for a few minutes.

We had learned in the school locker room that all men are not created equal. The Chief Theatre taught Willy and me that Negro and Mexican women also come in various shapes and sizes. This could be true for white ladies also, but we had no way of verifying that.

Well, we had some glimpses from Carla but no other comparison. And she had blossomed since we hunted night crawlers and went water skiing together.

"You I and will know never," Willy said. He stared down at the dirt.

"What do you mean, Willy?"

"My talk isn't so good," Willy said, "and you appearance different."

The lump in my throat grew so big I wasn't sure I could ever drink water again. I hoped Willy was wrong. Never, ever having a girlfriend sounded bleak. But maybe it would be worse if just one of us had a girl. Carla had already threatened our Solemn Pact and it turned out she had no interest in Willy or me.

What would we do when that real girl came along?

Or would she ever?

Anyway, our second benefit, that John Barleycorn bonus, came since the State of Iowa Liquor Authority outlet for Grundy Center County sat next to our theater.

"Jesus turned wine into water," Willy said, almost getting it right. What he meant was that since alcohol was a free miracle in the Bible perhaps it was meant to be so for us. After each show Willy and I slipped down into the Chief Theatre's basement. A window opened under the sidewalk. We eased through it and into a narrow walkway under the sidewalk, pushing away the cobwebs and took several steps over to the State of Iowa Liquor Authority's basement window. It lifted easy. We reached inside and appropriated one bottle every night, not so much that the State of Iowa Liquor Authority, SOILA, would notice.

Four Roses whiskey sold best to the migrants. That's what we handled most often. This made up for our daytime unemployment after the Mexicans and Negroes arrived. That field work made sense for the migrants, or why would they come so far? And the farmers got more for their money or why would they fire us? Everybody benefited.

Maybe it resembled stealing but taking whiskey from SOILA and arranging for the migrants to get some at half-price didn't feel like a mortal sin.

Pritchard's Modern Auto loaded up on used cars for the migrants. They bought junkers and put bananas in the transmissions to quiet the grinding. With some they put cardboard under the floor mats to hide the rustouts, and sold those folks vehicles after payday, when they felt rich and headed back south. We suspected most of those cars didn't make the Missouri border before they shelled out the transmissions, blew a rod or froze up.

One year the Mexicans arrived early and we got laid off July third. The next day Hank the Tank and Willy's dad did the "TURKEY DROP & COW PLOP," but nobody told the migrants. Another switcharoo developed that year when Willy's dad let Hank the Tank fly the plane while they dumped the coupons and the bird. By most accounts, our mayor wouldn't qualify as sober when he took the controls.

Hank the Tank buzzed the town. Everybody cheered, having just grabbed for the floating coupons with one citizen capturing the bird. They buzzed the campsites the migrants set up outside town. This may have disoriented Hank and Willy's dad. Or maybe the routine simply bored a couple of guys who had done it a dozen times before and weren't so alert.

No matter. What counts is that phone service was restored within two days to the north side of Grundy Center and power came back before noon the following day.

When they hit the power and phone lines those wires sheared off the wings flush from the fuselage. If that dead maple had been cleared like it should have been, the next stop for Hank the Tank and Willy's dad could've been Farber & Ottoman's, "Friends When You Need Them Most," with their bodies on display, cooling towards room temperature. That only meant a four-degree drop this holiday.

But as it was, the fuselage nestled in the top notch of that tree, and the upper half swayed until a crowd gathered under them. Willy's dad probably would've cursed if he knew how, but he didn't, he just shook his head, gently parted a few branches and eased himself out and slid down the trunk.

The fuselage bobbed up higher and the branches, still rocking, lifted.

"Your city officials are immortal," Hank the Tank shouted to the growing audience. His beet-colored face bobbled inside the cockpit and he waved at the people below, smiled at the empty lot on the other side until realizing there were no voters there, which took him awhile, and turned back to the crowd again.

"Are you getting photos of this?" he asked.

Somebody put an extension ladder against the fuselage. Hank waved it away. The crowd cheered. Hank stood, the fuselage shifted, started to slide but caught on another branch.

Hank the Tank lingered in the wreckage, aloft, waving, to the cheers of his voters. Some of the mayor's less enthusiastic supporters axed that maple the next day.

"Mother died today, or maybe it was yesterday."

Albert Camus

Chapter 8

"Where did Mom go, Grandma?"

Grandma sat in her rocker, not rocking.

"Grandma, where do you think Mom went?"

Grandma flipped a page in the Bible. She didn't look up. Dinner wasn't started so I took two wieners from the icebox and suggested to here that I could make 'Smores for dessert.

"Grandma, where?"

"The Lord is testing us, Moon."

"Where did Mom go?"

Grandma flipped another page and traced down the lines with her finger whispering the words. "Her note didn't say where, Moon. I would guess Chicago, since the Greyhound bus goes directly there, with only eight stops."

"What's Chicago like?"

Grandma turned another page.

"Grandma?"

"Big. Bad. She thought it was glamorous."

Mom's note promised that she'd be in touch as soon as she got situated. But we heard nothing for days, then weeks.

Grandma's face tightened. My insides pained, mostly for the situation, not blaming anyone. Well, maybe myself. Maybe Grandma thought Mom's life would have been better if I hadn't come along and upset everything. Mom did the best she knew how and others might have collapsed sooner. Mom fought through economic difficulties and won, but sometimes let people get to her. Grandpa had called this mood our "Irish Virus," or the "Dark Dog."

Luckily those "Dark Dogs" came and went for most of us, but Mom's didn't. Maybe Doctor Throckmorton's career help wasn't as charitable or glamorous as it appeared. That wouldn't surprise me.

"Mom's so spunky," I said to Grandma, "there's a good chance she'd soon be working for some fancy Chicago doctor and becoming a full-fledged nurse and wearing a stethoscope and using tongue depressors and carrying one of those pointy flashlights to peek into people's ears."

Grandma just groaned, fanning herself.

Mom must have told Grandma about her plan and how she would get in contact. I'm guessing that since the note Mom left wasn't in Mom's handwriting. It was Grandma's. I didn't mention this. Mom undoubtedly felt so bad about leaving that she couldn't even write and needed to have Grandma do the note for her. We didn't keep the note.

That "Dark Dog" bit Grandma hard when Mom left. Grandma's Irish too, like my dad, but she's Protestant. While Ireland produces music and poetry, there's a contrariness in our tribe that leads to melancholy.

Grandpa and Grandma were different but they coped. Grandma stayed Methodist after Grandpa died. By that I mean she was born and baptized Presbyterian and raised Republican. Grandpa came from a Methodist and Democratic family. After two years of courtship, they agreed that she could remain Republican but would switch to the Methodist Church. Grandpa converted to a Republican but could stay Methodist. That worked easier for him since his conversion was hidden by the voting booth, but Grandma's family refused to attend their wedding. They called them heathens. After seventeen years, her family started visiting again and almost became friendly.

So despite being Irish, my grandparents worked things out.

I started walking back to the "Bone Orchard" more often to review the situation with Grandpa. That canvas didn't make it through the first winter. I staked it tight over him but the freezing and thawing tore it up. In talking with Mr. Colvet, who cared for the cemetery, I learned the rain rarely got down as far as the boxes and with that ankle-high grass over Grandpa, he probably stayed as cozy down there as Grandma and I did in our duplex. That comforted me, and after Mr. Colvet left, I sat next to Grandpa's grave.

"Math comes easy to me in school, Grandpa."

I spoke loud enough for him to hear through six feet of dirt, but glanced around to make sure nobody else was around.

"I adjusted Grandma's spark advance last night." Then I backed up to explain how Grandma got a car and learned to drive, since he wouldn't know about that. I stood and looked over the cemetery again. Nobody else was there. I sat and pulled a grass stalk that had gone to seed, slipped the tender end between my teeth, sat and chewed it while explaining.

"The bracket that holds the generator also busted. Mr. Nordstrud could order a replacement for eight bucks. The warehouse in Des Moines would load it on a Greyhound Bus and we would have gotten it in about a week, if they had any," I said.

I stood, checked around to ensure we still had our privacy. We did so I finished the story.

"That car's fifteen years old, so parts aren't always in stock. Mr. Nordstrud said I could pay him a dollar a week for eight weeks if I wanted. I thanked him and said I'd think about it. But at that price, even though I knew he wasn't charging me for the bus freight, it seemed saving some money for my education made more sense.

"So instead, Grandpa, I took a two-by-four and cut off a one-foot length. Then I ran it through the band saw at school, making a diagonal cut the long way. That night I wedged that piece in between the generator motor and the engine block, hammering it in just enough so the belt connecting them tightened."

I scanned the "Bone Orchard" for visitors and there still weren't any.

"Grandpa, when I turned the key it started right up."

Grandpa heard my story and enjoyed it, that's for sure.

I didn't disturb him by mentioning Mom leaving for her new career. After Mom settled and we knew where she was, probably Chicago, I planned to run right back to Grandpa and report the good news.

I didn't mention the thought of Iowa State to Grandpa. That sounded outrageous until I knew I could get in and figured out how to pay. When I had those answers, I would hurry over to Grandpa and gradually mention going to college.

By mentioning that I was saving money for my education on this visit, I began to prepare him for the thought. On the next visit I'd mention, casually, how the best-paying jobs recently were going to college graduates. Maybe during the next visit after that, I'd suggest that I was thinking about attending a college, but just as a trial. Then finally I'd announce that I had enrolled at Iowa State.

That way, Grandpa would come to understand that this schooling would help our family advance in the world. My true interest wasn't only to get ahead with a college diploma. It also seemed like a way to help all of Grundy Center. Maybe I could show the citizens that asphalting Main Street would pay off and if Mom had a tough time in Chicago, her son being a college graduate might give her a reason to return.

After I had explained to Grandpa about how I fixed the generator, sitting there without a breeze, a few leaves fell. A Red-winged blackbird trilled from the cat tails in the ditch, going "reee-reee." Those birds are lucky, all with red shoulder patches; none of them look different, eliminating any trouble.

The birds stopped. I heard another familiar noise. In a minute, sure enough, Grandma's car coughed up the road. We had decided against investing in a muffler after the road salt and gravel ate up the old one, so I heard her coming from a half mile away. It was better she not see me being this strange, talking to the ground, so I jogged over to the Catholic side and ducked behind a tombstone. As our car pulled closer, it clanged. This told me my two-by-four worked loose, tilted and the fan blades ticked it.

Grandma parked outside, waddled into the cemetery and stood right where I had been sitting. She had some difficulty bending over and dropped to her knees while touching his stone. Grandpa didn't have granite sticking up but we proudly marked his spot with a flat limestone, which still clearly showed all the letters of his name, except the middle initial. Farber & Ottoman, "Friends When You Need Them Most," had got that letter wrong so I chiseled it off and ground the gap down smooth with a file.

I circled around and peeked at Grandma from the side. Her face softened, not to what you might call happy, just warm. She stayed like that for a spell. When she struggled to stand I had to restrain myself from running over to grab her elbow and help her up. She shuffled out to our car and that engine turned over after the second attempt. I wanted to walk over, lift the hood and straighten out that board before the fan belt snapped. But I didn't and she pulled away slow, our engine making so much racket you'd think it was doing sixty.

I wondered how often she visited Grandpa. The thought made me woozy. She never mentioned her cemetery trips to me and I never told her about mine. Grandma and I relied on each other without discussing it.

That same night I rolled Grandma onto her bed.

"You'll do fine on your own, when that time comes," she said.

"I'll not be leaving, Grandma, we are family."

"My dear Grandson, the Lord calls us all." She smiled, patted my wrist and slipped into sleep before I could think up an answer.

We played six-man football at school. I couldn't participate and didn't care to, are you joking? Get all banged up? Mr. Scarletti offered to fit me with custom padding in a helmet, but he'd have to get Doctor Throckmorton's approval for the expenditure, so why even ask? Do pushups and jumping jacks and wind sprints every day? Wear one of those silly jock straps? No thanks.

Something strange had happened at home anyway, and I had gotten more advice on handling King Throckmorton. The day before she disappeared, Mom had rattled through our place, dropping things into a cardboard box. Grandma wasn't home yet. Mom asked me to put my finger on the twine while she knotted it.

"Always remember one thing, Moon."

"What, Mom?"

"Life goes easier if you don't antagonize folks."

She tied the knot and lugged the box outside somewhere, then stepped back in and looked out the window.

"I'll try to not antagonize anybody."

"Just watch for certain people, dang it. Like Doctor Throckmorton, Moon, don't walk through his neighborhood during daylight and get somebody else to collect from him for your paper."

"Why?"

"Just do it. If you're smart, you'll do that. Don't be pushing yourself on Doctor Throckmorton. He's a busy, important man."

"But..."

"Do it, can you for once help instead of dragging me through the dirt?"

"What dirt...?"

She walked out. Like a hundred times before.

But Mom stopped.

She set the box down, turned and walked back toward me. I'd never seen her lower lip quiver before. Mom walked right up to me and put her arms around me so I knew something was wrong.

"You can't help it," she said.

I didn't know what to do. Her arms were wrapped around mine so I couldn't hug her back even if I knew how, and my hands kind of flared out from my legs like tiny wings and I stiffened.

She let go, walked away, picked up her box and went on. I didn't have a clue that she was taking off forever, but could tell something was different.

Since Doctor Throckmorton never attended away games, I served as water boy when we went to Oskaloosa, Eagle Grove, Britt, Montezuma and Sac City. Grandma tore up a jersey that nobody needed and took in the seams, so I was number 41 on those trips and had my own parka to stay warm on the bench. Most of the senior guys treated me okay. We were juniors now. Willy and I would be the top dogs of Grundy Center High in just a year. And the almighty, all-seeing omnipotent Doctor Throckmorton never knew I carried water on those trips.

Mr. Scarletti sent my name in to the National Park Service before Career Day came around. If you were in the Park Service you wore those flat-brimmed hats and green uniforms. After forty years you got a pension. Juniors like me and Willy weren't part of Career Day but Mr. Scarletti got an exception and drove me to Marshalltown where they set it up in the community college auditorium.

"Mr. Scarletti, why do I get to do this early?" I asked while we rolled over the hard road in the driver-training car. Floating along in that Buick, which had a Dynaflo transmission, we didn't need to look away from anybody while cruising through Marshalltown.

"Moon, two reasons. First is that if things don't work out for you, the Park Service takes hardship cases and gives them a graduate equivalency exam, so you might even be able to become a Park Ranger before next year."

I didn't say anything. Grandma and I were hardly poor and school was getting good.

"The other thing is that you should see this community college. These schools give kids a good start on a higher education, and you wouldn't be lost in some big city like Ames."

I said nothing. People like Mr. Scarletti knew more about the world than me, but this was not my plan.

We found the auditorium. Several companies had set up card tables and stapled crepe paper down their front sides. They put brochures on each but you had to talk before getting one. Maytag, Ellsworth Junior College, the United States Army, American Institute of Business, Marshalltown Community College, Fisher Governor, John Deere and about a dozen others all greeted me without any fuss. It turned out that the Park Service representative got caught in a Minnesota blizzard and couldn't make it that day.

On the drive back, Mr. Scarletti explained that being a Park Ranger meant I could watch for fires from a tower in the mountains of South Dakota or Colorado or Wyoming. Best of all, I would be out with nature where there wouldn't be people to bother me and my life could become peaceful.

"Mr. Scarletti," I asked, "wouldn't it be okay to just finish up at Grundy Center High and then think about what I should do?"

"That wouldn't be so bad, Moon, but there's one problem."

"Yes, Mr. Scarletti?"

"We know that the Park Service is hiring now. We don't know if they will be in a year."

"I might be willing to risk that, Mr. Scarletti."

He took a long breath and sighed. We drove on. A tractor seemed uninterested in helping us pass so we slowed to twenty miles an hour for a while, then zipped past at a crossroad. Mr. Scarletti also said that Marshalltown Community College had a clinic where our own Doctor Throckmorton was affiliated and that he was willing to make sure I got a job there. It wasn't clear to me what "affiliated" meant but it was quite clear that my job would be cleaning up their operating room after surgery, wearing a surgical mask and mopping floors at night. Oh. Wearing a mask.

"Doctor Throckmorton," he said, "thinks that might be a nice solution for your dilemma."

"What dilemma, Mr. Scarletti?"

He clicked on the headlights in the daylight. He turned them off. The road didn't rise or fall or bend and there were no other cars, trucks or tractors.

"Mr. Scarletti, what dilemma?"

He turned on the radio, fiddled with the clock, adjusted our seat, opened a vent and turned the radio off.

"I see no dilemma, Mr. Scarletti."

"Well, Moon, you know with it being awkward for you to fit in society comfortably, working nights in the Marshalltown clinic would give you some well-deserved solitude. And how about being a Park Ranger? What wouldn't any man give for that life? No parents to answer to, no school board, just the Park Ranger and the trees and the deer. You're one lucky guy, Moon."

We hit that section by Belmond where the grain elevators stood so high and close to the road that the winds could whipsaw your car, so Mr. Scarletti gripped the wheel tighter and we stopped talking. The car got through without veering.

"Mr. Scarletti, you know the high school kids have me play 45s at the sock hops now."

He knew what I meant. We put on dances after home football games in the gymnasium. Since I couldn't have a date, of course, the student council appointed me as 'DJ Moon' and I played records. I was a local star. Maybe they didn't have me mixed up in the middle of things, but it's not like I was ignored and snuck outside at night, alone.

"The powers that be," Mr. Scarletti said, "think it's better for Grundy Center that you not be in the public eye."

"Well, Mr. Scarletti, other people feel different. Who am I to say?"

"Moon, know your place. None of us control our own destiny."

It flattered me that Mr. Scarletti thought about my future so much. Mr. Scarletti liked me, I could tell. But he was only the school principal in Doctor Throckmorton's town. Mr. Scarletti was just another hired hand.

I picked up a clue while passing through the VFW one day. It was always smoky and dark in there, and the hanging lights over the pool tables made the green felt glow. The players' hands and faces lit up when they leaned over their cue sticks, disappearing when they'd rise back up into the smoke.

Nobody saw me come in the rear door. The guy shooting at the far end talked while bending over the table.

"Did you hear how Doctor Throckmorton described Moon to the school board?" He shot and missed the pocket but clicked several balls.

"No, what'd he say?" somebody asked from the shadows.

"Doctor Throckmorton said Moon is the pimple on Grundy Center's butt." Another guy studied the balls on the table. Nobody said anything. I snuck out the back door, walked down the alley, took my time coming up Main Street, swung the front door open wide so the outside light showed my silhouette to everybody. I walked through and sold few papers.

I'm not a pimple. Emperor Throckmorton, MD, is the one filled with pus. MD stands for My Deity he thinks.

Every year some seniors took the SAT tests. Mr. Scarletti brought a sealed box into the study hall. He ripped it open and the teacher passed out a questionnaire to those who had an envelope with their name on it.

I didn't get one.

The nurse took those aside who received the form, suggesting they go to bed early that night. None of the farm kids got forms. They had chores to do and our local harvest didn't need any more school distractions. Willy and Carla got forms.

The next morning I slipped into the front office.

"Why didn't I get a form?" The secretary glared and said she'd check.

"Moon, you won't need the SAT," Mr. Scarletti said, "for the Park Service or at Marshalltown Community College.

"I'd like to take the test anyway, Mr. Scarletti," I said.

He wrinkled his face, said okay and huffed out while the secretary groaned about trying to find an extra form. By nine o'clock she hadn't. The test had just started. I asked if she was having any luck, and she said it was probably too late. I asked to speak with Mr. Scarletti. He was tied up in an important meeting, so she slid a form halfway across the counter. I reached across, snatched it, filled out each sheet, took my booklet into the testing room and started.

This exam took four hours. I had missed the first thirty minutes. Willy looked up and flashed an okay sign. Carla glanced at me and stared back at her answer sheet. Nobody else moved.

These kind of tests cranked me up. Each year we had taken the Iowa Basic Skills exam. First they might ask which of the following four things don't fit, and there would be pictures of an apple, a banana, the planet Earth and an orange. If you're common-sense smart, the world doesn't fit with the fruits. If you're cocky you start over-analyzing, realize that the banana is the only non-sphere, and check the wrong answer. Those test makers aren't geniuses, so you calibrate your thinking towards their level. Next there would be a train heading west at twenty miles an hour with a second train heading east at thirty miles an hour, and they started fifty miles apart. When's the crash? Not too tough.

Then they'd ask if you would like to have a vocabulary that was:

1.) prodigious,

2.) heavily salted with porcupines,

3.) darker than a black cat in a tarpaper factory at midnight or

4.) moist.

That's how these exams always started but the test-makers jacked up the difficulty with each page. So I dove in and started figuring and guessing and hoping.

The SAT testing service headquartered itself in Princeton, New Jersey. That made sense. Albert Einstein lived there. Luckily they required that I fill out my own home name and address on the form.

The importance of this was that it helped avoid clerical errors. In my own case, for example, the school apparently didn't receive the results of my test. They announced the Grundy Center results without mentioning me. Our class ranked in the 76th percentile nationally. If Ole Ericsen's results were excluded, Mr. Scarletti confided, our school would have scored at the 88th percentile.

It turned out that Gloria Throckmorton won an honorable mention for her results. Although I beat her in math classes, it appeared that I scored a big, fat zero on the SAT test. That late start hurt more than I realized.

A month later, at home, we got a big envelope in the mail. It had an embossed return address, coming from the Woodrow Wilson Scholarship Foundation.

"A man can be destroyed but not defeated."

Ernest Hemingway

Chapter 9

Mr. Scarletti had said I didn't need to take the SAT test. I had started it thirty minutes late. My results hadn't been mentioned in the school's announcement.

But that envelope, the one that came a month later, claimed I won a Woodrow Wilson Scholarship.

It went on, saying they would loan all money needed for housing, books, meals and tuition to any accredited college, interest-free. All I had to do was graduate from high school and spend ten years teaching after college. For every year teaching, my loan was forgiven by five percent. After ten years, only half of the total would be due, without interest.

The letter said this scholarship was based on my exceptional SAT test scores.

Grandma fell on her rear while reading that letter. She stayed on the floor, open-mouthed, in our main room, not bothering to hoist herself back up. Grandma just kept reading it over and over, out loud, then silent, wiping her eyes with a sleeve and reading it again. She sort of looked at the ceiling and finally handed that letter back.

I made the first two long distance calls of my life right then, with Grandma's approval.

First I called information in Princeton, New Jersey, to get the phone number for the Woodrow Wilson Scholarship headquarters. Then I called them to make sure this wasn't a mistake. They were closed. I called the next day. It took them a moment to find my scores, then the person on the other end assured me that this was real, no joke, and yes, Iowa State would be fine.

That long-distance call cost us sixty-five cents for three minutes, and was worth every penny.

The Woodrow Wilson Scholarship Fund sent another signed letter verifying everything they said.

In this process Grandma and I discovered that long-distance information calls were free. Of course the phone company got us big time when we dialed those long distance numbers.

"God damaged you and now God blesses you," Grandma said.

"Why are you wearing gloves, Grandma?"

"It's warm, Moon, but my fingers are glowing and I don't want to stain your scholarship letter."

"What shall we do with the award, Grandma?"

She rocked, reading the letter again. The floor creaked under her chair.

"Careful, Moon, careful. Heaven placed its loving hand on your poor head today. But some Grundy Center authorities may disagree. This is a proud moment. But we must quietly celebrate. Not silently, quietly."

We talked for a couple hours about how to handle this. It wasn't the easiest thing, but I took that award letter and glued it down to a quarter-inch sheet of oak, leaving two inches around each edge. Then I rubbed a mixture of white paint and wood filler into the grain around the edges so the border looked filigreed. The harder part came when I varnished the board. To make sure I didn't mess up, I practiced on scrap lumber. One was also oak, so I wiped it with the white paint and wood filler concoction and experimented, testing several levels of stirring and painting. It became obvious how much mixing worked best for clarity, getting rid of the bubbles but not whipping the varnish up until it went milky. Now Grandma and I had a plaque, eleven inches by fourteen. I put two eyehooks on the backside, connected with a hanging wire.

First we hung it inside our front door. Everybody could see it there when they came to our place, but since nobody ever did that we started inviting them.

I switched it to the wall above my davenport a week later, but Grandma said that was selfish, just dangling over my head. She'd like to look at the plaque herself sometimes, Grandma complained. Of course she was asleep before I ever pulled my curtain, so she could always see it anyway. But no matter, we hung it over the doorway into her bedroom.

My Woodrow Wilson Scholarship plaque commanded attention there. This triumph deserved it.

Grandma invited the choir director from church, the janitor and two teachers from school over for coffee and desert. She made angel food cake, not devil's food, obviously, since religious crowds were involved.

"Oh, no special reason," Grandma said into the phone every night, "we just thought it was time we hosted you with some eats and refreshment." She'd repeat that in three phone calls every night and usually got one acceptance.

"We'll see you Thursday evening then," Grandma would say, smiling and nodding, "and don't you dare bring a thing." We got out some bubble lights and tinsel from the Christmas tree, wrapped them around the plaque, and plugged them in. Colors and flickering light bathed that award. This way we didn't need to point or mention it. Grandma just waited until they asked.

"Oh, that, Moon won a scholarship to any important, prestigious school he wants to attend, even Iowa State, due to his SAT scores," Grandma answered.

"We don't know if he'll accept this or not. Of course we're pleased for Grundy Center that one of our own would be so honored."

I stuck a note on Carla's locker early in the morning, when nobody would see, suggesting that if she and her dad cared to stop by we'd be happy to provide a soft drink and a sweet roll, but she didn't answer.

I invited Willy's folks over and they all came by.

"Carla visit?" Willy asked.

"No, Willy." I didn't say anything more. I wish Carla had come over. I felt bad that I wish she had. I felt worse that Willy would feel bad if he knew she had visited.

"Good," Willy said. He shook his head in a satisfied kind of way, and this shamed me, because I hadn't admitted to him that I pasted an invitation on Carla's locker. Or my second note to her.

"Stop, Moon, just stop," Carla had said when she saw me in the hallway. If I thought about this, and I tried mightily not to, it seemed that I had betrayed Willy by asking her. Plus I got scolded by Carla for it. I swore to never again let any girl jeopardize my friendship with Willy.

I had also asked Mr. Scarletti but he needed to supervise the baton twirling classes after school.

I never mentioned any of this to Gloria Throckmorton. She never talked to me anyway but we were the two smartest kids in our class and she knew that. Gloria probably respected my award, but with her dad's attitude, couldn't mention it. Besides, we had to handle this carefully. Grandma was my main cheerleader and would stay thrilled for life. Mom would have been proud, I guess.

"Moon, might the missus and I come over to celebrate your scholarship?" Mr. Nordstrud asked.

"Sure, Mr. Nordstrud, how about tonight?"

"Maybe, Moon. Will anyone see us, I mean, will there be others?"

"No, Mr. Nordstrud, just you and Mrs. Nordstrud."

"Fine, Moon, is 6:30 okay?"

"Yes, thank you, Mr. Nordstrud, yes."

Several others came by. But none who were on the city council, the bank, or who had loans from the bank visited, mainly because we became careful not to ask them. Mr. Nordstrud also suggested that nobody from the school board should be confronted with my award. We agreed, and since there were always others listening in to the telephone party lines, Grandma never mentioned anything but the cake and coffee when on the phone.

Finally the coffee and cake expense became noticeable and we stopped.

Two more farms failed to pay their loans that year. Doctor Throckmorton stepped in to save both, allowing the former owners to work his new properties, provided their crops covered the rent he charged them. The clothing store closed on Main Street. As farms grew, farmers became fewer, and surviving got tougher for retailers and others who serviced the public. The bank tightened loan requirements which made it harder for stores to carry as much merchandise as the bigger stores in Mason City, Fort Dodge and Des Moines.

One night Grandma and I pulled both chairs in front of the doorway. We positioned the Sears lamp under my award, which now looked like a jukebox and stared into it, relishing our great fortunes. She brewed herself a coffee and spooned in some sugar. We looked at the signature and commented on it. I had once dabbed it with an eyedropper to see if it was hand-written or printed, and it smudged, a true signature. We discussed the letterhead design, which featured a typeface so elegant you could barely read it. I sipped an RC Cola. Grandma talked about each generation getting a step farther ahead. We split a Hostess cupcake.

Her smile lines spread.

"Grandma, when I get that college degree, you and I might set up some special classes in Grundy Center. Students like Ole Ericsen and Dudley Stebbins, who are a little slower, might do better with extra attention," I said. Her face tightened.

"And Mom would probably rush back home when she hears how I've done so well." Grandma's head dropped.

"Grandma?"

"Oh my boy, don't set yourself up for hurt."

"Grandma, she'll come back. I won't be an embarrassment anymore."

Grandma shut her eyes.

"My grand, grandson, can you be satisfied with what is?"

"Does the imagination dwell the most, Upon a woman won or a woman lost?"

William Butler Yeats

Chapter 10

Willy purchased a '32 Ford coupe for two hundred dollars. I adjusted the spark plugs by slipping a dime in the gap and tapping it with a hammer. When the Mason City junkyard received a crashed '48 Ford with a perfectly good motor, Willy's dad picked that engine up for fifty bucks and we slipped it under the hood, making a true hot rod. I milled the heads down to boost the compression and Willy painted flames on the front.

With our big engine and flame paint we looked tough. But the car scraped anytime we accelerated hard or hit a dip. So cruising slow and racing the engine was as good as it got. The hard road to the west of town bumped up on a bridge far enough that we couldn't travel that way, and three miles south the gravel washed out so much that we didn't dare cruise there.

Carla wouldn't ride with us and we didn't know any other girls to ask. So now that we had wheels, bushwhacking became our favorite sport. Willy and I never switched to glasspak mufflers. That way we could sneak up quieter and bushwhack easier. All the guys who had dates parked on the empty shore south of Lake Poytawukie, called Lover's Lane. They chuckled about "watching the submarine races" there. We would let them sit for a while before we pulled up, headlights off, and bushwhack.

This meant one of three things.

First, if it was just Willy and me, he'd get the car turned in the opposite direction, about thirty paces away, engine running silent. We'd watch the car for ten minutes, unless their windows started fogging or the antenna swayed, indicated things were progressing faster. Then I'd creep to the side windows, stand up and shine a flashlight in, run back to Willy's car and we'd take off.

Since we were pointed away they never caught us. Once in a while some showoff chased us and we'd floor it until the first crossroad and switch off our headlights while turning left. They'd go straight through and we'd lose them. With the way Willy's car was lowered, there were only certain turns we could take, but nobody ever knew that.

Another trick required a gas can. Instead of popping up and shining a flashlight, I'd crawl around the car and trickle out gasoline in a circle around it, always staying twenty feet away. After splashing a little fuel all the way around, I'd toss a match and the flames jumped up about five feet high, making a big "crump" sound when it ignited. That fire lasted thirty seconds and lit up the area. Willy and I took off immediately, since the boy and girl inside usually got any loose garments back on pretty fast. Their car was safe from the flames but it took them some moments to realize that.

One time we caught Christina Dawson, the minister's daughter, playing kissy-face out there on her very first date.

She probably hadn't been parked for five minutes when that circle of fire illuminated the area.

Their heads popped up. Willy and I roared away.

Christina Dawson never dared to go on another date, all through high school.

The third bushwhacking tactic only worked when we had two cars. We'd just cruise right in next to them, one car on each side, turn on our lights and radios, and race the engines. They'd start their motor after zipping and buttoning fast, slap their car into reverse, stop, cramp their wheels, pop the clutch in low and fishtail through the gravel, spewing rocks all over our fenders. They never dared to jump out and threaten us since we outnumbered them.

Willy and I agreed over one thing and argued over another. We knew we would never park with a girl in the country like that. Any girlfriend of ours would be special for liking us, and we'd sit on their porch and go for walks and respectful drives, but never park.

But Willy grumbled one night while we cruised Main Street, saying we were both geeks, and shouldn't even think about having girlfriends. He said our Solemn Pact didn't mean a thing since no girl would ever ride around with either one of us.

"Who'd want any of those pretty girls anyway, Willy?" I asked.

He gave me a sad stare.

"They get spoiled," I said, "and when you and I find a couple of plain girls, they'll be easier to get along with anyway. We are lucky."

Willy just shook his head.

One night we pulled over to the Lover's Lane on the south shore of Lake Poytawukie and Willy spotted a Cadillac in the bushes. He turned our car around, pointing away from the dark blue vehicle.

"Moon, hand me the flashlight," he said.

"But you're the driver," I said. I handed him the flashlight.

"You try driving," Willy said, "I never get to peek."

He crept up alongside the Caddy, stood up, shined the flashlight in, ran back to our car and we took off. I drove a little slower than Willy but it didn't make any difference since the Cadillac didn't follow.

"Was Gloria inside?" I asked.

"No."

Our right wheels caught in the ditch, we stopped, I slid over and Willy jumped out, he ran around, hopped in behind the wheel, popped the clutch and freed us. We rocketed away.

"Could you tell who it was, Willy?"

"Uh, no."

"Did it look like Gloria?"

"Not. No Gloria."

"Then who, Willy?"

"Gloria, maybe."

I chuckled. "Who was she with?"

"I could not see."

"Willy, who would you guess?"

"I didn't see enough. Okay, I saw Gloria, the naked lady was Gloria."

"Gloria's a girl, Willy, not a lady."

"That's what said I, the girl was Gloria."

"No you didn't." We dropped the subject. Willy maintained fifty miles an hour and took several turns to be safe. Soon the red lights on top of the grain elevator appeared.

"Moon, your Mom left for Chicago to find a job?"

"Yes."

We pulled into Grundy Center.

"Moon, has you and your grandma gotten a letter?"

"No," I answered, "but that doesn't mean much, now does it? She struggles sometimes, but always figures a way, and it's just like her to not burden us with worry until she's landed something."

Willy rolled us to a stop in front of Grandma's and my duplex, slowly so the crunching gravel wouldn't wake her.

"That's pretty considerate of her, Willy, don't you see? When you look at it that way?" Willy stared ahead and said nothing. I got out.

"Moon?"

"Yeah Willy?"

"Oh forget it." I walked inside. Willy was acting strange, but this was fine. I have moods sometimes, so I tolerate that with others. Inside I noticed Grandma had taken the bubble lights down from around my Woodrow Wilson Scholarship plaque. We had decided to keep them up until I left for college, but maybe she decided to save the electricity, which I could understand. When I asked the next day Grandma glanced out the window.

"Don't taunt the authorities," she said, "make your way around them."

Two days later I had delivered ninety-two newspapers so there were five to go. The eastern sky glowed in the darkness.

What happened next proved the advantages of living without the distractions of a Chicago or New York. Some marketing genius evolves.

A buzzing came from the south when I crossed Main Street. It was too dark to make out, but a patch of sun illuminated the dust cloud chasing a dot up the road. I stopped. The noise grew. So did the cloud.

It seemed wise to get off the street so I edged toward Grifhorst's Drug Emporium and peeked around the corner. This thing in the road roared like some kind of motor and it gee-hawed back and forth, right and left, almost hitting each ditch. And it kept coming. In about two minutes the machine pulled into the center of town and I couldn't believe it. This was Willy's dad's old plane, reborn. The wings were still clipped off stubs where Hank the Tank met those power lines, the fuselage was painted red and the propeller roared, pulling it along while somebody steered it by braking either the right or left wheel. That crash must have snapped the cables to the tail as well, or whoever was driving could have steered with the rudder. It looked like the owner of our gas station driving, but was tough to see, then that new red paint on the side and the Texaco star told me that sure enough, that's who owned the machine now. He probably had been at Waldinger's implement yard south of town, fixing up the plane.

Grundy Center's gas station now had this unique advertisement, a wingless plane that would go to parades in the surrounding towns every summer and sometimes just zigzag down their main streets to remind folks of another place they could gas up.

Since there wasn't another station in Grundy Center, he didn't need to advertise locally. He just needed more of those surrounding community folks to come his way, instead of Coon Rapids or Bradgate or other places that had pumps.

He was a sale promotion whiz, some of Grundy Center's leaders said. Others shook their heads at that, and took a position that nobody could touch Mr. Hardcastle, who sponsored the "TURKEY DROP & COW PLOP" and did that handful of peanuts promotion for his grocery.

Willy discovered two car shows where his hot rod qualified as an entry. One was way off in Chicago and the other in Des Moines. Both charged a $10 fee to compete, so this was serious. They were scheduled for the same weekend.

"Tell you what, Willy, I like your car so well if we go to the Chicago show, I'll pay the entry fee."

"Really Moon?"

"Yup."

"You wouldn't go just to search for your..."

"Nope, the important thing is for your car to be seen in a big show."

Fortunately Willy couldn't pee if anybody else was in the bathroom with him. This meant we stopped twice as often on our Chicago trip; once for him and once for me. So I used that free long-distance information thing to write down all the Chicago phone number with initials that sounded like they might be Mom.

When Willy relieved himself in Oak Park at the Harold Johnson restaurant with that orange roof, I found the pay phone and checked all three numbers with the dimes I'd stuffed in my sock. Two weren't Mom. The other never answered.

When Willy used the D-X gas station in Elmhurst, I checked out four numbers in that town and eliminated two.

When Willy used an alley in Wheaton there weren't any pay phones nearby, so both of those numbers would have to wait. I checked them from the show later, but those calls cost me sixty cents each and neither one was Mom.

While Willy sampled the White Castle restaurant, I used their pay phone and eliminated all three numbers in Aurora that could have been Mom.

Of course when we left Chicago, after the car show, we had to stop again to empty our bladders, one at a time, and I faked a stop just to get near a phone where I needed to try a couple numbers again and told Willy I needed to call home, but it ended up that none of those numbers were Mom. So it cost another dollar and twenty cents to not find her, plus the ten dollars for the contest.

We didn't win anything at the car show, but a couple judges looked at Willy's car longer than necessary.

"Nice car," one said. The other judge nodded his agreement.

"It takes a great deal of Christianity to wipe out uncivilized Eastern instincts, such as falling in love at first sight."

Rudyard Kipling

Chapter 11

"Can you guess why they call it VEISHEA?" Mr. Nordstrud asked. He slapped a feather duster over his doorknob display, stepped around his cash register and patted my shoulder.

"Don't the first letters of Veterinarian medicine, Engineering, Industrial arts, Science, Home Economics and Agriculture spell VEISHEA?" he asked. VEISHEA was Iowa State's spring celebration. Students created floats for a procession that's over three miles long, second only to the Rose Bowl parade, without so many bands or horses. Each college put on demonstrations and visitors came from every county in the state.

"I've got to run down there tomorrow," Mr. Nordstrud said, "and it would sure be swell if you could ride along and help, Moon, could you spare me the time?"

I allowed as to how I could.

Mr. Nordstrud drove and we spent all day there. A college student took Mr. Nordstrud's watch in the Hall of Science, put it into this ultrasonic bath and we saw some dirt vibrate out from the wrist band that he didn't even know was there. They gave out small cherry pies at the Home Economics College, free. There was a steel ball, bushel-basket sized, on a cable, suspended from the ceiling about four stories up, right in the middle of Beardshear Hall. We could tell time by where that ball swung across the circle on the floor. I came back a couple hours later and sure enough, it was cutting that circle in a different spot, right on time. The earth's rotation did that.

The veterinarian department dissected a baby pig. Mr. Nordstrud agreed we didn't need to linger there. The agriculture field showed new hybrids of seed corn germinating.

Next week I started to write a report on my trip, but the school suddenly took on a new project. Everybody was assigned to write a paper describing why "Poytawukie" meant place "where deer drink" in Sioux. The Lake Poytawukie Chamber of Commerce promised a $25 savings bond to the best paper from each nearby school.

This was triggered by a Des Moines Register article on Lake Poytawukie, and their big city know-nothing reporter snooped around and came up with a different translation. He got some elder Indian, probably senile, to declare that "Potawuka," the original name, meant "Dead Skunk Waters" in Sioux.

His stupid story hinted that local businessmen knew that when they changed the spelling. Them Des Moines bigshots will stop at nothing to stomp on us little town guys.

Gloria's paper won. Doctor Throckmorton arranged for a Tama Indian to visit her for an interview and defend the translation of "Poytawukie." Tama Indians aren't Sioux, so that might have been fudging.

"Where's our plaque, Grandma?" After school I noticed that our plaque and its lights weren't decorating our home.

She wheezed and her glasses fell off. I picked them up and handed them to her.

"Did you move it, Grandma?"

She straightened out her glasses and tucked the wires behind her ears.

"It hung there long enough, young man. We were looking at it too much ourselves, so I loaned it to the church."

She coughed.

"Others may enjoy it there."

I liked that. I snuck in the church Monday, when nobody was around, but couldn't spot it. When I asked Grandma she got confused, but said she'd ask The Most Reverend Dawson where he hung it.

For Easter Willy got to go to PAG Church Camp at Lake Okoboji. There were kids there from all over Iowa. He invited me as his guest.

Lake Okoboji made Lake Poytawukie look shabby. There were so many trees around the shore that you could walk it all day without getting sunburned. We stayed in log cabins, boys and girls mixed with a minister in each.

On our first day we collected around the fire pit, all 300 Methodist kids from everywhere in Iowa, singing "Rock of Ages" while this blue-haired woman pounded out the music through their portable organ.

When she finished, a wild-eyed man stood in front and raised his arms.

"Amen," he said.

"Amen," everybody replied.

"Who loves you?" he asked.

"Jesus," we answered.

"Let me ask you this," he began, "have you ever met an escaped nun? If so, brothers and sisters, puhleez raise your hand."

Nobody moved a muscle.

"You see how they work? If a poor nun wants to escape, how can she?"

He slapped his thighs and stomped back and forth, shaking his head.

"They found nun skulls and pregnant skeletons all through the catacombs underneath Rome, children. Some strangled with their own rosaries."

He went on. It seemed biased, but that escaped nun question gave me something to ponder. I also worried about this and am sure that Dad saw the light, converting to Protestantism, before passing on.

Willy and I had prepared well for PAG Church Camp. We picked the lock on his dad's liquor cabinet and poured one inch of Kuypers creme de menthe in a mason jar, then another inch of Four Roses whisky, Manischewitz grape wine, Gilbey's gin, Blackbeard Rum and some kind of vermouth. Then we poured an inch of water back in each bottle, so Willy's dad wouldn't get upset by noticing. We sealed the top of the jar with tin foil, screwed the lid on tight and tucked it in the bottom of Willy's sleeping bag.

The Most Reverend Dawson arrived that afternoon, erupting when he saw me.

"God doesn't make mistakes," he said, leaning over me.

"Only the devil creates defects."

Apparently nobody had cleared my attendance with him.

"Why would we allow the dark side into a holy camp?"

I just did what I normally do, and tried to stay out of his vision. Usually our damp but Most Reverend Dawson buzzed all over, but this time he seemed different. He moved slower than usual, but I ducked him anyway. I didn't need to hear again about how my defect was "a slap from God's hand, due to the sin of my birth." It wasn't so bad when he shouted that stuff at me, but I didn't enjoy it when he preached so loud that others heard.

He dozed off early, and that jar of liquor tasted sweet, like liquid candy, except it burned.

Nobody spends much time thinking about toilets which is understandable. Sitting on the groaner is dignified in a strange way, since that may be the only privacy you experience with a door or curtain shut. But when the door is open and you're not sitting on the toilet but hanging your head down in it, retching your guts out, there's less dignity. If you considered how you appear from outside the room, rear in the air, face in the porcelain, it might humiliate a person beyond repair. The sting in your mouth and convulsions of the stomach keep one from fussing over lost pride. Everybody laughed about Willy's and my illness the next day but we learned a couple others did the same out on the grass, so we felt reasonable.

Luckily the Reverend Dawson was out of sorts that morning, slept until lunch and didn't see any of this.

A busload of Negro singers from the south sang that afternoon. It was nothing like a minstrel show. They sang louder and faster than you can imagine and stayed just one night in a separate cabin on the other side of the courtyard. Their music made me embarrassed by the half-live stuff we did.

A disabled girl, Ruthie, joined our cabin. You could hardly tell that she wasn't complete unless someone pointed it out. She almost kept up with that Negro choir. Ruthie's voice rang out crystal, piercing my bones until the marrow let loose with juices I'd never felt. Her voice, talking or singing, warbled like a bird. Her ponytail reached her belt, swaying when she walked, coffee colored with a single drop of cream. Each time Ruthie drifted into our cabin I became aware of nothing but her presence. Somehow she knew better than I when we were alone.

After lunch Ruthie mentioned that everybody was gone. I looked around and she was right.

"You smell nice," I said. I felt stupid right away.

Ruthie thanked me and said that the odor was vanilla. I stopped feeling like such a knucklehead. She tilted her head and that ponytail swung over a shoulder.

Ruthie asked what she should call me.

"Everybody calls me Moon."

Ruthie smiled, paused and asked me what I wanted her to call me.

I told her my name but said she could call me whatever she wanted, and I explained that everybody else knew I was an oddball, so if she didn't want to be around me, I'd understand and she could call me anything she wanted.

The amazing thing, I almost kept talking but Ruthie placed a finger on my lips so I stopped. Our cabin was still empty. She asked why I thought she might want to be with anybody else, and I nearly fainted.

"Well, most do, that is, Willy, who you met, doesn't and my Grandma pays lots of attention to me, but of course she has no choice. Mr. Nordstrud always helps."

Ruthie asked again why she should favor anybody else.

"Oh, lots of reasons, really, Ruthie, since I'm not so pretty and embarrass my town and yeah, I'm smart in school but the administration doesn't really like having me there so I don't know. Maybe I should leave."

She did it again. Placed one finger on my lips. I shut up. She asked me to stay. Her voice sounded more sing-song than talky, she said please and claimed that she wanted me to sit with her. I went light-headed.

After awhile, anytime the other campers might be around, talking and playing records, I wouldn't even realize it. For me, they vanished if she was near.

Ruthie asked me what I wanted her to call me again.

"Moon's okay."

She asked if I really meant that.

I'm embarrassed, but I have some pride and I lied.

"Yes. Moon's fine."

Ruthie knew chemical elements, could calculate square roots in her head and remembered all the words to "Diana," "Blue Suede Shoes," "Rockin Robin" and a million others. Her mother wouldn't let her wear perfume, which I understood, but Ruthie helped bake at home and got into the habit of dabbing vanilla behind her ears. Her mother never caught on to this, so

Ruthie had her perfume without getting into trouble.

She couldn't operate the oven, of course, being disadvantaged, but mixing the batter was easy for her.

Ruthie and I talked several times every day, which made Willy go cranky. One night while walking back from the vespers campfire, Reverend Dawson led the way. He sang Kumbaya and the others were right behind him. Ruthie and I lagged back so the Reverend would not get huffy with me.

I held Ruthie's hand to help her along. She didn't object.

Our cabin stood just ahead when The Most Reverend Dawson stopped singing and staggered in front of us. His knees folded, he sat on the grass for a second, tipped over and gasped. Willy ran for help. Reverend Dawson, leader of the John Wesley Pentecostal Redemption in Jesus Second Methodist Church, also known as Wesley Redemption Methodist, but never called WRM, left to commune with God before the nurse arrived. They carted his damp body off to the hospital in an ambulance, but there wasn't much point.

We all went back to our cabin.

We sat around without a chaperone. One of the girls said we might as well play spin the bottle. Ruthie and I, being not as normal, said we'd sit that out and watch, which they approved.

Willy glanced at me. I stared back. We nodded okay to each other. He and those other kids started playing post office and other kissing games.

It got dark out. PAG Church Camp didn't appear to have a plan for dead chaperones and we were alone. Somebody said we might get in trouble if we kept the lights on that late so we turned them out.

Ruthie whispered. I cannot reveal exactly what she said except that it involved her wanting to know if I thought she was attractive. I kind of stammered and said way too much back in reply, then felt like a complete dork until she asked another question.

This time Ruthie wanted to know if I thought I could like her, and wow, I started answering so fast and loud that she hushed me with a smile and my voice went squeaky just when I'd have given anything to sound deep and strong.

Ruthie whispered in my ear, and it felt like the base of my spine was jolted by electricity. She asked if I wanted to show her the porch.

We drifted out of the main room, unfolded the davenport and spread a blanket. She could tell, even in the dark, that the other kids were doing things, and we both felt more comfortable outside on our own. She could hear and smell what was going on inside, so we just stretched out in our own little area. Some things I had heard about but never understood became clear that evening with Ruthie helping me.

Gentle magic, that was.

If there was a way to keep that electricity forever I'd do anything for it.

The next morning all twelve of us, six boys and six girls, walked to breakfast. I guided Ruthie by holding her elbow, and before too many steps, she placed her other hand over mine. Her ponytail glittered like rusty nails flashing in sunlight, flouncing sideways with each step, and all I could smell was a vanilla heaven. Everybody kept quiet but we stuck together.

Willy's face flushed every time I glanced at him. I'd nod, he'd nod back. We were both amazed by what was happening, but our Solemn Pact was safe.

There were more sermons and singing but all I wanted was for night to come again. Ruthie too.

She whispered that she had no father, unlike me. I had at least met mine. Maybe that's why her mom was so strict.

We all probably sat too close together or kept our heads too low because this frowny woman in a blue dress with white dots and straw hat came to sit with us. She scrunched so many lines across her forehead that Willy said she must screw her hats on.

"You'll be well-supervised tonight," she said.

Before dinner some cars pulled up to our cabin. Mr. Scarletti bounced out of one, waved at me and said "Moon, you're going home," while somebody I didn't recognize headed toward Ruthie from the other car.

"Who's that?" I asked.

"I don't know," Ruthie answered. I had forgotten for a second that Ruthie was blind. After the woman spoke Ruthie told me it was her mom and that I must find a way to visit her in Pella, her hometown. I promised I would.

Willy's dad raised his voice when we returned early and stepped into his shop, but not because of anything we did at the camp.

"Boys, I don't mind you stealing the liquor," he said.

"But please stop diluting what's left for me with water, okay?"

Willy and I had a serious talk about our "Solemn Pact." We agreed that the girls we met at PAG Church Camp were wonderful, but not a threat to our friendship.

"Your Ruthie is a good girl," Willy said. His face flushed.

What a relief. What a pal. And Ruthie liked Willy too.

I saw Ruthie every week. Her mother acted okay with my presence, she even left us alone evenings in the living room and there was nothing ever like those times in this world.

It was a blessing that Ruthie was a Methodist. That eliminated a potential problem. The PAG Church Camp was a mixed Protestant group, so it could have been awkward between us. PAG stood for Protestants And God but the counselors had whispered that it really stood for Popes Aren't God.

Ruthie liked to touch my face.

"I sense your beauty," she said. Somehow Ruthie could tell how excited I got from across a room. She also knew when her mom was returning, which was a most convenient skill and saved us embarrassment.

"Do you think this is what they call spooning?" she asked.

"In Grundy Center I think it's called heavy petting, but, it's special for us, Ruthie, don't you think?"

She nodded. I always hid the Kleenex.

"What's this picture?" I asked after a session.

"Is it the one in the Kresge Deluxe frame?" Ruthie asked.

"Yes." I picked it up.

"That's Mom at her prom."

"Why is the photo cut in half?"

"That other side would have been my dad."

Her mother said it would be okay for Ruthie to visit me at Iowa State. I could describe the campus to her. She could help with Chemistry and Math. I could walk her to the campanile. She could tell me how different the sounds were when muffled by snow, what smells the spring breezes carried and we could make a tuna casserole together every Saturday. She knew how to cook better than me but, I could line up the ingredients for her and protect Ruthie from the stove.

One Saturday when I hitched over to Pella, Ruthie was gone, shipped off, to a special school on the east coast, wherever that is. I couldn't write her even, Ruthie being blind and telephoning that far cost a fortune.

"Moon, this is better for you both," Ruthie's mom said. She stood in their doorway, squeezing a dishrag.

"Better?" She was wrong, wrong, wrong. She said something about the dangers of cross-breeding two defects and some other stuff that made no sense. I didn't cry in front of her but ran down the street. After I got to the highway I squatted in the ditch and blubbered until no more spasms came, tried to look normal, stood next to the ditch and stuck out my thumb to go home.

Ruthie's father had run off when she was a baby. My chance to be the first dependable fellow in her life was ruined.

I worked at forgetting, but it took a long time. Maybe I should say it will take a long time, since I'm not yet cured and don't want to be.

I might remember her vanilla forever. And that ponytail, golden silky oak, drifted from side to side in my mind. I floated when her fingers ran across my forehead. You cannot imagine what it's like to be pretty and perfect and wonderful to someone who is all those things herself.

There was still Iowa State ahead, an excitement to consider, but Ruthie made me wish I could be two places at once. Or if I could live half as long, but hear the purity of her voice once a day, that would be a terrific trade.

Grandma started leaving earlier and returning later. I figured she wanted more time at school so my departure for college the next fall wouldn't be so abrupt.

I got home from school, fired up the stove and heard her car chug up the street. Her feet crunched the snow outside, and she struggled in.

"Grandma, I've been thinking."

"Yes, my lad."

"When I get to college, shouldn't I travel home every other weekend and tend to chores around here?"

This would make the change easier for Grandma, I was thinking.

"Wouldn't that make the adjustment smoother for me?" I asked.

Grandma unwound her scarf, jerked off one galosh in our boot jack, nodded, yanked off the other, unbuttoned her coat, hung it on the rack and plopped into her chair.

"And whichever of us hears from Mom first," I said, "should call the other one immediately, no matter what the long distance charge is."

Grandma looked weary.

"Maybe you shouldn't be so all-fired up about college," she said, so I hushed up and stoked our stove.

Two weeks before graduation Mr. Scarletti asked me to stop in his office after class. I wondered all day what he had in mind. Maybe it would be a special honor for my winning the scholarship. The school might want to brag that up a little at a ceremony.

Willy slugged my shoulder just before I turned into Mr. Scarletti's doorway. I would've popped him back but it seemed like a time to be on better behavior. When I passed the secretary she jumped up and scurried into the hall. This took away some of my cockiness, but not all of it. Since I'd be gone in two weeks, not much mattered now. Mr. Scarletti motioned for me to sit. I did. He strolled to the door, shut it with both hands, turned, shuffled back and sat. He didn't say a thing. He brushed a piece of invisible lint from his sleeve.

"What can I do for you, Mr. Scarletti?"

"Moon, in the big picture, we all must recognize our strengths and weaknesses." He stared at the top of his desk. "You, my boy, possess plenty of each."

"Thank you, sir."

"Moon, I report to a Board of Education, headed by very prominent citizens of Grundy Center. The Board must always consider the good of our town in all things. Sometimes this affects individuals." He bent and straightened a paper clip.

"Just like the rest of us, Moon, you'd sacrifice personal ambitions for the good of our community, if asked, right?"

"Yes, Mr. Scarletti."

"Well good. You will understand what I must tell you. We had a difficult meeting with the Board of Education. Your community is concerned for your safety in the world and how your presence affects the reputation of our good town."

"I'll study hard, sir."

"Not quite, Moon." He straightened another paper clip.

"What do you mean, Mr. Scarletti?"

He turned sideways and dropped the paper clip on the floor, bent over, retrieved the clip and placed it in his wastebasket.

"Awarding a graduation certificate requires the approval of the school board. What I must tell you today, and there is a good side to this, is that the board did not vote in favor of your graduation."

I didn't fall over or slide off the chair, I don't think, but my eyes kind of rolled up and for a second I couldn't see or hear.

"We told your Grandma about this some time back."

When a surprise hits you, the thing goes away for a spell and then surges back, like winds in a rainstorm or those larger waves on Lake Poytawukie. It doesn't matter if the shock is good or bad. There must be something in our brain that protects us and doesn't let any blast straight in.

"What do you mean, Mr. Scarletti?"

"Look at your failure to graduate, Moon, as the golden opportunity to become a Park Ranger. Or we can arrange to get you a night job in Marshalltown at the clinic Doctor Throckmorton influences. You could take some smaller daytime classes and not disrupt anybody as much."

I tried to consider what he said but felt so dizzy my main thought was to avoid falling off the chair.

"You were helpful, Mr. Scarletti, showing me those possibilities. But I think with the scholarship and all I'll go ahead and attend Iowa State."

Mr. Scarletti looked for another paper clip in his drawer.

"But you see, Moon, that Woodrow Wilson thing, which was a loan, not a scholarship, by the way, is only good if you are admitted. Without our diploma you cannot and will not get into Iowa State. And I am afraid you are going to turn out bad if you cannot learn to cooperate."

"Why can't I graduate?" I wish I'd said that better, not sounding so pitiful, but I couldn't help it just then.

"Why?"

"Well, mostly Moon, you see in a caring community like Grundy Center, we all know each other better than some metropolis like Ames or a sprawling campus like Iowa State. And the board members worry that such a change and so many people who are not used to you, like we are, could cause harm."

Forget the rest of what he and I said, because he just kept going around like that and I got whiny and my voice cracked just when I hoped it would go deep and strong. I walked out without saying good-bye or thank you, drifting home so Grandma could explain what had happened.

She wasn't home. I guessed she was still working at school, but that's the last place I wanted to visit right then.

It took three hours to hitch a ride to Pella. I strolled past Ruthie's house, slowly, so I could look at her window. From behind a bush I watched her mother washing dishes. Their kitchen doorway swung half open, swaying in the wind and drizzle.

I smelled vanilla. I started walking so nobody would see me and get nervous, circling the block and passed her house again and again, glancing up at Ruthie's dark window. For an instant I froze when the light clicked on in Ruthie's room, but her mom walked over, pulled the curtains inside, shut the drapes, walked away and the room darkened.

I walked back to the main road when I spotted a girl several blocks away. My eyes aren't so sharp at a distance, so I couldn't be sure, but her leathery ponytail danced as she walked.

I ran ahead.

She turned into a house and shut the door before I got close.

I stood outside, wondering what to do.

She began to sing, and I could hear her from outside. It was pretty, but an alto, not Ruthie's soprano and that hair was probably one shade too dark anyway. I walked away.

Getting back to Grundy Center took four hours. It was midnight and raining, a warm, light rain.

Grandma wasn't home.

This had never happened.

Grandma was always there.

I couldn't sleep, so I walked, paced around Willy's house once and drifted home for a slicker after I realized my shirt and pants were drenched and my hair was plastered flat by the rain. I passed the Wesley Redemption

Methodist Church and looked around but Grandma's car wasn't there. As I neared the school a flu bug hit me and I threw up. Since I'd forgotten to eat not much came out, but I heaved and gagged up stomach acid until my eyes watered. Grandma's car sat behind the school, but the light was out in her work room, so I dragged home.

Lying on my bed, I stared into the ceiling until sunshine peeked around our curtains, brightening the room. I rolled out and walked back to school in my same clothes. Nobody was there except the janitor. He was a slow guy, Grandma called him "lightning," but that morning he sprinted back and forth, trying to get someone on the phone. I walked into the front door and headed back for Grandma's classroom.

"Moon, don't go there," he said, too late.

Her door was open and Grandma was lying draped across her chair, behind the desk, mouth open. She gripped the Woodrow Wilson Scholarship plaque in her left fingers. Normally she carried it with both hands, one under each corner, like an item for the altar, but this time she clutched it in one cold hand. Her other arm wrapped around a chair leg.

Mom was gone. Now Grandma left me. Maybe Grandma and Grandpa could make peace with Dad in the Protestant Kingdom, play Canasta and Cribbage while listening to angels sing.

There were five bouquets at Grandma's wake. One came from out of town since all the local flowers were used up for her special day of remembrance. We didn't have a replacement minister yet, so the Methodist preacher who worked Hayfield and Titonka came over and brought that extra batch of flowers. He charged five bucks, which I didn't have, but he drove me home and I gave him a lamp with a good bulb. It was a genuine Sears model. I told him the catalog classified it as "good" quality and the minister looked satisfied. Sears offered "good," "better" and "best" for much of their items, but the "good" was what we went for. Doctors probably bought the "best." You can light a room with any of them.

Mr. Nordstrud walked over with two Cokes. We sat outside on the step to drink them.

"Moon, could you join me on a drive tomorrow?"

"Sure."

"There are some things I need to check on in Ames, and I could use your expertise."

"Okay."

"I could pick you up at seven, Moon. Would that work?"

"Fine."

Mr. Nordstrud handed me a cardboard box saying he thought I might have a use for it. I tore it open after he left and just before Willy stopped by. There was a large piece of canvas in it with grommets around the edge. There was a note from Mr. Nordstrud, explaining that this was "All Weather" canvas with a special wax in the threads. It would last much longer than the previous fabric, his note said. So Willy drove me back out to the graves. Grandma rested right next to Grandpa in the Protestant section. Willy and I staked out that tarp over them. It may not have been necessary, but for sure they'd have a dry summer.

"What you will do?" Willy asked.

His question grew bigger the more I thought about it. Mr. Scarletti grumbled that I had already waited too long for the Park Service this year. And the Marshalltown night job was also gone.

"You wasted that opportunity Moon," Mr. Scarletti said, "I hope this is not the beginning of a bad ending for you."

Our landlord came by and said we could work out something and that if I needed a few days to decide, that was fine.

"No more than a week, of course," he added. He promised not to squawk if I stayed all seven days, but would appreciate it then if I'd mow his lawn.

Willy thought the shed behind their house might hold a bed, and with a kerosene heater, might be some kind of new adventure for us. I could use their bathroom for a free newspaper. We looked into the shed, but you could tell his mother had the fidgets. She was canning tomatoes and green beans for the winter, so naturally would be going back and forth a lot, but even so, she peeked out their back window about three million times too often, so we figured that idea was going nowhere.

Mr. Nordstrud picked me up in his '55 Chevy. It turned out that he needed to deliver some hand tools to Iowa State. He's a decent promoter when you think about it, getting business from fifty miles away.

In Ames we stopped by the maintenance warehouse. Mr. Nordstrud took me to the front office and introduced me to the manager. He showed me around while Mr. Nordstrud went back to the car and opened his trunk.

"Got a problem with that contrary bolt on the lawn mower," the manager said, "any idea how we could fix it?"

"No problem sir," I said. I squirted some gasoline on it to cut the rust.

"May I borrow that crescent wrench, mister?"

The manager handed it to me.

"There." The bolt twisted loose.

"Clever," he said.

"Well, sir, that's not enough. Now it'll rust even more unless we squirt some oil back on it." He handed me an oil can and I did. I also lubricated the threaded hole.

"You are one sharp mechanic, boy," he said. I thanked him.

Mr. Nordstrud and I said our good-byes and drove away. This gave me an ache, being near that campus and not even seeing Beardshear Hall or a classroom. But I told myself it was better this way, since I knew if I looked at the school and remembered Ruthie and Grandma all at the same time it would be a combination of black dog thoughts I could never pull out of. I asked Mr. Nordstrud what tools he sold them. He said nothing much. It must not have been since his car didn't ride any different.

My newspaper truck dropped my bundle off at 5:40 the next morning, about ten minutes late. Pictures of Mr. Richard Milhaus Nixon and Mr. John Fitzgerald Kennedy debating spread across the front. Folks said Mr. Nixon did well on the radio but looked unshaven on television. Most worried about Mr. Kennedy being a fish-eater. They said America would be under Rome's thumb if Kennedy were President. I delivered the papers and ate a bowl of Cheerios. Our milk had spoiled. The Cheerios didn't taste so great with water.

Before Mom left town she had warned me to avoid Doctor Throckmorton. She said I shouldn't upset him. But I didn't care any more. Emperor Throckmorton MD and his wavy mop of permanent-treated hair, draped over a head that never won a Woodrow Wilson Scholarship could go to heck. Sure enough, when I trudged past his castle Doctor Throckmorton saw me through his picture window and motioned. I trudged over. He drifted across his covered porch, crossed both arms and frowned.

"Moon, when it took you so interminably long to pay for those skis, did I ever complain?"

"My memory is that you only mentioned it five or six times, Doctor Throckmorton."

He gazed at me that way that he often did, not moving. I stared back and only blinked once.

"Most folks, Moonboy, would not let you get away with that impudent comment." He went on about how grieved he felt that my Grandma passed on. I tried not to, really hard, but standing there with nothing, I couldn't help it, and I sniffled. I had no place to live anymore. My throat made little squeaky noises. Not loud, but my face wrinkled and tears ran. I needed money. If I started spending my college cash, I might never get there. I choked down the sobs so he couldn't see that deep into my hurting, but my chin and lips kept flickering in ways I couldn't manage.

"Moon, we all have times to live and times to die. Yours may be shorter than average, due to your affliction." He smiled.

"I never thought it was right that our town calls you Moon. To me, your head looks more like a comma. Shouldn't we change your name to Comma?" Doctor Throckmorton asked.

I couldn't answer.

"Your Grandma had three score and two years of life," he said.

If I could have turned and run, I would have, but things might get worse if I didn't pay attention. I went into a kind of trance, like I was somewhere else, hearing his words but not feeling them.

"You shall never, ever set eyes on your mother again, Moon, and you should realize what a blessing that is for her."

Some black ants were digging a new tunnel in front of my toes.

"Your Grandmother could have lived another ten years, Moon, but my suspicion is that your failure to get into college broke her heart, yet I wish you no harm."

One of the ants carried something white, about twice his size into the hole.

"You cause problems everywhere, Moon. You may not mean to, but that does not solve the problem, does it?" He walked inside.

Jesus.

I stepped on the ants.

Doctor Throckmorton ruled the school board. They decided Grundy Center shouldn't give me a diploma. Okay, it was my failure to get into Iowa State. Nobody else. That didn't perk up Grandma. And Iowa State certainly required a high school diploma. I found that rule mentioned fourteen different times in the Iowa State Catalog.

“To travel hopefully is a better thing than to arrive.”

Robert Louis Stevenson

Chapter 12

Maybe the world always bounces from good to bad. Or could it just be that jealous people swat at you when you're up, while the better people lend a hand when you're down? I don't know which. But Mr. Nordstrud asked if I knew why that maintenance manager in Ames asked about me.

"No, Mr. Nordstrud, I don't."

He stood behind his counter, wiping the crowbars, hammers and saws with an oily rag.

"Well, Moon, wasn't he impressed with the way you repaired that mower bolt? Hmm. Didn't I coat these tools just a month ago? See where a couple of them got rust spots, that'll keep me busy, huh? Anyway, you suppose they need talent like yours?"

"I don't know, Mr. Nordstrud. Gee, maybe. Well, I don't know. Could be, Mr. Nordstrud." Even at seventeen, sometimes I answered weird, especially if the question made me excitable. If they wanted to hire me, and if only they only had hired me a month before, Grandma would be proud. I'd be respectable. She'd be alive.

In the troubled pie of life, somebody served Grandma a large slice. My arrival, unplanned and all, destroyed her for a moment, but she fought back. Mom and Grandpa too. My failure to make college might have knocked Grandma over the edge. Sometimes when I'm alone, without Willy or anybody around, I'll look in a mirror at the way the side of my head kind of bends in on the right and how my eyes don't quite line up. And instead of wishing I wasn't so noticeable, I think about the problems I create and realize that maybe I am supposed to be made different.

"The Lord marked Cain just as the Almighty damaged Moon," Reverend Dawson said, "sin and it shall be shown."

Yet here was one more piece of luck, like the world wanted to give me another chance, with that maintenance manager from Iowa State possibly planning to hand me a career.

Mr. Nordstrud interrupted my thoughts. "Can you believe this? How could I forget part of Iowa State's order? Serves me right, doesn't it, that now I have to drive back tomorrow, alone? Care to tag along, Moon?"

"Yes, Mr. Nordstrud, yes, of course, okay."

Mr. Nordstrud and I washed his '55 Chevy the next morning so we'd look professional. He brought home a new jar of Turtle Wax from the store and we wiped off the water drips with a chamois. Then we rubbed in the wax. By the time we finished coating it, the wax had caked white where we started, so we tore up some worn out bed sheets and wiped it off.

"Moon?"

"Yes, Mr. Nordstrud?"

"Can we keep this trip secret?"

"Sure thing."

"When you finish delivering your papers, you end up in the south part of town, right Moon?"

"Yes."

"Would it be okay if I pick you up there, so nobody sees us?"

"Sure, Mr. Nordstrud."

It turned out Mr. Nordstrud wanted me to learn more about the college, but suspected a certain, prominent Grundy Center citizen wouldn't encourage this. I understood.

Cars from 1955 kept some status even when they weren't the newest. Those models were the first with hooded headlights. Before 1955, if you wanted "eyebrows," they called them, you had to build them yourself. I only saw that in magazines. But in 1955, Chevrolet, Ford and Plymouth all came out with hooded headlights as standard. They also, all three brands, introduced two-tone paint jobs where the color changed on the sides with chrome strip dividers, not just a roof of one color and body of a different shade. That was a great car year.

When Mr. Nordstrud and I rolled into the Iowa State maintenance warehouse, it wasn't like we were clinging to some tractor. We looked like folks deserving attention. The manager sauntered out and came to my side of the car instead of Mr. Nordstrud's. We stepped into the warehouse. This place was bigger than a house. It required two space heaters. They had welding equipment, hoists, a paint area, two machining tools and a grease pit.

When the manager asked me if I'd like to try working there awhile, I said yes.

"Don't you want to know about the pay?" he asked.

"Yes, sir," I replied.

"This is a state job, Moon, and it starts at $2.35 an hour. After a year, if you develop machining skills so your job class can be upgraded, you're eligible for an increase. Forty hours a week, time and a half overtime."

"Sir, what does time and a half mean?"

He explained. I asked what the seasonality was and when I might be laid off. He kind of smiled, and said there would be forty hours every week. Non-stop. You never got fired, he meant. I glanced over at Mr. Nordstrud and he nodded like I could trust that comment, which seemed stupendous, but Mr. Nordstrud never let me down.

I took the job.

While driving back to Grundy Center Mr. Nordstrud cautioned me that cities are different and I'd need to watch myself, as if I didn't understand that. But he told me not to go spending that $2.35 an hour, no matter how fat it sounded, since my rent would be shockingly higher, picture shows would cost fifty to seventy-five cents and taxes would take huge bites from those paychecks before I even saw the money.

"You know, Moon, it's not just the prices?"

"What else, Mr. Nordstrud?"

"Moon, did you ever see so many more ways a city can take your money? In Grundy Center the carnival only comes to town for what, three days every August? There, didn't that Iowa State calendar show something going on every weekend? Did you realize their restaurants are open every day, some of them for twelve hours? How can owners live like that, can you imagine?"

I nodded. These questions made me wobbly.

It's kind of embarrassing but it happened again. Mr. Nordstrud pulled over and I got the window down before throwing up. Some of it hit the side of his door; I grabbed a rag from the trunk and cleaned it off. With the new wax job, no damage was done. The humiliating thing was that Mr. Nordstrud didn't drive but another ten miles before I spit up another time.

When I said it happened again, well, when Doctor Throckmorton drove me to Woodward I got this same stomach upset and vomited inside the ambulance, which soured him. When Gloria slapped me, I didn't get sick just then, or even when Willy and Carla and I rode home. I never upchucked in front of them. Only when I was alone.

"Might your jumpy stomach, Moon, come from travel? Shouldn't I run you by Doctor Throckmorton?"

"If you can stay, Mr. Nordstrud."

"Do you want me to?" He drove us right to the doctor's palace.

"Can you believe this kid got a new job?" Mr. Nordstrud asked.

Doctor Throckmorton's eyebrows rose.

"Yup, isn't it a surprise?" Mr. Nordstrud asked.

Doctor Throckmorton grunted.

"How this happened," Mr. Nordstrud said, "is beyond me, but can you believe he'll be a janitor in Ames, on the campus?"

It seemed to me that Mr. Nordstrud had something to do with my getting the job, but I said nothing.

"I'll bet you're not surprised, are you Doc? Isn't it understandable why Moon got sick?"

Older, professional men in Grundy Center called Doctor Throckmorton Doc.

He whispered something to Doctor Throckmorton. Doctor Throckmorton whispered something to Mr. Nordstrud. Doctor Throckmorton handed me a bottle of white pills; tiny ones, smaller than aspirins and each one had a small line indented across it. He told me to take one the day before leaving for Ames and one every day until my body adjusted to the changes.

"You can stop taking them when you return," Doctor Throckmorton said.

"If I come back, Doctor Throckmorton."

"You shall return, sadly, with that bent head hanging down," Doctor Throckmorton said.

"Can you imagine my surprise, Doc, over this whole thing?" Mr. Nordstrud asked.

I told Doctor Throckmorton I would take a pill a day until I adjusted. Since I would leave for Iowa State tomorrow I swallowed one right there. Doctor Throckmorton said Ames and Grundy Center might have different germs and travel always presented risks. I saw him wink at Mr. Nordstrud. I mentioned that Iowa State sure seemed different than Grundy Center. Doctor Throckmorton corrected me and said I was going to Ames for work, not Iowa State, which could be argued either way but I didn't bother. Mr. Nordstrud asked how much the pills cost. Doctor Throckmorton said eight dollars. I noticed the label said "samples. . .not for sale" but I didn't bring that up. I was escaping. Mr. Nordstrud talked privately with Doctor Throckmorton and either paid the eight dollars himself or talked Doctor Throckmorton out of the charge. It was smartest to give the King his royalties in Grundy Center. I offered to pay Mr. Nordstrud but he claimed Doctor Throckmorton forgave the bill. I wonder. If either of us had known another physician anywhere, we would have gone to that doctor instead. We left.

"Moon, do you know how lucky it was for me that you tagged along yesterday?" He turned towards my home. "While you were talking to the maintenance manager, I met some of the other workers there, and guess what? Can I suggest they're a group you'll enjoy? And do you know how reassuring that is to me? But best of all, they've got some screwdrivers with heads so chewed up they do almost as much damage as good and their new budget allows them to buy another set, so I wrote an order right there, is that fortune smiling on me or what?"

That Mr. Nordstrud is one sharp cookie. We parked in front of my place.

"Guess what? That means I need to drive down to deliver again tomorrow. Care for a lift? You've got to get there somehow."

Mr. Nordstrud picked me up at noon. That morning was frantic, telling the landlord I'd be leaving, calling my boss at the Des Moines Register to let him know who would take over my route, packing my clothes in a box and taking my Woodrow Wilson Scholarship plaque over to Willy to save for me.

Willy was changing the u-joint in his car. He scooted out from under it, but his hands and face were covered with grease, so I stuck my plaque on his garage workbench.

"So I'll see you soon, Willy."

"I hope so." He looked at the wrench in his hand.

"We're still best pals."

"Forever."

"Remember our Solemn Pact?" I took a step backward.

"Sure." He sat on the garage floor. I stood in the doorway.

"See you soon."

"Take it easy."

"You too."

"See you around."

"Yeah. Don't work too hard."

I trudged off. Willy pulled himself back under the car.

I stopped at the corner to glance back. Willy stood with his hands in his pockets, watching me. I waved once, kind of a weak single swing of the hand. He nodded.

Mr. Nordstrud said he mentioned my new career to Mr. Grifhorst, the druggist, and Mr. Grifhorst packed up some toothpaste, a razor, shaving cream, a deodorizer stick, a comb and a toothbrush as going away gifts. When we pulled out Mr. Nordstrud drove a couple blocks out of the way, past Carla's house. He honked. Her dad staggered out and blinked at us, and then she stepped to the doorway.

"See this success story heading for Iowa State?" Mr. Nordstrud asked. Carla's dad turned around and stumbled back inside. Carla waved and smiled.

"Cool, Moon, go daddy-o," she said. I waved back and we accelerated toward my future, with Mr. Nordstrud's tires growling through the gravel. Right away I told Mr. Nordstrud not to worry about his wax job since I had taken another pill that morning. Everything seemed distant like I was watching myself do stuff instead of actually doing it and things happened slower.

Even though it was dreamy that day, I thought back about Carla and how she looked, waving at us as we pulled away, and how she cheered for me after not talking to me for so long and I wondered if she and Willy would get together.

If they did, could I still be their good friend?

Mr. Nordstrud said I should never take more than one pill a day. Being woozy I wrote that down for a future reminder, but I misplaced the note.

Carla sure looked pretty when she waved and smiled.

Mr. Nordstrud said when the supply ran out my body would probably be adjusted to the different germs at Iowa State. Then it wouldn't be necessary to take any more, he guessed, and thought these pills helped adapt to change, but could be dangerous if taken too long.

"They're like a crutch," he said, "necessary while you heal. But like a crutch, they weaken you if used too long."

Mr. Nordstrud drove three blocks east of Main Street, on gravel. I guess he didn't want certain people to see us leaving. He pulled back onto paved road near the south of town and we screeched away.

I heard his tires spin but fell asleep with my head kind of bouncing against his side window. When we pulled back into Ames, I woke. It felt different this time. Maybe these trips made me sophisticated. When we rolled below the underpass and out towards the college, on that four-lane road, I didn't get jumpy. I saw all this excitement again but like it was a motion picture instead of real and felt no urge to upchuck.

"What are you thinking, Moon?"

"It's embarrassing, Mr. Nordstrud."

"Can you tell me?"

"Mr. Nordstrud, somehow this puts my life on track. If I pay attention to what you told me, and save some money, I can find Mom in a couple years."

"You think so, Moon? Is it possible that might not be a good thing?"

"And Mr. Nordstrud, there's this girl, Ruthie, we really got along but her family moved her east and maybe I could find her and just possibly we could..."

"Moon, can our dreams be better than what we discover?"

We talked about that, and Mr. Nordstrud suggested I just do a good job and see what happens.

It turned out that the pill bottle contained enough for my first month. Mr. Nordstrud said he was due back in Ames about then, would stop by and we could go out for a pizza. I asked what that was. He explained and it sounded weird. You didn't even use a fork, he claimed.

"Mr. Nordstrud, can you tell Willy that you and I will be eating a pizza?" I asked.

"Sure Moon, anything else?" He patted my head. Nobody ever did that before.

"Could you explain pizza to Willy, Mr. Nordstrud?" He said he would. Mr. Nordstrud explained that besides rent another big expense in the city would be clothes since I'd be expected to change shirts every day. But Iowa State set up a clothing budget for new hires to ease their adjustment. I would get enough shirts and pants and socks for a full week of work, plus an extra set of shoes. All paid for.

We parked right in front of the JC Penney store on the south side of main, strolled in and a friendly guy walked up to Mr. Nordstrud, looking away from me. Mr. Nordstrud explained what I'd need. This sales person, who wore a Sunday suit despite it's being a Thursday, decided we could try more things easier if we left the main floor. He put me in a closet with a shrunken door that didn't even reach halfway to the floor or the ceiling and handed clothes over it for me to try.

Mr. Nordstrud figured seven shirts, two pants, seven pairs of socks and under shorts with one new set of shoes would fit my budget. All this filled three bags.

The salesman asked if this would be cash or check.

I explained that it all charged to "the Iowa State introductory clothing budget for new workers from out of town."

Maybe he wasn't as bright as his clothes. The guy gawked until Mr. Nordstrud took him aside by the arm and whispered a couple things until the salesman understood. I carried the bags to the car while Mr. Nordstrud further explained to that fellow how this clothing budget worked with Iowa State.

We went to my room which Mr. Nordstrud had set up two blocks south of Lincoln Way. I could easily walk over to the warehouse in any kind of weather. My room had a washbasin and hot plate. The toilet and tub was just a few steps down the hall. They called the bed a Queen, it was so big, but Mr. Nordstrud assured me it was okay for a guy to sleep on. I felt nervous in it the first few nights. My window looked over the ag fields.

A Mt. Rushmore painting decorated one wall while a red and yellow Iowa

State flag draped over the other. They called these colors "Cardinal and Gold" in Ames. The painting probably cost some money since the figures stood out in three dimensions from the black velvet background. The bureau had four drawers, so everything I owned could be tucked out of sight.

For $25 per month the sheets got changed every week or for $22 they switched linen monthly. I took monthly, of course. No reason to go whole hog.

I couldn't find the cord to pull on the light the first night when I took a bath. The soap didn't seem to lather either. The next morning I studied the bathroom and discovered the light switch was built into the wall. The soap hadn't lathered for me because it was store-bought and still in the wrapper.

Mr. Nordstrud surely understood the price of city living. There were all kinds of costs you wouldn't think of. First was the Laundromat, and since I didn't know how much bleach to use all my new shirts got splotchy by the third week. A bag to carry the laundry cost seventy-five cents at the campus bookstore. It pained me to see the same laundry bag at JC Penney's downtown a month later for only fifty cents. You've got to watch city people. They're slicker than goose droppings. On the other hand, the downtown bus costs a dime, roundtrip, and the bookstore was an easy walk, so that wasn't a total loss.

The first day of work, Friday, I forgot my pill and sure enough, some germ got me and I went dizzy and sick just outside the maintenance shed, but nobody saw.

We spent that first day getting to know the tools. Those machines were the likes you'd never see, except maybe at Waldinger's Implement yard, and even Waldinger's were smaller. If I could learn to handle this stuff, I could sure go back and show everybody a thing or two in Grundy Center. Well, maybe I couldn't show them since the town doesn't have any machinery this big, so I'd have to tell them. That, however, would be bragging and they might not believe it. I'd just make sure Mr. Nordstrud saw me running these giant machine tools so he could tell the town himself.

Maybe Mr. Nordstrud would see Doctor Throckmorton strutting down the street.

"Nice morning, huh, Doc?" he'd ask.

Doctor Throckmorton would nod, without stopping.

"Have you heard, Doc, how Moon's doing so surprisingly well?" Mr. Nordstrud would be careful with his words. Doctor Throckmorton would keep on walking and say nothing back.

Since I was learning to work with sheet metal, I might form a piece into a scoop shovel for Grundy Center and chrome plate it. Then I might engrave "Grundy Center, Finest Town, In the State" on the handle. Mom's piano customers would recognize that phrase. Word would get around.

Hank the Tank would carry this scoop shovel onto Main Street for the "TURKEY DROP & COW PLOP" ceremony.

"Citizens," he'd say, "we have an official city scoop shovel this year."

He'd read the inscription. The crowd would clap. And without Hank the Tank or Doctor Throckmorton even knowing it, pretty soon those music students and their parents would whisper things about Moon, and Doctor Throckmorton would hold up his hands for silence but it wouldn't work and he wouldn't understand what was going on right in front of him.

Since I forgot to take my pill that first day, and the Ames germ hit me, I puzzled over it and decided to take two on Saturday, sort of knock that thing out. But it had me, that germ, because about an hour after taking the two pills I could barely walk and by ten in the morning I went back to bed and didn't wake up until Sunday. On the Sabbath I took just one pill and everything went okay.

Monday went perfect. I hoped work would never end. But we were finished at five, my manager said. I ground the valves on a campus truck, and did all sixteen just right, well, maybe lost a little temper on one, where the blue color on the edge appeared, but not much and that engine purred when we finished. Quitting time came.

"Thanks for your help today, Moon," my manager said. He was walking straight to me, wiping the grease from his hands and arms with a red shop rag.

"Thank you sir," I said, "thank you for letting me work here." I stood straight and reached out to shake his hand.

"The pleasure, Moon, was all ours." We shook. I got thanked for a day's work, unbelievably, and made almost twenty bucks for it.

Tuesday we had to clean out a boiler. This got nasty. There were scales of rust all over the insides with a calcium buildup. I crawled in with a steam hose and blasted away until most of it was gone. My manager and I looked at the inside and tried to figure what was best to protect it. We sprayed sulfuric acid in there; you wouldn't want to breathe that for long, to dissolve the remaining calcium. Problem is this stuff ate the metal too. After flushing it out, we agreed a thick coat of Rust-Oleum was about as good as we could do. This was far cheaper than porcelainizing the inside, although it wouldn't last as long.

Pretty soon my manager and I did stuff like that every day. It was like me and Willy figuring out how to water-ski, except I got paid. How good can things get?

There was a challenging task, however. My next chore took place in the armory. This was where graduation, basketball, wrestling and ROTC drills took place. The first day they sent me to the armory I knew I was in trouble the instant I stepped inside. You could park six locomotives inside, without interrupting the basketball practice. I was supposed to sweep the floor. The team practiced on one half while I swept the other side.

But when I slipped through the door, first the noise, then the hugeness made me woozy.

Until that moment, I had believed we played basketball in Grundy Center. But this game wasn't recognizable. There was this chirping that didn't stop, like a sparrow chorus, until I realized it was the rubber shoes on twenty feet jumping, stopping, and turning on hard maple, every second, creating that sound.

I couldn't count Catholics because all they did was practice. If they'd played a game, you could tell because the Catholics crossed themselves before each free throw.

I got through that day okay after realizing the trick was to stare at the floor ahead, not glancing down court, never study the ceiling, far wall or anything distant. In Grundy Center you could never see that far inside. With all that echoing and squeaking, I could faint. So I studied things nearby. There were two more days of work there and the second day I swept the bleachers. Keeping my eyes down and remembering my pill worked. I didn't get sick.

I started to wonder if those white pills might not be so much for germs as for nervousness. So for that third day a couple of pills did the trick. My worry was that on the third day I had to set up two thousand folding chairs on the floor for a ceremony. They were to be set up straight, requiring that I stretch out a string to align them. This meant looking a long way across a lot of chair legs, further than I ever did before. Surely a sick spell would follow.

I took two pills and that seemed to work. But I had to stay until 8 pm to get the chairs all done and when they were finished they faced the wrong direction. My manager said it wasn't much of a problem to put the podium on the other end, so everything worked out, which was a relief.

Finally I got to spend Friday at the warehouse, and soldered cable connections all day, one of the most fun jobs there is. Being there in the warehouse, without unfamiliar people noticing, just doing something I knew, relaxed me. I only took one pill that day, but by noon, a little edginess swept over me, so I walked back to my room during lunch, eating my sandwich on the way.

Part of my room deal was that I got a section of the refrigerator for my stuff. If I wanted soup or a hot dog for dinner, I could manage that in style with the hot plate in my room. I pulled the pill bottle out of my underwear drawer and swallowed two. For a moment things got a little tense, since I forgot to pour a glass of water and choked. After sprinting down the hall to for a glass of water, it was okay and I headed back to the warehouse.

My manager's face was the second thing I saw, after the ceiling tiles of the college hospital.

"You awake, Moon?" he asked, looking scared.

I wanted to apologize, but didn't have the energy.

It was the next morning, I had missed work and they found me in a dead sleep with the alarm run down. How bad can things get? The best job in the world and already I screwed up. I tried to roll out of the hospital bed and did but my legs wouldn't hold up, so I tumbled across the floor, looking pathetic.

By noon my head came back, so I scrubbed up and ran over to that warehouse. When I stumbled through the door, my manager nodded at me.

"What do you want me to do?" I asked.

He eased into the chair at his desk.

"I'm ready to work."

He smiled.

"Anything you want, sir?"

He pointed at a broken trailer hitch.

"Think you can fix that, Moon?"

I had on the mask, gloves and goggles and sparks flew for two hours.

"All done sir," I said to my manager. He walked over and ran his finger over the welds I made.

"Not bad, Moon, looks solid."

"Now what, sir?"

"Just relax, Moon. Sir is what I call my dad." He sauntered away.

"Okay, but what should I do next?"

He turned.

"Sharpen that rotary mower, and let's call it a day."

"May I come in tomorrow to make up my lost time?"

"Forget about it. Never happened."

Unbelievable.

It turned out Gloria Throckmorton took summer classes at Iowa State and one day I spotted her bowling in the Union. She had always been snotty, not as bad as her father, yet I was happy to see a familiar face, especially since I was now a professional. I hustled back to my apartment and changed into my shirt with the fewest bleach spots. I put my identification badge on the pocket and hurried back to the Union but she was gone. A couple weeks later I saw her there again, with some friends. Like always, they giggled and whispered, stopping to bowl, not noticing anybody in the lanes next to them.

Iowa State had four lanes, not just one, like Grundy Center.

I walked past two or three times, a little closer each time until she spotted me.

"Moon. Hey Moon."

"Gloria Throckmorton? From Grundy Center?"

She waved. I walked over.

"Sisters," she said, "this is Moon."

I stuck out my hand but none of them had learned how to respond, so I crossed my arms and tried to look like there were a hundred other things needing my attention.

"Moon, these are the sisters of Pi Delta Phi." These Fie Pies, or whatever, lived in a house together, kind of a club. She said I should come by sometime. I agreed.

Now I started to realize those pills kind of relaxed me and I had eighteen left, but Gloria Throckmorton inviting me to visit was so upsetting I decided to take a pill ahead of schedule. Then it turned out not to be so necessary since she didn't leave a message telling me when, like she had promised. I checked twice a day. My boarding house kept messages, no charge for incoming calls. A couple of days I checked three or four times until my landlady started gritting her teeth loud enough to hear.

One Saturday I walked past that Fye Pi house until Gloria shouted "Hey Moon" out a window. She did that on my fourth pass.

I smiled. She came down and we sat on the porch.

"Could you come by after lunch tomorrow?" she asked.

"Of course."

I broke a pill in two, swallowed half with my regular pill that morning and strolled over toward Gloria's Phye Pi house about noon. If you've ever felt like you were looking through several panes of glass, when you weren't, that's how the world backed away from me that day. Everything stayed a little out of reach.

My shirt had a button collar and I wore polished cotton pants. I sauntered around the block several times.

A beekeeper yelled at me from Gloria's second story window.

I walked up to their porch. The beekeeper dragged out in a terry cloth robe. But it wasn't a beekeeper, it was Gloria, with her hair in curlers and a drying bonnet over them. She looked tired. Gloria must have been studying late.

"Moon, I'm happy you came by," she said. That kind of talk might have gotten me all confused without my pills, but it didn't, I just listened.

"You're supposed to be good with tools, and our toilet doesn't always flush. Could you fix it?"

I went home, changed my shirt and pants, got some tools from the warehouse and returned to fix their toilet. It was simple, I just bent the wire on the float and I could've done that without changing clothes. Gloria watched while I fixed it, but she had the dryer blowing into that bonnet.

She switched it off. "Christina Dawson still doesn't have a boyfriend," Gloria said.

She turned the dryer back on, ending our conversation.

Gloria clicked off the dryer again. "Grundy Center is getting anxious for her."

I thought about mentioning the time Willy and I surprised Christina when she and that guy tried to park next to Lake Poytawukie, but decided to keep my mouth shut, even if she turned off her hair dryer again.

She clicked it off. "Moon, do you remember when you stained our wallpaper?"

"Not really," I said.

"When you watched the coronation, Moon?"

"Oh, yeah."

"I never told dad what you did. I scrubbed it away myself."

"Gee, thanks Gloria."

"No problem, Moon. Are you finished?"

"Yup." I finished.

"Moon, maybe you could come by and have a Coke with one of my sisters some time." They called each other "sisters" in their club. I went back to work and tried to forget what she said since she probably didn't mean it. And I avoided that house again and steered clear of the Union for a month. But maybe Gloria had a better side.

A few weeks later I strolled past her Pye Fye club, and sure enough, out the window I heard her, after only circling twice.

"Moon. Take Millicent to the Union for a Coke." Gloria sort of nudged this girl out the front porch. All the sisters leaned out their windows. Millicent and I walked to the Union.

"I'm majoring in Home Economics," Millicent said.

"We learned the fourteen steps to make a bed today. I go to household appliance class tomorrow, and they've got this new device called a blender we get to study."

"Zowie," I said.

"What's your major?" Millicent asked.

"I'm in appliances myself, sort of," I said, "maintenance and design."

"That's keeno," she said. This was some girl. We got to the Memorial

Union, picked a table and she excused herself for the powder room. I told her I needed to do the same, but I ran next door to the drugstore, looked for some Old Spice or other sweet-water but they didn't have any, so I rubbed a pine air-wick on my shirt and scurried back to our table. She looked kind of funny at me and scrunched up her nose. We each drank a Coke and walked back. I thought about telling her, just a little, about Ruthie so she'd know I wasn't a beginner with girls but the proper moment for that subject didn't arise.

I sorely wish somebody from Grundy Center could have seen her walking with me. Carla or Willy or Mr. Nordstrud or Mr. Scarletti. Anybody. When we returned, I stood on the porch, not sure if I should shake hands or something else but Gloria hustled out and yanked Millicent inside by the wrist. All the girls peeked out the windows again, disappeared and chattered and laughed inside. I stayed on the porch. Gloria stepped halfway out, holding the door open behind her.

"Moon, really, leave now," she said.

"Millicent is a freshman, a pledge, so she must do anything I request. Eeeewww, what's that perfume stink?"

"Gloria, I don't know."

"Peeuuuw."

"I don't know what, maybe it's a bush or something spilled in one of your bathrooms or..."

"You don't think, Moon, that I'm forcing her to spend more time with you, do you? We discipline these young girls, but stop short of cruelty." She shut their door. I heard the lock click.

I never again walked that street. It was out of my way anyway. Several weeks later, while heading for work, I saw Gloria walking with three girls, each carrying books and chatting. They strolled up one side of Beech Street and I walked the other, all going north.

"Moon," she yelled. I didn't turn.

"Moon, Moon." I started to walk faster but not so quick that it looked obvious.

"Hey Moon." I glanced sideways, gave a half wave and turned east to avoid them, saying nothing.

"Moon, could you fix another toilet?" I walked faster, swung my arms high and looked straight ahead.

"Let early education be a sort of amusement; you will then be better able to find out the natural bent."

Plato

Chapter 13

A window air conditioner in one of the Quonset huts failed and they needed it for math classes. I trotted over to repair it.

I had figured out how my pills worked and had eight left. Mr. Nordstrud would come in a week and if I needed more, he'd arrange one last batch. But I knew not to take an extra pill that day, just the regular one. If I had to work around a crowd another pill might protect me from going detached, or if I had to work inside the armory. But this was a small class. And while more than one pill helped, at first, a second pill headed me for trouble too often.

Professor Max Cohen flashed a gold front tooth, and chalk dust followed him in clouds. After his math class left he watched me work on the air conditioner.

"Young man, just how does this apparatus perform?" He bent over while I kneeled into the cabinet.

"It compresses the Freon outside, Professor. Then the liquid Freon comes into these pipes in your classroom and it evaporates, chilling the pipes."

"And what occurs as a result?"

"The cycle repeats. The evaporated Freon goes outside, where it's compressed again."

I explained how you could calculate the cooling ability of a unit. He smiled non-stop and thanked me while the cold blew across us and began to fill the room.

"Are you finished for the day, young man?" Professor Cohen asked.

"Yes, Professor." He waved an arm across his desk, covered with papers and said that if I'd help him correct them he'd buy our dinner at the Union. This excited me. I agreed. I had never dined with anybody except Grandma, Grandpa, Mom. And of course twice with Ruthie at PAG Church Camp, but I was sort of unconscious when around her.

Professor Cohen complimented me at dinner.

"Your grasp of mathematics is solid," he said.

He must have meant it, because we did it again the next night and pretty soon Professor Cohen sent students with difficulties to me. I'd explain things and sometimes helped him correct tests. His brain had plenty of torque, but he needed a cane for walking more than a few steps.

Back in Grundy Center, Mr. Nordstrud told part of the town about the machine tools I operated. Mr. Nordstrud visited Iowa State every month, and always stopped by. My boss even let me talk with Mr. Nordstrud during work hours. That's how heavenly this job was.

"Can we make a point to not irritate the Grundy Center elite?" Mr. Nordstrud asked. He and I agreed that he should never mention my helping students. That would be fun but might invite trouble. Mr. Nordstrud brought me another bottle of pills.

"Can this be your last medication, Moon?" he asked while we split a sausage and mushroom pizza, eating with our fingers. That sounds strange, but it's like an open-faced tomato sandwich smashed down to flat bread. Most of the other diners ate theirs without utensils, except a jittery lady near the window who struggled with a fork, then a knife and finally rolled it up to take home. Mr. Nordstrud asked me a million questions about my math tutoring. I hoped to introduce Mr. Nordstrud to Professor Cohen one day.

If they wanted.

And if they had time.

They'd get along, I bet.

One of Professor Cohen's students met with me every Tuesday after work. We went through problems in his room and he gave me a dollar each time. This was a farm kid and he hadn't done much with numbers, but he caught on quick.

On Tuesday afternoon my manager sent me to the armory. I knew I would be lining up folding chairs again. This meant I couldn't use my trick of just looking at nearby things to keep from getting dizzy, so I risked taking a second pill. After finishing work, I floated home and couldn't get the energy to open my can of Campbell's chicken noodle soup. I stretched across the bed for a second but didn't wake until the next morning. My farm kid student said the landlady hollered and knocked on my door but couldn't wake me. So I missed him that night. He took his test the next day and got a D.

This was my fault. A college kid got a poor grade. My doing. It wasn't enough that I failed to get into college myself, now I started destroying other people's chances for success, ruining their reputations and dreams. Those pills relaxed me, but they were dangerous. I emptied the bottle out my window. My landlady's doghouse sat directly below, and it looked like it was being struck by a hailstorm, with white pellets bouncing off every shingle. And I noticed that her dog slept most of the following month and wouldn't bark anymore, even if I ran toward him.

Luckily, my student managed to schedule a makeup test. I tutored him free and he earned a B+.

I fell sick in that armory five or six times. When work required that I deal with a lot of people, I excused myself pretty often for the bathroom. All in all, this tiny inconvenience beat the gigantic problems those pills created. My life would just have to be jumpy sometimes. And I got nervouser, but learned to anticipate that, ducking away from people when the jitters set upon me.

After a couple months, Professor Cohen and my manager at the maintenance warehouse worked out a deal to share me. This went on all year. I spent every morning at the warehouse and every afternoon grading papers and tutoring the slower kids in math. I worked with my hands in the morning and my head in the afternoon.

Best of all, my pay shot up to $2.60 an hour by the end of those two years. Plus I got to use the tools in the warehouse for working on student's cars every weekend. Like anything, with practice, I got better and better at fixing cars.

I soon could mix in crowds without getting jumpy. Oh, there was the Kansas State basketball game incident in that cursed armory. Even then, I ducked into a stall in the bathroom before anybody knew.

Mr. Nordstrud visited again.

"Can you believe it? Where did this last bottle of those white pills come from, Moon? Aren't I a consarned fool for not remembering how I got these? Shouldn't I just throw them away since you don't need them."

"I don't need them, Mr. Nordstrud, not anymore."

He smiled and nodded.

"Isn't your adjustment a miracle, Moon? Isn't it great that you beat this, since there can never be any more pills?"

He stared at me. I smiled back.

"And weren't they expensive?" he asked.

"A shame to sprinkle them in a ditch, isn't it?"

"Expensive?" I asked.

"Can you believe it, Moon? Isn't my memory slipping? You remember, um, don't you, that these would have been costly, ah, if I hadn't gotten them as free samples?"

"Let me dispose of them at work, Mr. Nordstrud. We have containers there for dangerous materials."

"Do you think these are dangerous, Moon?"

"Mr. Nordstrud, I started sleeping too much from them, so I threw them out my window and I suspect my landlady's dog ate them. He didn't bark for weeks."

Mr. Nordstrud and I chuckled over that. He agreed I should dispose of the pills carefully.

I changed my mind later. The pills scared me no more. I thought it could strengthen me to glare at this last bottle of pills, keeping them next to my toothpaste, every morning. That would remind me of what they almost did to that college student who needed my help. Instead of tossing them, I'd look right into them and triumph over those rotten chemicals, from the start of every day. I would never miss work or end up in the hospital again.

Professor Cohen arranged for me to take advanced algebra at Iowa State. What a snap. I got an A. The next semester he set it up so I could be a part-time student, despite my not having a high school diploma. Professor Cohen told me I could graduate from college without it. He knew my experience in such things wasn't the best, so he took me to meet that skinny, bald Registrar again. The guy remembered me. He talked loud, jumped up and waved his arms, sat back down and confirmed that I could qualify.

I felt blessed. That makes sense. I was.

If I worked at the maintenance warehouse each Saturday, plus through summers, Professor Cohen showed me how I could cover my expenses.

Professor Cohen delayed things a few days, unintentionally. Somebody shot President Kennedy. That depressed Professor Cohen so much that he stayed home and didn't eat anything for two days. Then somebody shot the guy who shot President Kennedy.

"Where does this madness end?" Professor Cohen asked.

"Where has our culture gone and why?"

President Kennedy had sent some troops to South Vietnam. This would protect the world from the commies. Government folks warned us about the "domino effect" if Vietnam went pinko. President Kennedy even had their Premier Diem assassinated when that leader wasn't aggressive enough against the communists. Now we would wait to see if President Johnson would continue to protect America and our way of life by saving Vietnam.

I should have cared more about that stuff, but suddenly I was almost a student. Professor Cohen worried about the world when all I wanted was to get enrolled. After a week, he got his head back together and did just that. I became a college man.

With Grandma gone, earning a degree no longer meant that she and I could improve things in Grundy Center. If it was me alone against Doctor Throckmorton, well, that fight's scary to think about.

But my being an Iowa State graduate would mean everything to Mom and Ruthie.

Mom could hold her head higher. But with studies now, and working at the same time, finding Mom would have to wait until graduation. Then I'd have a big job, more money and time. Plus, she'd be prouder and happier to see me.

With Ruthie, I'd send her a copy of my grades.

"Wonderful, I am so proud," she'd say, in that flute-like voice. But if her mother doubted it, those grades would make it easier for Ruthie to prove I was becoming somebody in the world.

Well, of course, it would also encourage Ruthie to wait for me. She knew I'd come for her.

I smelled vanilla. Her ponytail, milk chocolate, fluffed through my mind. Ruthie being a Methodist made everything perfect between us. I felt like a Methodist, but because I missed out on catechism I didn't know all the secret passwords and stuff. But I liked everything about the Methodist Church except the ministers and the members, so she and I would be fine.

She'd have to wait a few years. That hurt. But in weak moments, when I felt alone and frustrated, it helped to imagine how great things would be when the world knew that I was an official Iowa State graduate.

"Ka-bam."

My window rocked. We towered over campus, four stories up. I looked out the window and down.

"Ka-bam." A ten foot flame burst out from the tail end of the Chevy. Several kids gathered around it in the parking lot. The driver raced the engine, it roared with each touch of the throttle, rapped when he let off and every few seconds it belched fire.

"Ka-bam."

I looked again, and Willy leaned out the car's window, driver's side, laughed and waved. He came down some Saturdays. We had agreed it might be better to not mention my college classes yet in Grundy Center. Willy brought my Woodrow Wilson Scholarship plaque on this trip.

The crowd shrieked, and pleaded for him to do it again.

"Ka-bam."

A security officer marched into the lot, Willy parked, the crowd scattered and he ran into our foyer. I took him up to my new room.

"How'd you do that, Willy?"

He stretched out on my bed and I slid a chair next to him.

"It's dual got glasspaks," Willy replied.

"Yes, but so do other cars, Willy. I've never seen flames like that."

Willy explained how he had installed spark plugs in the exhaust. When he pulled the choke, he could also flip a switch and those pipes turned into flamethrowers.

I had left my boarding house and moved into this dormitory, just like a normal college kid. I hung my plaque on a wall behind the study desk. I bought a leather case for my slide rule, wearing it on my belt. This told the world that I was a serious student, not somebody majoring in "Underwater Basket Weaving" or "PE."

This dorm was so big that several people would be missing every weekend, which meant Willy could visit and stay overnight, sleeping in somebody's unused bed, and he did. I think he liked it a lot. He showed up about every other weekend, which kept me smiling.

Our dorm section was Spinney House, and we were our own club. Spinney House showed spirit. Some thought we might be the best group on campus but we never claimed that. When the yearbook took our picture the guys asked me to sit front and center. I turned my head a little to favor the left side, so as to not embarrass the Spinney House guys, but I did that on my own. Nobody asked me to.

I received A's in math and chemistry and B's in English and History.

Professor Cohen was so smart he could help me in any class and sometimes I'd go to his apartment for dinner, since he lived alone. He even kept a blackboard in his living and dining area and had a cocker spaniel missing one leg, named Isosceles. Professor Cohen favored Isosceles so much that sometimes even that dog shook off chalk dust.

Usually Professor Cohen made a tuna, noodle and pea casserole. We'd split a six-pack of Schlitz afterward, in front of his fireplace.

Professor Cohen called his beer can opener a "church key," which was funny, but made me uncomfortable.

Isosceles snored near our feet. My grades pleased Professor Cohen.

"It is wholly unnecessary to score all A's, my young student." He split two grilled cheese sandwiches with me and gave the third to Isosceles. The dog whoofed it down so fast I feared he'd choke.

"Your B's are just fine, and with straight A's in math, you'll be a valued graduate."

Sure enough, Isosceles coughed up part of the sandwich and swallowed it back down. Professor Cohen, not having any farm experience, watched and shook his head.

"The better part of college is a social education, and you are absorbing much of that."

Isosceles nuzzled his leg. Professor Cohen poured milk in the dog's tray.

"Your story-telling is superb, in spite of not always using the most apt word," he said.

I didn't know what "apt" meant, but didn't ask, since sometimes what the professor intended to say became clear.

"Your being different blesses you with unique perspectives, and you should write that story one day. A book, would you agree?"

Yikes. A book. Moon, me, without a high school diploma, an author? Getting a B in English? They stretch thoughts, don't they, at college? Well, either that or Grundy Center limited our thinking. Who's to say?

Another night Professor Cohen asked me to tell him who God was. Me. Not some man of the cloth. That required a few days to answer. First I had to think about it some. And that was fun, despite never having learned from catechism. Looking back, the Professor asked me to decide things myself, the same things that Reverend Dawson and Mr. Scarletti preached at me before. It was kind of scary, but that's the kind of talk you had with Iowa State intellectuals.

The Most Reverend Dawson had waved his arms and sprayed perspiration like a dog crawling out of a lake when he trapped me in the church basement and explained why God deformed me. I became unsure that Reverend Dawson could have known any of that. I don't feel evil. I just look different.

Luckily, Professor Cohen didn't understand some details of my socialization. Our Spinney House engineers all took drafting classes. With a speedball pen they could draw a draft card in about an hour with any birth date you wanted for two dollars. Then one guy's mother, a clerk in the Wisconsin Department of Motor Vehicles, brought us some blank driver's licenses we could fill out. With those two documents we could drink in any bar. Spinney House guys always split up, so the bartenders wouldn't notice twenty guys carrying Wisconsin licenses showing up at once, night after night.

Professor Cohen probably understood generally what went on without being tested by hearing specific examples. He said that the better part of my education would be learning to live with others. And it was practical. I never ruined another shirt with bleach. I noticed Carl Hamilton putting a Gillette blue blade in the sink, shaving cream on his face, he put his thumb on the flat side of the blade, splashed some water in and the proceeded to rub the blade back and forth across the curved inner surface of the porcelain. I asked what he was doing.

"Sharpening the blade," he said, "this one got dull. You get a month from one Gillette Blue Blade by sharpening it this way."

I tried it. Sure enough it worked, and instead of buying blades every few months, one package of ten now lasted a year. Professor Cohen didn't even know that one. When I told him he flashed that wide smile, gold tooth gleaming and did it again when I returned, and he reported how this extended the life of his razor blade.

Ghazi Nasser lived down the hall. Jerusalem was his home. We all used to boast about where we came from at dinner, and some guys took to saying they were from "God's Country" before telling you about Spirit Lake, Osceola, Grimes, Reinbeck, Ft. Dodge or wherever. One day a new guy asked Ghazi where he came from and Ghazi said he, and only he, truly came from God's country. Everybody howled since in his case it was fact. But Ghazi wasn't a Christian, which confused things.

Ghazi kept a brandy snifter on his desk filled with mints. I popped through his door one night.

"Ghazi, how many forms does sulfur come in?" He was smart.

"Take a mint, Moon."

I chewed a mint, sat and opened my notebook. Ghazi explained the four ways sulfur exists in nature, plus its several different forms when heated.

He talked. I scribbled.

We never knew if refusing candy might be an insult to a foreigner. Having mints for visitors seemed a little unnecessary, but maybe they did that in his country. Possibly they lived in tents but always offered a mint to somebody who just got off a camel. How would we know?

After a couple years, we learned that Ghazi made the mints himself. He'd keep an eye out for toothpaste tubes in that bathroom we all shared. When he spotted one with a drop of hardened toothpaste around the top, he'd pick it off. Then Ghazi set the globs on a radiator near his windowsill and after a couple days of heat and daylight they hardened and became his guest mints.

They had factory-made mints at the West Street Grocery next door but the big item there was beer. This store had a walk-in ice locker at the back.

Some weeknights, even in late spring or early fall when it was hot, we'd stroll in carrying some books, look at the bread and slip into the locker when the cashier got busy. Being bundled up in two sweatshirts, we could sit inside that locker and chug several cans of Schlitz or Hamm's or Pabst Blue Ribbon quick, flip the empties out through a window without much sound and amble out. Other times, if somebody had beer or whisky, we'd go out and always invited Jimmy Threlkeld. He was wiry and short. Only Jimmy could fit up the chute of an automated ice delivery machine and get out, pulling a ten pound bag behind him. If the car we were using had a spare tire, we rolled it out of the trunk, filled the empty wheel well with ice and beer and drove out into the country for a party. Just us guys.

There were dozens of students who were different at Iowa State. Indians and Negroes enrolled.

Indians weren't the kind in cowboy and Indian picture shows, these were ones from India. They took harder courses like agriculture and engineering and mathematics. And they were both men and women.

Indian men came thin, and had a luminescence under their darker skins. Their pupils were coal black set in egg white eyes. They wore long-sleeved dress shirts all year.

Indian women wore robes that looked like they were made of Kleenex, except colored in pastels, draped as togas and they had red dots on the middle of their foreheads.

I never asked if they were born with those dots or if they put them on with lipstick. One reason I never asked was I never talked with any of them. They showed up at the Methodist Church, I heard, but other than that I'd just see them on campus. I'd try not to stare at them and they tried not to stare at me.

To prove Iowa State wasn't prejudiced, Indians lived in a special dorm on the highest campus hill, called International House. On Sunday afternoons there would be mixers, which meant the professors would take turns going over to talk at them, whether they liked it or not.

The Negroes were football, basketball, wrestling and track stars. They lived in special dorms built under the stadium. They also, like all the athletes, ate at what's called a training table and some Iowa State graduate who farmed would get credit each week for providing a cow or two for them. This also was a desegregated thing, with everybody eating together at the training table, just like they mixed it up on the playing field.

They didn't room together, of course.

Race relations were important to Iowa State. They worked hard to make sure the one percent who were minorities got special treatment, unless they were oriental. And when some dance committee had a theme of "Clap Yo Hands" for a fall dance, the faculty advisors to the student council suggested that the name should be changed since it sounded racial. Two thousand programs were destroyed to ensure no bigoted messages jolted our campus.

I guess that was good, but a couple of years later Iowa State gave three hours credit for "Afro-American speech," which encouraged certain phrases as part of their cultural pride. What was happening was coloreds became Negroes became Afro-Americans became blacks became African-Americans. If I came from Mexico I think I'd prefer to be called Mexican instead of Latino or Chicano or Hispanic, wherever those places are. Same for Apaches and Navajos instead of Indians, maybe, and Nigerians and Kenyans. But how would I know, being a chalk-faced Irish kid from Grundy Center? These "minorities" make up a majority of the world by the way, if schools could ever think globally.

One Spinney House Negro majored in astronomy. He borrowed a deflated weather balloon from the college and snuck it to his room.

"You hold this end," he said. I did while he rolled it down the hall after supper.

"Here's the vacuum," I said.

"Power on?" he asked.

"In ten seconds."

He hooked up the backend of a vacuum cleaner to it, I plugged in the cord, he tripped the switch, it blew up, knee high, nobody noticed and in a minute filled the hall, trapping everybody in their rooms.

"Hey, what's going on?" asked a voice down the hallway.

"Look at this," another said.

Every door opened but nobody could get out.

"What the hey?"

"Who's doing this?"

"Somebody's going to pay."

That thing looked like a milk flood, rising up to about shoulder height. The fabric unfolded by itself while it grew. A couple guys tried to get out of their rooms and made a commotion about it. When another door opened, the weather balloon puffed in. Some laughed. Others threw wet globs of toilet paper at us, over the balloon, but only half of those wads cleared it.

We didn't stop. The fabric reached the ceiling and filled the hall. The yelling got louder. Somebody stabbed the balloon with a pair of scissors. That stopped it, and the thing started to drift down. Other Spinney House guys did the same in their rooms.

One thing we discovered that night was the way our weather service keeps all that balloon fabric from sticking to itself. They coated the insides with talc. You'd have thought the first winter snow came early to Spinney House, and somehow arrived indoors. It was impossible to see down the hallway, even after the balloon dropped to waist level and finally flattened. After the talc settled, every desk, shirt, book and floor looked white. The engineers commented that their slide rules worked better for weeks.

Our astronomy student was a hero, a champion prankster for several minutes, until everybody started looking at the mess in their rooms. He and I quickly started to help clean up, so they wouldn't make a "torpedo run" with us. We scurried down to each doorway. I carried the vacuum and told them we'd be right back to finish. We needed to calm everybody quick.

I helped the future astronomer vacuum and mop since I had helped him. And also because I had suggested this project the day before.

My fellow prankster looked scared for awhile, but after it was all over I think he was glad he did it. Rolling up that balloon without the talc and with twelve new holes in it, you could hardly tell, and he returned it to the department the next day.

A "torpedo run," by the way, was when two or three guys grab and wrap you with belts, pinning both arms to your sides. Then they hoist you up, carry you into the bathroom and shove your head into the toilet.

They yell "fire one" and flush. Maybe they yell "fire two" and do it again. That sound and all the water gurgling is not my favorite college memory. But the fact that my Negro friend and I might be victims, just like anybody else tricking our neighbors, proved that Spinney House showed few prejudices for or against us, which felt right.

My earliest problem didn't come from my dorm buddies, but from the librarian. It had to do with a flashlight. We had a calculus examination coming up, and it seemed that if I did well, I could stay at the head of our class. But there were only three books with practice examples in the library and they couldn't be checked out. Taking turns with a dozen other classmates, I stayed late, looking and working on the problems.

They locked up the library at midnight. The guard was one of those guys who stared when I was around, always watching and I could tell he was on my case. This guard always checked the restrooms at closing, even looking under the stall doors to make sure nobody hid in there. But he never climbed up to the third story book stacks, just glanced at them from the second floor, so if I laid flat on the aisle up there I guessed he'd miss me.

I was right.

Luckily, they opened the library at six in the morning. That meant I could study inside until three or four, sleep a little and when the noise of opening would wake me, I could run back to my room, sleep another hour and be at the warehouse for work by eight. What's more, I'd know those calculus problems by heart.

The only problem was that this guard walked around the outside about two. I must have blown it and let my flashlight beam hit the window frame while I was reading because he was in there and atop me like stink on manure before I even heard the door open. The librarian and the guard conducted my hearing the next day at noon. Professor Cohen came to observe. A cloud of chalk dust floated around his corner chair for several minutes after he sat.

"There are only three books for a class of thirty," I explained, "so it's tough to prepare the lessons."

Nobody answered.

"About a dozen other students showed up that night," I said, "so I had to hang around late to get a chance at the lessons."

Silence.

"That does present a challenging situation," Professor Cohen said.

The librarian cleared her throat.

"But it seems he planned this violation," she said.

"Well, not so much ma'am," I said.

"Why, then, young man, did you bring a flashlight into the library?"

If anybody could have stopped the red color from spreading over the back of my neck just then, I'd have paid them twenty dollars to do so. It spread across my face while I stared at the wooden slats on the floor but I couldn't really see them. I was wishing I had replied that I always carried a flashlight on campus after dark but I couldn't warp the truth like that, especially with Professor Cohen's gold tooth shining at me from the corner.

"Perhaps," Professor Cohen said, "this student is guilty of planning ahead. While we never condone breaking the rules, part of education is learning to anticipate problems."

She marked my library card with a red X, which told all the staff to watch my behavior when I used it, and that mark didn't seem to speed up the help I got either. Each year we got new cards so that wouldn't plague me forever.

Later that week I started a few minutes late for dinner at Professor Cohen's. I stopped at the grocery and got a tube of day-old biscuits for a dime. We both liked those and at this price we paid about a penny a biscuit. Going up his front walk, every second turned into a minute. He might have been so dismayed by my library shenanigan that I would no longer be welcome, but when his torn screen door swung open, all I saw was that golden smile.

"Well if it is not my favorite student," Professor Cohen said, "We slipped past that fuddy-duddy librarian pretty well, did we not?"

What a peach. What a professor.

That evening we ate all ten biscuits with butter, had a package of Lipton's chicken and rice soup and some funny round green things that were kind of bitter, but I ate both of mine. He called them Brussels sprouts.

"Teaching might be the perfect career for you," Professor Cohen said.

We sat in his living and dining area, which also had a miniature stove and a sink. His bedroom and bathroom angled off to one side. He poked at the fireplace which could only hold one log at a time.

"With sputnik launched, the Russians have made a move to control space," he explained.

Isosceles lay at our feet, snoring. His head raised each time the fire popped, then sunk back down, eyes shut.

"There will be a surging demand for technical training through the next few decades," he said.

"Should the Russians overrun us, of course, we might be put to slave labor on farms without tractors."

That sounded awful.

"But you ought to write a book someday, use your perspective, help people understand."

"Understand what, Professor Cohen?"

"The isolation, the prejudice, the difficulties our handicapped face, my young man."

"But Professor Cohen, I'm not a cripple or a Negro or some retard or Indian, so how could I know about that?"

"Promise me you will just keep the thought?"

"Of course, Professor Cohen." That man with a non-stop smile, surrounded by a cloud of chalk, could imagine anything. I had trouble grasping his book idea, however.

But I added a teaching class to my curriculum the next semester.

It turned out Professor Cohen also checked back into the Woodrow Wilson teacher grant program for me. He said the lack of a high school diploma didn't matter now that I was in college, but that the few years' delay in my schooling disqualified me. This was okay. That award meant a loan, anyway, which means something you owe back. I liked working in the maintenance warehouse. And this way I could teach without starting out in debt. Getting degreed just might take two years longer.

So?

Would I even want a degree two years quicker if it put me in debt?

Well, maybe.

Because even if I owed money, I might find Ruthie sooner.

Ruthie liked me, a lot, but she's such a pretty girl, a real spirit and some other guy might horn in. I couldn't expect she'd wait forever. Those extra two years getting through might make the difference, and what would a life be without Ruthie? But there was no choice but to work and get through school, hoping things might work out with her later.

School went easy, work kept me busy with real things and my grades stayed up.

For a while, I tried tutoring again. It proved to be too much. There was this other thing. Some girls actually took math, believe it or not, but many of them seemed jumpy around me. I didn't appreciate their nervousness. Professor Cohen suggested maybe it was my apprehension of the opposite sex rubbing off on them. I respectfully disagreed. My heebie-jeebies were gone. Mostly. I understood the boy-girl thing thanks to Ruthie, so they didn't fluster me so much. Just a little. I could not explain this fully without violating my relationship with Ruthie.

I stopped tutoring in my junior year.

This gave me some spare time, so I'd research the east coast in the library. If I could get a summer job there, maybe I'd find Ruthie. But that part of the country had too many cities, I finally admitted to myself.

I called long-distance information in Boston, New York, Philadelphia, Baltimore, and Washington, D.C. to see if Ruthie had a phone listing, since that service was free. Well, there were several in each place. None were her. That little experiment cost me $84 in phone calls to hear a dozen voices that sounded nothing like Ruthie.

I tried Chicago, sending letters to every medical office and piano store, offering to work for the summer, but nobody answered. Finally I decided to work in the west with Willy.

"That fun sounds," he said. I didn't mention my Chicago attempt, since that always seemed to bother him when I searched for Mom, despite our "Solemn Pact."

So I got to work on Colorado and found us both jobs.

My manager at the warehouse said this trip was fine, since summers were slow and he'd have morning work for me when I returned in the fall. Willy told Mr. Nordstrud, who urged us to be careful drinking the water, but I'm not sure how anybody does that. I wanted to make sure Professor Cohen approved, so I walked over to his house. We sat in his living and dining area with Isosceles sniffing my ankles.

"Phillis Wheatley and Lord Byron taught us much," Professor Cohen said.

"Who?"

"A black slave woman and a clubfooted epileptic. Both wrote well," Professor Cohen replied.

He squinted at me.

"Isn't this trip a great idea, Professor Cohen?"

"You have a sensitivity that only pain can create," he said, "and know your way around our college now."

"That's right, Professor Cohen. I can even find my way in Des Moines." I blushed.

"With your sensitivity comes fragility. The larger world will test you again, but perhaps no more than the places you've already been."

"So this will be a great experience, right Professor Cohen?"

"I would hope so. Someday you must write a book, so others may taste real life. More stories may come with this summer work."

So that was that. In one year, just twelve months, I would be an Iowa State graduate, with summer work experience in those majestic Rocky Mountains.

Willy and I had never seen the Missouri river. That's the first landmark we crossed. The Missouri took Lewis and Clark on their journey. Some described that river as "too thick to drink, but too thin to plow." This is a guess, but if you lined up forty cars, end to end, that's how far it was across the Missouri river.

We might learn to like the Rocky Mountains. Maybe we'd live there one day. I could see Willy and me, riding horses out there in the sagebrush, herding cattle. Willy might sit on a palomino and mine would be gray. Maybe we'd bring along a dog and sleep around a campfire some nights. We could name Willy's horse Goldie. Mine's Dusk. We might carry carbines, holstered next to our saddles, wear ten-gallon hats, bandanas and cowhide chaps. My holster could have leather fringe around the edges.

There'd be a ranch house and Ruthie could live there. The dog would be her guide while Willy and I grazed cattle. I could tell her what the peaks looked like each morning and get food for us.

When meals were ready, Ruthie's voice would cut through the prairie air better than those lunchtime triangles they ring in every cowboy picture show. She could tell me how the cactus blossoms smelled after a rain and alert us when coyotes howled from the distance. I'd set things up so she could get around without stumbling. Ruthie could walk free in the open space outside, her ponytail fluttering in the wind, matching the wet adobe colors. I could read to her most evenings, she'd sing and vanilla would float through our cabin.

Mom would vacation with us each summer and those surroundings would calm her down. We'd live with our horses, cattle and a dog.

I would be normal to all of them.

Willy might get a girl too. Perfect.

By mail, I had lined up jobs at the Stanley Hotel in Estes Park. Willy would help the hotel's plumber, while I washed pots and pans for the cooks. Hopefully the hotel staff wouldn't be bothered by my appearance. We were promised one day off every week and if Willy and I could arrange that to be same day, we just might saddle up horses and practice roaming those mountains and countryside. Maybe with some cows around. Roy Rogers and Gene Autry were just picture show actors. We knew that, but this kind of living might suit us.

With the tips conventions normally gave the staff, I'd have enough to finish school.

"I can't get no girl reaction."

Mick Jagger

Chapter 14

Spring planting and fall harvests forced Iowa State to close sooner and open later than other schools. We took only two days off at Thanksgiving and four each Christmas, plus clipped a few off the Easter vacation to compensate for our shorter year. Willy and I had a week before the Stanley Hotel needed us and I had some unexpected overtime cash, so I hopped a Greyhound to Chicago.

The Museum of Natural History had guards with badges but no guns.

"Officer," I said to the first one, "there's a missing woman."

"Let me escort you to lost and found," he said, and pulled out a notepad.

"No, she's not missing today," I said.

"She's been gone for a few years and we think she might be in Chicago."

"Where in Chicago?" he asked.

"Yes, in Chicago. This is directly on the bus route."

"Son, I can't help you."

"Is it possible you've seen her?" I described Mom. He listened and shook his head. Maybe I exaggerated a little about there being $100 reward for locating her. But if somebody did I could send them five dollars a week until that was settled so this wasn't such a big fat lie.

And since I was in Chicago anyway, I might as well. I kept badgering that museum guard until he took me outside and waved down a cop.

This policeman listened to my story but didn't take notes. He shook his head and finally took me to the downtown library.

The library had a collection of phone books. Mom's name wasn't listed in any of them. I had to check two dozen, that town's so big. If you shot a

22-caliber long rifle bullet into the main Chicago phone book, my guess is that the slug wouldn't get beyond halfway through. That's thick. You could press every wrinkle out of a hanky by just setting any of those phonebooks on it overnight.

If Mom only knew how promising my life became, she'd burst with pride and want me to find her. She might be short of money. I'd soon be able to help.

Mom must have known that Grandma's dead, but she never got back in touch so I worried that she might be ill or worse.

I failed to find a trace of her.

In Grundy Center, when we wanted to call somebody, we just picked up the phone and told Sandy McEntaffer who we wanted to talk to. In Mason City, you had to dial their number, and there were so many people there that it took four numbers. But Chicago even had words in front of the numbers like Cedar 2-1917 or Blackwood 7-2810.

Nobody in Grundy Center remembered anymore that Mom and Dad were unable to marry.

"It just don't matter," Willy said. My head is still bent, sure, but Willy doesn't even see that. He said so regularly, and I appreciated it the first few times he repeated that. After awhile I told Willy he didn't need to keep saying it.

And Professor Cohen seemed unbothered by my circumstances.

"There are no illegitimate children," he said, "only illegitimate parents."

I liked that thought until I realized it reflected poorly on my parents.

In Chicago people kind of stepped aside on the sidewalks when they saw me coming, which was convenient.

I hopped a Greyhound back to Grundy Center. Willy picked me up and we took off, free as Red-winged blackbirds.

The "Mighty Muddy" flows gentle. This explains how Lewis and Clark rowed upstream. Willy and I took off our shoes and waded around the edge and our feet sank in the muck up to our calves. Willy had several changes of clothes packed so he jumped in and swam a ways but came back quick because the water was so muddy he couldn't tell what else might lurk in it.

We didn't see any Indians. Not a wigwam or a teepee or an arrow or a tom-tom. That's because American Indians are segregated onto their own land, called reservations, except it's not always where they originally lived, but new land that our government said they should occupy.

At Iowa State the India Indians walked all over campus and took classes just like us, except they didn't speak American very well. I didn't learn if American Indians talked like us, not running into any.

The policy was to segregate American Indians onto reservations of bad land but mix with India Indians on Sunday afternoons. Professor Cohen got agitated over this. He called himself a Jew but never went to the Temple in Des Moines, so I'm not so sure what that label meant.

Temples are what Jews call their churches.

The John Wesley Pentecostal Redemption in Jesus Second Methodist Church, better known as Wesley Redemption Methodist, taught me that the Jews killed Christ. But Professor Cohen informed me that Jesus was Jewish so this all muddled me. And when I looked it up in the library, it appeared that the Romans crucified Jesus. I wonder how the Christians got it so wrong.

Professor Cohen noted that Afro-American students were loaded on buses in the cities, spending so much time riding that they got worn out and couldn't participate in extra-curricular activities at school. This also turned out to be the perfect way to separate their moms and dads from the schools, destroy PTAs and reduce parental interest. Integrating Negroes and segregating Indians seemed contrary.

Lewis and Clark saw Indians every day, so the riverfront land must have been taken by the whites while the natives got moved back from the shore.

A bridge crosses that Missouri River. Willy shouted "Wooeey!" all the way over it but I kept quiet. When we got into Nebraska we pulled over at the first gas station. They sold Nebraska decals. Willy favored one that showed a guy in a straw hat, husking an ear of corn. I feared that might confuse folks with Iowa and Willy agreed, so we picked one that outlined the state and just said Nebraska across it. We stuck it in the lower right corner of Willy's rear window. We didn't have our own state sticker. To cross back for an Iowa decal, would run us another twenty-five cents for the toll, and then again to return to the Nebraska side. Spending a half-dollar to get our home state decal, plus the price of the decal itself, felt a little steep.

Of course, had somebody offered us a ride across that bridge at a carnival, for fifty cents, we'd probably have paid that in a minute. Willy reminded me that we weren't leaving forever and could slap an Iowa decal on the lower left of our rear window when we got back. By then, we might also have a Colorado sticker and a Kansas label, if we remembered to take the southern route home.

So Willy and I drove on to Ogallala, Nebraska. We pulled into the Ogallala Police Station for the night. They let us sleep in the jail in exchange for washing a couple of squad cars in the morning. Willy and I each had our own cell with a straw tick. We were too excited to sleep until almost midnight.

"Why they call it a bachelor's degree?" Willy asked. "If a girl got one, would be it called a maid's degree?"

"No, women get bachelor's degrees," I replied.

"Is that Fahrenheit or Centimeter?"

"Neither. Degree is just a word."

"After you graduate, do you decide things like that decal problem for us?" Willy asked.

"Naah. Who drives the better car in Grundy Center? The math teacher or the plumber?" I asked.

"Oh," Willy said. In a few minutes his breathing slowed and I dozed off too. The jail door clattered open at three in the morning. A new guest stumbled inside and the door slammed shut. The lock bolt clanged.

"Somebody's breathing," Willy whispered. We listened. Whoever it was shuffled around, fell to the concrete and started snoring. We could hear him but couldn't see him. The next sound came from Willy's cell door slamming shut. Then mine. About four o'clock another citizen got tossed in, hacked and coughed, finally lying down. We couldn't see this gentleman either. I guess they were tossing in the town drunks to sleep it off but we couldn't know that for sure. They might be axe murderers or Commie spies.

The Police Chief unlocked us the next morning. We stepped around the other guests and their puddles, washed both squad cars to pay for our lodging and headed on west, rolling like tumbleweeds. This took us to the panhandle of Nebraska, where we thought we might make some serious cash. Outfits drilled for oil there and supposedly paid $5 an hour. We figured a couple months of that work and Willy could buy new wheels and I might bank enough to carry me through my last year of school in comfort.

We made great time, cruising along at sixty. And Willy, being used to more money than most folks, always filled the tank when we stopped for gas. Grandma never bought over a dollar's worth.

Maybe Willy and I would grubstake ourselves on a ranch. Neither of us understood how a grubstake worked, but that could be possible, maybe. And I knew the Stanley Hotel would be okay without us. Lots of kids showed up at Estes Park each summer. Stanley Hotel's management forewarned me that if we were just one day late they'd give away our jobs to other applicants.

Pretty soon we saw pumps along the road, big as corncribs, pumping oil out of the earth, the same ball of dirt from which we harvested corn and beans. The soil here looked worse, kind of like brown clay or sand instead of the black loam we plowed in Iowa. They sucked oil out of that ground and grew alfalfa, hay and sugar beets in it. Those beets give all of us the sugar to sprinkle on cereal, make frosting or Kool-Aid. Willy and I rolled along, him driving and me cutting slices of Velveeta and putting them on Ritz crackers.

The oil rigs started out scattered but soon clumped up thicker and we stopped for gas. The attendant looked at me out of the corner of his eyes while he scrubbed the bugs off our windshield. I was used to that. Willy asked him about the oil riggers pay and the attendant said yes, they were paying five bucks an hour. He directed Willy to a hiring hall. I gave him a piece of cheese.

"Thank you," he said, "and be careful."

"Why?" I asked, and handed him an apple slice.

"Just watch your back." Willy and I took turns using the bathroom to clean up. Willy put on khaki Bermuda shorts and a bleeding madras shirt with a button-down collar. He'd gotten that outfit from the men's clothing store in Mason City. It looked pretty sharp and hadn't ever been unfolded. Fancy clothes like that couldn't be worn by Willy in Grundy Center, he said, or folks would start calling out of town for their plumbing work. I slipped on some clean jeans and an Iowa State tee shirt.

Pickup trucks circled the concrete block building they used for a hiring hall. Gun racks lined the vehicles' rear windows, and held guns.

When Willy and I stepped inside the place went quiet. It took a few seconds for our eyes to adjust to the dark. There were four tables of men playing cards and drinking beer and a counter where you signed up for work.

Willy walked straight over to the counter, and I lagged behind him. I heard several chairs pushing back from the tables but Willy didn't seem to notice.

One guy in a cowboy hat shouted across the room. "Looks like a college boy and a freak show to me."

Somebody smashed a bottle into the wall behind me. It didn't come close but that opened up my eyes a few notches. A guy with a crowbar strolled in my direction.

Willy scribbled our names on a clipboard chained to the counter.

He didn't see the guy hook his crowbar around my neck, pulling me towards a table of his buddies. They all stood.

Willy turned and saw.

"That stop," Willy shouted, which confused them for a moment.

The front door burst open and several silhouettes moved in from the sun. One was the gas station attendant.

"Best let him go, Gus," the attendant said. The guy with a crowbar paused but released me. Willy and I stepped over to the gas station attendant, who motioned us outside. His buddies stayed in the doorway.

"You boys get in your car and drive out of here fast," he said. He promised that his friends would keep the oil workers inside the hall for five minutes but said after that they would be free to go and might chase us. Willy and I lit out; our careers in the oil business seeming like a thing better pursued another day.

We couldn't see the Nebraska State Trooper's eyes through his dark glasses. He wiped his forehead with a hanky.

"You boys were clocking 85 miles per hour," he said.

His car was parked right behind ours, on the gravel shoulder, he leaned towards Willy. Willy looked at the ground.

"I said 85 miles per hour." He thumped Willy in the chest.

"Couldn't," Willy said.

"What'd you say boy?" The Trooper stuffed his hanky in a hip pocket.

I glanced down the highway, the sun baked the concrete and that watery look turned the road into a pond in the distance. The Trooper whipped out his pen.

"What he means, officer…," I started to say.

Whoomp.

A blast of air blew off the Trooper's hat. A pickup streaked past.

Whoomp. Another pickup roared by and the wind slapped our chests.

"Jesus H. Christ," the officer said, crumpling our ticket and running to his car. I grabbed his hat and tossed it through his window and he nodded.

"We didn't get over 70," Willy said, but the Trooper didn't hear, his tires crunched through the gravel, smoked across the pavement and he was gone. In seconds his siren whined.

Willy and I sat parked beside the road, breathing heavy, looking up at the rear view mirror once in awhile, but no more pickups appeared. We eased back onto the highway, rolled down the road at a respectable 60 miles an hour and in about twenty minutes spotted the trooper ahead, parked alongside the two pickups.

Sometimes I do childish things. Willy eased back on the throttle while we passed. The trooper's back was to us and the oil workers watched Willy and me cruise by. I saluted them in a special way.

Willy stomped on the gas when we got out of sight, turned at the next exit, went several miles south on gravel, turned west again at the first crossing and stayed on that back road for another ten miles.

We'd rehearsed this routine when bushwhacking around Lake Poytawukie. Willy and I pulled off and parked between two sand hills and slept in the car that night.

The Stanley Hotel became famous later as a movie setting for "The Shining," starring Jack Nicholson. We couldn't know that then but it goes to show how famous things and places come your way if you get out and around. We used to stare at that photo of Roy Rogers shaking hands with Mr. Sheetz, the owner of the Chief Theatre. Mr. Sheetz displayed that photo in the lobby, signed by Mr. Rogers himself. We were getting closer to fame ourselves.

The Stanley Hotel was built by the man who invented the Stanley Steamer, one of the earliest cars, predating the Model A Ford. The Stanley Steamer used a steam engine which gave it one, and only one, advantage over gasoline power. This was an ability to climb steep hills. Mr. Stanley designed his hotel to have a driveway just steep enough that only his Stanley Steamers could make it to the parking lot from the road.

Estes Park straddles the Big Thompson River. This is country so eye-popping that I don't dare try to describe it. In winter it just shuts down, blockaded by snow. In the summer tourists drive up over the continental divide and see forever from Trail Ridge Road.

The continental divide is the spot where, if you poured a bucket of water on it, half flows west and ends up in the Pacific. The other half bucket goes east, into the Gulf of Mexico and drifts into the Atlantic. Willy and I tested that but our bucket of water just soaked into the ground. Some things take faith. The Big Thompson pulsed from a babbling winter brook into a roaring river each summer. There's no doubt that water heads east.

Trail Ridge Road soars above what they call timberline. This is ground so high that no more trees grow; just rocks, scrub brushes and snow patches. I'm not reporting more. It strains me to put together the right words that capture these sights, so I'll stop trying.

Willy and I checked in and sure enough, they had jobs for both of us and a bunkhouse room. Our room had a set of drawers, more than we could fill, two beds and a bare light bulb overhead. All the men shared the showers and bathroom down the hall.

The women's dorm looked twice as big, which Willy saw as a good sign. Sure enough, lots of college girls rolled in for summer jobs. Willy borrowed my Iowa State tee shirt that summer and he fit in just fine.

Willy helped the plumber. I started out doing the pots and pans in the kitchen. This was a specialty trade and I caught onto it quick. My galvanized tub ran about three feet deep and had a steam pipe in it. When the water cooled, I just twisted the valve and steam gurgled through the water, heating it instantly, but you might scald your hands unless you remembered to pull out while doing that.

During meals, there wasn't time to change water, so I just kept throwing soap in, steaming the water and skimming off grease. After the rush I'd change water.

I scrubbed the pots with a chain mitt. Following dinner, it was my duty to go into the kitchen and polish the grilles with pumice. This was pretty simple work. The cooks acted crazy, however, maybe working in heat all the time does that.

A busboy from Beaumont who claimed to be a Tulane student but wore ducktails and said "ain't" regularly, whistled while hauling trays of dirty dishes. At 2:36, on a Wednesday afternoon, the pastry chef stabbed him in the belly for whistling. The busboy lived, they told us, but the pastry chef lit out and wasn't seen again.

One reason the staff tolerated me, from the start, was that they had people with problems bigger than my irregular face. But it wasn't smart to send a dirty pot back to the smoke, clatter, steam, flames and shouting of the kitchen. And you didn't dare let the chefs run out of clean pans.

Everybody treated me like a friend at the Stanley Hotel. Kids came from Kansas State, North Texas, Ole Miss, Colorado State College, a dozen others and of course, me from Iowa State with Willy sort of representing my school as well. Willy asked me a few things about classes and how semesters worked so he could sound official.

Marie, from Lawrence, Kansas, took a particular liking to me. Her smile, I can still see it, sometimes I try to sketch her face but it's incandescent. Her teeth and eyes brightened a room. Maybe she just lit me up, and the place seemed sunny because I glowed. She waitressed like most of the girls, except those few who worked in the laundry.

I owned a couple shirts with collars. They weren't so new and the collars sprouted those little balls of thread. Marie showed me how to take my razor across the collar to shave those things. Marie said a worn collar "pills" like that. Suddenly both my shirts looked new.

We ate in a room for employees called the zoo. They served stew or hash. This allowed the hotel to create our meals from scraps returned from the dining room, which was hardly touched sometimes. But a couple of times the crew got sick so we always looked out for fresher food.

I ate a lobster at the Stanley Hotel. It comes from the ocean and looks like a giant bug painted red, so you wonder what possessed the first person to ever cook one. But they are good. Marie ordered it for me, pretending someone in the dining room wanted a lobster. When this creature was ready she whisked past my gurgling tub and winked. I slipped down the back stairs to the bathroom in the basement. Marie came past the door, handed me the tray and kissed my cheek.

I only mention that she kissed me to show how well accepted I was, like a regular guy. She did that without hesitating and seemed natural doing it. She even took more time, placing her soft, warm, moist lips on my normal cheek, the left one, several seconds longer than would be technically considered necessary to call it a kiss.

It was warmer, longer and pressed tighter than Carla's kiss had been. I nearly dropped the tray when Maria kissed me, but then she was gone and I ducked into the bathroom with the lobster. This basement toilet was for the help only, and had one stall with a drain that backed up during rains. I locked the door and ate that lobster, balancing on the stool lid, which was cracked.

When I claim that lobster is good, it chews like chicken, except more rubbery but tender at the same time. You dip it in lemon butter. These cooks must have been foreigners since they made it a garlic lemon butter, something that we viewed with suspicion back home.

Maybe sitting on a cracked lid that squeaks with a sewer drain under my toes, balancing a tray on my lap wasn't the fanciest setting. But this proves how good lobster is. Of course Marie sneaking it and kissing me made things special. Maybe I'd have eaten a Firestone tire, mud-fried and relished it. But this reveals how some new people, like Marie, treated me almost as well as Willy always did.

Marie and I had a heart-to-heart talk that same afternoon.

"You see, Marie, I am committed to this girl named Ruthie, wherever she is."

"That's neat, Moon, so cool, I'm thrilled for you both. We can be special friends while honoring that relationship." I didn't bother mentioning the time I walked to the Iowa State Union and back with Millicent.

Every night after dinner we headed down the hill to Jax Snax. Most nights there was a band. Other hotel workers also gathered there every night, each group at their own tables. We'd drink beer and do the twist, the push, the stroll and other dances. When I say "we," of course I don't mean myself, but I'd sit with our group and drink beer and we'd laugh, and Willy got to where he could dance with them and that's how nights passed.

Marie and Willy would go off by themselves, sometimes, which was fine because it was an easy walk home for me. But we always spent the first part of every night together laughing and drinking.

Since I didn't get out on the dance floor, my appearance didn't draw any attention or trouble from the other hotel staffs. Since the music was loud, talking was tough, and nobody noticed Willy's talking impediment that much.

Marie never kissed Willy. Not that I saw, anyway. And I didn't ask him. But I failed to tell him that she kissed me, which was an error.

Marie understood I was attached to Ruthie, and Willy had blessed my relationship with Ruthie so nothing violated our "Solemn Pact."

It turned out, just like I never told Willy about my imagining having a girlfriend and driving her to Grundy Center in an MG, Willy also had a girl secret.

"Willy, we have our Solemn Pact about girls, remember?"

"Yeah."

"Well we both like Marie and she likes us, right?"

"It's not a problem," Willy said, "I maybe have a girlfriend back home."

Wow.

Either that sly old Willy had held out on me, or, he was overestimating the interest of some girl in him. I hoped, for his sake, that this was real.

After a month's work, we all got a day off without pay. They wouldn't let me take mine when Willy got his. Marie got the same day off as Willy, and she knew how much Willy and I wanted to go riding together, so she did my pots and pans for me that day. Willy and I headed for the T-Lazy-7 ranch. That tells you a lot about Marie. I got another waitress to spell Marie the next week, so she still got her day off to relax. I spent one night working on that other waitress's car, changing the universal joint so everybody got something from the trades.

Willy and I drove to the ranch, gave the foreman four dollars each and hopped on our horses. Each had a "T" branded on its haunch next to a number "7" except the seven tilted on its side. That's how the place got its name.

Willy, of course, dug his heels into his mare and tugged the reins. The horse reared up, kicked her front legs in the air and he shouted "Yippee-aye-oh." A cowpoke sauntered out from the stable, carrying boots, chaps and ten-gallon hats.

"You dudes might be more real," he said, "with boots, chaps and hats."

"Okay," I said.

"No siree, dude, two dollars extra."

Willy and I dismounted, walked to the other side of the corral, discussed that price and agreed that while two dollars was a lot of money, we should probably do it for safety. We agreed we weren't doing it because we thought we were Roy Rogers, or something like that. We quit playing cowboys years before, but it would be a safer ride with that gear.

I gave Willy a dollar. He handed two dollars to the ranch hand, who gave Willy boots, chaps and the hat. The chaps would protect our legs if we rode through sagebrush or cactus, keeping our jeans from ripping. We would almost save the two dollars right there. The boots protected us from being dragged to death. The reason those heels are there is to make it impossible for your foot to slip all the way through the stirrup. If that were to happen, in a fall, our ankles would be trapped, the horse would spook and run while Willy's and my skin, muscles, flesh and other parts would be spread out over a stretch of land, nothing more than two thin, moist films. We wouldn't attract a starving buzzard. The pointed toes made it easier to swing your foot into the stirrup, getting in with less than perfect aim. We didn't own a canteen, so the hats would be helpful when we needed water.

Cowboy dress was practical.

"I'll take those," I said, reaching for the other set of boots, chaps and the hat.

"Two dollars each," he said.

I looked at Willy. He looked away. We whispered to each other. This practical approach was becoming expensive. Willy dug another dollar bill from his pocket and wobbled over to me. His ankles weren't so steady in those high heels on soft dirt. I took the dollar, added another to it, got my outfit and put it on.

Willy asked about spurs.

"No spurs for dudes," the cowboy said.

We swung our legs over, Willy slapped his heels against his horse and it trotted off on a trail headed toward the peaks. My horse fell right in behind, no urging necessary. Our horses plodded along the path, which wound across a grassy stretch for a mile. Aspen and pine separated us from the Big Thompson but you could hear it gargling in wide spots and spit-roaring where the rocks choked in on the stream. Our trail took a right turn, into a notch between the peaks. The path climbed up, winding around the mountain.

These two animals probably had done this every day for years, but still wheezed on the slope and stumbled once or twice over loose rock. Willy stopped where the path widened, and I pulled alongside.

We stared. We were a couple thousand feet up. We could no longer hear the Big Thompson over the wind swishing the pines. The evergreens smelled clean.

"Wow," I said.

"Is this better than a paint?" Willy asked.

"It beats any picture I've ever seen," I said.

"Your turn to lead."

I nudged my horse, and we clopped ahead of Willy. Gophers scurried between the rocks alongside and the higher we climbed, the scrubbier the pines looked. Marie had appropriated some cupcakes for us from the kitchen. I threw one back to Willy. He caught it easily, even though my toss went high. We ate part and threw bits to the gophers while the horses struggled ahead.

A black cloud rolled over the canyon on the other side, but didn't seem interested in our direction. It stormed the opposite cliffs. We actually saw different weather, without being in it. We kept going. My horse jerked when it thundered over there, but I patted her neck, talked low and soothing and she settled down. Animals accepted me.

We reached the peak and it turned out not to be pointed, but kind of a flat spot behind what looked like a pointed top from below. We gathered some squaw wood, those are dead branches that still hang from the tree, so they're dry, put a few pine cones under them and lit a fire while our horses rested.

Lightning struck across the canyon and the startling thing was that the bolt was below us.

"Is God here?"

"Somewhere," I replied.

A few drops started to pelt us, not much; we had on big hats anyway and watched that storm roll across the other mountain while we huddled around our fire.

Willy and I didn't say one word.

We sat and stared. One of us would get up and look over the backside.

Maybe we'd toss a stone and watch it sail down. Then I mentioned we probably shouldn't because a ranger had told us that could start a rock slide. We knew that this came close to being a holy time, a unique moment, but it dazed us too much to discuss.

The sun beamed through. Another black cloud rolled over it. It shone on us again, lower in the sky.

"Moon, what if I get girl?"

"We're always friends Willy. Are you serious with Marie?"

"No, no, another girl."

"Who?"

"It may not work out."

We started back down. The rain swept over to our side of the canyon. The horses got soaked. Their eyes flipped white when lightning struck and they twitched. Willy and I dripped from the chest down, those big brimmed hats keeping our upper bodies dry. We didn't take turns leading down because you couldn't see that much in the downpour and our horses seemed to stumble more on the wet rocks.

There were a couple moments, where the trail narrowed and the edge dropped off so fast that if our horses slipped, there wouldn't be any noise, just air whistling past us, while our bodies accelerated toward rocks and trees.

"I'd rather hit a tree" Willy said.

"I don't think there'd be any difference between hitting a rock or wood, Willy. Dead is dead."

Our horses moved slower. We hoped they could see better than we. Our fingers stiffened in the cold, so we couldn't let go of the reins, even had we dared.

After another hour, which felt like three centuries, the land flattened and we knew we would survive. Willy and I started talking again. At about a mile from the T-Lazy-7 those horses broke into a gallop. Willy and I didn't do anything to cause that, they just took off. Willy whooped and pretty soon was waving his hat in the air. I just gripped the reins and held onto the horn, bouncing off the saddle with each stride. The corral gate was open, our horses stopped so fast at the water tank that I slipped over my mare's head, splashing into the water. That same cowpoke came out carrying a bullwhip.

He snickered and said if I'd get out quick he wouldn't charge extra for stiffening the chaps. Willy lent me a hand; we took off the outfits and sat around the stove in their bunkhouse to dry. Willy and I thought we might listen to the cowboys talk about riding the range, taking cows along the Chisholm Trail, fighting in saloons and things of that nature. But they discussed Ford pickups vs. Chevys, Social Security, baseball, who won the Korean War and the cost of milk. When Willy and I dried out, we thanked them and drove back to the Stanley Hotel.

We had experienced a day that nobody in Grundy Center could possibly imagine.

That kid who claimed to be a Tulane student stood behind our bunkhouse, target shooting tin cans when we pulled in. It turned out the story was true, he lived, but hid in the woods until he was sure the pastry chef was gone, and his stab wound had healed up in a week.

"Ain't that T-Lazy-7 a great deal?" he asked.

We agreed that it was some experience. A few other guys gathered around.

"Did I tell you what happened when I tried it?" the Tulane guy asked.

"I got saddled up," he continued, "and they tried to gyp me out of more money so I could dress up like a cowboy. Can you believe that? They were going to charge me a buck, a whole dollar, to play cowboy. They probably had an Indian outfit with a tomahawk too."

Willy and I chuckled, not replying.

We all headed down to Jax Snax that night, Marie and Willy and me in his car. We told Marie all about it, except that chaps and boots part. Marie talked with me in the early evening, then she and Willy danced so I headed home.

I've seen people work hard and never get a break. Not so with my life. I may hustle more, maybe I put extra effort into things but I've been rewarded generously. The Stanley Hotel was no different. The head of the kitchen, a Frenchman who trained the busboys and waitresses to hoist a tray overhead on three knuckles, came back to my station one morning. He always wore an ascot which is a fluffy kind of tie.

"Moon, we come across a professional washer wiz experience in pots and pans."

"I understand, Mr. Benoit," I said. My voice broke a little, but I don't think he noticed.

"Non, non, Moon," he said.

"Uh, then, what do you mean?" I asked. When the excitement gets me, I never talk so smooth.

"You, Moon, deserve zee promotion," he said.

What a relief. For a few seconds there it felt like I had failed again.

"I'll clear off the tables so fast and quiet, our customers won't know it's happening," I said. I wiped the grease and charcoal off my hands.

"Non, Moon. We cannot place you in public eye, you understand, but as of zees moment, you are promoted to glass washer."

This was a break. The glass washer station was away from the kitchen, between it and the bar and cooler. No cooks yelled at you there, the busboys and waitresses all came past several times an hour, making it a friendly spot. The regular glass washer fell into the habit of emptying glasses from the bar himself. He told us the alcohol protected him from the guest's germs. One day he'd only finish the scotches. The next day he'd drink all the wine. Another day he might suck down what's left of both the gins and vodkas, those being harder to tell apart. By only drinking one thing at a time he figured he'd never get sick.

It worked.

What his plan didn't protect him against was passing out and the second time he did it during a shift cost him his job. So my dependability and his drinking got me a promotion. The pay couldn't change, since the hotel was having a tough summer, they said. But as before, I would get a share of the blanket tips that conventions paid the hotel. Blanket tips came from groups at the end of their stay and were for the entire staff, replacing individual tips.

My new station had a rubber mat to stand on, which was more comfortable than the wooden platform in the pot washer's corner. Both kept your feet dry, but the rubber had more cushion, so your feet didn't die during the day. But the best part was that the pastry chefs were next to me, and if I walked past them it often smelled of vanilla, which brought Ruthie to mind.

I found many reasons to pass by the pastry chefs.

I won't reveal the previous glass washer's name. I'm not trying to damage anybody's reputation. It just seemed appropriate to explain how I managed to get a promotion in such a short period of time. Some of it was that I showed up for work on time every day and tried to never let the cooks down. But the other part was luck, and for the rest of the summer I enjoyed the status of being a glass washer. I hardly ever drank anything from the returned glasses.

Our head chef collected and distributed the blanket tips. He threw tantrums every time a busboy or waitress dropped a tray. This chef stood 5'6", wore checkered pants and a starched white hat and insisted all the chefs dress the same. Only he, however, wore a checkered bandana. All other chefs wore white bandanas.

My bet was that he weighed 210. I'm a decent guesser from working once in that "guess your age and weight" booth during Korn Kastle Days. Usually I worked at the Coke bottle tipping, but Doctor Throckmorton finally had that booth banned. The "age and weight" job was to guess about half of them within five years and five pounds. Do worse, and the cost of prizes meant we lost money. Do much better and folks stopped coming by with their quarters. So I never did my best until the last afternoon of the last day.

So if I got it right, and the head chef weighed 210, you can imagine how it looked when us scrawny college kids collected around him in the kitchen after the Premier Life Insurance Executives left.

"There won't be any blanket tip," he said.

Everybody looked at each other with shock.

"You entered so many wrong orders, dropped just enough trays and failed to clean enough dishes properly that this group won't be coming back and won't reward your poor performance."

"But they seemed delighted," Marie said.

"Oh sure, when they get liquored up," the chef said, "they'll be happy. But when it came time to settle up, they remembered your dreadful service."

For about ninety minutes, we felt inadequate. Our whole group understood, briefly, that we flunked that week. Everybody went back to their rooms and sat, maybe read a book, thought about how we could improve and soaked in embarrassment.

But before two hours passed, a secretary at the hotel, a woman whom the chef had insulted several times, mentioned to one of our crew that the insurance group actually left a $1,000 tip for us.

For us. Not him. And that word got around in minutes to every worker in the hotel.

This wasn't right. The head chef drove a white Thunderbird with gold pinstripes. He worked Estes Park in the summer and Palm Springs in the winter. Probably didn't work at all in between. And he was good, the guy made gelatin carvings you couldn't believe but he screamed anytime a busboy dropped a tray or when an order wasn't clear. His assistant, we called her Poll Parrot, due to the way she screeched from her tall stool next to the kitchen door, checking receipts, repeated every announcement he made. She produced soprano echoes of his tenor commands.

That night we drank less at Jax Snax. Partly because that money wouldn't be rolling in for the week. Some of our conversation involved justice.

Losing my share of that tip didn't mean I couldn't return to Iowa State. If I skipped lunch a couple days a week, my cigar box savings could cover that last year. So I'd still get the degree, a respectable job, help Mom and find Ruthie.

It seems the next day, at 2:15, when most of the dining room cleared but the staff was picking up or setting tables for dinner, a waitress dropped an aluminum tray. I'm not revealing who by name, but this was a lady with a radiant smile who had befriended me.

That tray clanged on the cement kitchen floor. The head chef scurried over, screaming at her.

Just as he got to Marie it seems eight other waitresses and busboys dropped aluminum trays in various parts of the kitchen. All we could see was the head chef's mouth and chin flapping but nobody heard a word. The clatter blotted out every sound he tried to make.

A half cantaloupe sailed across the kitchen and hit Poll Parrot perfectly in the face. This fruit had sat in the sun most of the morning so a reasonable debate could be held over whether it was a liquid or solid when it struck. After the impact it sloshed over her sputtering face and dribbled down the lace collar of her blue dress.

Willy's always been athletic. His ability to throw something so accurately from behind a lobby door that's only opened momentarily is a gift. I'm not implicating Willy. I'm just commenting on a skill.

The head chef's eyebrows flittered and fluttered, independent of each other, kernels of corn popping in the noise. He ran from one corner of the kitchen to the other, looking like he was shouting but we couldn't hear.

We knew he would rush into the dining room next, after the last guests left lunch, to salvage what he could of his gelatin sculpture and reshape it for dinner.

The last table cleared. He scurried to the centerpiece without noticing ten waitresses and busboys scattered across the dining room. Each one stooped, holding a single dinner plate. All stood their plates on edge and gave them a twirl, like a top. The ten plates whirled quietly on the hardwood floor. Every waitress and busboy hustled out. After a minute the plates still twirled. But instead of whirling on their edges, they began to flatten, making a "waller-waller-waller" noise that turned into an overture as all the plates went horizontal. Three doors to the dining room opened a crack. Several busboys and waitresses peeked at the head chef, running from plate to plate, swearing in Austrian. Willy, Marie and I stood watch in case Poll Parrot returned. She didn't.

(If part of growing up is that you don't do things like that anymore, then I hope to never mature. When somebody wrongs somebody, things should be done. It may not stop their behavior. It may not make things right. But it sure relieves a victim's bitterness.)

Another person poured sugar in the Thunderbird's gas tank. That repair cost the chef part of the tip he stole. And wedging several nails halfway into both rear tires meant he suffered a flat down the road, where it's not so convenient. A rear flat is safer than a front, so he received some consideration. Unfortunately, he might not understand that we did it, so after he patched those tires someone slashed them again in his parking spot, right next to his fancy room over the hotel.

He got the message.

I doubt he ever pocketed a convention tip again. That's important because the smallest amount anybody steals is their first theft. We did his later life a favor.

Willy got edgy in August. He rode a horse faster than me and water-skied better. We proved that on Lake Poytawukie. Willy could also unclog a drain quicker and toss a cantaloupe with accuracy. But he wasn't used to being so far from Grundy Center. I had lived in the apartment at Ames and later in Spinney House, so this cowboy life didn't unsettle me as much.

"That girl I mentioned?"

"Yeah Willy?"

"She lives in Kanawha."

"That's really super, Willy."

We sat on the mesa behind the Stanley Hotel, between meals. It was a five minute hike through the boulders to get on top of this overlook. Nobody bothered us there but gophers. If we didn't toss them food, within minutes they'd ignore us. We could see up most of the Big Thompson Canyon from there.

"Kanawha is what, about fifteen miles south of Grundy Center?" I asked, pretty well knowing the answer.

Kanawha was the intersection of two gravel roads, had one bar, two churches and a gas station with a single pump. If you wanted premium, you had to drive somewhere else.

"Kathleen letters sends," Willy said.

"If you'd like, Willy, I'll read them and try to explain what she's saying."

That seemed like a favorable offer, since Ruthie and I were such good friends.

"She graduate in 1962," he said, "and wasn't engaged so town is getting nervous for her."

We looked down the canyon. The sky was clear, but, by now we'd learned it could change fast.

"There's nothing wrong with her," Willy said.

We heard thunder up the canyon. Without a word, we looked up, saw the dark sheet draped below a cloud and the sparks below, and Willy and I started scrambling down the rocks to our concrete block dormitory.

"I'm happy to read your letters and help you understand them," I said.

"That's probably not right," he said, "her thoughts are private."

Willy made me proud sometimes.

"Maybe we could all go to Lake Poytawukie when we get back," I said, "before my senior year starts."

"I want to avoid embarrassment if things don't out work," he said.

Willy didn't go to Jax Snax as often in August. The few times that he and Marie and I did Willy didn't stay to dance with her. He and I started leaving early. Marie started dancing with those loud fraternity guys from Ole Miss which I don't think she should have. She had more class than they did. Those smoothies were always quick with jokes but that doesn't mean they're more fun to be around. A lot of the girls seemed to think so, but Willy and I didn't care. We had our own friends. I hate how Ole Miss frat boys act.

We left in August. I preferred to stay until the season ended but Willy got terribly homesick. The hotel said our early departure would be fine. They had a waiting list of workers, even that late in the season.

It took us about ten minutes to pack our stuff in Willy's car and we rolled down the Stanley Hotel's steep, circular drive.

"Willy, Moon, Willy and Moon," somebody shouted. Marie was running down the hill and nearly fell. We screeched to a stop.

"I'm going to miss you guys," she said, leaning through the window.

She wrapped her arms around Willy. I watched. That felt funny.

But right away Marie ran around to my side, leaned in and hugged me too. I glanced at Willy and he was looking out his window but his face drained white.

We pulled away slow. Marie stood in the middle of the drive waving and we both waved back.

Willy and I headed east, hardly speaking until the Kansas border. By the time we got to Missouri everything was okay between us again. We got those state patches and put them across Willy's rear window. That Missouri river seemed wider where we crossed it, farther south. There was no charge for crossing this bridge, so we did it three times. Once we crossed our home border, we got an Iowa sticker for Willy's window to show off alongside the others.

This made quite a display. Nebraska, Colorado, Kansas, Missouri and Iowa decals all across one window. We didn't do anything to call attention to them. Half the time we didn't need to. Many of the gas station attendants mentioned it when we stopped and we tried not to sound smug. You never knew, some of them could have been to another state themselves, so it's best to not to boast. Willy didn't complain when I asked that we stop in Ames so I could check my mail. Sure enough, there was a postcard. It showed Trail Ridge Road on the photo side. The message, handwritten so well it should be framed as art, said, "Moon, knowing you brightened my life. I'll always remember you, stay cool daddy-o. Marie."

She said that.

I showed Willy. He nodded.

It's important to understand that that Marie wasn't the kind of person who just says things casually. This woman had a careful mouth. You could bank on her comments. Oh, I know, saying she'd always remember me sort of meant we'd never see each other again but I imagined I might visit her school sometime. Since Marie understood that my lifetime plan was built around Ruthie, a visit would be okay.

And Ruthie would understand.

Marie was a pal. Ruthie was the world.

But I got excited anyway and that familiar pain arose behind my eyes. For a moment I thought about my bottle of white pills. Since I had vowed to never swallow them again, I dropped that idea and after a few hours the hurting stopped anyway.

"What do you think she meant by that?" I asked Willy.

He kept driving, and wrinkled his forehead.

"Those were pretty friendly words, weren't they Willy?"

"She just said that she liked you," Willy said, "that's all."

It was hot, in spite of the 4-65 air conditioning we used in Willy's car.

"Do you think she meant we'd never see each other again?"

"Yeah," Willy said.

"But do you think that's the way she wants it?"

Willy said he didn't think she meant anything one way or the other about that. Maybe Willy was right. But I thought Marie wouldn't mind if I showed up next year at her school. I'd bet she would introduce me to her friends. We wouldn't have to dance or anything like that. If she took me to a party she could dance with other guys and I'd go back to wherever I was staying before it got too late. That would be fine.

I didn't ask Willy any more opinions about Marie because he seemed irritable.

4-65 air conditioning means driving 65 miles an hour with all four windows down, and it kept us from sweating much. Willy and I pulled into Grundy Center the next day.

"Let's head over to Lake Poytawukie," I said.

"Naah," he answered, "I should go to Kanawha and let Kathleen know I'm back."

"I'll go with you, Willy."

"We'll do that," Willy said, "after it's positive things are going forward with Kathleen."

Willy's experience with girls now exceeded mine, so I accepted his judgment. He drove to Kanawha. I slept in the Smith's hayloft without mentioning it to anybody. Grundy Center enjoyed peace without my disrupting things, especially now that I was a college student. While Grundy Center raised me, much of the town stayed uncomfortable in my presence. There was no need to upset anybody.

I hitchhiked to Lake Poytawukie the next day. Two cars stopped without giving me a ride. Finally a meat truck stopped and picked me up, but he was zigzagging across the county, making deliveries and I noticed his vehicle seemed unable to pass any bars without stopping for a sample. What should have been a twenty minute ride turned into two hours but it still beat walking. I arrived in Lake Poytawukie with the sun overhead. Kaster's Kove rented me a rowboat and tackle for two dollars. I bought a fifty cent jar of dried chicken blood which made an effective bait. That night I caught three catfish. I smoked them on a grille in the state park and watched the sun nestle into the maples lining Lake Poytawukie's west shore, wondering at what a big world we live in. Once this water was all I ever wanted, but now Willy and I had seen and conquered the Rocky Mountains. Yet with all that glamour, Lake Poytawukie still fit me most comfortably, kind of a calming tonic. I swam way out and paddled back in the dark while stars blinked from each ripple. I kept the fire going and rolled up in my blanket next to it, waking at sunrise to the Red-winged blackbirds sang from the reeds. It's reassuring to hear those birds and the waves lapping on the rocks, just like they have for thousands of years. The Red-winged blackbirds would stop their "reee-

reee" sound soon and later head south, but the waves themselves would slap and splash for several more months until they froze.

Where I shoved the boat out, the same three rocks rose from the water and the center one showed the mica stain, unchanged, next to that fissure I'd scrutinized a hundred times before.

People change more than Lake Poytawukie. Willy preferred I not meet his girlfriend for some reason.

Getting back to Grundy Center went well, two cars stopped, one took me all the way and I walked around the town to Willy's house, making sure I didn't run into anybody. Willy had also received a postcard from Marie. It showed Trail Ridge Road on the photo side. Her message said something about knowing him changed her life and she'd always remember him, said "stay cool daddy-o" and some other dimwit comments like that, typical, silly girl talk. Sayings that they write in your yearbook. Willy said Kathleen wouldn't ever say stuff like that, except he knew what Kathleen felt and he was honored that her affections were for him.

I mentioned how pleased I was with this.

"Who knows?" I asked. Maybe this could end up with an engagement or marriage and a family.

Willy said maybe.

I mentioned that this was how it starts.

Willy said he hoped so, he really did.

I assured him that it would be a pleasure to meet her.

Willy said we would do just that, in time, when he had more confidence in the situation.

I asked him to let me know when the moment was right.

"Grundy Center has a new name for Christina," Willy said.

"Christina Dawson?"

"Yeah."

"What is it, Willy?"

"They her call 'Ragless' Christina," Willy said. He explained that they never did so to her face, or around the church. She still didn't date anybody and bought a supply of Kotex from Grifhorst's Drug Emporium every month. But somebody found boxes of perfectly good Kotex at the dump. The clerk at Grifhorst's Drug Emporium put a small code on the bottom of all their

Kotex boxes. Sure enough, next month there was proof that Christina Dawson was faking it. She certainly wasn't at risk of getting in the family way; a real late bloomer.

Willy kept hesitating over my Kathleen questions, so I headed to the cemetery to pay my respects. It was dark enough that I could get a Pepsi for a nickel from the outdoor vending machine at the Pure Oil Station, without anybody noticing, on the way. I thought Grandma and Grandpa would get a kick out of my cowboy experience so I told them the entire story. Well, some of it got left out.

I did not tell Grandma and Grandpa about Commander Neil Armstrong walking on the moon. That was important, if it was true. But several stories suggested the whole thing was faked by that new-fangled agency, NASA, and how could we know if those television scenes weren't just done in the studio that produced Captain Video before?

Myself, I believed Commander Armstrong walked on the moon. But I decided to delay reporting it to Grandpa and Grandma until we knew it for a fact.

It appeared that the planners who laid out the cemetery forgot that Catholic families grew bigger than the "Hypo-Protestants." That's what Dad used to call Methodists, Congregationalists, Baptists, Lutherans and Presbyterians. Still, Dad was probably one of us now. As a result of this oversight the Catholic section filled the south side before the Protestant part reached two-thirds of capacity. The departed Catholics were now also planted all the way down the west edge of the lot. So what was going on here was a flanking move by the Catholics, with their burial plots starting to surround the Protestants on two sides. Grandma and Grandpa stretched out far enough into the corner that they need not notice. But Reverend Dawson was right there on the Protestant front line and you can bet he was sweating.

Maybe Reverend Dawson still held bad thoughts toward me.

I tried to pee on The Most Reverend Dawson's headstone, but nothing would come out. I walked to the ditch around the "Bone Orchard" and relieved myself easily there.

I came back and finished my bottle. "Pepsi Cola hits the spot. Ten minutes later it hits the pot," went the joke, based on their ads. And sure enough, after a few minutes, it worked. I had to go again, failed to wet The Most Reverend Dawson's grave a second time, and went back to the ditch.

Two other bothersome things hit Grundy Center. Willy and I snuck downtown to check the first. There was no reason to lie about this, no imaginable reason, so we guessed the rumor to be fact. But we had to see ourselves. We walked, rather than driving, to delay facing the depressing news. When we got to the Coast-to-Coast Hardware Store, sure enough, a sheet of plywood was nailed across the front window. The door was chained and padlocked. The word "closed" scrawled across the plywood. I knew Mr. Nordstrud well enough to realize he had painted that word "closed" and I could tell he did it quicker than his habit. There were a couple of paint drops and a run line below two letters. That's the kind of craftsmanship he wouldn't normally accept. It turned out that the number of farmers had continued to shrink. Each year fewer came to town for supplies until finally Mr. Nordstrud couldn't pay his bills.

The deep shame of this became apparent when Willy asked around town and learned that Mr. Nordstrud had put his davenport and lamps on a pickup, piled a couple mattresses around the side and drove out of town. Folks thought he headed south.

Willy asked around while I hid in the shed behind his house, which now boasted a window and screen door. Willy learned that Mr. Nordstrud left owing the grocer, the power company, the gas station and the Copper Kettle. His debts were posted on the bulletin board at the VFW, coming to $386.

Willy started paying down Mr. Nordstrud's debts at five dollars per week, and would continue until I graduated. Then I would finish paying them off myself. We also agreed that if Willy were to get engaged, he could cut back to $3 per week. That would be enough so the creditors could sense something being done and would not hire a collector. We also decided that that if Willy didn't end up as a family man, we might head back to Colorado to be cowboys again. And Willy said if he did get serious with Kathleen and if she got serious with him, he would ask if it would be okay for the three of us to take a trip to the Rockies, riding horses up into the sky, down canyons and through the sagebrush. Willy said Kathleen was an agreeable lady and reckoned she would find this attractive. He said just the thought of that should make any girl even more interested in the kind of life he offered, beyond being the best young plumber in Grundy Center. He had a point. Willy said if I could find and attract Ruthie that would make our world perfect.

During this visit, good old Lake Poytawukie stayed familiar and friendly. Grundy Center stepped away.

Classes didn't start for two weeks at Iowa State, but I returned to work. For some reason, my boss delayed my start for a day until he checked something with Mr. Nordstrud. I swept out the armory once, lined up the folding chairs for summer graduation, did some chores at the warehouse and started reading my senior class books.

Professor Cohen and I ate dinner together every night that first week, and he got me to thinking beyond the next year and to my life. He made a meatloaf with ketchup once and hamburgers another time. He didn't move so well around the kitchen so I made chili for us the next time and pigs in a blanket another. I think Professor Cohen appreciated my cooking, although I put the wrong kind of beans and too much pepper in the chili.

He squirted mustard over his pig in a blanket that one night, I'll never forget how he paused. Professor Cohen looked at me, squirted the mustard again, looked away and asked:

"Have you considered Jesus and his disciples' preferences?"

"What do you mean, Professor Cohen?"

"It's reported that they traveled together. Clearly the group dined together, drank wine with each other and most of them never married, like good Jewish boys are supposed to. Might they have been queer?"

I nearly choked on my hot dog. That thought never quite cleared from my head. That Professor Cohen, there's nothing he couldn't think. Never feel sorry for me. Cowboy adventures in the Rockies, peculiar conversations with intellectuals, an enviable career developing, and my stunning Ruthie.

She was probably thinking about our days together.

Somewhere.

"The thought of suicide is a great consolation: by means of it one gets successfully through many a bad night."

Friedrich Wilhelm Neitzsche

Chapter 15

She was a snot.

Gloria Throckmorton graduated from Iowa State and moved to Omaha, becoming a teacher. She lived in that distant city, probably enjoyed being pursued by many businessmen who drove large cars and owned boats. They cruised the Missouri River which was so long you could float all day without seeing the same dock twice. Maybe Lake Poytawukie was smaller, but it also was cleaner. And maybe Gloria Throckmorton evaluated all those businessmen and ended up selecting a doctor or dentist or lawyer; some professional like her majestic father.

Gloria Throckmorton couldn't be remembered by herself. Anytime I thought of her, I saw several laughing girls around her, paying attention.

"Moon, what, just what is that stain?" she had asked in her living room, the only time I'd been allowed there.

They wore cashmere sweaters if it was fall or winter with a battalion of boys flapping around the edge of their circle, all strutting for attention.

"Moon's rising," she had shouted on that ride.

The girls waved their bouffant flip hairdos and beehives, and Gloria always seemed to be in the center even when she swept around the edge of her group.

"You're supposed to be good with tools, Moon, and our toilet doesn't always flush. Could you fix it?"

My guess would be that Pritchard's Modern Auto delivered a pastel Thunderbird to Doctor Throckmorton the week before her graduation. They probably wrapped a big pink ribbon around it and parked the car in the Fie

Pi driveway and handed her the keys after a fancy graduation party. She'd squeal and hug Doctor wavy-haired Throckmorton, MD, who would nod like a minister granting communion. Some other big shots from Grundy Center would visit that afternoon and they'd all go to a restaurant with tablecloths and appetizers. Maybe they'd even get a hotel room and play Canasta that night.

Following her graduation, filled with confetti, smiles, crepe paper streamers, air kisses, congratulatory cards, people looking past people to see who else might be watching, hats and neckties, Gloria cruised over to her four-room Omaha apartment with a balcony, in that new car, her trunk filled with shoe boxes and dresses.

"You don't think, Moon, that I'm forcing her to spend more time with you, do you? We discipline these young girls, but stop short of cruelty."

I bet her dad made a separate trip with more clothes and bought her some Danish modern furniture.

But what we learned for sure was that Gloria married, moved into a bigger place and two years later slipped a hose into the exhaust pipe of her car, inserted the other end in a side window and rolled the window almost to the top. She stuffed a percale striped sheet, with a matching pillow case, in the opening around the hose. She started the engine and never woke up.

I don't know what a "percale" sheet is, but that's how we read the story.

We learned this when Willy and I returned to Grundy Center. The Omaha World-Tribune obituary, which Willy's folks saved, said her passing was quiet and peaceful. The service was in Omaha since her social life now centered around that town. A private burial took place in Grundy Center.

The GRUNDY CENTER MONTHLY BUGLE, which by then came out about five times a year, carried no obituary, Doctor's orders.

Gloria and I had shared nothing, except an ease with learning in a small town.

How can we know what goes on in other people's minds when a Gloria Throckmorton kills herself? Her suicide stunned everybody. The more I experienced others, the less I knew them.

Except myself. I could not mourn Gloria. I did not feel terrible. Surprise, yes, but grief didn't visit my heart.

Professor Cohen discussed these questions when I returned to the college. He tried to comfort me and made great sense, but didn't erase my fear that a dark corner hid inside my soul.

"Nothing brings spring faster than a ninety-day loan taken out in January," farmers used to say. My senior year went like that. Even though I was headed for teaching, Professor Cohen urged me to interview with all the companies that recruited at Iowa State. Because my math grades were perfect, plenty of them scheduled me for a talk. He thought I would do better after several practice interviews.

Professor Cohen took me downtown to the JC Penney store, where I'd gotten my work clothes just six years earlier. This time I got a suit. That's where the pants and the jacket come from the same cloth. We decided I only needed one, and got a dark, gray flannel outfit for seventy dollars that looked pretty sharp. At that price, it ought to. This suit had a chalk stripe, they called it, yet it didn't look anything like Professor Cohen's coats which showed chalk dust all over.

Once you get the suit, then you need a belt and shoes to match. We picked a cordovan belt and shoes. Plus Professor Cohen bought me a can of cordovan polish so the belt and shoes would always shine. He advised me to use it several days before the interview, since the stain didn't always come off your fingers right away. Cordovan is pretty much a purple color and is horsehide. Now I had two pairs of good shoes counting my black lace shoes from ROTC. When they told me I couldn't be in ROTC, while it was compulsory for every other guy in the whole school, the commandant took my uniform back. I hadn't even worn it. But it was policy to not take shoes back and they charged me a dollar for those, so there was that lucky star shining on me again.

The wardrobe creation, however, still wasn't finished. I needed a shirt and probably two. And a tie for each.

The reason for two is that if you're lucky, there will be a second interview and you don't want to look like you only have one shirt and tie. The follow-up interview might be with a different person but you can't know for sure. The second shirt and tie are insurance. I planned to keep a notebook about what I wore to each interview to avoid repeating the outfit. The trick here is to make sure they're noticeably different. We picked out an oxford cloth shirt with a button down collar. We found a gray and blue polka dotted tie to go with that. The second shirt was white, plain collar and with a solid maroon tie. It was pretty hard to not notice those dramatic changes. And they both looked peachy keen under that gray suit.

There's a whole new thing to learn about the ties. First, there are two ways to knot a tie. You can do a four-in-hand knot or a Windsor. The first one is easier. The second one kind of balances out better, but the knot grows.

Professor Cohen got a little lost on this part so the salesman helped me until I diagramed the steps to tying the knot. I kept those sketches in the coat pocket. Now I could tie a tie.

Professor Cohen and I agreed that teaching would be the perfect career for me, but since the corporations who came to Iowa State showed interest in my grades, I might as well rehearse with them.

My first session came with Mason, Hanger, Silas & Mason Co. This company made artillery shells for the army and operated a plant next to the Mississippi river in Burlington. I studied up on the outfit. It turned out they designed their buildings just like Dupont did with three brick walls and one of light wood, facing the river. In the event of an explosion, the wood walls blew out but the rest of the building stayed put. Just replace the wooden part and any building could be back in operation within a week. Workers who got caught in a blast were said to have "crossed the river."

Employment should be good with this outfit, since the commies were pushing Vietnam around. Shells would beat those pinkos. Mason, Hanger, Silas & Mason Co. manufactured a special kind, with plastic shrapnel. When the enemy got hit with this stuff, no X-Ray could find it, so if they survived the battlefield they'd die in the hospital. It was clever.

This interview took place on the second floor of Beardshear Hall. I got there thirty minutes early, brought a second copy of my grades, signed in and sat on a bench outside the door. By leaning sideways, I heard most of the interviewer's questions and the student's answers.

They ran over the time limit, and were ten minutes into mine when they finished. I must have bent further with every question and answer, because when I tried to straighten up, my muscles and back had stiffened. I slid back sideways on the bench, so the door wouldn't crack my head when it opened.

The student left, the interviewer glanced at me and went back inside. I was half-crouched, trying to stand but my back still curved sideways when he looked.

By the time I got up, however, my spine mostly unlocked and I stood nearly straight. The faculty person called me in and introduced us, with me still tilting sideways a bit.

The man from Mason, Hanger, Mason & Silas sort of froze when he saw me. I waited a few seconds and he recovered, handing me his card. It said Personnel Assistant, Hiring, Mr. Robert "Bob" Smathers. I stuck out my hand and introduced myself.

"You can call me Bob," he said, but I didn't dare. He explained the position was a cost analyst.

"A few weeks of accounting training would be necessary," he said.

"But numbers don't seem to be a problem for you, do they lad?"

"No sir."

"Does, uh, your unusual appearance ever cause problems, son?"

"My pals at Spinney House had me sit in the front row for our group picture."

"I see, that's nice."

"The staff at the Stanley Hotel treated me like family, sir."

"Did they let you work with the customers?"

"No, I stayed in the kitchen."

"Well you're a remarkable fellow."

"Thank you."

After finishing his coffee, Mr. Smathers tore little pieces off the Styrofoam cup while he talked. To my great relief, my back was straightened out by then. Most of his cup disappeared after ten minutes. Since we started late, our interview only lasted twenty minutes. He had ten candidates to meet that day, he explained, but none had math grades as solid as mine. He shredded the base of the cup while he said that, swept the bits into his hand, dumped them in a wastebasket and shook my hand.

I told Professor Cohen about the interview, which went quite well, I guessed. While I still wanted to be a teacher, we agreed that the world might surprise me with other choices.

One week later I wore my maroon tie and white shirt to an interview with an IBM recruiter. He said most of their hires were in sales, and my abilities seemed stronger as a technical support employee. That sounded great.

For Easter weekend I bused to Omaha for an interview with Peter Kiewit Construction. They needed estimators and would pay half the gasoline cost for anybody who visited. That went well, except when the interviewer learned I took the Greyhound, since I can't drive, he needed an extra week to get my travel check to me. He said estimating was an office job, so not having a driver's license might be okay.

Mr. Smathers, meanwhile, sent me an extremely polite letter about how interesting it was to meet, but he said with sincere regrets that they had filled the position. He also said he was sure that with my "numbers skills," it wouldn't be long before some lucky company hired me. I wrote back thanking him.

Next came a big one. Gates Rubber, the largest producer of V-belts in the entire world, needed quality inspectors. Understanding statistics was critical to this position. I made straight A's in stat without breaking a sweat. And get this, Gates Rubber was headquartered in Denver, Colorado, right at the foot of the Rocky Mountains. A guy could ride horses every weekend, learn to snow ski, fly fish for trout, kayak and wake up at the base of those mountains every morning.

My career, of course, was important, so those things couldn't affect my decision. But can you imagine, driving up to the Stanley Hotel, just for something to do on a Saturday? And riding horses over Trail Ridge Road?

My IBM letter also said that the interviewer appreciated our meeting and that I should be proud of my accomplishments. Unfortunately, they decided to hire different skills than those "strong ones" which I possessed.

Peter Kiewit Construction sent me a check for half my bus fare and a letter.

"We congratulate you on your scholastic achievements," the letter said, "but regret we can't find an appropriate opening for your superb skills at this time."

I wrote back.

"When might a better time be?" I asked. After two weeks they hadn't answered, so I sent another letter.

"We cannot be sure when circumstances might change, but wish you the best in your career search, and are sure you'll do quite well."

That was a nice compliment. Things were going well.

My General Electric interview was quite promising. I told the man that I'd seen Ronald Reagan host their TV program. This impressed him. He came all the way from Schenectady, New York, which is pretty far but all their advertising media studies were done there. They needed trainees. Media analysis required a lot of number crunching. The interviewer spent most of our time looking out the window, wondering if it might rain and asked me questions about some of the buildings. He wondered where to eat so I offered to meet him for dinner, but he already had plans.

"The hiring committee admired your accomplishments," Gates Rubber's letter said, "which makes us regret that different criteria meant selecting other candidates."

I wrote thanking them, after looking up "criteria" in the dictionary to be sure, and asked about what those criteria might be and when they might change, but didn't hear back. I wrote again reminding them to keep me in mind for those changing criteria.

Professor Cohen helped set up my teacher interviews. He talked cranky after none of the companies made me an offer. I think he saw who got jobs, since he was a professor, and became downright angry.

It was uncharacteristic of Professor Cohen to use profanity. For a gentleman with hardly any practice, however, he soon excelled.

Professor Cohen and I walked downtown for a pepperoni and cheese pizza one night, my treat. I reminded him that these interviews were just for practice anyway. He nodded a sad nod.

Professor Cohen bit off the point of a pizza slice. "Persisto, damn them all, persisto," he said.

"Persisto? Professor Cohen, uh…"

"Latin," he explained. "Persist. Illegitimus non carborandum."

"More Latin?"

"Yes, of course, forgive me. Persist. Do not let the bastards grind you down."

"But Professor Cohen?"

"Yes?"

"I'm a bastard."

"No. I mean that is irrelevant, a wrong use of the word," he said.

Professor Cohen started speaking louder and faster, and the couple at the next table moved to the corner.

"The wisest King of all, Solomon, was biologically illegitimate. David conceived Solomon with Bathsheba," he said.

"Could you tell me more back at your apartment, Professor Cohen?"

He looked around.

"No," he said, "there is nothing for us to feel any shame about. True bastards are those who consume more than they produce. Matrimony comes from a superstitious ceremony and the commitment is commonly abused, and so has little to do with anything."

Professor Cohen knew math, understood history, spoke Latin and I felt blessed to get his advice, but it was getting awkward for some of the other customers in the restaurant.

"Persisto. To hell with them and may we cleanse ourselves by their rapid departure."

"Things are looking up, Professor Cohen. GE seemed interested and, maybe that job would be a good thing to start with."

"If so, young man, it would be my pleasure to visit as your guest in Schenectady every summer," he said.

This was a relief, since New York was probably too far for Willy.

The teacher interviews all took place in two days, June 15 and 16. Every school district's principals came to the Iowa State Armory and hundreds of graduates went from table to table, getting a dozen half-hour interviews each day.

Professor Cohen researched all the principals. He favored those who had majored in religion, sociology or physical therapy. He thought those might view my skills with respect and tend to favor someone like myself.

I'm not quite sure what that meant.

Professor Cohen knew I relaxed more in smaller towns and would be able to walk to school in them, so he ended up sending letters to the principals coming from Eagle Grove, Woolstock, Algona, Corwith, Blairsburg, Iowa Falls, Coon Rapids, Britt, Grundy Center, Sigourney, Independence and Lohrville.

Every one of them scheduled an interview with me. Every last one. That Professor Cohen must write a powerful letter, I tell you. He's a poet. And he wants me to write a book?

Graduation came before the teacher interviews and it was quite a ceremony. Senator Bourke B. Hickenlooper talked to us. Professor Cohen and Willy both attended, which honored me greatly. Nobody appreciated the alignment of those 2000 folding chairs more than me.

"Here is a small token for my favorite student," Professor Cohen said after the ceremony. He handed me a box. I was in my cap and gown. Some of the graduates tossed their caps in the air, but I needed the deposit back, so I controlled myself. But when I opened the box, I nearly fainted. It was a genuine Timex wristwatch. Can you imagine? "Takes a licking and keeps on ticking," John Cameron Swayze said on TV demonstrations. Once he attached a Timex to an outboard motor propeller and sure enough, after running the motor in water, he took the watch off and it still ran. Those Timex watches are tougher than a Bulova, and that matters. Nobody had ever given me something that wasn't necessary before. That Professor Cohen was saintly generous.

My career with General Electric collapsed on graduation day itself. The letter was well written and complimentary of my academic results.

Why would anybody in their right mind choose New York anyway? I had twelve teaching interviews coming up. Professor Cohen was having more difficulty walking and mentioned that he was incontinent. I think that means you can't travel far. And how did he expect to never buy another GE light bulb? That was going a bit far. I guess Westinghouse and Sylvania made bulbs so maybe he could boycott GE. I kept quiet since Professor Cohen was only looking out for me.

I didn't care. I was headed toward being a teacher in some friendly Iowa town and Ruthie would love it. Mom might join us.

Because the teacher interviews took place in June, the schools knew which of last year's teachers were leaving and how many vacancies they had to fill. Professor Cohen remembered that I got dizzy, sometimes, in that enlarged building.

"Would it be prudent to swallow one of your white pills before the interviews start?" he asked.

"No."

"And, my favorite graduate, just why not?"

"The secret, Professor Cohen, is to just look at things that are close, never the ceiling or distant walls. Those pills are hazardous. I only kept that last bottle to defy the drugs."

"What might you mean by that?"

"For two years they've sat there, untouched, next to my deodorizer and toothbrush. That makes me stronger."

"Bravo, cheers, huzza," he said.

"Huh?"

Professor Cohen's gold tooth beamed as he leaned back and clapped. Over the years, Professor Cohen had developed confidence in me. Sometimes I think I got better just to catch up with his growing opinion.

"You might also choose to say," he added, "deodorant, not deodorizer."

"What's the difference?"

"Deodorizers mask the smell of a room, in the usual sense of that word, while deodorants are used to control bodily odors."

What we didn't know was that the Armory was set up with partitions for those days, dividing it into 132 interviewing rooms, each with a curtain in front for privacy, so I didn't have a challenge with dizziness anyway.

This process would tell me in one week where I would live and teach. All the interview scores went into a computer and they balanced the results. This way some genius who talked smooth didn't capture twelve offers, leaving eleven other graduates without any. Nobody got more than two offers to ensure everybody's fair chances.

My interviews went perfect although the principle from Eagle Grove smiled too much. He went on and on about his love for nature and rural life. That fellow must have never stopped a cow from eating her placenta, castrated pigs or scraped chicken manure off the floor. And the Algona guy, the one with a four-mile strand of hair criss-crossing the top of his head, couldn't seem to look at me. I'm not making fun of baldness. Since my head appears slightly irregular I shouldn't say what I just said. Baldness is fine. It's just the silly wiggling of hair from the sides over the top and plastering it down seems a waste of time. Wind and water must terrify someone like that. Not only did that guy not look at me but he sort of stayed in the corner and never shook hands. All the other interviews went well.

The first night of waiting, I didn't sleep. Mostly I tried to imagine the school buildings in Woolstock, Corwith, Blairsburg, Coon Rapids, Grundy Center, Sigourney, Independence and Lohrville. I pictured the guys enjoying math so much they'd study weekends and the girls not being edgy around me so we could be friends. The principle from Britt showed me a picture of their school so I didn't have to dream up that one. His building was modern, single story, with a flagpole in front and a new gymnasium on the west side of town. The Iowa Falls lady gave me a sketch of her building to keep. It was a two-story brick building next to the river and ran its own cafeteria. The second night I dozed off just after midnight, I was so tuckered out after not sleeping the first night. I thought up the imaginary kids so many times that I started to know them.

I named them all. They learned math and liked me.

But would they be able to handle square roots? How could I make algebra and trigonometry and geometry fun? Just teaching math and understanding the numbers isn't enough. You've got to help them enjoy it, show how it works in life and make some games. If you do a good job of that their lives will be better, education becomes an adventure and America gets stronger.

It was kind of silly to spend most every night that week, awake, until late trying to guess what the kids and buildings and other teachers would be like where I landed. After all nobody got more than two offers and I was worrying about all twelve. Some of the time I planned the room I would rent and the shirts and pants I could buy. Maybe I would get my own chair and davenport, but not the first year.

My printout came on Saturday morning, sealed in a 9" by 12" Kraft envelope. We lined up alphabetically in the Armory and I got mine after twenty minutes. Some kids opened theirs on the spot, whooping and hollering. Others scurried off. That's what I did.

Professor Cohen agreed to meet for a celebration pizza. I wanted to get back to my apartment first and have an adventure opening that envelope without others around. Then if my choice confused me I could let Professor Cohen help.

I gripped that envelope tight.

Nothing happened in the first block walking to my study room, until the intersection. A car honked. Neither of us had seen each other. He drove on by. I crossed, but tripped on the curb.

This was disastrous. My envelope hit the sidewalk, I sprawled out, scraping it and the envelope tore. I looked inside and the papers were ripped, but not so bad that they couldn't be read.

I started walking again, this time looking carefully in every direction, and holding that envelope with both hands. Maybe I looked strange, but this was my entire future.

I waited outside the dorm until somebody came out, letting the door swing open, so I could duck in without using my hands.

I got to my room.

I stuffed the envelope under my mattress.

I walked down the hall to the bathroom, since I was excited, used the facility and walked back to my room.

It seemed too abrupt to just open the envelope, so I returned to the bathroom, carrying my washcloth, and scrubbed my face.

Feeling refreshed, I strolled back, locked the door and pulled out the envelope. I stared at my plaque for a few seconds, remembering how proud I felt with that honor, tore off an undamaged corner of the envelope and ran my finger inside, being careful not to damage the offers any further.

I read the printout.

Another of those drifting spells floated me away. It's like I left my body and hovered on the ceiling, looking down at myself, studying me studying that printout but neither of us understanding anything.

Nobody made me an offer.

Not one.

There was a nice note from the vocational guidance office, handwritten on the bottom, saying that many budgets had been trimmed this year since the corn borers damaged the Iowa crop. Illinois, Missouri and Minnesota had sprayed in time, so their yields held up and prices per bushel stayed flat. But Iowa yields dropped. Some of the schools feared that they might not collect enough tax to hire replacements that year.

"As a result," this note said, "an unfortunate few will receive no offers. Perhaps a consultation with a vocational guidance officer, between 10 and 2 on Tuesdays or Thursdays, is advisable. Please avoid lunch hour which runs from 11:30 to 1:30. Appointments must be requested seven or more days in advance."

I was one of the unfortunate few.

"No poor, rural, weak, or black person should ever again have to bear the additional burden of being deprived of the opportunity for an education, a job, or simple justice."

Jimmy Carter

Chapter 16

Professor Cohen went dead quiet at lunch. Over the months he had talked less as walking got tougher and his incontinence restricted travel. But this time he sat without a word for several minutes and his face drained white. A drop of spit rolled down his chin. I blotted it with a napkin.

He looked out the window and I don't think he saw a thing.

"Education betrays us," he finally said, "the pursuit of knowledge has been nothing but pursuit, never getting there, probably not even coming close. Damn them all to hell. We celebrate giant technology strides while tumbling from decency."

"Professor Cohen, I can go over to the maintenance warehouse and start work right away, without needing to meet new people or learn a different trade."

He looked away.

"Working there was fun and a place I fit."

I had never seen Professor Cohen cry before.

"Of course, I couldn't expect summers off," I said. I was also thinking that the money wasn't so great that I could track down Ruthie and Mom easily.

Professor Cohen mumbled something.

"What?" I asked.

"Persisto."

So I would. Working at the maintenance warehouse would get me some cash. And time to figure out how to reach Mom and Ruthie.

"Can you make it back home Professor Cohen?"

His head nodded but his eyes glazed. He whispered in Latin again, so weak I could barely hear.

"Then I'll go straight to the maintenance shop and get those paychecks coming."

He didn't look up. We did something we'd never done before, and tossed half of our pizza in the trash. I helped him stand. He wobbled to the door. I watched him stagger down the sidewalk and when it looked like he'd make it home, I sprinted over to the warehouse, running so fast my side hurt. It seemed important that I get that job back quick, if only to help Professor Cohen recover. My manager was there, spray-painting a file cabinet. The other workers were out relining the chimney in the generator plant.

"Can I come back now?" I asked.

"Just because I got a degree doesn't mean a thing on salary. My old rate would be just fine," I said.

My manager dumped his coffee into the sink without answering.

"One thing that schooling did," I said, "was to help me understand the way Iowa State operates, so I appreciate now how important it is to repair these things."

My manager stood, shoved his hands in his pockets and explained that his budget was fixed and that without Mr. Nordstrud providing those tools free, there was no way he could put me back on.

"What do you mean?" I asked.

"Your Mr. Nordstrud gave us free tools while you worked here, Moon."

"I didn't know that."

"Doesn't matter," he said.

I'm not a person who shouts. The JC Penney store manager didn't need to call the police. All I suggested was that they should take my suitcoat, pants, belt, shoes and ties back since I wouldn't need them now, and they were hardly worn. If I could get eighty cents on the dollar, with my savings I could repay Professor Cohen for his expenses. Just because I made a mess of everything, Professor Cohen shouldn't be out of pocket. They said since the pants were cuffed to fit me, they couldn't accept them back. I pointed out that at my height, a little above average, somebody could buy them and need them shortened.

When the manager claimed I shoved him, that was not accurate. When I held up the pants to his chest, maybe my hand bumped him a little. It was more that he lost his balance than me hitting him.

My argument made sense, so expressing it again, after the officer arrived, struck me as reasonable. When the cop told me to stop shouting I yelled that I was not speaking with him. Putting me in the Ames jail was overreacting. I wasn't about to make that one phone call they allowed.

Forty-eight hours alone, food provided, when I didn't have much money or a place to go gave me time to plan. And sitting alone in that cell, with a straw tick on a slab, a stainless steel toilet with no lid, no sheets for the bed, no belt on my pants or laces in my shoes, you can't do much but think.

The instant they released me I went to the dorm, collected my clothes and the Woodrow Wilson Scholarship plaque, taped everything in a cardboard box and stopped by to see Professor Cohen.

Once again, that walk up his sidewalk seemed to take about a year. Had he read about me being tossed in the clink? I rapped on his door. His shades were shut. Normally he'd shuffle over, open the door, smile and greet me with some startling intellectual comment.

"Come in," he said from inside. I almost couldn't hear him. He slouched in his living and dining area, half sitting, half lying on the davenport. I turned on the lamp. A couple dirty dishes laid on his table, so he must have been ailing. I picked them up, washed and dried them as best I could, since there was no soap and the food was crusted dry on the plates. Isosceles's bowl was flipped upside down and stuck to the carpet but the dog wasn't anywhere to be seen.

I told Professor Cohen about my new career plan. He nodded.

The professor thought, given my situation, that it made sense. He didn't smile, just mumbled that in a strange way, I might now lead a life that other Iowa State graduates could envy. He did not know about my residency at the jail since he had canceled the paper. It seemed best to not distress him further with that information. I got halfway down his sidewalk when I heard the professor whisper through his screen door.

"Persisto. May those recruiters and principals roast slowly in hell's flames. Put your life in a book, that shall explain all we need know about the human spirit. Damnation on them. Illegitimus non carborandum."

I hitchhiked to Lake Poytawukie in one full day, getting three rides. I took my jungle hammock, which had mosquito netting sides with a canvas roof, and slept in the woods near the north shore. I slipped my genuine Timex into my sock before going asleep in case somebody robbed me during the night.

In better times I'd bought the hammock for $10 from Richard's Surplus Store in Des Moines. During a summer I could almost live in that thing, with a blanket and nothing else. The trick was to tie short strings on the cords near both ends, just at the canvas edge. That way the rain gets pulled away and won't seep under you.

The Red-winged blackbirds called me at sunrise. "Reee-reee" they said and I got up slow and quiet so they'd keep singing.

Their sounds reminded me of Ruthie, pure notes, high ones. I found an untended boat in the rushes and poled around the shallows. I picked night crawlers and sold them to the boat place, getting plenty of change for a burger and malt each day and swam at the public beach to stay clean and proper.

After a few days I hitched over to Grundy Center. Two rides got me there by noon.

Willy, my pal, always proved to be as good a friend as any guy could want. I mention that to keep his big news in perspective. It seems Willy had gotten engaged, quietly and quickly. He went over to Mason City and found a ring with a 1/4-carat diamond for $100 and son-of-a-gun, he bought it and Kathleen accepted it. The jeweler didn't care how much Willy paid down as long as he made some kind of weekly payment.

"Did you ask Kathleen about taking a cowboy trip west with us?" I asked. Willy didn't exactly answer.

By now I understood that when my brain went into a frenzy, it stepped back from the world. This is a good thing and protects a person from getting too wound up. It's sort of like having a shock absorber built into your head. And Willy getting married was sure a milestone in our lives and I couldn't wait for the wedding or to meet her.

But I didn't get to see Kathleen. The reason, it turned out, was that she already was in a family way. They always said in Grundy Center that "the first child sometimes comes a little faster than the others," and while I'm not saying this was proper, the point is to remember how Willy stood by me, even when it wasn't easy for him. Kathleen probably is also a decent person. They just made one mistake and we should look at the entirety of people's lives before judging, if we ever judge.

Since Kathleen lived in Kanawha, her delicate condition needn't be known in Grundy Center and Willy thought they might rent an abandoned farmhouse until the child arrived, moving back into Grundy Center after a few months. Luckily the GRUNDY CENTER MONTHLY BUGLE was then only coming out every ninety days, so the birth announcement could be set whenever Willy and Kathleen wanted without the "month counters" in town catching it. That way they could also use their real anniversary date.

Willy said my career plan sounded like a picture show and he wished that he could join me, but then he stopped.

"I'm proud of my new responsibility," he said, looking away, "and we're always best friends."

The carnival came to Grundy Center right on time. The manager remembered me from Korn Kastle Days. He introduced me to Mr. Mick McSweeney who ran the race car business. Mr. McSweeney explained the job. Some lucky guy would tune and examine the race cars, which were a separate part of the carnival. This fortunate person would also work in the pits. If they liked how the individual performed, he might even get to be flagman some day.

Mr. McSweeney wore white jackets and a red bow tie, standing 6' 4", waving both hands when he talked, skin white like he never knew the sun and his red hair puffed out in front and slicked back on the sides.

Mr. McSweeney interviewed me in his trailer. I stood. He sat behind his desk.

"Might work, boy, might work," he said.

"It'll work, Mr. McSweeney," I replied.

He stood, picked up a driver's helmet and handed it to me.

"Boy, try that on," Mr. McSweeney said, tugging at his bow tie. I slipped on the helmet. It slid around until I peeked through the earhole. Mr. McSweeney chuckled, and handed me a smaller sized helmet. This one fit.

"Stand straight, boy," Mr. McSweeney said. He walked around me, nodding.

"You see boy, we need to look professional. I'll want you in uniform, and wearing that helmet from dawn until dusk."

"Do I get the job, Mr. McSweeney?"

"There are plenty of fellows begging for this position, boy," he said.

"None more than me."

"Ah, there's something about you. I'll turn away the others. You start tomorrow, boy. Keep that helmet on." Mr. McSweeney agreed to let me take a week off and leave the race cars, no matter where we were, when Willy scheduled the wedding. I wouldn't get paid and he couldn't promise to hold the job for me when I returned, but that all seemed fair. I got to bunk with four other guys, two of them friendly, all tattooed but me, in the Airstream trailer that hooked onto the Tilt-A-Whirl. Popcorn, cotton candy, foot-long hot dogs and peanuts salted in the shell were free, but we'd be fired if they caught us reselling any.

Let me say that again. All the midway food, a chili dog, Dairy Queen, caramel apples, whatever, came strictly at no charge for us performers.

It was always loud, sledgehammers driving iron stakes into blacktop and dirt, bells ringing at booths, barkers hustling people into the tents and the sounds of race cars.

And until you've stood on the edge of a track, and felt a race car rip past, the fumes deadening your nostrils with exhaust sounds so loud you stuff cotton in your ears, which still doesn't stop the sensations, because the noise vibrates your chest and the draft from each car buffets you, it cannot be imagined how much power can exist in cars.

This explains why salary isn't so important.

Sit in some office without windows? Under neon lights?

All my needs were covered, plus the excitement couldn't be believed. Our trailer had a shower. I had a closet in the Airstream where I stored my stuff, kind of keeping the Woodrow Wilson Scholarship plaque and my Iowa State diploma taped up in the box, since that might strike the other folks as high-falutin.

Why would anybody want to work for General Boring Electric? Walk in at the same time every day, wear an ID badge, and say predictable things? Look a certain way? Attend lots of meetings?

Sure they get paid a lot. Those poor suckers should. They'd die for a job like mine. We scheduled races in Dayton, Ohio and Winchester, Indiana and Anderson, Ohio and Knoxville, Iowa and Muncie, Indiana. How's that for glamorous? Why would a guy in his right mind want to work at a desk for GE when you could promote races and see the world like this? We were modern day cowboys.

By August we'd hit the state fairs in Sedalia, Missouri and Champaign-Urbana, Illinois, St. Paul, Des Moines and Pierre, South Dakota. After that, we'd head all the way to California and race in San Bernardino and Sacramento. We had ten trailers and just as many trucks in our caravan with fifty employees. Mr. McSweeney told me that if we all hustled and the rains didn't come too often, we could make a half million dollars in a good season. That's five hundred thousand dollars. My agreement with Mr. McSweeney was that I'd get one percent of the profits at the season's end. If I proved myself, he said two percent might be possible in a second year.

"Mr. McSweeney, numbers come easy to me. I could help do your bookkeeping."

He pursed his lips.

"Boy, we've got that covered."

I let that drop, figuring my skill would show with time. For now, in my first year, all my food was covered, they gave me two uniforms to wear and a professional driver's helmet. I slept and showered in the trailer, got fed by the carnies and stood to make $5,000. I never took off the helmet in daylight, just as Mr. McSweeney asked.

If the season went as it should, I could hire a private investigator with my bonus. Maybe I'd not let Mom know when I found her right away. I'd just put some money in her mailbox with a mysterious note. Or maybe I'd arrange for her employer to give her a big bonus, so when she saw me, she'd have her own pride, and could hold her head up, while we hugged and such.

I'd tell Mom about Ruthie right away and send that private investigator off to find her too. Ruthie's so radiant and magical that I might be too late. Some guy might make a move on her at that East Coast school. But she'd hesitate, remembering our nights on the davenport at PAG Church Camp and those dreamy evenings in her living room.

"It is with a pious fraud as with a bad action; it begets a calamitous necessity of going on."

Thomas Paine

Chapter 17

After several weeks of writing letters to Ruthie's mom in a bunch of possible towns I finally connected. Ruthie had gotten her degree from the Iowa School for the blind in Vinton and moved to Massachusetts with her mother.

Her answer didn't have a return address. But the postmark said Quincy, Massachusetts. Information gave me their phone number. I cashed three dollar bills and stacked thirty dimes, six rows of five, on the counter below the pay phone. That may sound extravagant, but I sure didn't want to be cut off after all these years.

"Ruthie's finishing music school and plays three instruments," Ruthie's mom said.

I knew she'd overcome all.

"She composes in Braille, and I play it on the clarinet and she rewrites based on how it sounds." That Ruthie, she is something.

"Moon, you know she's a pretty girl, and there's a young man she's committed to."

The handpiece dangled over my head when I regained consciousness. It made that "eeeeeeeee" sound that phones do when you forget to hang up, my dimes were scattered all over me and the floor outside the booth. Nobody noticed so I must have not been crumpled up for long.

Now I knew.

Mom would be the only person to find. Ruthie was lost. I was blessed to have known her.

Mr. McSweeney's races would help me find Mom. If we didn't get rained out too much, this was certain. I'd pay attention to my job, and help that tall, pale man in the white jacket and red bow tie succeed.

Right away I learned lessons in my new career. Mr. McSweeney pushed one hand through his red hair and waved his weenie finger at me.

"When you're on the racetrack, boy, always look upstream. Never, ever watch the cars go by. Keep your eyes on where they come from," Mr. McSweeney said.

He was looking out for me.

"The car that will kill you hasn't passed by," he explained. A loose tire, a vehicle tumbling end over end or skidding sideways, he said again that I must always watch where they're coming from and never where they're going, unless I'm behind a fence.

A second lesson, and one that's important for drivers is that if you ever see a crash ahead, you should aim for it. That doesn't seem natural, but all race drivers know that when a car spins, or a couple of them tangle, the most likely spot they won't be, when your car gets there, is where they are at that instant. They'll spin to one side or the other. Aim right at them. That could save your life, but it's an unnatural instinct.

Our first race was booked in Winchester, Indiana, on a high-banked asphalt track. This was a sprint car race which means the cars were open-cockpit types like you see at the Indianapolis 500, but a little smaller.

To get there Bubba White, a hot driver, let me sit in his sprint car on the trailer. He and Lulubelle, Bubba's girlfriend, rode in the pickup, while I sat in the racer with my uniform on; helmet and all.

Bubba radiated glamour. Besides winning races, he smoked Pall Malls and lit his Zippo in a single motion, rubbing it fast over a pant leg, flipping up the lid and sparking the flint at the same time.

Mr. McSweeney made signs promoting our race and when we got to Indiana, Bubba White dragged Main Street of every town a couple of times to promote the race. I'd wave from the car.

"Boy, with that crash helmet on," Mr. McSweeney said, "you look like a regular guy." I became a bit of a celebrity. This didn't mean a lot, though it was interesting being normal.

Mostly I wore that helmet since Mr. McSweeney pointed out that it helped business. Bubba loaned me money to buy two more, so I had a white helmet, a black one and a metallic blue number with a red stripe and white star on it. This added more pizzazz and excitement.

I wore my jump suit and a helmet from morning until sleeping so we promoted the races heavy.

Bubba's car was white, of course, but you could barely tell. A big STP decal covered the hood, we stuck two Delco decals on either side of the hood, painted a Red Man Chewing Tobacco logo on the rear and slapped Midas Muffler stickers just under the cockpit. And every one of those big corporations paid us for this.

It was kind of like Iowa State where rich alums gave the school checks and got their names on places like Friley Hall, the Reiman Gardens, or Brenton Hall.

Mr. McSweeney said it was all the same. "Just peddling the real estate, boy."

We drove all over Winchester and the nearby villages. Bubba and Lulubelle stopped at every intersection and I'd hop out to tack posters on the telephone poles. My marketing career took off.

On race days I also served as the technician, due to my mechanical background. This meant inspecting the cars before the race and checking the winners to make sure they hadn't cheated.

Of all the racing groups in this country, Mr. McSweeney's wasn't the biggest, but we certainly were famous for putting on the best show. Some of the other groups called us outlaws; out of jealousy

On the day of our Winchester event I inspected the vehicles and they all checked out okay. I knew Bubba's better than any, having ridden in it on his trailer through every town, one day with a plastic sheet over me while it rained.

Bubba and I worried about this new Florida driver, Roy the Raging Rebel. Bubba's car was an Offenhauser, a classic four-banger engine. The Rebel had some rich orange grower for a sponsor, drove modified Chevy engines and smoked Tiparillos.

Those Chevys raced fierce. The eight cylinders, even though they displaced the same as our four, gained traction by being smoother. They were tough to beat. One day I saw the Rebel pull out his lighter, he had a

Zippo too, put his thumb on the bottom and middle finger on the top. Then it was like he snapped his fingers, flicking the top off and the lighter flamed, not touching anything. After Bubba saw that, he stopped making a show of lighting his on a pant leg.

Bubba needed to win about every third race or Lulubelle would have to return home and go back waitressing at Woolworth's Five and Dime lunch counter in Red Oak, Nebraska. The Rebel got a new engine for each race from his sponsor. Bubba and I stayed up all night rebuilding his engine every time we hit the next town.

Our Winchester race started on a Saturday night, under lights. All the cars passed my inspection. The hot laps came first.

Hot lap money made our group famous. Every driver got three laps, alone, around the track. The fastest driver got $500, second got $400, third $300 and the next seven fastest each got $200. A driver could cover all expenses right there. It encouraged fast times but Mr. Red Svenson from Muncie got too excited. He'd retired three years before, came back and lost a tire going into the number one turn. What happened next illustrates what high-banked means. Mr. Svenson's car went straight into that curve, right up the bank, through the retaining fence without being delayed a second, cleared a large tree, not disturbing a leaf and came down in Skunk Creek.

Mr. Svenson was pleased that Skunk Creek existed, but his car owner wasn't. Without that water cushion, Mr. Svenson might have ended up several inches shorter. But in that creek his vehicle became a sizzling, rusted loss with nothing to salvage.

These races were so exciting that I could get through a whole day without visualizing her ponytail, tinted a baked apple color, or smelling vanilla, almost.

Anyway, Bubba pushed his car through a hot lap at 96 mph, then 98 and clocked in at 102 on his third, a track record. (This was later challenged by some of those bigger race organizations, which came out with tape measures and pronounced the Winchester track fifteen feet short of a quarter mile. Mr. McSweeney charged the official race groups used rubber tape measures but let the record go.)

I got so excited when Bubba broke 100 mph I fainted. When I woke up, Lulubelle had me stretched out on the infield and draped a wet mechanic's rag over my face. I bounced right up before Mr. McSweeney saw, tugged that helmet back on and continued to watch the cars, making sure no mischief took place.

It was too soon to celebrate anyway, since the Rebel went last. When the Rebel fired up his engine I stopped watching the cars on the infield. He knocked off his first hot lap at 96 mph. This was scary. His second lap timed 99 mph. I couldn't watch anymore. But his third lap came in at 97 mph.

Bubba won the $500. The Rebel had to settle for $400. Him with his brand new engine every race, staying in a fancy Holiday Inn, while Bubba and Lulubelle and I stayed in the trailers and worked all night rebuilding before each race. I didn't clap or yell since I worked for the official organization.

Next the genius of Mr. McSweeney showed. The crowd loved these hot laps, but more than that, they created a buzz leading to the main event. Mr. Svenson's getting airborne added to the spectacle. But the big event was thirty laps, twenty cars, and unlike all those formal race organizations, we put the fastest cars in the last row, and the slowest first. Talk about passing. That's why our races were exciting and other groups called us outlaws.

Just to keep everybody trying, the race itself paid $1,500 for first place, $1,000 for second and $500 to the next five. A driver who wanted to do more than cover expenses needed to score in the hot laps. Then he needed to charge through all those slower drivers in the final race for the last purse.

This was real racing, with passing and almost 100 mph traffic on a quarter mile oval in front of 5000 people who paid between $2.50 and $15, depending on where they sat. Mr. McSweeney kept half of the gate and paid the prize money, so it worked out well for all of us.

On this race day, the Rebel won. Bubba came in second.

In our next weekend race, both Bubba and the Rebel worked their way through the crowd and by the twentieth lap, Bubba had the lead. But somehow, with only two laps to go, the Rebel seemed to just stand on it in every straightaway, pulled ahead and won by several lengths.

It didn't make sense.

"Something's wrong," Bubba said, "Chevys are hot, but he's untouchable."

"Why do they carry so much alcohol and nitro?" I asked.

"How do you mean?" Bubba asked.

"We carry a couple gallons," I replied, "and that's plenty for cleaning off grease and oil."

"So?"

"The Rebel's got a ten gallon drum of the stuff."

Bubba's eyes widened. He explained what was going on. But we had tested each race car's tank for gasoline before the race and didn't detect any illegal fluids in the Rebel's. This was mysterious.

These racers carried lots of tires and changed them, depending on the track conditions. Bubba didn't carry so many but did have a branding iron. This was a metal rod that we plugged into an electrical outlet to heat it up. If we had only slick tires left and found a dirt track that paid well, we'd heat up the branding rod and cut grooves in the tires. Then we could compete on dirt.

One of the luxuries of this life was spending evenings in that trailer, since it was air conditioned. Getting cool every night gave me energy that lasted most of the following mornings, until the afternoon heat wilted everybody.

Several nights a week I'd sit in the cool air of our trailer and write on a Big Chief red tablet. Professor Cohen encouraged me to do this. He said I showed promise as a story teller.

I tried making up stuff. That didn't work. So I wrote down my Grundy Center stories, which went better, but there was a problem with that. Too much of my life was ahead and not much was past, and I would make Grundy Center better somehow, someday, so the full story couldn't be told yet.

We were becoming pals, but I never mentioned my writing to Bubba. Bubba and I mostly talked racing. I explained to Bubba how we might test our suspicion of the Rebel's cheating. I told him how alcohol and nitro had a high flammability and some other characteristics that gasoline didn't.

It's necessary to be vague, but if anybody left a branding rod accidentally turned on, near fuel fumes, there's a way chemistry might deliver justice if someone is cheating. If it's only gasoline and the branding iron's set to a precise temperature, there would be no problem.

Probably the strangest thing about a race car burning, if it's filled with alcohol and nitro, is that you can't see flames. Water, if sprayed on the car, won't put out an alcohol fire.

We said nothing when Roy the Raging Rebel lost his fancy racer in that accidental blaze. Folks noticed that the emergency firefighters couldn't see much flame and that made it tougher to put out. That also verified what was going on.

Afterward, Bubba and I dug through the wreckage.

"Lookie here," I said.

"What?" Bubba asked.

"See these fuel lines?"

"So?"

"They are way fatter than necessary. They could hide the nitro or alcohol in here, and we'd never find it when sampling the gas tank. This could siphon in and last for a whole race."

"Moon, you're a whiz kid," Bubba said. "Smart, Moon. Genius."

Demand for orange juice must have been strong that year, because it wasn't even two more weeks into our schedule before the Rebel came back with a brand new car. We chatted with him about the fuel lines, and the Rebel didn't cheat that way anymore.

But Bubba started coming in second again, not always, but often enough that Lulubelle had to hop a Greyhound back for Nebraska to work the Woolworth's Five and Dime lunch counter. She said it was an okay job. The Rebel wasn't carrying any nitro or alcohol this time, and I never did figure out his new method of cheating.

The Rebel quit our group halfway through and joined the United States Autoracing Club. He got a ride next year for the Indy 500, did well in their time trials but didn't respect the speed. After he qualified, he stuck his right arm out of the cockpit to wave at his crew and the slipstream jerked his shoulder out of the socket, ending that year for him. Those Indy cars move.

We mostly did two races a weekend through June and July, going to daily events when the State Fairs kicked in. Every race had a poster. I always tacked hundreds of these posters on telephone poles, near intersections where traffic slowed, in every town before the race. I kept a sample of each tucked under my mattress to show Mom. She'd be impressed. And her jaw would drop when she saw my genuine Timex watch. Half of these races were for sprint cars and half were stock cars.

We also did a couple of "Local Daredevil" events.

At Knoxville, one of the stockers won way too easily, but after the race I couldn't find anything funny in his gas tank. He didn't have any strange fuel lines. The engine looked legal. I lifted the heads and measured the displacement. Luckily, I used a steel ruler. If it had been wooden, I'd have missed this. When I moved the flywheel to get the piston down to its bottom position and jammed that ruler in to measure, it didn't clunk like it should have. It clinked. It should've clunked.

Even luckier the mechanic had a magnetized screwdriver, so I slipped that down the cylinder, and sure enough, pulled out a fake top to the piston. They'd cut off the tops of eight pistons and slipped one down each cylinder before letting us measure. It looked legal and measured legal but wasn't.

Mr. McSweeney came over. He and I and the driver huddled. The winners had already been announced. Mr. McSweeney thought it was best to keep this quiet so as to not confuse the crowd. But this driver needed to disappear without his prize money and not race for another month as a penalty.

The driver agreed, pushed his car onto a trailer and we never saw him again. I did read in Speed Sport News that he was winning big time in Tennessee and the Carolinas, places we never went.

When I asked Mr. McSweeney if it would be fairest to redistribute the prize money among the drivers, he explained that then they'd have to announce it to the audience and newspapers to keep the drivers happy, and this quieter way the right thing was done. Besides, he laughed, you just made some more money on your share of the split.

"Mr. McSweeney, if it's all the same to you, I'd rather not have any part of that money," I said.

"Don't worry, boy. You won't, and I won't. What we'll do is be more generous with the 'accident' bonuses. That way, boy, this evens out and nobody's the wiser."

Accident bonuses were paid to drivers to help them rebuild cars that crashed. Mr. McSweeney awarded those as surprises in front of the grandstand after giving out the trophies and winner's cash.

Drivers sometimes got $200 if they crashed in front of the grandstand. Those who wiped out on the back straightaway got $50, but only if there were bleachers and spectators there. By giving away more than normal, Mr. McSweeney and I wouldn't be benefiting unfairly from that money we withheld, but I didn't notice that the accident bonuses changing much. Maybe they did. It was all Mr. McSweeney's judgment.

The money we made mattered, of course. That was how I'd find Mom. It's just that we had to make that season bonus, but we ought to do it fairly.

My first public relations lesson came in Sedalia, Missouri.

The carnies' trailers parked near ours, next to the fairgrounds. I got to talking with Fritz, their elephant handler. It frustrated him that the local paper, radio and TV weren't emphasizing our carnival. After eating a couple of foot long hot dogs with mustard, no charge, Fritz and I waited for sunset. We slipped over to the elephants and he patted the oldest animal's ear. She nuzzled him with her trunk. Fritz pulled the restraining stake out of the ground. He did that with one hand, rather easily.

"Zee elephant eez not zee brightest," he said.

"Eef you stake them down when zey are babies, from then on, zey do not challenge zee stake, no matter how easy it eez to pull out."

Maybe an elephant never forgets, but they don't think too hard either.

This elephant was African. We could tell by the ears, which are larger than an Indian elephant's. More amazing is that African elephant ears are shaped like Africa and Indian elephant ears are shaped like India. Fritz and I were always baffled at how that came to be.

Fritz led the elephant off the grounds. I slipped ahead, looking out for people or dogs. Fritz followed. It was getting dark, but my helmet and jumpsuit profile could be seen, plus Fritz in his knee boots and this elephant twice our height, swaying behind him.

I found an alley without any back door lights shining. We worked our way down it.

Fritz stopped at a row of garbage cans.

The elephant raised a front foot and crunched them down, one at a time, to a fourth of their size, popping the sides while garbage spurted through the split seams.

I spotted an apple tree near the alley.

Fritz guided our elephant to it, and poked him behind the ear.

"Crack."

The tree split.

Fritz nudged the elephant again, it raised a foot, stepped up on the trunk and the tree quivered, splintered its trunk and fell.

No lights came on.

We shuffled to the neighboring yard and tore down a clothesline.

Fritz staked the elephant there so she wouldn't move and we draped some of the clothes over her. Fritz and I slipped back to his trailer and he called the police.

"Zere is a runaway elephant tearing up zee neighborhood," he said.

The police station asked him the address. Fritz got flustered and handed me the phone.

"Three blocks south of the carnival," I said.

They asked the street address.

"Three blocks south of the carnival," I repeated, "but I've got to go now before we're all massacred." I hung up.

We asked the contortionist, a lady who could put both ankles behind her neck, but who talked normal, to place another call and give them our location. She did.

It took about ten minutes for the squad cars to roll up to our trailers. Fritz got up, acted surprised and promised the police that we'd handle it, gave them each a box of caramel corn and thanked them. He explained that they shouldn't use their sirens, but that he and I would calm the animal through the night and return her during the day.

"Zis animal goes crazeee in dark, but viz me in za daylight," Fritz said, "ve control za wiolence."

The police walked over with Fritz and me. We carried blankets to sleep through the night. We stopped and shook our heads at the smashed garbage cans which the police hadn't noticed. We walked past the destroyed tree hoping somebody would see. They didn't, so we stopped, stepped back, looked at it and loudly proclaimed that it undoubtedly fell over by itself. The Chief of Police arrived and said he'd check on that when the sun rose, and that we'd better hope that was the case.

Fritz and I got to the elephant and rolled out our blankets nearby, after he spent more time than necessary patting the animal and talking to her. The police parked down both sides of the alley, locked their doors and dozed off, taking turns, in their black and whites with guns unholstered.

Luckily they hadn't notice that our elephant was already staked when we arrived.

Fritz and I woke up as the sky began to glow and took off the bedspread and clothesline draped across the elephant. We replaced it with a white shirt, clothesline and some black pants.

"Betta contrast for za newspaper photographs," Fritz explained.

And sure enough, the TV and newspaper and radio crews showed up, interviewed Fritz and the next day headlines trumpeted "Mad Elephant Rampages Through Sedalia." Photos showed the animal with one white shirt over her forehead, black pants straddling her neck and clothesline entangled with her tusks. Inside pages showed the flattened garbage cans and the destroyed tree.

The next day Mr. McSweeney and Fritz were photographed with the homeowner receiving $50 for the clothesline loss and inconvenience. Another citizen was pictured receiving a $200 check to cover the downed apple tree, which Mr. McSweeney complained was $40 over budget. We held a garbage can photo session at Montgomery Ward, with Mr. McSweeney loading up four new galvanized garbage containers in the pace car for delivery to the citizens with crushed cans.

Each story and photo happened on a separate day, so we covered the media all week and the grandstand filled up for every race. The midway picked up too.

I had become a public relations professional.

By September, the Midwest fair circuit finished. We put on a couple more "Local Daredevil" events before heading to Sacramento and San Bernardino for their fairs. I began to wonder if Mr. McSweeney wasn't another slicky-tricky guy. There was no doubt that he promoted shrewdly. When there was an empty week on the schedule, he'd get on the phone and book a "Local Daredevil" show in some town along our way. The first "Local Daredevil" event was in Limon, Colorado. I got excited about seeing the West again until I saw Limon and realized we might as well be in the flats of Kansas.

Mr. McSweeney got the Jaycees in Limon to sponsor their "Local

Daredevil" race. The Jaycees committed to buy at least 1,000 tickets at $3 each and we used their names while selling the rest.

We ran a newspaper ad to get drivers. They had to wear a helmet and seat belt. If they didn't have a belt Mr. McSweeney sold them six feet of triple strand rope for $5, showed them how to tie a square knot and they lashed themselves onto the seat. He also encouraged each "Local Daredevil" to drive fast, explaining that race car owners were in desperate need of new drivers.

Those who didn't have helmets were urged to borrow football helmets from the high school.

We paid a farmer $500 to cut hay or alfalfa to the ground, creating a figure eight track.

Picture that. Inexperienced drivers, racing in front of their hometown crowd, for money, meeting at an intersection twice every lap.

We stacked hay bales around the inside to keep the drivers on the course. The site sloped on both sides so all the folks could see, sitting on their own lawn chairs and blankets. Temporary fencing insured that most of the spectators paid. We recruited eight ambulances from the nearest hospitals and paid them $50 to stand by. Mr. McSweeney claimed that was for show, but we used five or six or seven, usually.

When this race started the fastest went in front, since we wanted the field to stretch out. That created immediate conflicts through the intersection. Winners got $500, $400, $300 and the next five got $100. I was a flagman and we black-flagged, that means eliminated, any car that got two wheels off the track or grazed a hay bale.

Imagine a thirty-lap race where the twenty jalopies start to meet at fifty miles per hour in an intersection after the second lap. They get disqualified if they swing too wide and they get rear ended if they slow down.

Limon's "Local Daredevils" event lasted five laps before we stopped it the first time. Wreckers cleared off seven cars and two ambulances took drivers away.

We restarted with thirteen cars and twenty-five laps to go. It was less crowded and the speeds picked up. Sometimes cars barely missed. A few times they totally miscalculated and smashed straight into the side of a crossing car. Several times their bumpers clicked, showering sparks.

In five laps we stopped again to clean up the carnage. Only one ambulance was required that time. The race finished with four cars after one more stop.

Mr. McSweeney had arranged that we all parked our trailers to the west side of town, away from the track so we could finish the "Local Daredevils" event and head out quick, stopping late that night in Elko, Nevada.

"Leave 'em wanting more, boy" he explained, "and leave 'em wanting more quickly." We did, and some aspects of my new career became downright bothersome.

We drove into the sunset. Fast.

California was weird but exciting. They didn't surf in Sacramento or San Bernardino. There's less water there than Lake Poytawukie. Mr. McSweeney said my geographical choice was to be an Iowa outcast or relocate and become just another Californian. I'd heard they slept on waterbeds in California, went swimming on Christmas and other stuff that sound immoral, but decided not to judge yet. Besides, Disneyland was supposed to be the most magical spot in the world, south of Los Angeles in a bunch of orange groves; so famous Nikita Khrushchev insisted on seeing it when he visited from Russia.

Maybe I could too.

Professor Cohen once asked me if I thought Jesus, Mary and Joseph made snowmen in Jerusalem and that got me rethinking the holiday anyway. For sure Californians dressed in brighter colors and talked louder. It was like they were all actors making impressions with everything they said, and never speaking in even tones. A lot of them talked about themselves and their feelings, stuff that's not polite in public.

I mean you'd hear people saying things about "society" and "relationships" and their "needs," even when surrounded by people they didn't know. If I were to do that, it would be like whining about Doctor Throckmorton years after I last saw him, to people who never knew him. Nobody in our traveling show knew about Ruthie and me. Only Bubba heard anything about Mom. And nobody, not even Willy or Professor Cohen or Mr. Nordstrud ever heard my wondering, my thinking that the world might be better off if I disappeared.

Besides, that thought passed. It came logically, when I thought about all the pain and disruption my existence caused people. But good feelings returned when I imagined going west with Willie and Ruthie or saving Mom from her current situation.

Whatever Mom's situation was.

And Professor Cohen's smile when I returned, I knew just how that gold tooth would glisten. But the story I wrote for him was coming slow. I hid it in my bedroll, thinking to polish and finish it later, after living more of life.

We did the races in Sacramento for the fair, driving all day in the same state and hit San Bernardino in time for the Orange Show race. When I say we drove all day and stayed in the same state, California, that means that we drove straight all day long and hit some pretty high speeds. What's more, while they call Sacramento northern California, it's actually only two-thirds of the way up, while San Bernardino isn't even all the way to the bottom. So California's sizeable.

Bubba White won the race in San Bernardino, a perfect way to end the season and he drove me to see the ocean before we settled the bonuses with Mr. McSweeney.

Besides California being such a long state it changed from side to side. If California was somewhat looney, that craziness magnified near the water. The people twenty miles inland didn't look, act, or dress the same as those within sight of the Pacific. They weighed more inland. The temperature rose or dropped by one degree every mile due east from the water, at least for the first thirty. Everybody near the water wore slicker hair, more makeup, less clothing with brighter colors and fancier cuts. Some of their houses had sliding glass doors, which was a neat invention.

I could walk that entire state in my jumpsuit and helmet without anybody looking twice. In Grundy Center that same outfit would earn a one-way ticket to the nuthouse.

We had to wait a couple days for payday. I picked up mail at San Bernardino general delivery and read a few newspapers. Willy had written that Donny Zrostlik was missing in action, somewhere north of Saigon. He said nothing about married life or business.

"Christina 'Ragless' Dawson found out that everybody in Grundy Center knew about her problem," Willy wrote.

"She packed up, left town and got a fine job as a book stacker in the Burlington library."

Elvis had grown fat and his new songs sounded like anybody else. The Beatles studied with Maharishi Yogi. What was that all about?

Ruthie's mother wrote.

"Tell us more about your life," she said.

I'd neglected to fully report in my letter to her.

"Ruthie was delighted and ecstatic to hear about you," she said, "but remains committed to her current beau."

I scurried around San Bernardino, found a dictionary and looked up "beau." This copy of Webster's Collegiate Dictionary said "beau" means a man of fashion or a lover.

Which? A man of fashion, it had to be, but why would Ruthie notice that?

To learn more, it seemed I needed to give Ruthie's mother some details. I sent her a letter every day except Sunday for three weeks. Once I mentioned my genuine Timex watch, but worked carefully on the words so it sounded casual, and not like bragging.

Robert Kennedy and Martin Luther King got shot. These were disturbing things. That made car racing seem peaceful, compared to the rest of the world. Still, I'd have rather not done another "Local Daredevils" event. Or a high-banked track, unless they could afford better spectator fences.

I sent more letters to Ruthie's mother. That seemed smart, as long as I didn't get pushy and just told her about new things I was seeing, like California. I didn't mention our races. If I could ever see Ruthie again, I'd tell her everything, of course.

Willy liked the letter I sent him, giving complete approval and enthusiasm over his marriage. I explained that our Solemn Pact looked good for a lifetime, since he'd already given Ruthie approval also. I also explained that she most likely was lost forever, but that without her, I would never be friendly with another girl. I couldn't.

Bubba and I hadn't seen an ocean until that first day off. We got to Santa Monica in the afternoon and just sat there on the pier; Bubba puffing on a

Tiparillo. First we stared at the water.

"There is no other side," Bubba said.

He was right, meaning when you looked for the opposite shore, it was not visible. After awhile, we gawked at the Californians milling around and that entertained, but we kept glancing back at the Pacific just to make sure it hadn't changed. It hadn't. The waves kept breaking and we watched guys and a girl surfing on them.

Surfing looked stranger than water skiing. There's no boat.

But if some artist painted an accurate painting of this beach at sunset, with the flowers on the cliff and the sun licking the waves with their whitecaps folding over, it couldn't be sold. Customers would call it garish and tacky. There was stuff on the dirt called ground cover where grass should have been. That ground cover flowered purple, yellow and red so bright it almost hurt my eyes. That's how pretty things are in selective spots. I said selective, because other California neighborhoods featured stucco box houses on postage stamp lots with an oilrig next door and developments that make the word ugly inadequate.

"Bubba, you know what's strange?" I asked.

"What?"

"We're the farthest west anybody can go, right?"

"Yup."

"Well if we wanted to see the old west, and cowboys, from here we have to travel east."

Bubba lit another Tiparillo.

"Hey Bubba?"

"Yeah."

"We're having some pretty wild adventures, aren't we?" He smiled.

In Iowa, maybe things never got so stylish as this but they never decayed so far. California stretches for the extremes while on average Iowa gravitates towards average. Those Californians planted trees in their parking lots. Nobody would waste space like that in the Midwest. But it kind of looked nice. Not practical, understand. How do you water the trees? And a car might bump into them. That's why it's probably not right to plant trees in a place designed for parking.

I began to respect the Vikings and Columbus, looking at that horizon and realizing there's no way to know what's beyond.

"There's another," Bubba said, pointing. And sure enough, another ship appeared. And just like before, the smokestacks showed before the decks, and the decks before the hulls, proving the earth is round. Maybe that was a clue to those explorers that the world wasn't flat. It would take more proof than that, before I'd risk my life sailing into the unknown.

We'd seen it all now. The sun set so Bubba lit another Tiparillo and we headed back to our trailers. Since I wore and owned a genuine Timex, I also knew it was time to leave.

When we got there Mr. McSweeney and everybody had vanished.

Gone.

The guy who rented us the space said he didn't know where they went, but he'd like to, since they neglected to pay the water and dumping fees for their spaces.

Bubba and I pulled out a Speed Sport News and saw a racetrack event posted for Yuma, Arizona. Some of the drivers we knew were advertised. So we hopped in Bubba's pickup, chained his car down to the trailer, paid for our space and took off for Yuma.

I rode in the cab with Bubba this time since Lulubelle was back home at Woolworth's Five and Dime.

Sure enough, we drove all night and caught up to them along the Interstate 10.

"Can't let McSweeney see us," Bubba said. We dropped back. Bubba lit a Tiparillo, we stayed just far enough back to see them but not close enough that they could recognize us.

Dusk made it tougher to see.

"He'll start to sleep now," Bubba said. McSweeney dozed in the back of his trailer during longer trips, while a worker drove.

We shot past the whole caravan, passing them all on the left, dropping back to the right lane after they disappeared in our rear view mirror.

"Surprise him here," Bubba said, and parked our pickup and trailer crossways, blocking the entrance to the race track.

Mr. McSweeney lost his composure, for a second, when he arrived and saw us there.

"Boy, Bubba," he said, "I'm sure glad you got my message back there. We had to leave so fast I was afraid of missing you."

Bubba and I suggested we do the accounting for the season right then. Mr. McSweeney invited us into his trailer. Bubba needed me to get compensated so I could repay his loan for my two extra helmets.

"The rain insurance prices jumped, Bubba," Mr. McSweeney said, "and we hardly made a nickel."

"What's rain insurance?" I asked.

"Boy, you're lucky you don't have to worry about it. Bubba, I have to buy rain insurance before every race. It's not cheap."

Our talk went on like that, with Mr. McSweeney saying again how relieved he was that his message got to us and with us not saying anything except asking about my bonus. Mr. McSweeney said he could probably manage to pay me $2,000, yet he had no choice but to ask that I wait until this race finished.

Bubba and I stepped outside to discuss. It seemed to us that $2,000 was both a lot of money and a lot less than Mr. McSweeney had originally estimated.

This world is full of decent people, but some worse thoughts about Mr. McSweeney entered my mind. The man never once called me Moon. I didn't mind being called Moon so much, but it was nice that Mr. McSweeney never called me that.

Yet Grandma always said when I didn't get along with somebody, I should work extra hard to find something about them I could like. Suddenly, with Mr. McSweeney, I was working real, real, extra hard to accomplish that.

I figured I could still find Mom with the $2,000 if I watched my expenses and could make it through the winter until the next season. To help Mom, when I found her, I'd have to get some extra work but that would be okay. I'd proven I could get jobs in the world. Bubba no longer felt comfortable waiting until after the race for payment, however, due to Mr. McSweeney's recent habit of traveling a little faster than us.

Vanilla smells and ponytail filled my head. If I got paid now, I could confirm, face to face, the truth with Ruthie. Most likely, this would be painful. But the agony of never being sure felt awful, and with that bonus I could spend a few weeks staying at the YMCA in Chicago while searching for Mom. She's my only family left.

So that $2000 started to look better.

We walked back into his trailer and agreed to take the $2,000 but insisted it be paid now. Mr. McSweeney said he couldn't imagine how he'd find it before the race.

Bubba went a little darty-eyed on Mr. McSweeney. His words came out faster and higher pitched.

Mr. McSweeney said okay. Just like that. And he pulled twenty "Benjies" he called them, hundred dollar bills, out of a locked briefcase, slipped them into an envelope and handed it to me.

I recounted them.

My eyeballs aren't the best. But when Mr. McSweeney opened that briefcase he turned it so the hinges faced Bubba and me. I saw a reflection in his trailer's window and I spotted more stacks of $100 bills in that briefcase. A lot of them.

Perhaps Doctor Throckmorton was correct. Could it be that he detected something evil in me? Maybe Reverend Dawson sensed my bad side, something I couldn't admit. Perhaps neither would be surprised by what I did next.

I was.

I snatched Mr. McSweeney's jacket off his dashboard and ripped off a sleeve. Mr. McSweeney stared, not moving. Bubba's eyes opened wider than I'd ever seen. I rummaged through the jacket, taking my time and found a matchbook. I stepped outside and opened his gas cap, stuffed the sleeve in it and tore off a match.

"My God boy," Mr. McSweeney shouted, "you'll go to jail. What do you want?"

"It's not respect Mr. McSweeney, because now that means nothing from you. But all that money left in your briefcase suggests you're stealing from me."

I struck the match.

"Boy, Bubba, can we talk reasonably?"

I moved the match closer to his sleeve. It was turning dark from the gasoline wicking up.

"Mr. McSweeney, why don't you sell us that old briefcase of yours for $2000?" I asked.

"Boy, Bubba, yes I have a lot of cash in there because we haven't paid the racetrack owner yet or the drivers."

Bubba explained to Mr. McSweeney that he'd like to enter this race but planned to drive in the opposite direction as the other cars. Bubba might have meant it. I owed Bubba some money.

Mr. McSweeney's chalky skin flushed to watermelon pink. His chin shook. That blaze of hair, normally puffed out and slicked back, scattered from his fingers shaking through it.

Bubba's voice went deep and he whispered.

"Have you ever," Bubba asked, while handing a monkey wrench to Mr. McSweeney, "been in a wrench fight?"

Bubba pulled a crescent wrench from his pocket.

"Mine's smaller, so if you've never done this before that evens things out. Moon, tell McSweeney how the Rebel lost his first car."

This seemed like a time for me to not linger on the technical details, so I didn't, but I explained to Mr. McSweeney how easily we found him, without the message he didn't leave for us and asked if he'd be sleeping in his trailer that night. Bubba chimed in with a few thoughts about the thrill of making a bigger man scream from pain. Mr. McSweeney unlocked the briefcase again and took out another twenty bills, stuffed them in an envelope and handed it to me. I opened it and recounted them.

I'm ashamed of what I did.

But it worked.

The third store we went to had enough change to break a bill, but I had to buy a stocking cap before they'd do it. That was okay. I could use the stocking cap as a liner for my helmets, since I thought I'd keep wearing them. I paid Bubba the $48 I owed him. We went to a cafe. I ordered a club sandwich. Bubba got pork chops with applesauce and I paid.

We were pretty rich, but Bubba and I weren't going crazy. The jukebox had selections and buttons to push for a dime in each booth, but we just flipped through the songs and waited, hoping someone else would pick something good. Ray Charles came up singing "What'd I say" almost immediately, and we hadn't spent a penny.

"Where can I write you?" Bubba asked. I hadn't thought of that. But it reminded me that I left some stamps in the trailer, so I told Bubba I'd write him when I got settled, but first I'd go back to get my stamps.

"Don't go back there, Moon. Leave the stamps behind."

"Why?"

"We beat Mick McSweeney," Bubba said, "but he's dangerous."

"All we did was get what he owed me," I said, "and even then a thousand dollars less." We said good-bye, and I promised to write Bubba in a few weeks.

"What in hell are you doing here, boy?" Mr. McSweeney asked. He noticed me going back to the trailer to get my stamps.

"I forgot something."

"You stay right where you are. Boy, you and that driver beat me out of a lot of money. I ought to call the cops."

"Okay. Call the cops," I said.

Mr. McSweeney walked halfway around me. I stood with one foot in the trailer, one on the ground, my helmet on. Mr. McSweeney circled back, just out of reach.

"Boy, nobody else will treat you as well as I did."

"You mean pay less than they promise, Mr. McSweeney?"

"See what I mean, boy? You've got a smart mouth on that weird face, and damned if others will take you in like I did. Think you can hide under that helmet forever?"

"Mr. McSweeney, I got along fine before you."

"I doubt it, boy. You scare people."

I stepped out of the trailer. Mr. McSweeney moved back.

"I have more friends than you, Mr. McSweeney."

"Yeah, boy. Freaks and misfits. Did you pay for that helmet?"

"I figure I paid $1000 for this helmet, Mr. McSweeney. Would you care to buy it back?"

"Not if you're going to take it off, boy. Keep that head covered." I walked away and left my stamps. His talk didn't bother me. I've heard that crud before. It doesn't eat at me or make me feel inferior, really, it doesn't at all, especially from some slob like McSweeney, I can take worse than that, no sweat, no problem, I'm not bothered. Still. Never mind.

Whoever torched Mr. McSweeney's trailer that night was probably a thoughtful person. Apparently the guy who did it walked around the trailer thumping on the sides so Mr. McSweeney would be awake, and could escape the flames, which Mr. McSweeney did. Perhaps the person who did this also wanted Mr. McSweeney to understand who did it, without giving him any proof.

His trailer burned down to the axles.

Bubba drove us to Red Oak, Nebraska, asking me a couple times if I knew anything about Mr. McSweeney's fire, but I changed the subject and Bubba snickered the first time and chuckled the second. When I stopped to buy stamps he looked puzzled, and didn't ask about Mr. McSweeney's fire again.

But Bubba discovered in Red Oak that Lulubelle had become interested in a fellow who lunched at Woolworth's Five and Dime more often than necessary, so he and she needed to talk.

Bubba took me to the nearest depot. We didn't discuss much, I guess we both had personal problems to work out. I took a Greyhound to Chicago. I spent $500 for an investigation, covering all of Illinois, but there was no trace of Mom. The YMCA cost $2 per night. Postage to Ruthie's mom ran about $4 per week.

In March, I stopped by Grundy Center. Willy said he'd ask around about my mom again, and let me know. Willy promised that next time I visited I'd meet his wife and new son and that almost turned out, but not quite.

Ruthie's mom finally wrote back. She said that Ruthie's "beau" accepted a job in GE's management training program and they had big plans.

She said my suggestion was a bad idea. She said I should not visit. My insides died.

Nothing mattered anymore.

Lake Poytawukie froze solid. Willy was busy in his marriage. My racing outfits caused Midwestern folks to stare. Professor Cohen moved into a convalescent home. He said that was a bad name, since most residents died there. Professor Cohen also nudged me again, suggesting I should write a book. I told him I'd started. He nodded with a big grin.

I hopped a bus back to California. You can wear whatever you feel like there, and I owned three helmets and jumpsuits.

I was thinking I'd try to find Mom, but needed more money first, to do it right.

El Cajon's inland. Like San Bernardino, the folks get closer to normal there than they do next to the ocean. It's kind of exciting because it's like the old west. Maybe not like the Rocky Mountains, but more like Apache and Navajo west, yellow and tan dirt plus cactus, while trees are scarce.

Bubba's luck ran out with Lulubelle, and now he raced at the El Cajon Speedway without traveling. He had told them I was the best mechanic who couldn't drive a car that he ever knew. I won the job on Bubba's say so. They raced every Saturday, year round, so it was steady work on weekends and I got an apartment nearby.

"How come we're such good pals," I asked Bubba one day. We were flat on our backs, under his car. He handed me a wrench.

"What do you mean?"

"You and me, Bubba, we help each other out more than most partners, don't you think?"

He loosened a bolt.

"Bubba, is it because you lost Lulubelle and my Ruthie's gone?"

Bubba lit a Tiparillo.

"Lulubelle fooey," he said.

"But Bubba, you sure, well, never mind."

"She don't matter."

"Okay."

We bolted the oil pan back on.

"Moon?"

"Yeah, Bubba?"

"Did we fix McSweeney?" Bubba whooped and hollered and I couldn't stop laughing myself. I doubled up, hit my head against the crankcase and looked at Bubba. He almost choked laughing since black grease smeared over my forehead. Bubba rubbed his hand across the transmission and slapped grease on his forehead and I nearly split a gut. No more work got done for ten minutes.

Wonderful things happened. I helped my apartment manager fix a water heater and he asked if I'd care to be the maintenance man for his wife's preschool. It was several miles away, but she'd drive me there and back.

Now I had work every weekday and the races on Saturday. My bank account grew. What's more, there wasn't that much to do at the school, so pretty soon I watched over the kids at recess. Indirectly, you see, I was becoming an honest-to-goodness teacher. I'd mop every morning, clean the toilets twice a day, do the windows once a week and started a schedule for repainting each room; something they'd never done on a regular basis.

It was interesting how different the boys and girls acted. If I handed a stick to a boy, he'd be shooting it like a gun in a minute. Hand it to a girl, and she'd cradle it as a baby. Now the teachers and I discussed this, some thought it was parent's expectations. Others said the boys didn't develop small muscle control as early as the girls, and they couldn't hold a pencil as well, so the guys ran and shouted, using the large muscles that worked for them. This was interesting and none of it came from a textbook. Those teachers let me talk with them about it, and asked my opinions after a while.

Pablo's mother enrolled him so she could clean houses during the day. Her husband hadn't returned from the field work for eight years then, she needed money and Pablo acted shy. I gave him a horsey-back ride his second day and he looked scared at first, started smiling, laughing and soon spurred me to go faster and faster.

His mom waited for me in the parking lot the next morning.

"Mr. Moon?"

"Good morning, and hello Pablo, buddy boy."

Pablo hid behind her skirt.

"Pablo wants to know if you'll give him a horsey-back ride again."

"That would make me very happy," I said.

Pablo stepped from behind his mom, looked up at her, she smiled and motioned at me. He ran over. I stooped, he jumped on, I pretended to buck, he shrieked a happy sound and we ran around the lot.

His mom waved good-bye and Pablo didn't cry, just waved back and we galloped into the playground. That became our routine every morning. Maybe I looked forward to that as much as Pablo. His bashfulness went away.

This was all I ever wanted to do and it didn't happen the way I planned, but what the heck, I got there. Sometimes it made me so happy I cried, just a little, when the kids tugged my shirt or tossed me a ball. A teacher asked me about my tears and I told her allergies bothered me from the El Cajon dust. A couple times I laughed so hard it startled a couple of the kids, but when you're ecstatic, that just happens.

How great can things be? I made more money than I could spend and was good at both jobs. If I could keep this up for a few years, maybe the idea of going through life alone wouldn't be so bad. I'd have races on weekends and kids to play with on weekdays.

You don't have to be special to someone to survive. I guess.

I hadn't been there but one semester and my apartment manager's wife raised me from $5 an hour to $5.25. She suggested I try to not laugh and cry so much, since kids weren't used to that. But she gave me the raise.

Maybe I'd even visit that new place, Disneyland. After doing a good search for Mom, of course.

"For de little stealin' dey gets you in jail soon or late."

Eugene O'Neill

Chapter 18

Things went best when I wore my jumpsuit and helmet at the school. The boys called me Captain and the girls seemed less skittish. We played hide and seek in the yard, when the weather permitted, which was nearly every day. It felt like California sat under a statewide plastic bubble, keeping all the clouds, rain and temperature away, letting them blow over into my Midwest. The weird thing about this school was that it had no hallways. Kids just stepped outside to go from one room to another. Later I learned all California schools are like that, and it didn't feel proper.

The kids never knew which shrub I'd hide in, so they ran in a pack from one bush to the other until they spotted me, pointed and shrieked. I learned to act scared when they found me, since the first few times, when I shouted "Boo!" it over-excited a few of them. When I let them scare me they giggled and screamed.

This delicate kid, Jessica, acted jumpy, no matter how I behaved, so I stayed away from her. The teachers thought that was smart. Her mother had a dependency problem, they said, and Jessica was born a nervous girl. So even when it was ninety degrees in the playground, I kept my helmet on and stayed in a corner so Jessica could run most of the place without feeling trapped. Luckily one of my helmets was white, so it didn't feel that uncomfortable in the sun. Pablo ran to me, Jessica stayed away and if I didn't laugh or cry the other kids just milled around and I could joke with them. The teachers noticed Jessica withdrew more in her second semester. Her mother's eyes were deluded, or something like that, they said. Jessica's mother always had a runny nose.

Our school ran half full in the summer. The air shimmered with heat across the playground, so we stayed inside a lot. And the air conditioning bills jumped.

"Makes me think we should shut down until fall," the owner said.

On June 13, 1971 a dry wind gusted. Sand ticked the windows. At 10:43 in the morning, two squad cars spun into our school parking lot. When they stopped, their dust cloud caught up. Both cars disappeared for a moment.

I cleaned out the grille on a classroom air conditioner, balancing myself on a stepladder. Keeping those coils clean helped them run better, holding down our electricity costs.

Three policemen kicked the door open.

"You the one they call Moon?" He held a baton in one hand and a pair of cuffs in the other.

"Yes sir," I replied.

"Get down," he said.

"Okay officer."

"Now," his partner said.

I did. They jerked the wire brush from my hand, tossed it on the floor, grabbed both my arms and threw me against the wall. Some of the kids outside peeked in, wide-eyed. Pablo screamed.

"You sick scum," one of the officers said. He hit the backside of my knees with his baton and I fell.

"Stop resisting or we'll shoot." The children shrieked, most running away but a few, like Pablo, slipped into the room and hugged the wall.

"Get up," one officer said. I did. Pablo ran over and slapped at him with tiny hands. The cop flipped Pablo away with his baton and my little pal fell into a corner. I bit the cop's wrist. He clubbed my head and whacked my ribs while I crumpled to the floor.

It hurt to breathe. Later I would learn that three ribs cracked. It felt strange, lying in the back seat of the squad car, hands cuffed, policeman swearing and not knowing what was going on.

Then it came to me. Mr. McSweeney must have named me as a suspect for burning his trailer.

They transferred me to the San Diego County Jail. I had my own cell, alone. Everywhere I looked there was nothing but steel and concrete, not a bit of paint. They stuck a few bricks in the wall of the exercise yard, and I tended to stare at them for relief.

The place was always chilly, yet smelled like sweat and concrete. You could usually hear somebody yelling in the distance, often several far off voices and not understand what they were saying but it was never happy talk.

My appointed attorney arranged to meet with me in a separate room without any bars, but I was handcuffed and we sat at a table next to a wall mirror.

"Did you ever fondle a student named Jessica?" he asked while removing his glasses.

I said no. I hadn't.

I never touched her and avoided even looking in her direction, after sensing that I made her nervous. Next a psychiatrist came in and asked about the other kids in the classes. She wanted to know if I ever had a girlfriend, so of course, I told her about Ruthie at PAG Church Camp, without revealing impolite details.

"This 'girlfriend' was blind?" she asked.

"Yes, but she went to college and plays three instruments. She didn't let a little thing like not seeing hold her down."

"Have you ever had a normal female relationship?"

"Yes, with Ruthie."

I told her about the date I had with the friend of Gloria Throckmorton. The psychiatrist pursed her lips. Then I told her about Grandma, how I protected her grave and explained that my mom and I might become close again, if I could find her. This shrink had to take a break after an hour, and came back with a new notebook.

"Ruthie, you see, and I became friendly."

"What does that mean?"

"Well, we understand the boy and girl thing."

She scribbled for a couple of minutes without looking up.

"Her hair is golden brown," I said, "she smells like a cake baking and when she talks her voice sounds like a flute."

"She talks like a flute?"

I could tell this expert wouldn't get it. She also got confused about my getting a college degree without a high school diploma, and seemed interested in Willy. That's understandable; you don't find many as loyal as him.

"You understand," she said, "that you shall probably never enjoy a normal female relationship, do you not?"

"No," I replied. "When I find a girl that likes me, she'll be special. That girl will be better than most, because she will see beyond my affliction."

"Do you not see the problem?" she asked.

"There's no problem. My wife will have more character than girls who chase pretty boys."

"The awkward thing is," she continued, "that those rare girls who may be attracted to you one day will be attracted because of your disabilities. That's not healthy either."

"No, they'll see beyond our physical differences."

"I hope you're right." She left. What a jerk. But nobody even mentioned McSweeney's trailer fire.

Another fellow marched in and put sensors on my chest and arms with little caps on each fingertip. He hooked all that up to a machine and asked a bunch of questions. He paused several seconds after each question. When they finished, a guard shoved me back into my solitary cell. The next day my lawyer explained.

It seems Jessica told her mother that I drove her and several girls out to Cuyamaca Park where we all took off our clothes and slaughtered zebras. Jessica said I ate the hearts from the zebras and drank their blood.

Did I mention that California is strange?

It turned out, however, that preschool teachers were being jailed in Massachusetts on similar childrens' statements that were impossible. Of course that's the state where they once burned witches. And now Ruthie lived there. That scared me some.

My attorney carried a fat file of papers the next time we met, and we had our own cell to talk in, but a guard stood ten feet away on the other side.

My lawyer took off his glasses to look at me. This was always a bad sign.

"Other children have corroborated Jessica's story, Moon. Expert social workers interviewed them and the other children are now giving the same story."

"But sir, I have difficulty driving."

"Yes, Moon, but you can drive."

"But sir, to get from the preschool to Cuyamaca park, after lunch, would require loading those kids in a car without any of the other teachers seeing, and driving 140 miles an hour both ways to get back before it would be time for the parents to pick up the children."

"Yes, Moon, the prosecution does have some holes in their case."

"Holes, sir? Where did the zebras come from? And where are the zebra remains?"

"Moon, our legal system will take those arguments into consideration. Unfortunately, you fit the profile of a sex offender."

"I've had girlfriends."

"Hardly a normal relationship that we can discover, Moon. Your unusual appearance probably makes that, unfortunately, preordained."

"Prewhat?"

He put on his glasses with both hands, my deodorant was failing and he began to button his coat. I almost told him more about Ruthie, but, to protect her, I decided any more details of our relationship should remain confidential.

"Moon, there are other factors."

"What? Sir, please tell me."

"Jessica's grandfather is Chairman of Great American Resorts, a fast-growing franchise for campgrounds."

"Yes, sir."

"His wife heads the 'Blessed Believers' which holds strong opinions about respecting the Bible."

"How does that effect me, sir?"

He glanced at the guard who seemed busy unwrapping a stick of gum, leaned forward and lowered his voice.

"They are politically active, and the District Attorney in San Diego is elected. This family causes about $200,000 to be contributed into the DA's campaign."

"But sir, I don't understand why that matters."

"Not so loud, Moon." He slipped his glasses down to the tip of his nose.

"They believe every homeowner should keep a loaded gun and nobody should ever have an abortion."

"Sir?"

"Yes Moon?"

"What does any of this have to do with me?"

"Don't you see the patterns, Moon?"

"What patterns? Are you leaving already sir?"

"I face several other cases today, Moon. There are a couple of things here, one good and one bad."

"What are they sir?"

"The good thing, Moon, is that hysteria dies with time, and the longer we delay your trial, the stronger your case gets, for reasons I cannot disclose yet."

"The longer I stay jailed, sir, the better my chances are of being declared innocent?"

"Yes, Moon, trust me."

"What's the bad news, sir?"

"The teachers at your school said you laughed and cried too much."

"Hmm."

"Hmm what, Moon?"

"I thought laughing and crying were strange behavior for Iowa, but normal stuff in California, sir. I still get rattled by all this."

So it appeared I fit the profile, was jailed for an impossible crime but might get declared innocent if they kept me locked up long enough.

My lawyer stood.

"Here, sir." I handed him a scrap of paper. A guard stepped over, looked at it and nodded.

"What's this, Moon?"

"Bubba's phone number. Can you tell him what's happening?"

"I'm happy to." He left.

The San Diego jail was the third largest in America. Only Chicago and Los Angeles were bigger. New York would have been, except it was divided into five boroughs.

I wish I didn't know any of that.

"Under a government which imprisons any unjustly, the true place for a just man is prison."

Henry David Thoreau

Chapter 19

They locked me up alone twenty-three hours a day. For one hour, I mixed with other inmates in the exercise yard.

Word got around instantly about the charges against me. The Aryan Brotherhood attacked me the first week but guards broke them up with tear gas, after a few minutes delay. I got stabbed in the stomach, slashed on my cheek and forearm, both eyes blackened, one tooth knocked out and my nose broken. None of that hurt as much as my ribs, which hadn't healed yet. The infirmary taped me so I could breathe with less pain.

Those nurses were nice.

The cuts and bruises healed, but it had shocked me to see a bunch of bald white guys, teeth clenched, veins standing out on their necks, swinging at me and yelling "freak" and "baby..." well, words that were vulgar and not true. I can't even imagine the acts they shouted about so they're sicker than me.

I got sympathy from the black bikers. They helped me, partly to irritate the Aryan Brotherhood. But the black bikers turned into my best friends.

Stubbyclaw ran the Aryan Brotherhood. He got his name from the four end knuckles cut from his right hand. His group claimed he chopped off those fingers out of shame when a Mexican gang ambushed his top four staffers in a drug deal. Their initials were tattooed on each stub. Other groups said he was stealing a battery from a car when someone slammed the hood on his hand. The truth is scarce behind bars. There was a swastika tattooed on his scalp.

My lawyer said the law required I get some free time in the yard, so they had to put me back out there and the black bikers looked out for me. I had no problems after that.

Blade, the black biker's leader, gave me one of his bandanas. I tied it around my head and man, you should've seen the looks in the yard. I stuck near Blade after that. He was dark but not so black that tattoos didn't show. He had a snake coming out of his rear and coiling up his back. I saw that in our gang showers. A series of periods circled his neck and just below his chin the words "cut on dotted line" kind of dared any reader to follow the instructions.

Blade made it clear to the other inmates that he would take care of anyone who bothered with me. After that, some of them even moved out of my way when I walked around, but I always stayed within a knife toss of our black section.

Blade used his power. The jailers knew his associates on the outside could do favors for them, and did. Blade carried money inside, but it turned out he couldn't count. This had helped to put Blade in jail, when he thought a clerk short-changed him at a drive-in, so he robbed the place. Blade and I spent five to ten minutes of every hour we had in the yard, trading nickels and pennies and dimes. He was no dummy. In a few weeks he could count. Sometimes we'd review it in front of others, just so his gang could see that he understood math now, and Blade gained status from that.

Blade and I strolled in tight circles, staying within our territory. One day at the beginning of my hour in the yard Blade stopped. He whispered.

"Moon, don't trust any screw," Blade said, "except Guard Snicker." They called him Guard Snicker because he always grinned, upper teeth bucked and often drooled and giggled when somebody got hurt.

"But Blade, he's evil."

"Have I took care of you, Moon, white boy?"

"Yeah, Blade, sure."

"I got Snicker, he's ours. Okay?"

"Okay."

The northern California Mexicans stayed in their area, the southern California Mexicans in another, the Aryan Brotherhood in a separate corner, my black bikers with me in theirs, Crips and Bloods took other turf. The few Philippine and Vietnamese gang members merged, while imprisoned, for safety. There aren't so many Asians in jail, except from those two countries, where our military taught them some attitude.

Talk about time to think. Twenty-three hours a day alone in a concrete cell, one steel toilet without a lid, a concrete cot sticking out from the wall and one frosted tile window. Minutes felt like months and months passed by in minutes. Time lost meaning. It got so that if they served any fruit I knew how it would feel and sound gurgling in my stomach several hours later. The same for chicken, vegetables, or milk. I could tell what was digesting by the noise, feel and timing.

It cheered me to think of Grandma, Mr. Nordstrud, Ruthie, Professor Cohen, and Willy. Mom and Dad too, of course, but did I destroy both their lives? Was there something rotten in me, considering that I'm in jail and so many people left me, and was that why the Lord made me different?

Ruthie joined me every Thursday noon when they delivered a piece of cake with glaze. I smelled her then, heard her voice chimes and saw her cinnamon ponytail.

I had mail privileges. But I never wrote Ruthie's mother again. It terrified me to think that a postmark or something on my letters would show that I was a prisoner. So I was probably fading fast from Ruthie's mind. Which, in this situation, was the best for her life.

When Ruthie slipped into my thoughts it took awhile to recover and she came by often. Blade could tell. He said women were grains of sand.

"There's always another piece of sand on the beach, Moon."

"Not like Ruthie, Blade, truly, never like her." He'd cup his hand behind my neck and shake me a little, laughing. I appreciated that. But I also felt bad for Blade, him not knowing how one grain of sand, only one, can smell vanilla, speak soprano and comb a ponytail into a honey brown waterfall.

Somehow a little colony of ants found my cell on the tenth floor. The trays of food they slid under my door usually contained a biscuit, or a cube of corn bread and sometimes a slice of white bread. After testing crumbs from that, against the corn kernels or green beans, it became clear the ants preferred the white bread. I saved a corner of that for them after each meal and would crouch down to watch them carry tiny pieces away. After awhile, no telling how much time, I talked to them, gently so it wouldn't be like some giant voice booming out, and tried to name each of them, but could never be sure I was telling them apart. I pretended to know each and we became great friends. They appreciated the bread I gave them and liked me for it. Unfortunately, more and more of them arrived and pretty soon they started biting me when I lay in bed. I hated to brush them off but they hurt, chewing my ankles and ears and back. More and more of them rampaged through my cell and I told Blade. He gave me a can of lighter fluid.

How he got that remains a mystery. The last thing any guard wants a jailbird to have is a can of inflammable fluid. A prisoner could, with a match, set a guard on fire by squirting through the bars and tossing a match.

I sprinkled fluid between the ants' entry points and my bed. This restricted them into their dining area. We got along great after that.

I fed them. They didn't bite me.

Stubbyclaw must have planned his move for months. Two skinheads started punching each other near the weights. The guards moved in, firing rubber bullets and tear gas. Blade and his bikers stepped forward to watch.

Stubbyclaw walked backward, in my direction, but I didn't notice until he turned and hurled a brick at me. It hit my stomach and broke two ribs again. He strolled back toward the weights without being seen, while I curled up on the ground, gasping for air but sucking in tear gas.

Blade saw. He shouted and the bikers circled me. I spent another two nights in the infirmary. Guard Snicker woke me.

"Up, Moon, up."

I sat up, wheezed and clutched my sides. Guard Snicker smiled.

"We're taking you out to a real hospital," he said. Snicker cuffed me. I rolled off the bed and into a wheel chair.

I got a special room at the hospital with Snicker standing guard. After the Doctors left for the night, Snicker came in, uncuffed me and unlocked the chain between my ankle and the bedpost.

"Moon, here's our secret," he said, grinning. "I got a girlfriend in town and I'm going to see her. I'll sneak back in the morning before dawn."

"Okay, Guard Snicker."

"Don't you call me that."

"Okay, sir."

"Now I trust you to not escape and embarrass me, okay boy? Because you could be out of state before I get back. And there's a whole set of clean clothes in that closet."

"Okay, sir, I won't sir."

Guard Snicker chuckled, wiped his mouth on a sleeve and slipped out the door. I slept.

My door opened and a dim light from the hall outlined somebody, but my eyes couldn't focus, it was still dark outside and black in my room.

"Is that you?" the figure asked.

"Am I who?" I asked.

"Is that you Moon?" Guard Snicker asked.

"Sure, sir."

"You are still here, then?"

"Well, yes, sir."

Guard Snicker snapped on the light, looked at me without smiling, chained me back to the bed and cuffed my wrists.

"Did you have a good evening, sir?"

He didn't answer. We returned to the jail at dawn.

Stubbyclaw couldn't even get that one brick loose without weeks of careful work. There was a masonry strip on one side of the exercise yard, but the guards inspected it regularly. So Stubbyclaw must have worked it free, covering up the broken mortar with toothpaste after each day of chipping away. He spent weeks working on the attack. The two skinheads got ninety days of solitary. Stubbyclaw flung that brick with surprising accuracy, considering that his fingertips were gone.

Hatred pushes some folks into extraordinary effort.

Those concrete walls are perfect for honing down a toothbrush into a sharp blade. That's probably how Stubbyclaw dug the mortar out around the brick.

For months things stayed quiet. I studied and memorized the cracks in the concrete. One ran out from under my bed and if the top of it had only curved left instead of right it would be a perfect replica of the Missouri river.

So I spent several weeks remembering the true path of the Missouri. Then with a pencil they let me have, I scratched out the proper direction for the upper river and think I got it close. Then by pushing soap and toilet paper into the crack where it went the wrong way and rubbing grit from the concrete surface over that, I created a true map of the Missouri river.

I marked the spots where Willy and I crossed it, putting both bridges in. They weren't to scale. The river was.

I was luckier than most inmates. I'd learned to live inside my head as a kid, due to my afflictions. That helped the time pass.

My lawyer requested that the city replace my tooth. He wanted me presentable for a hearing. The jailhouse dentist had fixed my tooth, putting in gold. My lawyer complained, saying they were making me look worse, whatever that meant, so they took out the gold and put in porcelain that nearly matched. Personally, I preferred the gold since Professor Cohen had one, but I wanted freedom worse so I agreed to the change.

"Up, Moon, up," Guard Snicker said at midnight.

"What, sir?" I sat up on my tick. He unlocked my cell door, slow so nobody would be disturbed.

"Taking you to the dentist again, Moon boy." He muffled a giggle with the elbow of his sleeve.

"No cuffs, sir?"

"Shhh." We slipped out, he checked me into a motel three blocks from the dentist's office and told me to walk over at noon. I peeked out the curtain all morning, amazed at how much traffic the road carried and how happy people sounded, mostly, and the trees and bushes and grass almost hurt my eyes with color.

The dentist examined my tooth repair and seemed satisfied.

Guard Snicker didn't show up.

The dentist called him. Guard Snicker came in another hour, cuffed me, chained my ankles, drove back to the motel and picked up a pair of shoes, pants and a shirt.

"Those look small for you, sir," I said, trying to be friendly.

"You didn't see these in your closet?" he asked.

"Yes sir, but they weren't mine."

Guard Snicker's jaw muscles tightened and we drove back to jail.

They sent by more psychiatrists, lie detector tests, doctors to evaluate my vision and driving aptitudes, lawyers, and so on, for the first eighteen months.

"Moon, I bring positive news," my lawyer announced during one of our weekly meetings, and he kept his glasses on.

"Sir, that guard is listening," I replied.

"It does not matter, Moon. Jessica's mother, who has an addiction problem, was arrested for shoplifting last week. Her cocaine usage will be part of her trial. Her parents will probably arrange to have her placed in a rehabilitation center and agree to a probationary period."

"Well, sir, that's terrible for Jessica."

"But Moon, it is good for you. Now Jessica's mother cannot testify without revealing this drug problem and her relapse. Jessica's grandparents will do anything to hush this up. I don't care if the guard is listening."

"Sir, I haven't heard a thing from Bubba."

"I am unsurprised, Moon."

"Did you, sir, tell him where I am?"

"Of course."

"I haven't heard from him."

"Moon, guilty or innocent, most people stay far away from accused child molesters."

"You know I'm innocent, sir..."

"Moon, nobody understands that today but you and me, and only you know for sure."

Two nights later, unannounced, a guard opened my cell and told me I had a visitor.

I guessed Mom had found me. Or maybe it was Bubba.

It had been two years.

I always hoped to rescue Mom from difficulty, but now here she came, maybe, to save her college grad son.

My head went light in the corridor. The guard helped me get back up from the floor. Everything cleared and I hustled into the visitor's area

It was Willy. That same red tie that was knotted around his neck when we watched the coronation dangled halfway over his belly, and it appeared he hadn't missed many meals.

My buddy. Willy Geiselman from Grundy Center. Nothing or nobody ever looked better to these eyes.

We sat for an hour staring through the glass, talking on phones. Willy was making something of himself, leaving his plumbing career, and now representing a famous steel company. At first he tried to sell pipe for them.

That didn't go very well. Willy's speech was almost normal by then, but sometimes he still confused words with strangers. So he became their trouble-shooter, helping plumbers with unusual installations. He was called in on the toughest plumbing problems in thirty Iowa counties.

"Moon, when will you get out?"

I wished he hadn't asked that but I said something back without sounding pathetic, which wasn't easy. He didn't need to say I was innocent. We both knew he believed that; no discussion required.

"Remember Dad's plane?"

"Sure."

"And that Texaco guy who drove it around without wings?"

"Yeah." I grinned.

"Well," Willy said, "that thing sold to the Prohaskas. They glassed-fiber the bottom and turned it into a duck boat at Grundy's Marsh. They haven't shot a duck yet, but other hunters claim they've scared plenty of flocks away." This was too much. Amazing things never stopped in Grundy Center. Willy said the Texaco station converted to three grades of gasoline but nobody else bought premium. Willy figured that since his car used plus, by filling the tank half with regular and half with premium, he got plus and saved two cents a gallon. We chuckled.

"Willy, you still gas up in the morning when it's cool, so you get more?"

"Hey Moon, my papa didn't raise any dummies." And we reminisced about how we once mixed used crankcase oil with gasoline to create diesel fuel during a shortage.

For a couple of minutes we ran out of things to say, but, just like old times, that was okay, but the guard edged towards us every time he noticed the silence.

"Willy, was it tough to leave your dad's business? I mean, how did you first bring up the idea?"

The guard relaxed and stepped back.

"I didn't, Moon. Grundy Center's drying up. Bigger farms mean fewer farmers, so the population's shrinking. Dad and I knew. Mr. Sheetz closed his picture show theater. Dad's thankful we together rode as long we did."

Willy said the farmers' joke was that the only way to make any money today was to install another mailbox. This was in hopes that you'd get more government checks.

"Willy, you're so, I mean in here it's, well, seeing you and talking, you can't..." I was trying to thank him.

"I know," Willy said. He mentioned that it took thirty minutes to get to my jail from his motel.

"It costs $40 dollars for one single night, but the city pays."

"Huh?"

"Yes, San Diego covers all my costs. They interviewed me to see if you're all right. We'll get you out and cross the Rocky Mountains again on our way back. You'll meet my wife and ball a roll to our boy. We carpeted wall-to-wall."

Willy mentioned that Christina "Ragless" Dawson married the librarian she worked for, had a baby and all three of them spent a week's vacation in Grundy Center. They visited half the town to show off their new son, which pleased everyone.

I clapped. Willy smiled. We said nothing more about Christina "Ragless" Dawson. It was a relief that the fire we lit around her parked car hadn't frozen her up so tight that she'd never reproduce. We both knew better than to say a single word about that through the jailhouse phone.

"I talk with the doctors head tomorrow," Willy added.

We figured I'd be out soon after that.

Our guard, however, who pretended to not be listening got confused by Willy's mixed words, and probably thought we were talking in code. He motioned and Guard Snicker stepped in.

They'd whisper after every couple of Willy's or my sentences.

"I'll tell them about you and Carla and me and how we saw her in swimsuits times many without doing anything crazy." Willy smiled. He was talking gibberish on purpose, knowing I'd get it.

Guard Snicker strolled past, faked a yawn, studied his watch and listened harder. Then he bent over Willy's shoulder.

"Your boyfriend's moving to a new cell," he said.

"Oh," Willy said.

"He'll have a cellmate now."

"Okay." Guard Snicker stepped back and laughed.

Willy and I stopped talking. Guard Snicker slapped his thigh, giggled and turned away.

"Could you mention Marie, also?" I asked.

"Why I should?"

"She was pretty special to both of us, Willy."

"Okay, she's but fake friend a."

"Anything will help, Willy."

Guard Snicker walked over to the other guard, shaking his head, whispered something and walked out. Somebody somewhere cut our phone line dead. We hung up. Willy nodded to me. I nodded back.

Grundy Center was sounding pretty good to me by now. Iowa State and Lake Poytawukie too. Those were the only places I was headed, the second I got out. I had left Iowa but Iowa hadn't left me.

Willy reported that the town changed, of course. Always did. Folks died. Babies came. Willy's boy and I might become good friends and I'd work hard to deserve that. Mr. Hardcastle closed his grocery. Willy thought it couldn't be avoided, with fewer farmers eating. Others in town groused that Mr. Hardcastle got too fancy, trying to get people to spend more, starting a gourmet section with apricots and bagels and ocean fish and other stuff nobody knew how to cook.

Mr. Sheetz left the theater and Grundy Center without paying his last month's electricity. Everybody agreed that this was typical behavior for show business people. Television didn't help, what with a fourth channel reaching town, if your antenna was tall enough.

The theater got converted into a craft shop for locally made items, like birdhouses and needlepoint light switch covers, aprons and arrangements made from painted dead sticks.

Farber & Ottoman, "Friends When You Need Them Most," kept pumping formaldehyde and selling caskets, and Willy said the price of dying edged up each year.

Willy's one hour visit kept me going, since I couldn't guess when my eyes would see Lake Poytawukie again. I replayed every word that Willy and I had said to each other. I remembered how he just nodded when he left and that's all I did back, one quick gesture. Those two motions said more between us than any observer could imagine.

Long before, I had learned to talk in my head to Grandpa, and with Grandma after she passed. So I knew how to have conversations without anybody knowing. But I'd pretty much covered everything with them, so Willy's visit gave me some desperately needed new material. I had also held conversations in my head with Mom, but now that had to stop, based on what Willy revealed.

Willy's information about Mom was not a big deal.

Well okay, it was.

What I mean to say is that I can handle it, really.

She wasn't the only person in my life, so this news was manageable.

If I could remember precisely what we each said about Mom, I'd report that, but my mind goes fuzzy when I think of this part of our conversation. It turns out, Willy said, that my mother wouldn't likely be coming back, since Doctor Throckmorton, it appears, had been paying for her keep while she attended a nursing school, rumors had it. Willy said he wouldn't have believed a word of it, or thought a thing about that possibility, except for our earlier bushwhacking incident.

That was the time he and I had snuck up on Doctor Throckmorton's parked car. Willy shined the flashlight inside and we raced off. Willy said it had looked very much like my mom inside that car with Doctor Throckmorton. He said he would have mentioned this to me before but he just couldn't be sure and none of that made any sense until he heard stories, years later, around Grundy Center about the two of them.

After Mom got through nursing school, so the citizens whispered, Doctor Throckmorton arranged for her employment with a friend of his in Mason City. This was far enough, but not too distant from Grundy Center and he became partners with that Mason City doctor. This required frequent partnership meetings, all conducted at Mason City, with none held in Grundy Center.

Mason City also wasn't so far that Willy couldn't manage a trip to investigate himself. He wore dark glasses, which kept him from being spotted by my mother, but this nearly got him arrested, just for looking suspicious. That's the same "profile" thing that kept me jailed for over two years.

Willy wasn't about to tell any of this stuff to me unless he knew it to be absolute fact, and I guess he did by the time he visited me in jail, having seen my mother for sure. Willy found her in Mason City. He saw Doctor Throckmorton pat her on the rear, standing in front of his partner's office, right on the public sidewalk.

"It didn't look," Willy said, glancing away and his face burning red, "like she was," his eyes got puffy, "wearing a girdle."

This presented an impossible task for Willy, telling me that my mother shacked up with Doctor Throckmorton. He knew this might be painful, so he had taken extra effort to get the absolute truth before telling me. And he showed no joy in the mention. In fact, he stammered around so much I almost didn't get what he was trying to say.

"You can sprinkle sequins on horse manure to make it pretty," one of the cowboys had said in Colorado, "just don't bring it in the bunkhouse." Willy sprinkled the sequins on his report, but didn't hide the facts or push them on me.

Another point is that Mom, no matter what she did, struggled to get by. Maybe Doctor Throckmorton had a different side to him that I overlooked and she got to know it. And after all, her problems with the town and money all began with me. I don't blame myself much, but facts are facts. I'm a bastard.

Maybe Mom went slutty but that Doctor Throckmorton forced her into it.

I don't know. It could be that Doctor Throckmorton was her only non-family friend. It's tough to decide. And it's fairly stupid to mope around over something like that, there were thousands of worse stories in this place.

I've got to stop being such a crybaby.

But my dizzy spells did return. Blade noticed.

"Check the sock under your bed," he said. We sat in the shady side of the yard. Blade slapped me on the back.

"Don't touch that sock until the screws are gone and the lights go out."

"A sock?" I asked.

"Inside," he whispered, "got you some help, white boy. Sniff a little of what's inside. Ease your pain."

They marched us back to our cells. Sure enough, I spotted a knotted sock that wasn't mine under the cot. They locked the doors. The lights went out. I rolled off the bed, grabbed the sock, untied it and shook out what looked like rock salt.

It was crack.

"Snort one at a time," Blade had said.

"Smash it into a powder first. Another thing."

"Yes Blade?"

"Pay attention, Guard Snicker get you free."

I crushed the crystals.

The steel bars on my window melted and the concrete convulsed. Did everything bad happen to Mom because of me? My gums pulsed and after a few minutes, I think, I could feel every heartbeat in my mouth. Mom left. First a red cloud, then exploding stars covered my ceiling. Ruthie's peanut butter ponytail flicked through my cell, her voice chirped and vanilla blasted through the bars. I laid back on the cot, riding the galloping horse up that mountain. Professor Cohen's gold tooth illuminated the pine trees and the canyon.

For three or four or nights I spun. Okay, maybe eight or ten. Then one day I drifted out to the yard for my free hour, and sat with Blade.

"I'm out of medicine," I said. We hung back in the shade again, where less happened and the guards didn't watch as much.

"Feeling better, my man?"

"Yeah, Blade. Relaxed. But foggy. Got any more crystals?"

"Sure nuff," Blade said, "but now I do you a bigger, the biggest favor. No more stuff. It's time. Time you slap them demons around, hit back, and do it with a clear head."

I knew Blade understood things I didn't. And he knew I understood stuff he didn't. So I thanked him. He squeezed my shoulder and smiled.

"Maybe, my friend," Blade said, "your mom messed up. Maybe you had nothing to do with her trouble. Could that be?"

It took a week for me to feel normal. When they served fish I ate it every sliver, hoping to restore any damaged brain cells. The San Diego fleet docked three streets away from the jail, so we saw tuna regularly and I never wasted a scrap.

It occurred to me, as a shock, that if I had kept up with that crack, I'd be just like Jessica's mother and our whole case could crash down if it became one junkie's statement versus another junkie's.

Guard Snicker stopped in front of my cell one morning, and stood with his back to me.

"Moon boy?" he asked. The back of his shirt started jiggling, so I knew, without seeing his face or hearing him laugh, that he found something funny.

"Yes, sir?"

"Next week you move." His head started bobbing.

"Okay, sir."

"Know who your cellmate will be?"

"No, sir."

"Stubbyclaw."

"What? That can't be."

It was near impossible to hear what he said next, Guard Snicker was snorting so hard and wiping drool from his mouth, but the gist was that the jail separated prisoners by race to reduce tensions and he said several times that since I was white, this made sense.

"My lawyer won't allow this," I said in a squeaky voice.

"He already knows."

He was teasing. They couldn't do this. My attorney wouldn't let them. Guard Snicker sauntered away.

I reminded myself, over and over, that when I was given a chance, I had done a good job for the El Cajon preschool. Okay, maybe I messed up by being so emotional in front of those kids, but I'd never let that happen again.

And the speedway drivers knew how well I tuned engines.

This imprisonment would end, I said to myself, and wrote it on my wall where a narrow beam of sunlight hit each morning. And they'd never put me in with Stubbyclaw.

Bubba never showed up.

Neither did my lawyer.

But Guard Snicker came back several days later, at midnight again and slipped open my cell door.

"Got another dental appointment for you, Moon boy," he said. "Say good-bye to this cell. You and Stubbyclaw bunk together when you return."

Guard Snicker took me to the same motel, unlocked my ankle chains, and uncuffed me.

"I got other duties," he said, "and the dentist can't see you for three days." He opened the closet.

"Looky here. Shirt. Shoes. Socks. Pants. Underwear. All in your size, huh?"

"You show up at the dentist's office in three days, okay? Here's fifty dollars meanwhile."

"When I return can't I stay in solitary?"

"Sorry. Budget cuts. You'll like Stubbyclaw."

He stepped out, shut my door and laughed himself into a coughing fit so loud it must have woken other guests.

So there I sat, staring out into the dark, not much traffic, wondering if this was my last look at the world.

The sun came up and cars whizzed past until a roar of three motorcycles rattled the windows. Black bikers parked in front of my door, swung their legs off the wide seats, flipped out their kickstands and swaggered to my door.

It was a quiet knock.

I chained the door and opened it a crack.

"You be Moon?"

"Yes sir."

"Sir? Us'n? We're with Blade."

I opened the door. The talker waved me toward his saddlebags and pointed inside.

My jumpsuits and helmets were inside.

"Look there," he said, pointing to the saddlebags on the second motorcycle.

My white pills, Woodrow Wilson plaque, my genuine Timex and an envelope with all my money was tucked inside.

"You wearing this?" the biker asked. "Or you putting on the threads in the closet?"

"Probably I'll keep on this prison uniform," I replied.

"No, man. You free. Ain't no dentist waiting."

"How did you know about that?" I asked.

"How'd we get all your things?" he said. "Blade says go, Guard Snicker says go and the lawyer gets all your stuff for you."

"Where?"

"Phoenix first. Here be your ticket." He handed me a Greyhound pass. It seemed like everybody thought about everything, except how to carry the stuff, so we went to a grocery and I bought some trash bags and slipped back into my jumpsuit and helmet, which felt so good I floated.

"I should tell the dentist I won't be coming," I said. The bikers laughed.

"What?" I asked.

"Everybody be in on the plan, Moon," one of the bikers said. "You free."

"It doesn't seem official. Shouldn't I call my lawyer?"

"Moon, he vacationing. But here's his number for tomorrow." That made it seem okay.

Three bald black guys roared through the streets with me teetering on the back of the middle bike, in my jumpsuit and white helmet, with two garbage sacks stuffed full hanging over each shoulder, fluttering in the wind.

The few cars on the street swerved over to the curb when we came alongside. A couple just hit their brakes and we shot past. We got to the depot, I thanked them, hauled my stuff inside and waited for the bus to Phoenix and good old Lake Poytawukie.

Eleven hours later, at the Phoenix depot, there was another bald, black biker waiting when I clambered down the bus steps. He offered to drive me to Colorado, free, but I told him I was headed all the way to Iowa. He asked if I needed any cash, and I said no. He asked if I wanted some weed and I said no thanks. He shook my hand and roared off.

When I say roared, it wasn't that "potato-potato-potato" sound of an Indian or Harley. Black bikers don't ride those, Blade had explained, they ride Hondas and Yamahas and Kawasakis and other rice bikes. They go faster, vibrate less and can blow the honkies and their Hogs off the road.

An elderly man strolled past the Phoenix depot with his cocker spaniel on a leash. I stared at him, and followed them for a block, just amazed by the vision. They walked where they wanted as fast as they cared to. So did I, for the first time in years.

I stepped into a drug store, out, back in, out and in again. It had palm trees growing from open circles in the sidewalk, marble walls outside up to my waist and dark wood frames around the windows. I sat, ordered a Dr. Pepper, then a Green River, and drank only half of each, burping quietly. This felt heavenly. I walked around the block, saying hello to everybody, a flower pot with red blossoms spilled over one window sill, the next store had a green awning and the only concrete to be seen was the curbs. I studied the people's clothes, bought a newspaper and ordered a Coke. I drank only half and left a quarter tip.

"Like as the waves make towards the pebbled shore, So do our minutes hasten to their end."

William Shakespeare

Chapter 20

They were struggling towards a cease-fire in Vietnam while I started writing the last part of this journal. Professor Cohen suggested I write what I know, so I finished this about the time that war cooled off. But it can't be read before the first few years of the 21st century, after Willy's son graduates from high school.

Here's how I pulled that off.

They returned the exact money I had when jailed, $338.45, so it didn't earn a single penny of interest during those years of jail time. My genuine Timex still worked after winding it again. I kept wearing one of the helmets and my jumpsuit. That was easier than packing everything, the September felt cool anyway and people stared less.

My garbage sacks didn't look professional for the grand return, so I stopped at a grocery, got a couple cardboard boxes, taped them up and put "Lake Poytawukie, Iowa" under my name on the outside, using the Magic Marker a clerk loaned me.

Since I had plenty of cash, I hopped a bus for Colorado, stopping in Ft. Morgan and bought a five pound piece of flat limestone.

The Ft. Morgan depot had a pay phone. I broke a $5 bill into quarters, shoved my boxes in, perched on top and dialed my lawyer.

"Moon, this is most disturbing," he said.

"But I thank you, sir, for getting me free."

"Excuse me?" he asked. "Excuse me? You are an escapee. There is a statewide warrant out for your arrest."

"What?" My pile of quarters spilled from the top of the pay phone, rattling all over the boxes, some rolling away and I let them.

"You have broken another law, Moon, and there are limits to what I can do for you now."

"Sir, I've been released, I have all my things."

"There may be an investigation into that, Moon, but I doubt it. There's some good news here."

"What?"

The operator asked for another quarter but I'd dropped them all by then and she disconnected us. By the time I picked up the ones I could find, and stooped over while walking around the floor outside I'd probably scraped back up about $3 worth, so I dialed him back quick.

My lawyer's line was busy.

I dug through the slits in the top of my boxes and got back another two quarters.

I dialed him again.

"Sir, you said there was something good?"

"Well, yes, Moon, listen carefully."

I knew he was taking off his glasses just then.

"You see, Moon, the City of San Diego might be afraid that you'd sue them for being wrongfully imprisoned all those years, the way I have been constructing your defense. And the drug rehabilitation of Jessica's mother makes her testimony weaker."

"You mean maybe I didn't kill Zebras, drink their blood and drive all the kids into the mountains at 140 miles per hour, sir?"

"Precisely, Moon."

One of my boxes crumpled and I fell on my rear into the phone booth. The telephone flipped out of my hand and banged the wall. I scrambled up and grabbed it again.

"What was that, Moon?"

"Nothing, sir. But I'm returning to San Diego and the jail right now."

"No, Moon, you cannot. They will add years to your sentence and your escape makes you look worse."

"I didn't escape."

"You have fled, and are described as potentially dangerous. Any officer spotting you is authorized to use full force to detain you. It is not terribly difficult to identify you, Moon."

"But this is wrong."

"Your escape was wrong, but the warrant will not go beyond the California border. If you never return to this state, there is nothing to worry about. And, luckily for the San Diego taxpayers, they have zero liability now to pay for wrongfully jailing you. Everybody wins."

"Did you say 'everybody wins,' sir?"

"Is that not how it appears, Moon?"

All people have their better moments. This was my worst. I should've returned so they'd know I didn't escape, God help me. But nothing had gone right up to then. Maybe I'd find Ruthie.

I failed to return.

That rock slab wasn't the most convenient traveling companion, but now I had a mission, so the rock, the taped boxes and I rode another Greyhound Bus to Ames, Iowa. I tied twine around the slab to make it carry easier. The moment to square up accounts approached.

On the way, one passenger tried to sell me a Norelco razor for five bucks, all the way across eastern Colorado. A couple of field hands offered to split their whisky with me while we rolled through Nebraska. We took turns ducking below the seat backs, so the driver wouldn't notice. The guys asked me to pay for my share, I told them all I had was a dollar, which they took and stopped passing the bottle my way. This was okay, because an ultimate duty lay ahead and distractions weren't appropriate.

Getting off at Ames, I hustled over to the warehouse. I understood they wouldn't hire me back, on account of Mr. Nordstrud subsidizing my earlier employment, but my old boss said he had a present for me from Professor Cohen.

Professor Cohen had passed away.

The manager shuffled around in his desk, and pulled out a sack, which contained Isoscele's dog collar, and a rather personal letter. There was a trace of chalk dust inside that collar, where the leather isn't so smooth. Just like I would have predicted, Professor Cohen didn't do it traditional. Nobody funeralized him. His body was trucked down to Des Moines for cremation, and the remains came back to Iowa State.

I trudged over to Professor Cohen's office. His name was gone from the door and some guy in a bow tie and wire glasses sat at his desk.

"Where did they put Professor Cohen's ashes?" I asked.

"What?"

Professor Cohen's chair squeaked, like it always did, when this guy turned towards me.

"Professor Cohen's remains, where are they?"

"Who are you? Who was he?"

This clueless new professor didn't have any idea about what might have happened to Professor Cohen's ring or his gold tooth but he recalled hearing that some ashes of some dead math professor had been scattered around the campanile.

I changed my plans. I borrowed a stone-cutting tool from the warehouse, cut my limestone in half, and inscribed a message on it. I borrowed a spade and walked over to the campanile. It was summer, so at six in the morning the grounds were vacant, and I put his memorial stone on the south side, where he and I had sat grading papers so many Saturdays.

The message on his marker was pretty standard, but worded in a way that carried a second meaning, which only he and I would understand.

That'll stay between him and me, and it's in Latin, anyway.

The marker being from Colorado would please him, since he encouraged that trip. I knew that stone would likely stay forever, since nobody on a campus really knows who's in charge of anything. And I leveled it off smooth, butting the grass right next to it, professionally done. Any landscaping workers noticing it for the first time would assume it was authorized. If a supervisor ever spotted it, he'd probably just get irritated, wondering why nobody told him about the memorial. Or maybe he'd just wonder how it had escaped his attention before.

I could see Professor Cohen chuckling at all this. He and I kind of laid that flat rock down together, and we had a grand old time at it.

It only took three hours to hitchhike to Grundy Center. Wearing a jumpsuit and helmet, with my boxes taped up neatly probably helped. The first ride took me all the way, stopping just once for a beer and a bump while I sipped a cherry Coke. He was a 3M salesman. I gave him a dollar to help with the gas.

He let me off at the DX Gas Station, the only one left in Grundy Center, and I borrowed their phone.

"Willy, I'm here."

"Willy, I can't quite hear."

"Willy, can you pick me up at the DX station?"

It was hard to understand Willy since I kept my helmet on. The kid running the station kind of glanced at me, trying to talk on the phone with that plastic earpiece covering the side of my head, but I figured he'd stare more if I took off the helmet.

I couldn't figure out which family this young man came from, but didn't want to stir up things by asking. He could just assume I was a traveler.

"Ka-boom!"

Flames belched out of Willy's tailpipe. We both laughed, I ran over and tossed my boxes in his trunk. Willy drove me right over to his home.

"It's a ranch house," I said.

"Now they are acceptable," Willy said.

"Remember the scandal when the first one was built in Grundy Center?" I asked.

"The city called it a 'sheep shed' and almost passed codes against them," Willy replied.

But modern trends didn't pass by Grundy Center forever, and a couple dozen ranch style homes eventually went up. Willy's even had a brick fireplace and a garage with electrical outlets. He used an electric blanket to keep his car engine warm in winter, so it started no matter what the temperature.

"Wow, garage heat, brick fireplace and a basement," I said.

"The basement's paneled with real Masonite," Willy added, "looks like brick."

We stayed parked in front, just looking at his place, and talked of our good fortunes. Willy's house was painted sky blue, which his wife Kathleen selected from the paint store in Des Moines, and they covered their roof with genuine asbestos shingles.

Their mailbox set back a yard from the curb, where rambunctious teenagers would find it difficult to knock over, but the postman could fill and empty it without much stretching.

Kathleen stepped out and stopped, wringing her hands around a dishtowel.

She was solid, you could tell right off. Kathleen tilted towards shy, not cluttering the air with words, except that she'd appreciate it if we didn't interrupt Willy Junior's nap yet.

So we didn't. But I couldn't wait to see him.

She waved us in.

Willy Junior slept in the basement where it stayed cooler.

"You sit my in chair," Willy said. He pointed to a leather upholstered Lazyboy. I was honored. This was his chair. It turned out that a fertilizer plant in Mahaska County awarded this prestigious piece of furniture to Willy after he fixed a puzzling pipe leak for them.

"Willy, you must be one of the richer men in the county." He chuckled. We talked about our Colorado adventures while Kathleen studied their wall-to-wall carpet. Grandma and me had gotten by with linoleum, which was respectable if waxed and clean. Those with more cash walked on hardwood floors with throw rugs. The truly rich carpeted wall-to-wall and here was Willy, among them. It was a two-inch green shag, and you could tell Kathleen had heard many of these tales before. She started laughing before we got to the funny parts of most, like the time we dropped all the trays in the kitchen to drive the head chef crazy.

Willy got up and turned on their lava lamp and we watched it for a few minutes until we heard a noise.

"He's up," Kathleen said. She scurried down the basement stairs and carried Willy Junior back up. He couldn't quite walk yet, but could stand. His eyes were puffed from sleep. He grabbed the doorjamb with one hand and his mom's finger with the other. Willy Junior lost his balance, but his mom steadied him.

"How's my big boy?" Willy asked.

Willy Junior looked at his dad, at me, his dad again and me.

He shrieked.

Willy ran over and scooped him up. That child could cry. I'm guessing the neighbors on three sides, even if they were air conditioned with windows shut, could hear Willy Junior scream. They all went into the kitchen and after several minutes, Willy Junior quieted down. Pretty soon I heard him sucking on a bottle.

Willy sauntered back into the living room.

"Great lungs," I said.

"Yeah," Willy replied.

"That's a good sign," I said, "the boy's got energy. Probably bright too."

"Moon, uh…"

"Yeah, Willy?"

"Well, you know, the missus thinks…"

"She's a good wife, Willy, I see that.

"But Moon, I argue with her, you see, her viewpoint, not knowing you and me and all…"

"Willy, I bet she's going to be a world class mom, too."

"So Moon, she thinks it's best that you stay away from our boy."

I don't recall quite what I said next, except that it took me a few seconds to collect a thought and probably I said something like "Oh, that's okay, I understand," or some such, but concentrated on not getting woozy and embarrassing anybody and wanting to understand that this was not personal, just a frightened child, and that there was no need to make that worse, really. So, needing to respect Willy's request, and not wanting to disrupt his new life, I stared straight ahead. My hand slipped off the arm of the chair. But a second effort worked. I lifted myself up, stood, turned and walked out.

Life never stops twisting.

Willy Junior's fear changed my plan. It required something different now to make things right. I could still prove Mr. Scarletti wrong and end up okay.

So I took a bus to Titonka, and had the stonecutter inscribe my remaining piece of limestone. I came back, and at dusk, checking to make sure nobody was around, slipped into the "Bone Orchard," Protestant section, and began to work a bit on Grandpa and Grandma's place.

Since I might not be returning, I scraped the turf off their spot and laid it aside, using one of my helmets. It would have been easier with a shovel, but to borrow a tool from anybody might attract attention, so I turned my black helmet, which was too hot to wear anyway, into a scoop.

I laid the stone.

I scraped and carried dirt from outside the fence, spread that over Grandpa and Grandma's plot and recovered them with the original sod.

Now they had a slight rise over them, like a roof, so there'd never again be a need for a canvas to protect them, and the rain and melting snow would all trickle off to the sides. They would rest, forever dry.

I slept with them, putting on two pair of coveralls to stay warm. At sunrise I hung out the outer pair to dry off the dew. Even though Grandpa, Grandma and I could never really be apart, this might be my last visit to their resting place, so I sat there and remembered them and all the things they did for me.

Being with them was good.

At the same time, the "Dark Dog" bit me for the first time that night and wouldn't let go. Grandpa and Grandma soothed my thoughts. But then that "Dark Dog" took over.

It took about an hour for the coveralls to sun dry on a bush. I rolled them up, stuffed them in my box and hitchhiked to Lake Poytawukie. This only took an hour. It seemed like the most uneventful journey ever to my lake.

The manager at Kaster's Kove said this rated as one of his strangest requests ever, but yes, he did have a couple leaky rowboats, and I could purchase either one for $6, as is, no returns.

Water seeped into the first boat at a rate that threatened my plan, so I returned it, the gentleman agreed to trade, and I tried his second boat. This one allowed about one gallon in every five minutes, which was perfect. I rowed, bailing out the water as I went, to a spot on the shore where I knew there was a garbage can and some shade. The bank was shallow enough that I could drag my boat out without help. It would drain itself there.

By the way, I don't think I'm a pervert. I've never thought those kind of thoughts. But the shrinks who said I fit the profile, well, maybe they know more about me than I do. I just don't think so. And I certainly never touched any kid in a wrong way or wanted to. The thought makes me ill.

Anyway my luck, sometimes, seems to never end. A length of logging chain coiled around the bottom of that garbage can. Sure, it was so rusted you wouldn't trust it to hoist anything, but for this project, that just didn't matter. It had no hooks but there were some wire clothes hangers in there that would help.

Up until now, I thought that I'd be spending four to five dollars for a length of chain at the hardware, and this discovery saved me from that waste. Now I had the day to finish the project, neat and clean, so I walked the main street of Lake Poytawukie, stopping in all three lawyer's offices, until I found a Gary E. Sutton, esq., who didn't know anybody in Grundy Center.

That was critical.

Mr. Gary E. Sutton will become important to explain what happened next.

Then I set up an account with my money at Lake Poytawukie Commercial Bank and walked back to the water.

My boat was there, drained and dry inside. I sat in it, on the shore, thinking that when innocent children yell with fear at the first sight of someone, maybe, just maybe, they can recognize the devil, a dark force hidden in a person. Maybe it's some sinful trait that hasn't surfaced. Humans survived this long on instincts, not by being the fastest or strongest animals. Perhaps it's best for everybody, me too, that I fade away.

Oh, I stopped thinking these thoughts at sunset. Too many boats remained on the water. Some die-hards pushed out for evening fishing, so I waited until they settled.

I put those white pills on the front seat, with my Woodrow Wilson Scholarship plaque and laid the chain on the bottom. My other two helmets, clothes and spare jumpsuit were already in the garbage can, neat and tidy. Wearing the cleanest jumpsuit and my white helmet, I started to row out towards the center. I'd stop to bail every ten minutes, using a coffee can.

Professor Cohen always said I'd conquer all odds and triumph, and I was thinking he'd probably applaud this gesture.

Lake Poytawukie's respectably deep near the middle, so I stopped there and dipped the can into the water. I opened the pill bottle. I popped the first two into my mouth, took a gulp of Lake Poytawukie and did several more. There appeared to be about twenty, maybe two dozen of those little white tablets, and to do a proper job, I swallowed them all. Then I draped the chain around my shoulders, tucking the Woodrow Wilson Scholarship plaque under my shirt and against my chest, leaving my arms free to bail water.

This way I'll run into Mr. Nordstrud, Professor Cohen, and introduce them to Dad and Grandpa and Grandma sooner. My head might be normal then, not that it bothers me a whole lot, but in the next life, it seems unlikely that they wouldn't keep a fellow deformed. It felt proper to drink of Lake Poytawukie, since this water formed my sharpest and happiest memories. This way it became a part of me, a place I always trusted. My feet were soon under water, so I bailed until the boat bottom was no longer sloshing wet, only damp.

Grandpa and Grandma worked hard for me. They knew I wasn't quite right. I burdened them heavy, and certainly destroyed Mom's chance for a decent life, but Grandpa and Grandma took care of me. They knew much of the world wished I had never happened, and most of Grundy Center didn't care for reminders of my existence. I think they'd both smile at me now, doing this to get closer to them. Dad too, and he could be respected and I'd have a regular head so I could hit home runs with the bat he gave me and Dad would have a huge farm. Doctor Throckmorton would be in an entirely different section. It's lucky, Dad would understand, that I wasn't Catholic so my plan was not a sin.

The marker at Grandpa and Grandma's toes would be my official tombstone. It would mystify the grave keeper until he got the check from my Lake Poytawukie attorney, Mr. Gary E. Sutton, esq. Then he wouldn't touch it. Especially after he understood that I wasn't really buried, just marked as their grandson. Cemetery rules didn't allow an illegitimate person to rest there, especially one who wasn't baptized. All I wanted was my name next to Grandma and Grandpa. Avoiding disruptions to others, and the embarrassment that caused them, was the whole idea.

What I planned on doing now, and did, was to keep bailing every five or ten minutes, as long as I could stay conscious. This way, by the time those pills totally knocked me out, and we know for sure that twenty of them will do that, the medicine would have another hour to work, before the boat and I sank. The chain would carry me, my jumpsuit, helmet, and the Woodrow Wilson Scholarship plaque safely to the bottom, unconscious and painless.

Writing this story was not difficult. Professor Cohen got that right. All I had to do was sit down and remember my life, except this last part, which was planned to happen after I wrote it.

I am lucky. This book tells you about my good friends, and a few who weren't so helpful along the way. Unlike anybody else, I've documented my life and exactly how it concluded. Everybody else gets struck dead as a surprise.

I mentioned that this was written about the time Vietnam was winding down. You're reading it much later. That's because the story was held in trust by that Lake Poytawukie attorney I mentioned, Gary E. Sutton, esq., and the bank two doors down from his office. It was scheduled for release in 2006. By that time Willy Junior will be through high school, and might even have his own family. I hope so. My pal Willy would make a terrific grandfather.

Professor Cohen always thought I could tell stories in an entertaining way, so if somebody publishes this, Mr. Gary E. Sutton, esq. arranged that all royalties go to you, Willy Junior. You and I owe Professor Cohen some gratitude if that happens. He encouraged me to do this, and if you read this as a book and receive some royalties, I've lived up to Professor Cohen's hope for me.

That's huge.

I apologize for scaring you as a baby, but in a way, you're my only descendant, so I wanted to leave you this story. Mr. Gary E. Sutton, esq., will also arrange that you receive my genuine Timex. It runs a little slow, but if you adjust it once a week there's no problem.

Spend the money any way you want. You might consider using some of the cash for a trip to the Rockies and see those peaks and sage, if you want. You don't have to. Just if it sounds good.

Remember Moon and your dad were best buddies, and one summer we rode like cowboys, way out west.

"After the first death, there is no other."

Dylan Thomas

Chapter 21

My name is Gary Sutton. I am the Lake Poytawukie attorney Moon picked to manage his final affairs. If you will forgive this interruption, Moon left out a significant chapter. Moon agreed that I could add any missing facts.

Neither Moon nor I guessed that his hand-written tablet would actually turn into this book; but with surprisingly little effort, it has.

My secretary transcribed it before submitting to publishers.

You have nearly finished. There are some more details that matter, some pleasant, others less so, which I will now explain.

First understand that in our conversations I never called him "Moon." To protect his anonymity and those affected by this disclosure, I chose to not reveal his identity. Notice that in his autobiography he never mentions himself by proper name.

That's because Moon did not want to embarrass others.

I suggested that their reputations should be able to withstand the truth. Moon's last request, however, was that nobody feel exposed by his story. So be it.

Moon also hoped to cast a favorable light over his mother, leaving out certain facts. I shall say no more about that.

I warrant that the names "Doctor Throckmorton," "Gloria Throckmorton," "Mr. Scarletti" and "Mr. McSweeney" were fabricated but based on actual people. Their occupations were altered enough to make them only identifiable by those who knew them well. This is a lawyer's way to avoid libel.

Perhaps you wonder how I could cooperate in a suicide, and why would I confess this publicly? It happened that Moon held back the last few pages of his story and mailed them to me just before he rowed out onto the waters of Lake Poytawukie. Therefore I could not have known his ultimate plan. He spared me that conflict.

In my final meeting with Moon, he walked by my office, standing outside on the sidewalk, waiting until I noticed and waved to him.

"Good afternoon, Mr. Sutton," he said, stepping in and looking sideways. The crotch of his pants, his armpits and waistband under the belt were darkened, as if he had been drenched in a rainstorm and had worn the clothes until they almost dried. He was barefoot.

"Sit, please."

He eased into my client chair. Perhaps Moon was unaware that he often turned the right side of his face away from people, looking out from the left side of his eyes. That morning, when he gazed straight at me, I felt I had earned his trust.

"Mr. Sutton, I hope I did the right thing."

"Well I bet you did. What was it?" An attorney spends a lot of time on boring projects; reading contracts, researching points of law, with surprisingly few hours in courtroom drama. Still, once in a while I hear startling facts, even here in Lake Poytawukie.

"As you can see," Moon said, "I just couldn't do it. Was that a mistake? Should I have stuck to my original plan?" He squirmed in the chair.

"Could not finish what?"

Moon stood, placed his palms on my desk and leaned forward. "Didn't you get my last pages?"

"There is more, Moon? No."

Moon slumped back into the chair. He revealed his suicide plan. Moon told me his final section explained how his death would occur. He expected those pages to be delivered in my morning mail. I shook my head, shocked. He told me how he believed that the world would be more comfortable if he disappeared.

It came naturally and I am proud of the words that surged out of me, explaining how he showed a unique beauty to those who knew him.

Moon didn't move.

To be fair, I also told Moon he must always expect some rejection, just as I do. The public meets my expectation rather consistently. I told Moon what he already knew; that he'll always attract more enemies and friends than those of us without physical abnormalities.

Moon nodded slowly.

"I need to remember the folks who help me and not think so much about the others," he said.

"It also would not hurt," I replied, "to be less critical of yourself. Sure, you need to concentrate on the good people and ignore the bad. We all should." Moon and I were talking beyond a client and lawyer. This honored me.

"I tried to kill myself last night," Moon said. "I guess you'll get the details in tomorrow's mail. It took me twenty minutes to row out where the water's deep enough. Thinking I'd be dead in less than one hour sharpened my thinking. Grandma came to mind, her sitting on our floor in Grundy Center and staring at my Woodrow Wilson Scholarship plaque. I remembered Mr. Nordstrud and our trips to Iowa State. And I wondered where Ruthie was and if she had started a family and if she might remember me occasionally.

"But those thoughts faded when I heard a fisherman and his daughter talking. They were anchored but I couldn't see them. They had no lights and neither did I. He was offering to put the worm on her hook but the girl thought she could try herself. They discussed this so kindly it reminded me of Professor Cohen."

Moon extended both arms. He rarely gestured, but this time it seemed natural.

"The fisherman and his daughter's voices trailed away while I rowed towards the center of Lake Poytawukie, making sure I didn't splash. My boat leaked. I bailed it again. Once the water was out I felt ready. I would no longer disturb others by dissolving into my lake

"I stopped rowing," Moon said. "There weren't many waves, just a gentle rocking. You could barely hear the water lapping the boat.

"So I took out the pills," Moon said, "and gripped my Woodrow Wilson Scholarship plaque. Lake Poytawukie water tastes awful, but I

was ready for that and needed to swallow a lot to get enough pills down. It took awhile to let go of the plaque. But I couldn't wrap the chain around my shoulders and chest unless I let that Woodrow Wilson Scholarship plaque float between my ankles."

Moon mixed details of our pond in with this ghastly story. The descriptions came from a man who loved Lake Poytawukie. A dreamy memory of dawns past and Red-winged blackbirds trilling from the reeds floated through the back of my mind as well. Those birds saw the light before we did, so our ears woke us before our eyes.

"The chain couldn't be loose," Moon said, "or my body's flotation might free me and I'd surface. Then folks would have to retrieve my pathetic, bloated carcass and bury me someplace that accepts unbaptized bastards. There was no reason to bother others that way. I wrapped those chains tight, bent the clothes hanger wire and looped it through the links."

Moon's face took on a quizzical look. He seemed to be trying to understand the moment while he explained it. There were no more gestures, only a gentle rocking in his chair, forward and back, non-stop while he talked. I think I nodded each time he glanced toward me.

"Something unexpected happened," Moon said, "just as I finished wiring the chain I heard him."

Moon stopped rocking.

"Persisto, persisto."

Moon slumped in the chair.

"I felt his disappointment, so I flung all of those little white pills overboard. Some of the gosh-darn things drifted back into the boat, which reminded me that it was barely afloat.

The chain was wrapped tight around me."

Moon's head dropped. He stopped.

"And then?" I asked.

No answer.

"Are you okay?"

Finally he looked up and into me. "The boat started slip under. Water sloshed over my thighs. I remembered waxing Mr. Nordstrud's car. I cut my fingers trying to untangle the coat hangers. I couldn't get them loose. It must have been my imagination, but even while fighting that wire I smelled chalk dust. I wanted free. But I couldn't get the chain off."

Moon held up his hands. Every finger was crusted with scabs.

"When Lake Poytawukie splashed around my neck I almost had the wires untangled. Small ripples wet my nose. The chain slackened but still coiled around me. My face went under and I plunged towards the mud at the bottom, still unwrapping the chain."

"Persisto."

Moon's brow furrowed. "I got free. I surged up and gasped at the surface. I swam for shore. For a moment I wondered where my plaque went. It should have floated. I couldn't see it. 'Persisting' seemed more important so I stopped looking, slipped off my shoes and started stroking toward shore."

Moon explained that he bumped into the boat with the fisherman and his daughter. They pulled him in and rowed to the beach. He lay there, not asleep but not clearly conscious until dawn. The public showers were only a half mile away; he stumbled to them in the early light and washed.

"Did Professor Cohen know best? I've been wondering all morning if I did the right thing."

Moon agreed that I could finish his story, adding this to the end. Moon also asked me to run a lost and found ad, in case his Woodrow Wilson Scholarship plaque floated to the surface and somebody found it. That gave me a sliver of hope. Moon just might persist.

He mentioned a possible trip during our last meeting. I encouraged him to take it. Moon still had money, but decided to conserve his cash by hitchhiking to the East Coast.

This journey risked everything.

It could shove Moon back over the edge.

Yet I believe he had no choice.

Moon called two weeks later. "When I showed up at Ruthie's home," Moon said, "her mother was uncommonly flustered. Ruthie wasn't there. Ruthie's Mom kept me at bay but I showed up every morning, bringing doughnuts and coffee. And she knows I don't drink coffee or eat sugar, so I won some points.

"Finally she arranged for Ruthie to visit me with her 'beau.'

"They would come from school at two in the afternoon. I arrived at noon so Ruthie's mom had me sit on the porch. I asked for permission to walk to the corner gas station for an orange crush. Ruthie's mom said that would be fine.

"I got into the gas station's restroom and splashed water over my face. I swabbed on an extra coating of deodorant. I tried to walk slow back to Ruthie's mom's house so I wouldn't sweat. Excuse me, so I wouldn't perspire.

"I sat on the porch again. Then it happened.

"I don't see so good at a distance, but there was no mistaking her, walking, almost running, a block down the sidewalk. That ponytail waved to me. A fellow was guiding her and carrying a trumpet. He wasn't blind. Ruthie started clapping and smiling the instant she stepped onto the porch. She knew I was there before I said a word.

"We shook hands.

"I nodded at the boyfriend who introduced himself, and I've forgotten his name. Something was wrong. He turned out to be a music student. It didn't seem logical to me that GE would be hiring a musician as a Management Trainee. Later I would learn that the Management Trainee and Ruthie never got serious because of that medical procedure Ruthie suffered through as a child. That's all anybody ever needs to know about him.

"Ruthie giggled and said they rehearsed a piece for me.

"Ruthie walked to the davenport without help and pulled a guitar from underneath. The boyfriend hit a note on his trumpet while she tuned her instrument.

"Suddenly her fingers flew across the strings and his trumpet ticked out notes in a beat to her tune. I was excited and scared. This was Ruthie, but prettier and shapely and with new curls on her forehead but the same vanilla ponytail making me dizzy and caressing an instrument I'd not heard her play before.

"I focused on her guitar strings to avoid fainting.

"Ruthie began to sing a song about PAG Church Camp and me. Her boyfriend put a mute in the trumpet and tapped out a background tune.

"A boy who is a friend, by the way, is an entirely different thing than a boyfriend.

"Ruthie finished and stretched out one hand. I got up but my right foot hooked behind my left ankle and I fell. I pushed away from the floor and stood. Her hand, palm up, reached to me. I walked over. Ruthie's friend patted my shoulder, walked out and down the sidewalk, twirling his horn. Ruthie's mother stood and strolled towards the kitchen.

"I now know Ruthie's mother to be a decent woman, who only wanted the best for her daughter. She had exaggerated about the boyfriend to protect Ruthie."

Moon ended our call by asking if anybody reported finding his plaque, and I told him no.

My phone rang a year later. It was Moon. "Ruthie's mother and I are friends and can even joke with each other about how she tried to discourage me. It turned out, Mr. Sutton, that she worked hard keeping every boy away, not just me.

"So I wasn't being discriminated against. She agreed that Ruthie should escape from that noisy coastal city after we married. Ruthie and I settled in this village with a blind college nearby. Her mother visits every few months and we all look forward to those get-togethers."

Moon asked if his Woodrow Wilson Scholarship plaque ever turned up. I told him no.

"This is a small town," Moon said. "If it weren't in a different state you might think it was Grundy Center, but the winters tend toward more gentle. I am the only mechanic. It's been fun keeping up with the new engines and not always easy, but some of the neighboring villagers bring cars over for me to fix, so I'm no simpleton."

Moon got disconnected. He was at a pay phone. Moon and Ruthie did not have their own telephone, and still don't. Only Ruthie's mother and I know their mailing address. In minutes, my phone rang again.

"Sorry Mr. Sutton, but I ran out of dimes," Moon said.

"After fixing several council members' cars, one suggested I could

serve as assistant street commissioner for a term," Moon reported.

"This was such an honor that Ruthie agreed it would be okay if I got up at five every morning and walked the town to check the streets and curbs." Moon mentioned that this impressed the council so much that he was urged to run for city office.

"We decided against becoming that public, but it was nice they asked. Ruthie teaches chorus and math at the school for the blind. She could easily find her way to the building if anything ever happens to me. It's just six blocks from our home, with only one turn. But we like to start our day together so I walk her there anyway. It's almost on the way to my service station." Moon mentioned that he found another Timex identical to the one that Professor Cohen had given him, but with a Speidel Twist-O-Flex band, and he bought it.

"Professor Cohen wouldn't mind," Moon said, "that old leather strap caught too much grease and oil."

Moon was as surprised as I when his story sold. And that is how this book came to exist. He was ecstatic to learn that Willy's son already had a daughter and that the Lake Poytawukie Bank escrowed the royalties in a college fund for her.

"With interest, that might pay her first two years at Iowa State," he said.

"It's like we have a granddaughter.

"There's a freeway not far from our village here," Moon continued, "and a couple truck lines respect my work enough that they turn off the main road and come to our shop for maintenance. Most of those contracts renew every year. It keeps me hopping and lets us mix some hamburger in with our beans."

The operator interrupted and Moon put two more quarters in the payphone. Moon said he wanted to explain another point, and did not want to risk getting cut off.

"Ruthie's mom feared having a blind grandchild. We understand, but we kind of wish her mother hadn't permitted that operation when Ruthie was just a girl."

He stopped.

"Moon?"

"Sorry, Mr. Sutton, I had a dizzy spell."

"Are you all right?"

"Just a minute, Mr. Sutton."

He didn't speak for a few seconds, coughed and continued in a hoarse voice.

"Ruthie's mother said the welfare official insisted that sterilizing Ruthie was in everyone's best interest.

"Sterilizing Ruthie wasn't in everyone's best interest. It wasn't.

"Sterilizing Ruthie was in everyone else's best interests. Not ours. At least welfare paid the costs.

"Still, Ruthie and I would have liked to have decided ourselves whether to have children or not. That welfare official did what she thought was right, we guess. Anyway, we always have Willy's granddaughter to follow."

Moon asked if his plaque ever showed up. I told him no. Moon said he guessed it was lost.

"Mr. Sutton, is the Timex I gave Willy Junior still ticking?"

"I'll check on that, Moon."

He thanked me for that.

"Ruthie and I have been married ten years. I come alive every evening after work, stepping through our door and smelling vanilla. She smiles when I serve breakfast and Ruthie laughs in a jingly bell tinkle when I wake in the morning. With every move, her ponytail swirls over her shoulders, Colorado sage colored but softer. What more could a guy ask?"

"You never know what life means till you die..."
Robert Browning

Chapter 22

This is Gary Sutton again.

There is more.

First, some background. If Lake Poytawukie sounded familiar, you must be a hardcore crossword puzzle fan.

During a controversy over the Indian meaning of our lake's name, the Chamber of Commerce campaigned to change the spelling from Potawuka to Poytawukie. After that resolution passed the council, we became the only lake with a name containing all the vowels. Lake Sequoia comes close, but doesn't use a "Y" and doesn't fit the same number of spaces, so that's how our community gained a small amount of fame.

Each January, the newest member of the Lake Poytawukie Chamber of Commerce gets an assignment to look up the current Cruciverbalist Association membership, and mails a Lake Poytawukie postcard to every one of them. The message on each postcard reminds them that Lake Poytawukie is the only body of water in America that uses every vowel and is ten letters long.

A "cruciverbalist," by the way, is a person who writes crossword puzzles. There are about 200 active and published most years. A handful of them end up using our name each regularly, so hundreds of thousands or millions of crossword puzzle fans learn about us annually.

The daily crossword puzzles, it turns out, start out easy on Monday and grow more difficult through the week. Poytawukie ends up being a Thursday or Friday kind of word. It took Rand McNally two years to catch up and make our change.

That's how we promote things around here. It also eliminated an embarrassing Indian interpretation of our prior name.

This lake is Moon's place, as the following letter from him explains.

Dear Mr. Sutton:

You've been a trusted gentleman. I was honored to be your client.

While you'll never hear from me again, I'll soon be close by.

My life was blessed. There's been much more good than bad. I apologize for burdening you with extra information, but feared you might worry if you never heard from Ruthie or me again, and wanted to make sure you understood why Ruthie and I disappeared.

There were some complications to Ruthie caused by that operation the welfare officials authorized when she was young. I guess they never paid top dollar for medical help. In Ruthie's case, they hired a traveling surgeon who specialized in sterilizing girls when their parents or local authorities requested. This fellow did lots of operations in Wisconsin, Illinois, Iowa, Missouri and Nebraska. It turned out some of his credentials weren't in order. He did Ruthie's operation on the countertop of dry cleaning shop in Waterloo, after dark. Ruthie barely remembers it.

There was an infection.

One result was that Ruthie ruptured inside later. It happened twice in high school, once again while studying music and three times during our marriage. She healed every time, building up scar tissue. Finally, this year, it was too much and we lost her.

I'll be free of this pain soon. You should know I'll be at peace, in a place that knows me. Should you sense my presence from time to time, that'll be real. I won't be far.

I respect your past advice, Mr. Sutton. Can you accept that this time, I need to head for my next life? Your assistance will never be forgotten and I hope the rest of your mortal experience will be as wonderful as mine was.

You helped me realize I was worthwhile. By getting my story published, you created a college fund for our "granddaughter" without us disturbing her, Willy or her dad, Willy Junior.

Mr. Nordstrud and Professor Cohen knew me longer than you, and I'd like to assure you that they would be happy to see my later life. I'm not so religious, but somehow I think they know about it. And I'm also confident that they would now approve of this departure, since my loss of Ruthie.

Mr. Sutton, these gentlemen await me.

And you see, Mr. Sutton, I'm missing Ruthie terribly, and just couldn't wait longer to join her. It took me weeks, all those years ago, to admit I'd been jailed. It took her minutes to assure me that didn't matter. But I never confessed that there was a warrant out for my arrest in California. I need to set that right with her and accept her judgment.

If she'll still have me, I'll introduce Ruthie to all the others. And maybe even Dad. I imagine he's a Protestant now, and it grieves me to think he lived without ever having a wife. My life was blessed by marriage.

Everybody dies. I just moved up my time.

Moon

Typically, "Moon" did not burden us with the specifics. I had coffee one morning with a clerk from the Rexall Drug Store on main about a week after getting "Moon's" letter. This clerk, a nice kid, mentioned that a man had come in the month before who looked like that fellow he saw leaving my office once, the one with a funny head.

"Know who I mean?" he asked.

"Not really," I said, "what did he want?"

"Oh nothing that I remember, except he bought three bottles of sleeping pills."

That told me all I needed to know. I envy Moon in a way. I'm not sure I've ever felt passions as strong as his.

I felt obliged to do more checking while "Moon" lived. He was gone before I could pass on these facts, and maybe that's best.

For five years, I ran a classified ad after the spring thaw, asking if anybody found "Moon's" plaque. I never got a response.

"Moon's" mother, it turns out, vanished when Throckmorton's medical practice shrank. Throckmorton's business was another victim of the dwindling farmer population. In his last twelve years, Throckmorton drove the same Midnight Blue Cadillac, claiming it was the best car ever made, but left town for a retirement home in Dubuque, where he bought a used Buick with rusted rocker panels. It turned out that the farms he acquired were bought with borrowed money. All were reclaimed by lenders during a three-year slump in crop prices. He discovered Protestants to be a minority in Dubuque, but had already made his non-refundable deposit to the home, and spent his last years grumbling about being surrounded by Catholics.

This must have been tough on Throckmorton.

Of the dozen doctors and nurses I asked in Mason City, several thought "Moon's" mother went to St. Louis or Denver. Most didn't know or care. They agreed she left town with a Blue Cross salesman.

Willy Junior got his bachelor's degree from Iowa State in Biology. He received an MD from Johns Hopkins, interned at Leesburg, Virginia where he now specializes in ear, nose and throat. His wife teaches history at their community college.

Since Willy's plumbing consulting work went well, and Willy Junior's wife taught school while he studied medicine, they managed to graduate without owing any student loans.

Their daughter is nearly a straight-A student, is happy about the college fund she has from the sales of this book, but hasn't decided yet where to attend or what her area of study will be. She has a younger brother who wants to be a pirate or a cowboy.

Willy enjoys describing the Rocky Mountains to these grandchildren, and tells them his adventures there with Moon.

"Fiction lags after truth."

Edmund Burke, 1729-1797

Acknowledgments

Thank you for believing that "Moon's" story deserved an audience, Stacy Williams and Allan Shaw.

Willy's granddaughter writes PublishAmerica a note twice a year, thanking them for depositing the book's royalties in her college account. With a lot of coaching from his parents, Willy's grandson also expresses gratitude, but his understanding of what all this means is uncertain. He's young. Give him time.

Many comments and critiques came from "Willy Geiselman," Jeremy Rosenblatt, L. J. Skeie, Gary Kirk, Donna Swaffar, Dave Johnson, Jan Meaker, Lou Wilcox, Laura Walcher, Bob Evans, Lindsay Walker, Amy Romaker and her screenwriting brother, Beth Obermeyer, Sandra Holtzinger, Irene O'Brien, Drusilla Campbell, Michael and Valentina Jones, Dale Steele, Rachel Laing, Mary Kay Gardener, Sheila Schreiber, Jim and Toni Schwartz, Joe O'Connor, Sandra O'Neal, Linda Shaw, Barry Armentrout and my traditional first reader, Nancy Sutton. "Mr. Nordstrud's" daughter verified a few details.

The class and staff of the Santa Barbara Writer's Conference lent enthusiastic support and guidance; thank you all.

Later comments from Rozanne Mack, John and Carolyn Hanson, Mitch Woodbury, Ed Tuck, John Essig, Bill Yungclas, Cheryl and Allan Abbott, Bob Middlemiss, Mary Carroll Moore and Don Scott helped much. Also Bob and Judy Wilhelm.

Some helped catch typos. Others pointed out where "Moon's" language, charming as it always was, defied comprehension. Those parts were edited with care, his original intent always protected and I think "Moon's" feelings remain correctly expressed. It took careful digging and remembering by some of the people credited to verify parts of this story, without exposing the book to those characters that still live.

A contract for the film rights was refused. As trustee for Willy's heirs, I need to be careful about this, but the initial payment was to be so modest that we all felt comfortable declining that offer. This movie adaptation would have made "Moon" more physically attractive and photogenic, deleted much of his childhood experiences and placed his story in modern times, to better attract current moviegoers. I'm confident "Moon" would have also said no. Moon, this book keeps our bargain and gives you a heritage of sorts. Your name and village remain confidential, but now there's a group of readers, not so few, who admire what you were. Somehow, I think you know that.

You are missed.

Printed in the United States
47057LVS00004B/157-204

9 781424 114917